WHISPER
OF THE
TIDE

Also by Sarah Tolcser

Song of the Current

WHISPER OF THE TIDE

A *Song of the Current* NOVEL

SARAH TOLCSER

BLOOMSBURY

NEW YORK   LONDON   OXFORD   NEW DELHI   SYDNEY

BLOOMSBURY YA
Bloomsbury Publishing Inc., part of Bloomsbury Publishing Plc
1385 Broadway, New York, NY 10018

BLOOMSBURY and the Diana logo are trademarks of Bloomsbury Publishing Plc

First published in the United States of America in June 2018 by Bloomsbury YA

Bloomsbury books may be purchased for business or promotional use. For information on
bulk purchases please contact Macmillan Corporate and Premium Sales Department at
specialmarkets@macmillan.com

Library of Congress Cataloging-in-Publication Data
Names: Tolcser, Sarah, author.
Title: Whisper of the tide / by Sarah Tolcser.
Description: New York : Bloomsbury, 2018.
Summary: Caro and Markos must decide if their love is more important than the fate of
Akhaia when a powerful Archon offers to help Markos fight for the throne if Markos will
marry his daughter.
Identifiers: LCCN 2017040025 (print) | LCCN 2017053182 (e-book)
ISBN 978-1-68119-299-4 (hardcover) • ISBN 978-1-68119-300-7 (e-book)
Subjects: | CYAC: Fantasy. | Love—Fiction. | Arranged marriage—Fiction. |
Inheritance and succession—Fiction. | Racially mixed people—Fiction.
Classification: LCC PZ7.1.T623 Whi 2018 (print) | LCC PZ7.1.T623 (e-book) |
DDC [Fic]—dc23
LC record available at https://lccn.loc.gov/2017040025

ISBN 978-1-5476-0074-8 (Aus)

Book design by littlemissgang and John Candell
Typeset by Westchester Publishing Services
Printed and bound in the U.S.A. by Berryville Graphics Inc., Berryville, Virginia
2 4 6 8 10 9 7 5 3 1

To find out more about our authors and books visit www.bloomsbury.com and sign up for
our newsletters.

For Michael, who has supported my writing career for thirteen years, ever since he read my short stories—which, frankly, I'm not even that good at

AKHAIA

AKHAIAN PENINSULA

Trikkaia

Edessa

Eryth

River Kars

Siscema

Valonikos

Four Mile R

River Thrush

RIVERLANDS

ESSA

Iantiporos

N

W

S

Southwest passage to Ndanna

WHISPER
OF THE
TIDE

CHAPTER
ONE

There's no law on the Pirate Isle.

Or at least that was how Pa's stories began. When I was little, perched on my father's knee in the cockpit of our wherry, he whispered the old pirate tales to me. The way he described it, Brizos was a magical island ruled by a dread queen who wore a man's finger bones as a necklace and rode a talking whale.

Striding between ramshackle wooden buildings, I dodged a puddle of water—and other things best left unmentioned. The wind blustered, tossing rain at me in sheets. My left boot, coated with clumps of mud, slipped in the street. If this was a magical island, I would eat my hat.

Which was also covered in mud.

From the gloom of a nearby alley, a cloaked man watched me.

Lightning flashed on his keen eyes as he sized me up. I pulled my coat back to expose my flintlock pistol, setting a hand on it. The threat of a bullet in the skull was enough for my would-be assailant. He shrank back into the shadows and let me pass.

Brizos was dangerous at night—that part of Pa's stories I certainly believed. I'd never had occasion to come here as a child, of course. This island was too far out in the sea for a wherry of the riverlands to brave the passage. And Pa would never have brought me anyway—he said it was full of scalawags.

Well, I had a bounty on my head now. I was a scalawag myself.

I continued on, sticking to the dark places under the eaves, where water streamed down broken gutters into slimy barrels. At the bottom of the hill, the island curved to make a natural crescent-shaped harbor. The wharf was empty and the ships deserted, with sails furled and awnings drawn tight against the weather. Pelting drops flattened the sea.

I tugged my hat lower to hide my face. What would my father say if he could see me now? Everything I wore was either borrowed or stolen. My prized gold-handled pistols were gone, one taken from me and the other lying at the bottom of the sea. And while right at this moment Pa and Fee were probably chatting across the red-checkered tablecloth in *Cormorant*'s cabin, a warm lantern swinging above them, I was combing the grimiest part of Brizos for a man who didn't want to be found.

I halted in the mud. This was it—the sign I'd been searching for.

It swung in the wind above the entrance to a dilapidated

shack. Through the rain I could barely make out the scratched letters that spelled The Black Bittern. Glancing over my shoulder to make sure I hadn't been followed, I shoved through the door. A spray of rain dampened the wood floor.

An old man's querulous voice rose up from the shadows. "Close that gods-damned door!"

Candles flickered in cloudy bottles on the tables. Above the bar an alchemical lamp sputtered and swayed in the draft that whistled through the cracks in the walls. Two patrons in dark clothing sat in dark corners. Otherwise the tavern was empty except for a man hunched over the bar and the bored bartender.

Water streamed off my coat, pattering in a black line behind me, as I crossed the room. My curls were frizzy and bedraggled, and my wet boots squeaked on the planks. It wasn't exactly the entrance I'd been hoping for.

The man at the bar turned.

Dark eyes glinting under the brim of a battered hat, he threw me a sour look and tossed back a glass of rum. His clothes were concealed under a long patched coat, but I caught a flash of dirt-encrusted brass buttons engraved with the symbol of Akhaia, a mountain lion with its tail coiled around itself.

The thin white line of an old scar crossed his cheek, under his right eye. Someone had given him another to match—a fresher cut, still angry and red, on his left cheekbone. Where a lone scar might have lent him a rakish look, two made him disreputable, an impression heightened by his straggly beard and unkempt hair.

Without a word, I slipped up to the bar.

The scarred man acknowledged me with a nod. "Didn't reckon I'd see you here tonight."

The bartender uncorked a dingy bottle, sloshing rum into a glass. Twisting on the stool, I assessed my surroundings. I'd expected a reputed pirate tavern to be raucous, with sailors singing bawdy songs off-key while pickpockets darted through the crush. But The Black Bittern's clientele stared moodily into their drinks, straight brown liquor without a trace of juice or sweetness. I had the feeling if I tried to strike up a conversation with the wrong old sailor, I'd end up with a dagger through my hand.

My rum was horrid but mercifully strong, a bootlegger's brew. I turned back to my companion, raising my eyebrows. "Out of all the taverns in Brizos, *this* is where I find you? This is an old man's bar."

He glanced at me from under the hat. "It's the kind of bar where people go while they're waiting to die," he conceded.

"So, an old man's bar."

"Ayah?" He cracked a grin. "Then what are you doing here?"

I steeled myself. This was it. What I'd come for.

"We need to talk." I shoved my glass away. "I don't plan on dying in Brizos. Not today. I have a plan to get us off this island."

"Half the Akhaian navy's searching the streets for us. There's a blockade of twenty ships floating in the harbor." The alchemical lantern gleamed on his left eye, which was blackened. "And don't think I be forgetting your boy Emparch."

"You know that's complicated," I said, following a long pause.

"Maybe it's complicated for you, but it ain't for me." He stared at the bar, where decades of spilled spirits had left pitted wood and circular stains. A muscle in his jaw moved. "No, I reckon this is where we part, the two of us." Suddenly I realized how tired he looked. "I like you, girl, so I'll warn you this once. You ain't cut out for this game. Mess around with lords and Emparchs, and men get killed. Men like you and me."

"I'm not a man," I said.

He gave me a lazy wave. "I was forgetting, *Lady* Bollard."

"I'm only half Bollard."

"Lady Andela, then," he said with a smirk, causing me to inhale sharply. Catching his eye, I knew he'd said it on purpose to get a rise out of me.

I swallowed. "No."

"Well, girlie? I know what you're here for, but there's no use asking," he growled. "I ain't going to come back."

Outside the wind shifted, rain suddenly battering the window. It pelted down on the roof, echoing through the quiet tavern.

I took a deep breath.

"I know," I said. "You're going to betray me."

CHAPTER
TWO
Three months earlier

So far revolution had turned out to be extremely dull.

"Unless we unseat Konto Theucinian from the throne, the Akhaian Empire will never join its neighbors, ushering—" Pausing, Markos shuffled his notes. "Um, ushering in the modern age of democracy. Other more enlightened countries are empowering the workers and encouraging free thought. We cannot expect that from Theucinian. He will keep power at all costs, even going so far as to murder his own blood."

From my table in the back of the theater, I silently urged him on.

Markos's voice grew steadier as he continued his speech. "My father, the Emparch. My mother, your Emparchess. My brother, the heir. Theucinian is ruthless, and he cares not for the plight of the common man."

"You was raised in the Emparch's palace, boy!" a man yelled from the pit in front of the stage. "What do you know about the common man?"

A ripple of laughter traveled across the pit. The theater was split into sections—elevated tables around the outer edges for folk who could pay, and a private balcony above for those paying even more—but the men who packed the floor were a rough crowd. My fingernails dug into my palms, but I knew I couldn't jump to Markos's defense.

He hesitated, a red flush creeping up his cheeks to the tips of his ears. Turning, he addressed his reply to the man who'd yelled at him. "In the three months since my father was assassinated, I've traveled the riverlands on a cargo wherry." Up in the balcony, a man in a silk robe rolled his eyes. "And spoken with many working men and women. I've learned a lot," he said in a rush. "And I'm willing to keep learning. And listening. As your Emparch, I would pledge to do the same."

Alone at my table, I smiled. What Markos told these people was true. He'd changed so much since the day I'd recklessly disobeyed my orders and opened that enchanted crate, discovering him inside. My gaze drifted to the faces of the Akhaian nobles sitting in the balcony, separated from the boisterous tradesmen and sailors who stood in the pit. It was their support he had to win.

Antidoros Peregrine rose from a chair on the stage, setting a hand on Markos's shoulder. "His Excellency is a victim, as much as you are, of what happens when men strive for power, with no thought for their fellow man." He projected his voice. "In the words of the great lawyer and philosopher Gaius Basilides . . ."

As he launched into his speech, Markos slipped down from the stage and wove across the floor toward me. He was half a head taller than most men, his wavy black hair visible above the crowd. One or two people stopped him to say a few words, and he nodded back politely. Most were too wrapped up in Peregrine's speech to pay attention to Markos, but I noticed that the man who'd shouted at him pushed through the audience to shake his hand.

Dropping into the chair next to mine, Markos groaned. "They hated me."

I pushed a mug of cold ale at him. "It wasn't that bad. They weren't throwing rotten fruit or anything."

"Yet." He slumped to rest his forehead on the table, an unwise decision in a public theater.

Antidoros Peregrine had convinced three local Akhaian lords to listen to Markos speak, which was the real reason we'd come to Edessa. He'd also insisted the event be open to the public, but looking up at the balcony, I wondered if that had been a good idea. As I watched, an usher tugged a lord's sleeve to ask if he wanted a drink. Insulted, he pulled his arm back, readjusting his robe.

I turned to Markos. "Did you think it was going to be easy to start a war?"

He sat up. "Gods damn it, Antidoros wants to put me on the throne to *avoid* a war." He took a long pull from his mug. "It's the only reason I let him talk me into making this speech in the first place. A political revolution without blood."

I tore my eyes away from the nobles. Antidoros was an idealist. Myself, I didn't think it was going to be so easy. The common folk and the nobles wanted such different things. And so far the lords had been wary about supporting Markos's claim.

Markos watched Antidoros Peregrine work the crowd. "This all comes so naturally to him. I envy him that." A crease appeared between his eyes. "*He* was once a lord, but you'll notice they don't shout at him."

"Your father exiled him from Akhaia for writing about the plight of the common man," I reminded him. "He stood up for them and lost everything. Folk respect that."

"And he's earned their respect, no doubt about that." Out of habit, he reached up to tug his earring, then caught himself. The bottom part of his left ear was missing, taken as a souvenir by a particularly unscrupulous pirate.

"You will too." I tucked a piece of hair behind his ear. "Someday."

"If only I could speak like he does." Markos sighed. "Oh, I suppose my tutors drilled it into me well enough. I can recite all twenty-six stanzas of the *Epic of Xanto*, but I'm not a natural orator. Not like Peregrine." He shoved away his mug. "I guess coming here was still worth it, for the practice."

I tugged his collar. "Markos Andela." I didn't usually call him by his full name, so that got his attention. "I could never do what you just did. So you're not a natural speaker. Most of us aren't. You're trying."

"I only wish I knew if any of it *mattered*." He glanced at the lords in the balcony. Two of them had stopped listening to Peregrine and were whispering behind their hands, while the third sat stony-faced, clearly disapproving of what he heard. They weren't looking in our direction.

Grabbing my chin, Markos kissed me. Part of me felt a thrill of delight, because I liked kissing him. Twining my fingers into his hair, I leaned closer. But the more practical part of me knew this was a terrible idea. With a sigh, I let go of him.

"Caro, why are you looking over there?" He tried to tug my lips back to his.

I resisted, ducking away to scan the crowd in the pit. "I'm supposed to be watching out for assassins." He trailed his mouth down my ear, while I tried to see around his head. "What if someone murders you while you're kissing me?"

His lips curved against my skin. "Then at least I'll die a happy man," he murmured, the words tickling my neck.

"Markos, don't be romantic and stupid." With a thump, I moved my chair several inches away from his. Even if Markos was willing to let himself become distracted, I couldn't.

To come here, we'd crossed the border into Akhaia. Antidoros Peregrine was of the opinion that it was worth the risk, since after all, Edessa was only a small whaling town far from the heart of the empire. I wasn't sure I agreed. In the three months since Markos and I had taken up residence in Valonikos, we'd already had two run-ins with assassins. No doubt they'd been sent by Konto Theucinian, the man who'd murdered Markos's family and stolen his father's throne. Drumming my fingers on my pistol, I studied the crowd. None of these folk looked like mercenaries, but some men were willing to do horrible things for the promise of coin.

I sighed. Ever since the day I'd opened that crate, nothing was safe anymore. Back then I was perfectly content to be Pa's first mate on *Cormorant*, trading up and down the riverlands of Kynthessa, my homeland. Until Konto Theucinian, Markos's father's cousin, had captured the throne of Akhaia in a bloody coup and I'd gotten mixed up in all of this. When I first met Markos, he was the sheltered and arrogant second son of an Emparch. Together we'd fought the Black Dogs and rescued his sister—and done our fair share of bickering.

We still bickered. A smile made my mouth twitch. But now we usually finished by kissing, which I admit was much more fun.

After Peregrine's speech ended and the theater cleared out, the three lords in the balcony descended. I'd already forgotten their names and titles. In the past months, we'd gone through so many of these meetings. I was bad at titles, and anyway, these men never looked at me.

Markos shook their hands. Stiffening his shoulders, he said, "Thank you for coming today. I hope I can count on your support."

The first lord glanced at the others. "You'd be better off trying your luck on the peninsula. They're far enough from the capital that . . . well, they can afford to be a bit more reckless. Lord Pherenekian is a progressive." His nose wrinkled as if he smelled something bad. "You might speak with him."

Markos didn't bother to keep the disdain from his voice. "You stood in my father's wedding."

"Yes, well." The lord gestured to his valet, who rushed to drape a velvet brocade cape around his shoulders. "You aren't your father. If you were Loukas, it might have been different."

Markos's nostrils flared. "I'm just as much my father's son as my brother was."

The second lord finally spoke, brushing an invisible piece of dirt off his robe. "Loukas Andela wouldn't have been seen dead in a public theater, pandering to the riffraff."

I balled my hands into fists to keep them from flying to my pistols. How dare he? Loukas *was* dead. That remark was meant to sting, and one glance at Markos made it clear the blow had landed. His face had frozen in a rigid mask.

Markos drew himself up. "I give you my thanks for coming today," he said regally, looking down his nose at the lords. "You'll pardon me if I don't walk with you to the door." Turning his back on them, he strode away.

I winced. They were lords of Akhaia, and he'd cut them down as if they were dirt under his boot. I supposed we could check these men off the list.

Catching up to Markos, I squeezed his arm. "There are plenty of other nobles. Some of them are bound to lend you their support. Reckon it's going to take more work than we expected, is all."

His lips flattened into a line. "Let's just return to the ship."

As we made our way back to the harbor, Markos and Peregrine walked ahead, while I stayed two paces behind. I'd be damned if anyone assassinated Markos on my watch. People on the street cast curious glances at us, but especially at me.

Most folk in the southern part of Akhaia had olive skin and dark hair. My face was light brown and freckled, and my hair a cloud of auburn corkscrew curls. But Edessa was a coastal town with whalers from all over the world. Likely it wasn't my looks that made people stare but the fact that I was heavily armed for a seventeen-year-old girl. I stalked through the dockside streets wearing a man's jacket, open at the waist to display the flintlock pistols on my belt, which had lions on the handles fashioned from real gold.

I felt the ocean before I saw it. Behind the murmur and rattle of the town, I heard seagulls shrieking. Their wild voices sounded like tantalizing scraps of a language I couldn't quite grasp. I sensed the up-and-down rhythm of the waves, though my boots trod cobblestones. Being chosen by the god of the sea was still so strange to me.

My first memory is sitting on my pa's knee, staring out at the slow muddy river. Dragonflies dart above the reeds and frogs splash in the shallows. "There's a god at the bottom of the river," Pa whispers in my ear.

Eight generations of the Oresteia family before me were chosen by the river god, who guides wherrymen through the winding marshes. I always knew exactly what my fate would be. I couldn't wait to be one of the brave wherrymen in Pa's stories, smuggling rum and dodging magistrates and having adventures with frogmen and magic crocodiles.

But just as there's a god at the bottom of the river, there is a god who lies under the ocean. And she had other plans for me.

Vix bobbed gently at the dock, her fresh blue paint gleaming. She was a one-masted cutter, swift and small, built to flit around the islands and bays of the coast. I'd heard folk whisper that I was too young to captain a smuggling ship. But the newspapers claimed I'd stolen her from a pirate by the name of Diric Melanos, who'd disappeared under suspicious circumstances.

So I reckon they weren't inclined to say anything to my face.

Nereus, my first mate, jumped up from his game of dice. His sun-whitened hair fluttered in the breeze. "How'd it go?"

"Not well," I said under my breath. Peregrine was deep in conversation with Markos, hand resting on his shoulder. I watched them descend belowdecks. Surely if anyone could talk Markos out of his mood, it was Peregrine.

"So, back to Valonikos, then?" the second mate asked. Patroklos was a rangy man with a north Akhaian accent and dark red hair in a plait. It made me feel at home to see him yelling orders on deck or hauling on the halyards, I think because he reminded me of Pa.

"Ayah." I felt the wind whispering to me. "Let's get under way. Coming here was a waste of time."

We left Edessa, sails puffed out to catch the fine southerly breeze. I steered with a hand draped over *Vix*'s tiller, keeping the coast on my right. A pod of dolphins tunneled through the water off the starboard bow. Nearby a rocky shoal lay underwater, invisible to the eye. Tonight the waves would be flattened by strong gusts, and rain would rush in. I knew these things like I knew my own name. Ever since the sea god had chosen me, I'd gained a sixth sense.

Ahead of us, a naval ship was setting out to sea, square white sails gleaming in the afternoon sun. At her masthead flapped a triangular red flag with a golden mountain lion, marking her as a vessel of the Akhaian Lion Fleet.

Pressing my lips together, I stared moodily at the ship. Three months ago I'd promised Markos I would sail for him as a privateer. But ever since then, *Vix* had been stuck in Valonikos harbor, while Antidoros Peregrine dragged Markos to meeting after meeting. Today's journey to Edessa was the farthest we'd ever sailed.

Though I was reluctant to tell Markos, it bothered me that I didn't know where I fit into this rebellion. *Vix* was like a mosquito, tiny and pesky, with the ability to bite hard. Surely there was *something* we could do—a blockade that needed running or an Akhaian ship to hunt down. I believed in Markos, and I wanted to be with him. And yet . . . I couldn't help feeling a bit like a bird whose wings had been cut off.

With a flapping of gray feathers, a seagull alighted on the rail. Turning its head to fix me with one beady eye, it whispered, "You want it, don't you? The cannons. The chase."

Its beak never moved, but it didn't have to. I knew the voice wasn't really coming from the gull.

"What good is a ship in a harbor?" the sea god scoffed.

I squeezed the tiller. She didn't just mean *Vix*.

Images flashed through my head, flooding me with unfamiliar sensations. I felt the thrill as *Vix* plowed across the waves. Cannonballs smashed into the hull of my enemy with a satisfying explosion of splinters. The Akhaian ship plummeted through the swells ahead of us, listing to one side. Fat and heavy, she was built for hauling supplies. She was no match for *Vix*.

Ropes tautened as grappling hooks pulled the ship—my prey—closer and closer—

I blinked. I'd never even sniffed a sea battle before, but somehow the vision had felt as visceral as a memory. I realized the gull was watching me with a knowing smirk.

"Stop that," I told the sea god, pretending my heart wasn't pounding.

"This is what you were born for. The rush of battle. The power of the sea." The gull swiveled its head to look at the red roofs of Valonikos on the horizon. "I grow weary of this port."

"Well, I don't," I snapped, though I suspected she knew I was lying. "And don't go putting things in my head again."

The god had never done anything like that before. It had felt intrusive and—a small part of me whispered—exhilarating. Hand sweating on the tiller, I reminded myself sternly that the bloodlust I'd felt wasn't me. It unnerved me that the god could make me feel something like that. For a moment I'd thought it was real.

There was still so much about the god I didn't know. Sometimes I wasn't sure I wanted to know.

When we reached Valonikos, a man was waiting for us on the dock. He wore a velvet cape and a three-cornered black hat, looking very official. My danger sense whirred to life. I gripped the handle of my pistol.

Snapping his heels together, the man bowed. "Markos Andela?"

Markos and I exchanged uneasy glances. We tried not to speak his name so loudly in public. It was too dangerous.

I cocked my gun. "What do you want?"

The stranger's eyes widened slightly. "Please, miss." He fumbled in his pockets, producing a letter with an ostentatious wax seal. "I'm a courier, come from Eryth. I promised the Archon I would place it directly in His Excellency's hands. In—in private."

Peregrine shot an amused look at me. "Peace, Caroline." He touched my arm. "Let's give the man a moment to explain himself before we go pulling pistols."

"Sorry," I told the courier, stowing the gun. "Mark—His Excellency—was recently attacked in the streets of Valonikos. So you understand my caution."

Markos gestured up the street. "If you please, why don't you follow me back to my rooms, where we shall be free to discuss your message without interruption." Turning back to me, he dropped a kiss on my forehead and said in his regular voice, "We'll be safe enough at Peregrine's house. Dinner at the usual place?"

"Ayah," I promised, squeezing his hand. "I'll change and meet you there at eight."

I watched their backs as they strode away, uncomfortable letting Markos leave with this stranger. He had his swords, I reminded myself. Markos always carried two matching short swords, and he was an expert with them. Besides, Peregrine would be right outside the door.

Still I kept my eyes on them until they disappeared into the crowded street.

"Pa will never let you," I heard a man scoff behind me. "You're not strong enough to handle the machinery."

I turned to see Docia Argyrus, the salvager's daughter, coming up the dock, skirts swishing around her ankles. Her dark brown hair was twisted up in a no-nonsense bun. She carried a bundle of maps tucked under one arm and an account book in her hand.

A man trailed after her. "And anyway," he went on, "salvage crews are rough. The men won't listen to you."

"It seems to me *you* started working on the barge when you was fifteen," she snapped. "And, I might add, a skinny squeak of a boy at that. I'm a better diver than either you or Hadrian. Pa taught me just the same as he taught you two. Oh hello, Caro." She waved at the man. "This is my brother Torin. He's an ass."

Torin was a burly man with tanned skin, wearing muddy boots and a fisherman's sweater. "Give it up, sister." He clapped her on the shoulder. "Salvaging ain't women's work. Besides, who'd want to be all day on a barge, diving and hauling and wading in the muck, when you could be taking it easy in the office? Ask me, you be the lucky one."

"You think doing all the contracts and all the paperwork is easy?" she demanded. "If I ever decide to leave Argyrus and Sons, none of you will know what hit you."

"What's this leaving talk?"

Docia rolled her eyes so only I could see. "Go home and bother your wife," she told Torin. "I'll just be in the office taking it *easy*."

Her brother shrugged, ambling off down the pier. She made a rude gesture at his back.

Docia Argyrus and I had struck up a friendship during my time in Valonikos. I hadn't seen my cousin Kenté since she left for Trikkaia to train as a shadowman, and I'd missed having a girl to talk to. Docia was two years older than me, but we had a lot in common. Both of us were the daughters of boat captains, working-class girls who'd grown up on the water.

I winced at the bitter look on her face. Trouble was, her pa was a bit more backward thinking than mine.

Docia nodded up the dock. "Pub?"

I hesitated. The envoy had seemed exceedingly eager to put that letter into Markos's hands, so it must be important. But I couldn't just barge into their meeting. Not when he'd asked to speak to Markos alone. I supposed there was no harm in having a pint while I waited.

"Ayah, let's," I decided. We started walking up the dock. "But only for one drink. I'm meeting Markos at the Net of Plenty."

"Oooh, *Markos*," she teased. "Wouldn't want to keep you from dinner with your young man."

My cheeks warmed. "He's not my young man," I lied. "What's this about leaving Argyrus and Sons? Do you think you ever would?"

She snorted. "No. But it would serve them right if I up and left. I could get premises across the street. Call myself Argyrus and Daughters." A grin stole across her plain face. "'Course, I'd charge ever so slightly less, so as to undercut them and take their business."

"Well, that's only proper," I said.

At the end of the dock, I cast a glance in the direction of Antidoros Peregrine's house. Curiosity burned inside me, but I would just have to wait till dinner to hear what the urgent message was about.

I only hoped this time it was good news.

CHAPTER
THREE

Markos was hiding something. I knew it even before he took the box from his pocket.

Brass lamps dangled from the rafters of the Net of Plenty, casting intricate patterns on the white stucco arches. Tantalizing smells leaked out from behind the swinging kitchen door. Breen, the frogman proprietor and cook, had an excellent reputation. Mottled green and brown, he stood in the doorway, surveying the busy tables. Catching his eye, I gave him a nod. The restaurant served the best seafood in Valonikos, and we came here often.

"Well?" Markos nudged the paper-wrapped box. "Open it."

To my surprise, he'd refused to discuss the mysterious courier. Instead he ordered a carafe of wine, and then proceeded to drink most of it himself. We were on the second course now, and we still hadn't talked about the message.

I untied the velvet ribbon around the box, feeling the curious eyes of the other patrons on me. They knew exactly who Markos was. I could almost hear the whispers. *Emparch*. But also *Exile*. *Pretender*.

With a wary glance at Markos, I ripped the fancy paper off the box and lifted the cover.

Resting against a cushion of snowy white was a bracelet. Blue and red gems sparkled under the flickering lamps. I pretended not to notice the hush that had fallen on the nearby tables, as people strained to hear us over the clattering dishes.

I stared at the box in confusion. A bracelet? I never wore jewelry.

Markos leaned back in his chair, twirling the wineglass between his fingers. "Call it a birthday present."

My mouth was dry. "You know my birthday's not for another month."

He shrugged. "An early present, then."

Even I, who had no knowledge of such things, could see the bracelet was exquisite. Mounted on an elegant gold cuff, a lozenge-shaped red jewel nestled inside an arc of sapphires. An *enormous* red jewel.

I hesitated to touch it, though my hands were clean. "That's not—it's not a real ruby, is it?"

"Do you honestly think I'd give you gemstones made of paste?" he scoffed.

The Emparch, as it had turned out, held accounts not only in Akhaian banks but in the neighboring countries as well. With the help of the Akhaian consul, Markos had wrestled through the months of paperwork required to officially apply for asylum in Valonikos. But once his identity had been established, there was some confusion about whether the accounts belonged to the Andela family or to the Emparchy. By the time everything got cleared up, representatives of the Theucinians had managed to empty out most of the gold and silver.

I shuddered at the memory of the day Markos found out. He'd dashed a bottle of ink on the floor. It had made an awful mess.

The *Daily Hierophant*, that detestable rag of a paper, had taken to calling Markos the Penniless Emparch. It was better than the Pretender, but not by much. If I ever caught up with Fabius Balerophon, the fool reporter who'd come up with the name, I was going to punch him.

My fingers brushed the cold gems. Markos couldn't afford this. "It's beautiful, but . . ."

He exhaled, a crease appearing between his eyes. "I admit this isn't going the way I imagined."

"All I was going to say is, wasn't it awfully expensive?"

His nostrils flared. "I'm an Emparch, not a pauper, no matter what that loathsome paper says. Anyway, I didn't buy it. It belonged to my mother."

"I thought all her jewels were taken by the—" I watched him stiffen, and hastily corrected myself. "Um, were lost."

From my father I'd received my freckles and the reddish-brown color of my hair, as well as a smuggler's instincts. Now those instincts rattled ominously. I remembered how arrogant Markos had been when we first met, masking his intense pain under haughty manners and formal speech. Tonight he reminded me of the old Markos.

Something was wrong. And he didn't want me to know it.

"Cousin Sophronia found the bracelet at her house," he explained. "My mother left it in her keeping years ago, before I was born, on a trip to the seashore."

When Markos had first arrived in Valonikos, he'd stayed with Tychon and Sophronia Hypatos, his distant cousins who lived on the Hill—as they called the sedate, elegant neighborhood at the center of the city. Although Markos was tight-lipped about what made him leave, I suspected Sophronia had said something rude about me. Whatever would have made him go up to her house tonight?

Markos cleared his throat. "I wanted to surprise you with something pretty. To show you how much I—how I feel about you."

He wasn't looking into my eyes. My stomach clenched. "Markos, what's going on?"

He swallowed. "Nothing's going on."

"Yes, it *is*," I insisted. Realizing people were staring, I lowered my voice. Gesturing at the bracelet, I said, "This is . . . it's too much. We never needed things like this before. I thought—I thought everything was perfect between us. Don't . . ." I held my breath. "Don't you think so?"

Markos gripped the table edge, knuckles going pale.

"Not that the bracelet isn't nice," I quickly added.

He made a choking noise.

"I didn't mean nice. Lovely—it's lovely," I stammered.

I was saying all the wrong things. It had belonged to his mother, and I'd gone and stuck my foot in my mouth, implying I didn't like it. I eyed the gems in their ornate setting. Where would I ever wear such a thing? It was meant for an Emparchess, and I was a sea captain.

Which was the real problem, wasn't it? Ever since I found out I was chosen by the sea and not the river, I'd felt uncomfortable in my own skin. Back on *Cormorant* I always knew the right thing to do. I no longer had that confidence—the feeling of knowing where I fit in the world. Markos thought he was just giving me something pretty, but he didn't understand.

This bracelet wasn't me. The ruby twinkled tauntingly up at me under the lamplight, yet another reminder that my whole *life* wasn't me anymore.

"Let's just forget about it." Markos downed the last of his wine, slamming the glass on the table. "You don't want the bracelet. I get it."

It was as if we were in two separate boats, the tide washing us farther and farther apart. I wanted to throw him a rope, but I didn't know how. He was so angry and I was so—

Scared.

My fingers closed on the box. "Yes, I do."

"Caro, I'll take it back. It's *fine*."

I knew it wasn't fine. With clammy hands I shook the bracelet out of the box and slid it onto my wrist. The gold lay heavy and cold against my skin.

Markos reached across the table, grabbing for the bracelet. I ducked away. "I didn't know you were this terrible at giving gifts!"

"Not as terrible as you are at accepting them," he muttered.

"Now." I turned my hand this way and that, making the ruby catch the light. "How do I look?"

"Gorgeous, of course." I sensed he wanted to say more, but he hesitated so long that the silence grew awkward.

"Markos Andela," I said, pretending to be stern, "you didn't sound very certain." Desperately, I cast about for anything that would lighten the mood. "Perhaps if I were wearing *only* this bracelet, you'd be able to summon up more enthusiasm?"

As soon as the words left my mouth, I winced. I'd just tried to flirt with him while wearing his dead mother's jewels. Even if he'd never seen her wear this particular bracelet, it was wildly inappropriate. If only I'd paid more attention to Ma's insistence that I learn manners and etiquette.

Markos smiled, and I exhaled in relief.

Then he crumpled, sliding sideways off the chair.

My heart rose into my throat. Behind me a lady screamed. I flung myself onto my knees on the floor. "Markos?"

He was alive, but his eyes were squeezed shut in pain. Had the wine been poisoned? I felt his forehead. Impossible—we'd both drunk from the same carafe. Wincing, Markos grabbed his right thigh. A red mark bloomed on his trouser leg.

I stared in horror. "Gods damn me."

Blood spilled out between his fingers. How had this happened? I'd never heard a shot. Over my dress, I wore a high-collared jacket trimmed in ribbons. Whipping it off, I pressed the fabric against the wound.

Something whizzed over my head. The wine carafe exploded. Red wine dripped down the tablecloth, as bright as the blood pooling on the tiles. I'd certainly heard *that* bullet.

The room seemed to freeze in shock. Across the sea of tables I spotted movement by the floor-length window that led to the garden. A gauzy curtain swirled and fluttered, and a man, clad in a black coat, swiftly retreated into the dark.

At the sight of Markos's blood, a waiter dropped his tray. Dishes crashed to the floor and shattered. The crowd came to life and pushed in, clamoring excitedly. The toe of a man's boot hit me in the leg.

Markos swore through clenched teeth. His face was always pale, but now it was practically translucent, his blue eyes slightly unfocused. With trembling fingers he reached for my hand, but missed.

"Get back!" I snarled at the people around us, shoving with my elbows. My forehead broke out in sweat. "Give him some air!"

Something greenish-brown landed beside me.

Frog toes.

Breen, the cook, pushed a heap of towels into my hands. Bundling them into a ball, I pressed down on the wound. So much blood. A bullet in the leg was better than one in the heart, but what if it had nicked an artery? Markos could still bleed to death.

Or lose the leg.

Through the curtain, I saw the assassin heading for the hedge at the back of the garden. "That's him!" I raised my voice. "Someone stop that man!" But no one heard me in the confusion. Lifting Markos's shaky hand, I kissed it. "I have to go after him."

"Caro," Markos gasped. "No!"

Breen set his hand over mine on the bloody towels. There was something steadying about the touch of his webbed fingers, each ending in a round green ball. He reminded me of Fee, the frogman who was my father's first mate on *Cormorant* and who I trusted with my life.

Breen's round yellow eyes swiveled up at me. "Go."

Dropping Markos's hand, I sprang to my feet. A hoop skirt was a cursed impractical thing, but it was handy if you wanted to conceal a lot of weapons. I lifted my petticoat to my knees, eliciting a gasp from the crowd, and rummaged under it. My fingers found my matched flintlocks. Jerking the guns out, I broke into a run.

Vaulting over the threshold, I landed on the garden patio. A lady shrieked at the sight of my bloodstained clothes, dropping her spoon. Belatedly I realized all the garden tables were full. I'd leaped into the middle of these people's dinner. They stared at me, silverware poised in their hands. One woman tittered nervously.

The man was gone, but the hedge branches still shivered where he'd passed through. Dodging around tables, I raced after him.

To fire into a crowded restaurant was madness. Flintlock pistols do not have a reputation for accuracy at long distances. The assassin's shot had hit Markos in the upper thigh, when surely he'd been aiming for his heart or his head. He might have killed an innocent merchant having his supper, or a waiter, or any of these people.

I dove into the hedge, branches catching my hair and skirts. The lace on my bodice snagged on the twigs, holding me back. Snarling, I pushed through. The lace tore from my dress. Ruined, just like my hair and jacket.

Bursting from the hedge into the street, I glanced wildly in both directions.

They called this the merchant district, a misleading name. There were no market stalls or tradesmen hawking wares here. Sedate stone buildings rose up from the street, their ornately carved doors flanked by urns of flowers. This was where the wealthiest shipping companies had their offices. The Bollards, my mother's family, were one block over. Lampposts illuminated the cobblestone street, where traders scurried about with account books full of figures and captains in three-cornered hats puffed on pipes. There were people from all over, with skin ranging from the deepest brown of Ndanna to the blue-tinged pale of northern Akhaia.

I caught a sudden flash of motion. Farther down the block, the assassin had seen me emerge from the hedge. He burst into a run, elbowing through the people on the sidewalk. Light glinted on something metal at his waist. He was armed with a blade as well as a pistol.

"Murder!" I screamed. "Stop him!"

At the gate of a nearby building, two guards stirred, but I couldn't afford to wait and see if they joined the chase. The assassin ducked into an alley and I pelted after him, flinging myself around the corner.

The alley sloped sharply down between whitewashed stucco

walls. It smelled strongly of rotting fish. In the gap between the buildings, far below, I glimpsed masts and spars. He was making for the harbor.

My shoe slipped on wet stone. A twinge shot through my ankle, but I ignored it. This time the assassin wasn't going to get away. Pulse pounding hot in my temples, I kicked my tangled skirts out of the way. From now on, I swore I'd wear boots and trousers *everywhere*.

Far ahead, the assassin's coat was a bobbing black dot. My fear for Markos simmered under the surface, clawing at me with dark fingers, but I forced it back down. I had to catch up.

I skidded out between two warehouses, and the city suddenly opened up around me. Valonikos harbor lay under a purply twilight sky, a sprawl of masts and sails. Smokestacks and wagons and warehouses, their wide doors open like mouths, dotted the curve of the bay. At the smell of the sea, my spirits lifted. With renewed strength, I kept running.

The man raced down the pier, dodging stacks of barrels and seaweed-coated crab traps. With a flick of his wrist, he untied a dinghy from the post, yanking the rope to bring it alongside the dock.

I raised my pistol and fired, but the shot glanced off the wooden bow of the boat with a shower of splinters.

Turning, the man drew his sword. I squeezed the trigger on my second pistol, but it jammed. Heart in my throat, I fumbled in my pouch of additional shot. But my hands were shaking so hard, the lead bullets slipped through my fingers.

The briny salt breeze stirred my hair, and suddenly I had an idea. Casting outward with all my senses, I reached for the sea. I didn't need guns—not when I had the power of the whole ocean at my fingertips. I concentrated on the water, trying to recall the way it felt that day when the waves had parted for me. My nostrils flared. The muscles in my arms tightened, and the sea—

The sea didn't move.

The assassin stepped closer, raising his sword.

I heard a resounding smash, following by the tinkling of broken glass. The man toppled forward onto the thwart, sword clattering harmlessly to the bottom of the boat. The dinghy rocked, sending out a rippling wake.

Wiping sweat from my eyes, I looked up at my rescuer.

Docia Argyrus stood on the dock, gripping a broken brown bottle. "Reckon this fellow ain't going nowhere."

CHAPTER
FOUR

"How—" I braced my hands on my knees, out of breath. Red spots danced before my eyes. "How did you—?"

Docia examined the jagged edge of the bottle, setting it on a nearby barrel. She jerked her head toward a low squat ship whose paint spelled out *Catfish*. "Was heading back to my pa's barge when I spotted you hightailing it after this fellow."

"Ahem." A guard captain in a dark blue coat approached, clearing his throat. "Young misses, what's going on here? Which of you accosted this man?" He jerked his head, and the other two guardsmen jumped to collect the unconscious man from the dinghy. Looking back at Docia, his eyes narrowed. "Is there blood on that bottle?"

"There'd better be," she said—quite flippantly, given the

seriousness of the accusation. "Bashed him over the head with it good, didn't I?"

"He's an Akhaian assassin," I told the guard. "She just saved my life."

"See here, miss, you can't go running through the streets screaming 'murder.' You're disturbing the peace." He tugged a notebook from his pocket with a beleaguered sigh. "If ma'am will please describe her grievance with the gentleman in question—"

"Ain't she just said?" Docia snapped. "He's a gods-damned assassin."

I didn't have time for this. "He shot a man in the Net of Plenty, in front of at least thirty witnesses."

The captain's eyebrows drew together.

"Come back with me, if you like," I said, "and talk to Breen. He'll tell you. But I have to go. My—" I swallowed, fear washing over me like a dark current. "My friend might be dying." I started to leave.

"I must have both your names for the report!" he called after me.

Docia rolled her eyes. "Eudocia Argyrus," she told him. "Which I daresay you know, Bendis, seeing as we learned our letters together. 'Young miss,' my ass." She nodded up the dock. "Go, Caro. I'll handle this lot."

The captain signaled his men to follow me to the restaurant. As I hurried up the street, I didn't bother to check if they were keeping up. I needed to get back to Markos.

When I burst into the restaurant, sweaty dress sticking to my shoulders, the other diners had dispersed. I supposed the dark bloodstain on the floor had put them off their food. I glanced frantically around the empty dining room.

A waiter paused, cleaning rag in hand. "He ain't here. A man come and took him."

"What?" My voice came out as a yelp.

I heard a chirp. Silhouetted in the kitchen door was Breen. "Sent for Peregrine," he told me. Spotting the guardsmen, he raised his voice and croaked, "Closed."

"Begging your pardon, Breen, but we got to get your statement," one of the guards said. "About the incident. We got the man in custody."

I didn't have time to hang around for that. I left the Net of Plenty and limped up the street, dread settling in my bones like a chill wind on a stormy day. Peregrine had taken rooms in the merchant district, not far from here. He graciously allowed Markos and Daria to live with him on a temporary basis. I knew it made Markos, who had grown up with every imaginable privilege, uncomfortable to be beholden to Peregrine for lodgings. But they'd also become close in the past months, and I rather thought Markos enjoyed spending his evenings arguing about politics by the fire.

I ducked into the courtyard of Peregrine's town house, my turned ankle stinging with each step. Round splotches of blood dotted the cobblestones. I felt suddenly faint, my head floating high in the air, disconnected from my body. I tried to swallow, but found I had no spit left. Panic mounting, I took the stairs two at a time.

Markos would be fine. He *had* to be.

I barged through the first door on the left—to see Markos awake in bed, his leg propped on a pile of pillows. Our eyes met. For a dazed moment I stood in the doorway, silently drinking him in.

Alive. He was alive.

My path was blocked by something metal. "No farther."

"It's just Caro," Markos said quickly, and I realized there was a sword in my face.

Antidoros Peregrine lowered his blade. "Caro." He exhaled in relief. "I apologize. I saw movement, and reacted with haste." But I noticed he did not put the weapon away.

Another man was in the room—a physician, I guessed from his black leather bag. Tucking a metal instrument into his pocket, he rinsed his hands in a bowl of pink-tinged water. Markos's trouser leg had been cut away and his right boot removed. The wound was dressed with a wad of fabric.

"If you heal well," the physician told Markos, tying off the bandages, "I think it likely you'll keep the leg. You were lucky, son."

"Your Excellency," I corrected him. Crossing the small room, I took Markos's hand in mine. It was cold.

The physician shrugged. "Begging your pardon, miss, but that's not my place to say, is it?" He turned his attention to the wound, and his tone became businesslike. "The ball went straight through the muscle. It seems to have come out cleanly." Noticing my glare, he added, "Just because I don't care to opine on the Akhaian succession doesn't mean I can't do my job. I took a vow to help all men, and I suppose that includes exiles and pretenders."

I put my hand on my dagger. "Theucinian is the real pretender—"

"Caro," Markos said, a soft rebuke. I was worried about the sickly pallor of his skin, and the feverish flush on his cheeks even more. "He just dug a bullet out of my leg. I would rather you refrain from stabbing him over his politics."

My voice broke. "How can you say that?"

Markos glanced at the doctor. "I don't blame him. It's hard for people, not knowing what's true and what's rumor."

"That's fair." Surprise flitted across the physician's face. He studied Markos more carefully. "You do have the Andela look about you, I suppose."

"You *suppose*," I muttered. "Why else do you think people keep trying to assassinate him? Calling him the Pretender is ridiculous, when you all know perfectly well he's exactly who he says he is. Just admit you're a bunch of cowards, trembling in fear of Theucinian."

"You'll have to excuse her," Markos told the physician. "She's . . . fiery."

The physician quirked his lips in silent agreement and began to pack his bag. "I'm not afraid of Akhaia, miss. Valonikos has been a free city for years. I only meant it's difficult for folk to know what to believe, when all the papers are saying different things. Now," he said, "the sleeping draft should start working in ten or fifteen minutes. You're to be confined to bed for a week. Absolutely no walking. Send for me at once if you develop an infection or a prolonged fever." He peered at me, raising an eyebrow. "And no . . . *exercise*. Of any kind. I trust I shan't have to elaborate, young lady."

I stared hard at the bed linens, my face warming with embarrassment.

Lord Peregrine escorted the physician out, leaving me alone with Markos. The moment he was gone, I curled up on the edge of the bed, not caring if my shoes muddied the sheets.

"How do you feel?" I snuggled close to Markos, savoring the solid feel of his body.

He shifted to put his arm around me. "It hurts like hell."

"I can't stand this," I said, feeling the sting of tears. I squeezed my eyes shut and buried my face in his neck. His skin was clammy. "This is the third time someone's tried to kill you. People aren't meant to live this way."

"I don't see any other choice," I heard him say. "Caro, don't cry."

"I'm not crying."

I felt his chest move with a stifled laugh. "You're crying *on my neck*."

We'd only been in Valonikos two weeks when the first assassin showed up. He'd infiltrated the Hypatos kitchens and been caught standing over the stove, a tiny bottle in hand. The cook had shouted at him and he'd scuttled off. Afterward none of the servants could remember seeing him enter or leave the building, which could only mean one thing—he was probably a shadowman. Tychon Hypatos ordered all the food to be thrown out, and that was the end of it.

Or so we'd thought, until a man lunged at Markos in a crowded street. Luckily Markos had taken to wearing an armored vest under his coat whenever he went out in public. The knife glanced off the stiff leather, but the assailant disappeared.

"At least this time we caught him," I said. "The city guards have him in custody." I related the story of how I'd pursued the assassin through the market district and down to the harbor, finishing with Docia Argyrus and her bottle. "Gods-damned lucky I was that she happened to be there."

"This time," Markos muttered darkly. "But what happens when our luck runs out?"

Grabbing his chin, I turned his face toward mine and kissed him slowly and deeply. I knew I should let him sleep, but I couldn't help delighting in the shivery feel of his fingers in my hair. Close. Tonight had been so close.

"We could go away," Markos said when I pulled back. "I don't mean somewhere in Akhaia or Kynthessa. *Far* away, where we won't have to constantly watch our backs. To, I don't know, Ndanna maybe. Isn't that where the Bollards come from?"

I rolled my eyes. "Hundreds of years ago."

A vast mountain range separated Ndanna from the rest of the continent, which was why Jacari Bollard's discovery of the Southwest Passage had rocketed him to fame and fortune. You couldn't get there by wherry. I'd never been to Ndanna, and what I knew amounted to no more or less than what most folk knew. The capital was called the Clockwork City, and the servants there were automatons, built from gears and metal and imbued with a magical life spark. The Bollards had lived in the riverlands for over two hundred years, but my mother, being a trader, knew how to speak the language of her ancestors. I had never learned.

Markos swallowed. "It was just an idea."

"I thought you wanted to get your throne back."

"You don't have to tell me what my duty is," he said with a sigh. "Believe me, I know. No one born into my family has ever been free." He stared at the bandage on his thigh. Gesturing at the splotch of blood seeping through the cloth, he said, "It's just . . . this is disgusting." He touched his scarred ear, still angrily red. "Konto Theucinian keeps sending people to take bits out of me. Even if it's slowly, piece by piece, someday he'll get me."

I'd never heard him sound so hopeless.

Leaning back on the pillow, he closed his eyes. "Someday there'll be nothing left."

He was quiet for so long I thought he was asleep. Easing myself off the bed, I crept to the door.

"Caro."

Hand on the doorknob, I turned. My heart ached at how vulnerable he looked, wrapped in bandages and surrounded by pillows.

"Tonight at dinner—" Markos cleared his throat. "Was that a real fight?"

My left hand itched to fly to the ruby bracelet, but I held it clenched at my side. He still hadn't told me what was in the letter.

I had not forgotten, but I didn't want him worrying about it right now. He needed to focus on getting well.

"I don't know what you're talking about," I lied. "We fight at least six times a day."

"Not like this, I think," he said quietly.

My voice stuck in my throat. Without answering, I slipped into the hall and shut the door behind me.

A tangle of ratted black hair and disheveled lace flew at my waist. "You can't keep me from him!" Daria shrieked, kicking me in the shin.

"Ow," I said calmly. Seizing Markos's nine-year-old sister by the arm, I detached her from my clothing.

Antidoros Peregrine appeared at the top of the stairs. "Little one, your brother was injured. He's just taken a powerful sleeping potion. It is imperative that he rest." Smoothing Daria's hair, he smiled. "In the morning you can bring him breakfast."

Daria's tear-streaked face looked as if snails had been crawling on it. She wiped her nose on her sleeve. "The kitchen girl said they were going to cut his leg off."

"That's a pack of lies," I snapped.

She eyed me suspiciously, then turned to Peregrine. "Is it?" she asked, squinting up at him.

He touched her cheek. "Little badger, the physician says his leg will be fine."

It rankled that she was willing to take his word over mine, but they'd grown close over the past months. I shifted guiltily. Living on *Vix* with Nereus, I didn't spend as much time with her as I should have.

Daria dug in her pocket, producing a fish skull, a bit of soiled ribbon, several wooden beads, and a dull kitchen knife. She plopped cross-legged on the floor outside Markos's door, clutching the knife in her lap.

Peregrine sounded bemused. "What are you doing?"

"Guarding Markos."

To my surprise, Antidoros Peregrine slid down the wall to sit next to her. Laying his sword across his knees, he said, "Well, then, let's say we guard together for a little while."

I knelt beside Daria. "I have to get back to *Vix*," I told her. Reaching under my skirt, I pulled out my best dagger. Mountain lions hid among the curlicues on its bone handle. "This is my lion dagger." I held it out to her. "Best be careful. It's not a toy. It's the weapon of an Akhaian bodyguard."

Sniffling, she took it. One side of her mouth tilted up in a tiny smile.

"Caro, are you certain it's wise to leave?" Peregrine asked. "Perhaps you should stay here for the night, where my men can protect you."

"I reckon I'll be safe enough with Nereus." Staring at the closed door, I swallowed. "Send word at once if—if anything changes."

I left the house, striding down the dark street. The sea before a storm has a certain wildness. I felt it whistling through the air, bringing crispness to the wind and a heightened anger to the waves. Beyond the rooftops and masts I could make out white crests, rolling in lines toward the harbor. I buried my hands in my skirt pockets. We were in for a blow. Inhaling deeply, I searched for the familiar whiff of salt under the human smells of the city.

The faint sound of the waves centered me, bringing me back to myself.

Only then did I remember what had happened earlier tonight, when I'd tried to summon the power of the sea—and failed. Had I done something wrong? That man had been ten seconds away from murdering me. Why hadn't I been able to call on the sea for help?

Perhaps I was wrong, and that wasn't the way it worked. Or I just didn't understand the sea well enough to do it properly. I cast a sour glance at the black water. Or perhaps *she* was lurking under there watching the whole time.

And whispering, "*Laughter*," in her mocking voice.

A lone lamp dangled from *Vix*'s forestay. The lettering across her square stern was deep blue, bordered by gold. Her name was newly painted in curly letters, with her home port of Valonikos underneath in a smaller blocky print. Fog whirled around me as I stepped onto the dock.

Reaching out, I touched *Vix*'s planks. A reassuring feeling warmed me. I'd grown up on my pa's wherry, *Cormorant*, so I knew that a ship was a touchstone. Something you could always come back to. A home on the water.

In the privacy of the captain's cabin, I removed my blood-stained outer skirt. I never wore stays, so I had no need for a maid, but it was a struggle to reach the laces of my bodice. Markos's blood had seeped through to my petticoats. Hastily, I wadded my clothes into a ball and threw them in the corner.

Clad in only my linen underwear, I could finally relax.

Women's clothes had so many cursed layers. A damp draft seeped in through the open porthole. I slumped into my desk chair, the cool air tickling my sweaty shoulders. The tiny desk was wedged between the bed and the wall, barely leaving room to sit. A cutter was not, after all, a full-sized ship, but a small vessel built for speed. I was lucky to have my own cabin at all.

Now that I was finally alone, my tears threatened to overflow. Why hadn't I said yes to Peregrine's offer to stay the night at the town house? I wanted to be with Markos. I felt every inch of the city separating me from him.

A bottle of brandy sat on the corner of the desk. Dragging it toward me, I uncorked it to take a soothing chug.

And halted.

A letter was pinned to the desk with a dagger. Danger sense tingling, I examined the envelope. *Caro Oresteia* was scrawled on the front in a sloppy hand I would have recognized anywhere. Jerking the dagger up, I freed the letter.

Cousin Dearest,

I hope this letter finds you well. Unfortunately I shall have to skip the pleasantries — the magic I've learned and the boys I've kissed and all other such intriguing topics. I'm writing because I overheard something I think might be important.

Last night two men came calling for the headmaster. I don't know their names, but I recognized one of them. He's on the Emparch's council — I think he might be a Theucinian relation. As it happens, I was lurking behind the parlor drapes.

(Oh, all right. I was sneaking to the kitchen to get some cheese. The cheese is not the point of the story.)

The headmaster offered the men some port, and they all sat down. I shall not recount the first half hour of their conversation, as it was quite boring. If you were here, I daresay you would ask why I stayed, if it was all so dull.

Well, you know how I love secrets. Presently my curiosity was gratified.

"There's still the problem of Andela," one of the men said, and my ears perked right up.

"Don't worry," said the councilmen in reply. "They've put the Lady Dressed in Blood on it. It won't be long now."

By now my cheese was quite forgotten as I skulked behind the drapes.

The headmaster screwed up his face in disapproval, a look I admit I recognized because it has been turned upon me more than once. "I'll pretend I didn't hear that," he said sternly.

"Oh, don't get all high and mighty on me. You run a school that trains assassins for hire."

"A gross oversimplification," said the headmaster, and off they went into an argument about whether it is moral for the House of Shadows to concern itself in the affairs of nations, which, while intellectually fascinating, is neither here nor there when it comes to Markos's plight.

The Lady Dressed in Blood!!!

Don't worry, I've made it my business to discover everything there is to know about her. I haven't found any clues yet, but

with a name like that she has to be Up to No Good. Tell
Markos he must be careful. As for you, I send the enclosed. It's
a talisman to protect you from shadowmen. Wear it & be
watchful!

K. B.

I turned the envelope upside down and shook it. Something
hit the desk with a clunk. Kenté's talisman was barely more than
a rough blob of gold, stamped with a crescent moon and suspended from a brass chain. I wondered if she'd made it herself. If
so, she'd progressed quite far in her study of shadow magic. I lifted
the talisman to sling it around my neck, and then paused. Tonight's
assassination attempt had put me in a suspicious frame of mind.

Shrugging my jacket on, I made my way through the main
cabin and climbed up to the deck, where Nereus and two sailors
sat in a pool of lantern light near the bow of the cutter. I'd avoided
them on the way in, not being in the mood to talk. The wind
whipped Nereus's hair as he shook a pair of dice in a cup. He wore
a half-open leather vest, exposing the tattoo on his chest, which
was of two mermaids and was even more obscene than the single
naked mermaid on his arm.

"Did you see who brought this letter?" I asked.

He glanced up at me. "What letter?"

I held out the envelope. "I found this on my desk."

He shook his head. "Impossible. We been here all night, love.
I saw no one."

"Nor I," his companion agreed.

"It's from Kenté," I said. "I only wondered if . . . maybe she brought it herself."

"Ah." Nereus grinned. "Well, why didn't you say so in the first place? That explains everything, don't it? No one sees a shadowman if he don't want to be seen." He took a swig off his flask. "Or she. Though it do seem to me that if Miss Bollard were here in Valonikos, she might've said hello to an old shipmate."

I knew he was right. She would have said hello to me too. My hope faded, leaving me feeling a little foolish. It had just been wishful thinking. I was worried and lonely, and I missed my cousin.

Back inside my cabin I studied the letter again. Kenté could have sent it with a fellow shadowman who had business in Valonikos. It was the most likely explanation. *Unless* . . . I leaned my elbows on the varnished sill of the porthole, staring out into the misty night.

Unless it was a trap, from yet another person who wanted me dead. When had my life become so cursed complicated? Like Markos, I was mightily sick of being on edge all the time.

Making my decision, I picked up the talisman and put it around my neck. The handwriting had been Kenté's, I told myself. The letter had sounded like her. I only regretted that we hadn't come up with some kind of code phrase between us, so I'd know everything was all right and she wasn't writing under duress.

The sky opened up, rain beating down on *Vix*'s deck above me, but the rhythm was somehow less comforting than usual. I stared at the ceiling, unable to sleep. Not when I knew Markos was wounded, tossing back and forth in pain.

Flopping onto the pillows, I squeezed Kenté's lumpy talisman. *Cousin*, I thought hard into the black dark, tears stinging my eyes. *I miss you.*

I only hoped the god of the night would deliver my message.

CHAPTER
FIVE

The following morning dawned gray and damp. I woke to the cries of gulls wheeling above Valonikos harbor. As I blinked away the haze of sleep, an uneasy foreboding crawled through me. Something was wrong.

Then I remembered.

Markos.

Rising from bed, I tugged on comfortable trousers, boots, and my knee-length green jacket. Kenté's talisman I slung around my neck, its weight heavy and reassuring on my chest.

All was quiet on *Vix*. I slipped through the main cabin and up the ladder. Patroklos blew on his hands, coat collar turned up against the morning chill. Last night's bad weather had brought with it a change in temperature, which was only to be expected in late summer. I returned his nod, relieved that he didn't want to talk.

The fog had not yet dispersed from the streets of Valonikos. On the way to Antidoros Peregrine's town house, I stopped to purchase hot coffee from a vendor's cart. As I sipped, a stab of homesickness washed through me. Back on *Cormorant*, I used to drink coffee with Pa and Fee on cold damp mornings like this. I wondered what port they were waking up in today.

"What news?" I asked the coffee girl, whose black braid wrapped around her head like a crown.

Her gaze swept me from head to toe. Taking in my jacket with its brass buckles and the gray knit cap covering my hair, she must have concluded I was a sailor whose ship had just put in.

"The papers is over there if you want one, miss." She nodded at a small boy who listlessly waved a printed sheet at the empty street. "Price of fish is up, whale oil's down. Sailors from Brizos be saying Dido Brilliante's ship ran an Akhaian blockade. And best walk with your knife at hand. There were an attempted murder last night."

I'd heard of Dido Brilliante. Pa's stories called her the Queen of Brizos, but it wasn't a real title. She was nothing more than a pirate who ruled over an island full of outlaws. I was more interested in the murderer.

"Ayah?" I curled my hands around the mug. "Did they catch the fellow?"

"They got him down at the lockup, but Fabius Balerophon says he ain't opening his lips, not for bribe or beating. You ask me, where there's one murderer, there may be more. Trouble breeds trouble."

"Ain't that the truth." Setting my empty mug on the cart, I flipped her a coin. "My thanks."

Climbing the hill to Antidoros Peregrine's house, I squeezed through the gate. In a flurry of wings, a seagull took off from its perch on the fence. Watching it wheel up into the gray sky, I wondered if the sea god had sent it to keep an eye on me.

I pushed through the courtyard door and pounded up the back stairs. As I approached Markos's bedroom, I heard a woman's voice inside.

"—was a mistake. She's not an appropriate match for you. An Emparch is exclusive about the people on whom he bestows his company."

I rounded the corner just in time to see Markos roll his eyes. "I was exclusive in Akhaia," he said. "I went almost nineteen years without ever meeting anyone interesting." He spotted me in the doorway, his face reddening. "Caro."

He was sitting up in bed, a writing desk across his lap. On it was a cup of tea and a plate littered with crumbs. I exhaled with relief. He was eating. That had to be a good sign. Letters and books were scattered on the blankets.

The finely dressed woman seated in a chair beside the bed glanced up at me, guilt flitting across her face. Behind her Antidoros rubbed his beard as he stared out the window. From everyone's awkwardness, I knew Sophronia Hypatos had been talking about me, but she made no apology. I was perfectly aware that she didn't approve of me.

Likely she was right. I came from a long line of river smugglers and scalawags. While it was true I'd become captain of a fast cutter at a remarkably young age, that was only because I'd more or less stolen it. I wasn't proper company for Markos.

And I didn't care.

Antidoros Peregrine cleared his throat. "Never mind, Sophronia. He has a gunshot wound. It can wait."

"Don't indulge him, Antidoros," she said. "The letter has to be answered immediately."

Peregrine's voice sharpened. "We are hardly speaking of an indulgence. The physician has given him strict orders to rest." He picked up a bottle from the tray beside the bed. "Isn't this your pain draft? It's full."

"I took some earlier." That was the lofty tone Markos used when he didn't want anyone to question him. A long silence followed. Crumpling the paper on the desk, he dropped it on the quilt. "Oh, all right. I'm trying to compose a reply, and I wanted my mind to be clear."

"I won't sit by while you run your health into the ground. That's enough writing." Peregrine raised his voice, beckoning to a servant. "Remove these pens. And the books. His Excellency needs rest. You'll take this potion, Markos. And you'll sleep."

Markos's gaze darted across the room to me. "You're right," he said quickly. "It can wait."

Sophronia stood, skirts rustling. "I'll take my leave now." She and Peregrine went out, leaving me alone with Markos.

The letter has to be answered immediately. Had Markos told everyone what the message from Eryth had said—except me? I swallowed down my hurt. He didn't even like Sophronia.

Pretending I wasn't upset, I perched on the edge of the bed. "You look much better."

Actually, he looked a bit feverish. Markos smiled, blue eyes shining bright against bruised sockets and flushed cheeks.

"You know," I said casually, keeping my tone light, "what with the assassin ruining our dinner, we never did get to talk about that letter."

"Oh . . . um . . ."

Daria tore past me and jumped on the bed, causing Markos to wince.

"Hello, little badger." He flipped one of her plaits. "Why don't you go down and play in the rock garden?" he suggested in an overly cheerful voice. "I want to talk to Caro."

Daria was not fooled. She bounced on the bed, kicking her legs. "Konto Theucinian's son is the same age as me. We used to play together in the rock garden at the palace. Which was much nicer than this one," she said blithely to me. "I suppose I'll never see him again."

"Why not?" I asked.

"Because Markos will cut his head off, of course."

"Daria," Markos told her sternly, "that's not a very nice thing to say. Now, go on."

"I don't want to," she said with a pout, and immediately launched into a rambling tale involving a cat and a fishmonger. Restraining my irritation, I tried to listen. The mysterious letter would have to wait.

It wasn't long until Markos's chin began to nod. The physician's sleeping potion was powerful. Watching his chest rise and fall, I reached out to stroke his hair. That little gesture seemed so raw and intimate. When I was with Markos, I felt myself teetering on the edge of a great chasm, terrified of what might happen if I tumbled over the precipice.

My fingers drifted to the ruby and sapphire bracelet, a cold lump under my jacket cuff. I wasn't sure yet how to be with Markos and still be me. In the last three months, so much had changed. I couldn't help thinking the old Caro had somehow gotten lost along the way.

Of course I couldn't tell him how I felt. He would misunderstand, just as he had last night when I'd expressed my hesitation about the bracelet. He'd think I was blaming him, and that was the last thing I wanted.

And anyhow, I thought sourly, remembering the courier's message, it wasn't like I was the only one with secrets.

"He's sleeping," Daria mouthed across the blankets.

I jerked my head toward the bedroom door. "Let's go," I whispered. Together we tiptoed out. Pulling the door gently closed, I said, "I didn't know Theucinian had a son."

Daria shrugged. "We're third cousins or something. I used to like him, but now I want all the Theucinians to die." Before I could decide how to reply to this rather bloodthirsty remark, she continued, "I wish we could just stay here. I like this city. There's a man with one eye who sells whalebone carvings and a street where all the houses are pink. Oh, and a garbage barge that goes by every day at six o'clock, and—"

"Well, I have to be going," I interrupted, for fear the garbage barge would turn into another long tale. "Still got your knife?"

She nodded up at me, pressing a hand to the pocket of her dress.

"Good girl," I said.

Leaving Peregrine's house, I headed for Argyrus and Sons alone. The salvager's premises were located farther down the hill, close to the harbor. I owed Docia a visit, to thank her for saving my life last night.

The morning fog had lifted. From the creak and sway of the wooden sign, I could tell the wind was rising. The sixth sense in my mind whispered that it was from the southeast. I pushed through the door of the salvager's office, a tiny bell tinkling overhead.

Docia sat behind a desk, rearranging a stack of papers. Cabinets large and small lined the office, overstuffed with maps. Argyrus and Sons was a salvage firm whose expertise was recovering shipwrecks and cargo lost at sea. An old anchor, nearly eaten away by rust, leaned against the wall under a painting of an Akhaian frigate. A giant ball of rope sat in the corner beside a tea table, presumably for use as a chair. Across the room was a dusty display case full of interesting old coins with foreign symbols.

Docia jumped up. "Is Markos going to be all right? Bendis told me they were worried about the leg."

"The physician says it was a clean shot. He'll be able to walk again." I perched on the ball of rope. "What else does your friend Bendis say? About the man who tried to kill Markos?"

She rolled up a map, stuffing it on the shelf. "He ain't saying who hired him, that's for sure."

I sighed. "He doesn't have to."

How long could we afford to stay in Valonikos, where Theucinian's assassins would just keep finding us? All at once I remembered Kenté's letter. *They've put the Lady Dressed in Blood on it. It won't be long now.* Last night's assassin had definitely been a man. But maybe he was in the pay of this mysterious lady.

Either that or she was just one more addition to the long list of people trying to kill us. Neither prospect was particularly cheerful.

"I came here to thank you," I told Docia, pushing my worries aside for now. "You bailed me out of a tight spot."

She waved a hand. "It weren't any trouble, Caro."

My eyes were drawn to the mess on the desk. The corner of a pencil sketch poked out from under an account book. It had numbers scribbled on it. "What are you working on?"

She shoved the drawing under the book. "Nothing."

Quick as lightning, I grabbed the paper, pulling it out. I recognized the outline of the Akhaian Peninsula, with lumpy circles representing the islands to the east, far out in the ocean. Lines and figures connected the islands. "It doesn't look like nothing," I said. "This looks like a map."

"It's . . . just a project of mine," she relented. "I've been cross-referencing some old dates with the tides, and with historical accounts of sea travel. Trying to figure out which known rocks and shoals would have been around when the *Centurion*—oh, never mind."

"So it's part of a salvage job?"

Docia stared at me in disbelief. "Ain't you never heard of the *Centurion*?"

I dimly recalled hearing someone tell this story at Bollard House. The *Centurion* was a legend. She was a royal Akhaian treasury ship that had gone down with all hands two hundred years ago. I hadn't realized Docia was talking about *that Centurion*. The ship was supposed to be lost without a trace.

But then, they also said the city of Amassia was lost, and I was almost certain I'd been there. The sea god had brought me. Nothing could vanish without a trace in the ocean, unless the god wished it to.

"Wasn't the cargo hold full of gold?" I asked.

"Ayah, gold bullion, they say." At my quizzical look, she explained, "Bars of raw solid gold. But there were also boxes and boxes of gold talents. They would've been very heavy. Likely she went down like a rock."

"Wait, *gold* talents?"

"Ayah, they used to mint 'em from gold," she explained. "Before they was changed to three parts silver, one part copper."

"What kind of ship was she?" I asked, curiosity aroused.

"There's a picture of her right here." Docia nodded at the painting on the wall. "Something of a legend among salvagers. Reckon every firm's got that painting in their office." She took something rectangular from the drawer. "But we got this too. Bought it off a collector in Trikkaia."

Docia passed it to me carefully, handling it like a relic. The drawing was very old, trapped under glass to protect it from prying fingers. On the yellowed paper, a detailed plan of the lost ship's cabins and sails was sketched in faint, faded pen. A three-masted frigate with square sails, she had boasted twenty cannons on her deck, likely to ward off pirates. Lowering the diagram, I passed it back.

"*Centurion* lore is, you might say, a bit of a hobby of mine." Docia wiped dust from the glass with the corner of her shirt. "I collect things here and there. I have a theory about where she is." She traced the curve of the ship's hull. "Well, half a theory. But then, most all of us do. The *Centurion* is a find," she said wistfully, "that could make a salvager's career."

"Would you ever think of going after it someday?" I asked her.

"It's only a fancy." A sad smile curved the corner of her mouth. "To pass the time in the office."

We chatted for a few minutes more, and then I bid Docia goodbye. During the short walk to the docks, my thoughts leaped from one worry to the next.

Markos had been wearing himself out for months, staying up into the night to pen letters to his late father's friends, asking for their support. He'd grown more and more discouraged when the letters went unanswered. Or worse, came back with insincere words saying how happy they were that he was alive, but ignoring his plea for help. Absently I twirled the ruby bracelet on my wrist. I remembered how Peregrine had taken Markos's pens and paper away. His leg would never heal if he kept pushing himself like this.

I strode up the plank onto *Vix*'s deck. Jerking open the hatch, I swung myself onto the ladder.

"Caro, wait!" Nereus called.

I was already halfway down. As I dropped to the cabin floor and my eyes adjusted to the dim light, I realized what he'd been trying to warn me about.

Sophronia Hypatos sat, gloved hands crossed primly on the rough table, her aquiline nose illuminated by the candle lantern.

"Hello, Caroline," she said.

CHAPTER
SIX

"Where are my men?" I demanded, taking in the deserted cabin.

Sophronia waved her hand. "I dismissed them."

I started to say she couldn't do that, and then realized there was no point. She could and she had. Facing her across the table, I asked, "What do you want?"

She studied me for a moment, while I studied her right back. Her silver-streaked black hair was elaborately coiled and pinned, and her olive skin meticulously powdered. Everything from her shimmery cloak to her perfume reeked of wealth. No wonder my crew had obeyed her without question—she was every inch a councilman's wife.

She unfolded her hands. "Let us speak plainly."

I regarded her dubiously. In my experience, whenever

someone said that, what followed was likely to be the opposite of simple.

"Markos has received an offer of marriage."

My stomach dropped through my feet, or at least that's what it felt like. I swallowed, mouth suddenly dry. The ruby and sapphire cuff felt like a lead weight around my wrist. My fingers itched to touch it, but I didn't want Sophronia to guess my feelings. I balled my hands into fists behind my back.

So this was Markos's secret.

"The Archon of Eryth will support Markos's claim to the throne—if, in exchange, Markos accepts his daughter's hand in marriage. The girl would become Emparchess."

I heard a fierce rushing in my ears, like breakers dashing on the rocks. Images popped unbidden into my head—Markos and another girl laughing over tea. Her hair on his pillow, fine and loose where mine was tight and curly. My stomach clenched. Markos, older, holding a child on his lap. In my mind I could not see the girl's face, but I knew she'd have highborn Akhaian looks, unlike me. And she would be, as Sophronia had said earlier, *appropriate.* Also unlike me.

Our first night together, Markos had warned me he could never promise me marriage or an engagement, and I'd just laughed at him.

Marriage. I'm going to be a captain and a privateer. I'm going to be the terror of the seas. *Whoever marries you will have to wear pretty dresses and go to parties and learn the names of a hundred boring politicians.*

At the time, I'd meant it. Marriage seemed a vague thing that happened to other people, far in the future. Or possibly never—my own parents were not married at all. But now that the idea of Markos marrying someone else had been thrown in my face, I felt numb.

"Where's Eryth?" I burst out, louder than I'd intended. "Is it a big territory? How many men would this alliance bring?"

I detected surprise behind Sophronia's dark eyes. She'd apparently expected me to collapse in tears.

"Questions worth asking," she said with approval. "The province of Eryth is large enough, and the Pherenekians are an old Akhaian family, very respectable. Don't you want to know about the girl?"

I squared my chin. Pa might be a wherryman, but my mother was Tamaré Bollard, a skilled negotiator who was feared in boardrooms up and down the coast. Ma would've squashed this woman like a bug beneath her boot.

"No, actually. I want to know about the deal." My voice remained steady. I sent up a quick prayer of thanks to the god of the sea. "Have you ever met Lord Pherenekian? The lords we spoke to in Edessa said he was a progressive thinker."

"We've met," she said. "The Archon of Eryth and his daughter visited Valonikos three summers ago. But that's not what you're asking, is it? You're asking if I think this is a trap."

"Do you?"

She shook her head. "To be entirely truthful, I believe the offer is as much about the daughter as the Akhaian throne. Oh,

Pherenekian is open-minded politically, that's true. But Agnes is, well . . . she's not particularly marriageable. She did a grand tour, when she was fifteen, and frankly she was a disappointment."

"Why?"

Sophronia sniffed. "Fancies herself an academic. A *scientist*." She said this as if it was a dirty word. "I believe she even had the gall to have a paper published. Something about moths or bugs."

"So what?"

"That sort of thing isn't attractive to men. No son of a lord is going to marry a girl who's smarter than him. At least—" The corner of her lip curled. "At least, not if she's so obvious about it. Going around with ink on her hands, talking all the boys' ears off about insects and chemistry experiments and the rotation of the moon . . ."

Despite everything, I found myself liking the picture she painted of Agnes Pherenekian. I didn't want Markos to marry at all, but at least this girl didn't seem too bad.

Sophronia went on. "The Archon has spoiled the girl. Her mother died young, and he's indulged his daughter's every whim since. I know what he's thinking. A dozen young lords have refused Agnes, but word's gotten about that Markos is unconventional. The Archon sees him as perhaps his last opportunity to marry off his daughter—and who knows? They might even suit well. When Markos was the second son of an Emparch, such a match would have been out of reach. The province of Eryth is rather remote and the girl is no great beauty. But now . . ."

Thinking of Pa, I knew he'd be willing to take a gamble, no

matter what the odds, if he thought something would make me happy. Perhaps this wasn't a trap. Perhaps it was only a man trying to be a good father to his beloved daughter.

"I'm surprised at the Archon for promising fifteen thousand men," Sophronia mused. "For I doubt he truly has that many. It may be that he's lined up some of the other lords to join him, once he's publicly declared support for Markos." Lifting her head, she addressed me directly. "We are both intelligent women. I assume you understand now why I'm here."

"Probably to tell me I'm not good enough for Markos," I muttered, covering my wariness with sarcasm. "Again."

She held up a hand. "You know that's not why. The messenger arrived yesterday, and Markos still hasn't told you the truth. He wants to spare your feelings. I, however, have no such compunctions."

"Thanks."

She scrutinized me, eyes wrinkling slightly at the edges. "You and I are women of the world. It falls to us to face things, when men cannot. Myself, I would rather know the lay of the land, in order that I might make an informed decision. I think you are the same."

"It's Markos's decision, not mine," I pointed out.

"My dear, I came here today because I'm afraid my young cousin is about to do something abysmally foolish."

"Markos isn't a fool," I shot back.

Sophronia pursed her lips. "That's not what I said." She looked at the bracelet I was wearing, the ruby sparkling under my jacket cuff. "When he asked me for his mother's jewels yesterday, I knew," she said. "I raised two boys. Don't think I don't recognize that puppy look they get." Leaning forward, she peered into my face. "He thinks he's in love. Did he propose marriage to you?"

"What? No!" My face flooded with heat at the word "love." "He—he wouldn't do that."

She said nothing.

I gripped the table edge. The Markos I'd met on my father's wherry would have accepted the Archon's marriage offer without hesitation. He would've spouted something about duty and honor and then sent me packing. But he'd changed so much since then. Was he really thinking of giving up his family's throne for me? He wouldn't be that stupid.

Would he?

"Markos Andela is penniless," Sophronia said quietly, "without support from the nobles. This offer is all he has—"

"He has me," I retorted. "And my ship."

Pushing back her chair with a scrape, Sophronia stood. "This little blockade runner is sprightly, and the artillery is enough to give a merchant ship pause." She looked down her nose at me. "But you can't stand toe to toe with the Lion Fleet. All but the smallest ships of the line will blow you right out of the water."

I opened my mouth to defend *Vix*, and then closed it. She was right.

With a smooth rippling motion, she shook out her cloak. I didn't have that kind of elegance, and I never would. I wondered if that wasn't exactly what she meant me to see.

When she spoke, her voice was commanding. "Do you believe Markos is the true Emparch of Akhaia? And did you or did you not swear to serve him?"

I swallowed.

Her expression softened. "I was your age when I was married, but for me it was the culmination of years of dreams and training. I always knew I was meant to be a politician's wife. Not so, I think, for you."

"I like *Markos*," I whispered. "Not the Emparch of Akhaia."

"I believe you," she said, surprising me. "It's why he's so drawn to you. But when an Emparch makes a decision, he must always think first of his country. Not himself. If Markos can't make the right choice, it's up to you to make it for him."

Pausing at the bottom of the ladder, she set one gloved finger on the wooden handrail. It came away blackened. Rubbing her fingertips together, she sighed. "We do what we must."

I watched her ascend the ladder, heeled shoes clinging to the rungs. After she was gone, the faint scent of her perfume lingered, smelling like roses and doom.

Nereus spoke, startling me. He leaned in the doorway separating the cargo hold from the main cabin. "You all right, girlie?"

I shot him a glance. "I suppose you were eavesdropping." The cargo hold could be accessed via a second hatch on the deck. I had no doubt he'd been listening to us. "How much did you hear?"

"Enough." He took a swig of rum. "You know, I once knew a girl who was destined for the sea, who became Emparchess instead. The whole ocean was changed, and the world was never the same."

The girl he spoke of was his sister, Arisbe of Amassia. She'd forsaken her destiny and married the Emparch of Akhaia, one of Markos's ancestors. Arisbe had been a favorite of the sea god, just like me. The god had been so angered by the girl's betrayal that she'd destroyed the island of Amassia, sinking it forever beneath the ocean. Pa had told me the legend when I was young.

"Markos hasn't asked me to be Emparchess," I protested, cheeks warming.

"No, but make no mistake." Nereus tapped the cuff on my wrist. The ruby glowed red in the lamplight. "He *is* choosing you."

Nereus was hundreds of years old, having sold himself into the service of the sea god. He didn't have much of a sense of time. I'd always gotten the feeling he existed outside it.

"Do *you* know?" I asked. "What I'm meant to do?"

"Ah." Nereus looked down into his flask. "Figured we'd get to this part. Even if I did know your fate—and mind you, I ain't saying I do—I couldn't tell you."

"I'm not stupid," I said. "I knew something like this might happen someday. Just not . . ." My voice cracked. "Not so soon."

He jerked his head in the direction of the deck. "Fancy a game of dice with the fellows? Might take your mind off things."

"No." I sighed. "I want to be alone for a while."

I left the docks and wandered down Valonikos beach. The waves battered the sand in an elusive rhythm, sounding almost like language to me. I caught snatches of words, only to have them whisked away. Removing my boots, I let my bare toes sink into the wet sand. The sea wind twisted my hair, wrapping the thick smell of salt around me.

I remembered the hopeless look on Markos's face last night. *Konto Theucinian keeps sending people to take bits out of me. Even if it's slowly, piece by piece, someday he'll get me. Someday there'll be nothing left.* I never wanted to see him look like that again.

Tears sprang into my eyes. I was happy with Markos. I didn't want to lose him. I didn't want things to change.

The sea god did not speak, but she didn't have to. I remembered her whispered words. *What good is a ship in a harbor?*

Towering clouds bulged above the flat line of the horizon, climbing all the way to the peak of the sky. With every bone in my body, I felt the ocean calling me. I wanted to feel the surge of the waves under *Vix*'s hull. To sail into the blazing orange sun. To travel the world like Jacari Bollard, my famed ancestor, who had also been chosen by the sea. Ever since I'd left the riverlands, I had been so lost. Looking out at the sea, I knew the only place I would find myself again was out there.

A ship was not meant to sit at anchor in the harbor, and neither was I.

Finally I forced myself to face the truth I'd been denying for months. Markos's dream was to avenge his family and reclaim his throne. But the Emparch of Akhaia ruled from a city bound by mountains on three sides. Living in a place like that would slowly kill me, as surely as staying here would kill him.

It wasn't the Archon's marriage offer that made us—Markos and me—impossible. It wasn't that he was an Emparch's son and I was a wherryman's daughter. The truth was we had always been impossible. I just hadn't wanted to see it.

Clenching my jaw, I stared into the crashing waves. I knew what I had to do.

⁓

"There." Leaning over, I opened Markos's bedroom window. It was the following morning, and the cloudy weather had passed. Sun shone on the red rooftops of Valonikos, spread out below us. "That's better, isn't it? The sea air will be good for you."

I perched on the edge of his bed. Inside, my heart was pounding. Sweat collected around the neckline of my dress. Somehow a frock had felt right for the occasion—more somber. Below my lace-trimmed cuff, the jeweled bracelet glittered on my wrist.

I knew what I had come here to say. I just didn't know how to start.

The breeze stirred Markos's hair. He looked alert, the shadows gone from under his eyes. I hoped that was a sign his leg was healing well.

"Caro," he began, "I'm glad we're finally alone. You remember that messenger who came the other day? There's something I've been wanting to . . ." He fumbled a little, his gaze dropping to the blanket. "That is, I need to tell you . . ."

I stopped him. "Markos. I already know."

He squeezed his hands into fists, the tendons turning white.

When he spoke, his voice was low and strangled. "Peregrine wasn't supposed to tell you."

"He didn't. It was Sophronia."

His nostrils flared. "It was not her place to do so."

The more formally Markos spoke, the angrier he was. I knew that from experience. "She was only trying to protect you," I said. "She had good intentions."

"Protect me from what? You?" A crease appeared between his eyes. "I'm not in any danger from you."

I thought otherwise, but perhaps Sophronia was mistaken about Markos's intentions. "So what are you thinking?" I braced myself. "About the Archon of Eryth?"

"Well, he wasn't one of my father's particular favorites." Markos picked at something invisible under his fingernail. "I wasn't expecting the offer. But I suppose it makes sense. He has no sons, and what man wouldn't want his daughter to be Emparchess?"

"Have you ever met her?" I asked. "The daughter—Agnes."

"At the winter ball, years ago. The Pherenekians don't often come to the capital. I was perhaps thirteen. I remember . . ." He screwed his face up. "She refused to dance. She was always scribbling in a notebook. And she didn't have—" The tips of his ears turned red. "Um. The kind of figure thirteen-year-old boys are interested in."

"But was she nice? Do—do you think you'd like her?"

He stared at me. "How on earth would I know that? I saw her once." Glancing at the stack of paper on the bureau, he exhaled. "I've started three letters, and I've crumpled up every one of them. They were all rubbish. There's got to be *something* I can say. Some way I can get this alliance without having to agree to the marriage."

"Markos." I hesitated. "You already tried asking nicely for the lords' support, and it's gotten you nowhere so far."

He clenched his fists. "This is intolerable. The Archons should be supporting me because I'm their rightful Emparch. I have nothing to trade but the Andela name, which no one seems to care about." Kicking the bedsheets, he said sourly, "Nothing to trade but myself."

"Then . . ." I swallowed. "Perhaps that's what you'll have to do."

His voice grew quiet. "Are you really suggesting I say yes?"

"All the nobles who are loyal to the Theucinians want you dead. The others are too afraid of him to support you. Except for this Archon of Eryth. If you reject the marriage, you'll offend the only person who wants to help you."

"Sometimes I hate your cursed common sense." He stared at the blanket. "Caro, how can you stand to be so reasonable when this is *us* we're talking about? You and me."

"But it's not only about you and me, is it?" I asked. "It's about Akhaia. Theucinian will be a bad Emparch, one who hurts people. You're the only one who can stop him. It's like you said—no one in your family has ever been free. You have a responsibility to your country, and I think you know that."

Markos reached up to touch the ruby earring that represented the Andela family, and then cursed, remembering it wasn't there anymore. "He's already taken everything from me. Hasn't he had *enough*?"

"Markos." My voice wobbled, and I fought to steady it. "You can't say no to this marriage because of me." I slipped the ruby and sapphire cuff from my wrist. His mother's bracelet sat in my hand, cold and sad. I held it out to him. "Here. I can't keep this."

"Well, you have to." His eyes flickered. "I refuse to take it back."

Inside I was screaming, but I couldn't let him see. More than anything, I wanted to see Markos avenge his family and take his rightful throne back. I'd sworn an oath to help him. He was meant to be the Emparch of Akhaia.

This was the only way.

"You shouldn't have given it to me in the first place," I said, the bracelet dangling between us. "This was meant for an Emparchess, and I—I can't be that. Not ever."

"I don't want an Emparchess." Markos stuck his hand in his hair. "I want you."

"But you *need* Agnes," I made myself say, though his words hit me like a dagger to the heart.

He punched the blanket in frustration. "Gods damn it."

Akhaia had better be grateful to me for the sacrifice I was about to make. They'd better put up a gods-damned *statue* of me.

"The truth is . . ." I drew a deep breath. Nothing I was about to say was the truth. "After we met, both of our lives got turned upside down. We . . ." I swallowed over the ache in my throat. "Well, we were both having a lot of strong feelings. Perhaps . . . we mistook those feelings for something else."

His face froze. "You think I don't know what I'm *feeling*? Caro, I—"

"Don't." My voice was ragged. "Don't say it. You'll just regret it." Lowering my head, I fixed my eyes on the carpet. "You see, I . . . don't feel the same way."

I felt rather than saw him recoil, the bedclothes shifting. Tension thickened the air between us.

I forced myself to go on. "I always knew this wasn't real. Only I could never find the right moment to tell you. Your family had been killed, and I felt sorry for you. It seemed . . ." I shrugged, though my heart felt like a blackened hole in my chest. "Well, it seemed like you needed me."

He made a choking noise. "You felt *sorry* for me?"

"Not that it hasn't been fun." Gently I took his hand, uncurling his fingers. "But when you gave me the bracelet the other night, that's when I realized I had to tell you the truth." I set the jeweled cuff in his hand. "Give this to your wife. I'm sure she'll think it's lovely. It's just . . . not for me. None of this is."

"I don't believe you," Markos said flatly. "I don't believe any of this."

"Well, it's true," I snapped.

"It can't be." He shook his head, as if in a daze. "Caro, what—what happened? Was it something I did? There has to be a reason . . ." His voice trailed off.

I couldn't stand to look at him, so I swept to my feet, smoothing my skirts. My gaze circled the room, taking in everything one last time. On the bureau was a newspaper. Only last week I'd ranted and railed at Fabius Balerophon, the reporter who insisted on calling me the Rose of the Coast and writing romantic trash about us, while Markos listened in amusement. Hanging from a hook by the door was the blue and gold coat Markos had worn at Bollard House, the night we'd danced together.

My eyes filled with tears. Everything in this room was a little piece of us.

When I'd composed myself enough to turn back to Markos, I found him looking down at the bracelet in his hand. His shoulders were slumped. The ruby and sapphires sparkled in the sunlight, absurdly cheerful.

I reached out to touch his face one last time. "I'm so sorry."

He pushed my hand away. "Walk out of this room."

So I did, my lips trembling. Desperately I pounded down the stairs. By the time I got to the bottom, my face was wet. I couldn't go back to *Vix*. I didn't want the crew to see me crying. Stumbling into the nearest alley, I slid down the wall. Moisture dampened my back and garbage stained my skirt. I didn't care.

"You need cheering up, love?" A drunken sailor lurched toward me.

Pulling my flintlock from under my dress, I brandished it at him. He scuttled off to find another alley to piss in.

I rested my head on my knees and cried.

CHAPTER
SEVEN

The next morning Sophronia knocked on my cabin door, probably to congratulate me for doing the right thing.

I pretended I was asleep. Doing the right thing had made me
miserable. I'd already resolved never to do it again.

Catching sight of myself in the cabin mirror, I made a face. I
looked puffy and dreadful, and I'd barely slept. My head ached as
I stared at an empty page of the ship's log. I had optimistically
purchased the blank leather book a month ago, hoping to record
the tales of my grand adventures.

Nothing had worked out like I expected.

Part of the problem was I didn't know what to do with *Vix*
anymore. I'd made a vow to Markos, that day we shook hands on
the sidewalk by the Valonikos docks. *I will always be your friend. I
will sail for you. Not for Akhaia. For you.*

I doubted he wanted that now.

Perhaps I should visit the Kynthessan Consul and ask if they had any jobs for a courier. *Vix* was a fast cutter with six four-pound cannons, perfectly suited for the task.

I sighed. Or I could sail for Bollard Company. It would be Ma's dream come true, but . . . I'd always fancied the idea of striking out on my own.

Someone scratched at the cabin door. I glanced up from the log, expecting Nereus. Or, gods forbid, Sophronia again.

"Oh," I said.

Antidoros Peregrine stood in the doorway. "I came to see how you were doing," he said. Crossing the room, he leaned on the shelf opposite my desk. "I was young once too, you know."

I eyed his beard and silver-streaked tail of hair skeptically.

"I'm sure it must seem like the end of the world right now. But I wonder . . ." He hesitated. "I've been where you are, on the outside of an arranged marriage. It doesn't always have to be the end. Much depends on the young lady in question."

"What do you mean?"

"Her expectations for the marriage." His face turned slightly pink, and I understood he was casting about for a polite way to explain. "Agnes Pherenekian is the daughter of an Akhaian lord, so of course she will understand her duties. But Caro, to her this marriage may be only that—a duty. It's quite possible she might be open to . . . well . . . an arrangement."

My cheeks lit on fire as I realized what he was saying. Peregrine was trying to give me hope.

Though Markos rarely spoke of his childhood, I knew the

coldness of his parents had cut him deeply. I remembered too well how his voice had been completely devoid of emotion when he described them to me. *Once my mother did her duty to my father and gave him two sons, she went to our summer house in the mountains. She only visited a few weeks out of the year.* The Emparch and his wife had given Markos the best of everything. The one thing they had not given him was a real family.

What Peregrine was suggesting . . . that wasn't Markos. He would be determined to make the marriage work, if not for himself, then for their future children.

"No." I swallowed. "I'm going away. Far away. I don't want to spoil this for him." I stared down at my logbook, the lines blurring, until I had control of myself again. "Why are you so interested in Markos anyway? Don't forget, I know you were stockpiling muskets. You wanted to overthrow his father."

"I'm almost afraid to admit it, for fear you'll call me a mercenary, but Markos Andela is a great opportunity. The Theucinians are imperialists, and they won't give up power. He's different." He exhaled. "Before, I never dreamed political change might be brought about peacefully. If only Markos was Emparch . . . He could establish a senate, with representatives from the people. He could do so much good for our country."

"But there's more common folk than there are lords," I snapped in frustration. "They have the numbers to take on the Emparchy. So why don't you just do that, and leave Markos out of it?"

"The common people would suffer the most if it were to come to all-out war," he said gently.

I felt stupid for not realizing that myself. I was so upset about losing Markos that I'd lashed out at Peregrine. When he'd only come here to try to make me feel better.

"But you're still going to have to start a revolution to get Markos into power," I said. "Isn't that the whole point of him marrying this Agnes Pherenekian—to get an army?"

He drummed his fingers on the shelf. "Well, I'd hoped the Archon's support would turn the other lords to Markos's side. Who would then put pressure on Theucinian."

"But you can't count on it," I finished.

"You look disappointed in me, Caro."

"It's just . . ." I wasn't sure how to say this without offending him. He had been a good friend to me. "When we first came to Valonikos, Markos was so excited by that book you wrote about the rule of the people. About a new Akhaia where he wouldn't have to be the Emparch. Then you convinced him that if he was Emparch, he might bring about a revolution without blood. But . . . that wasn't really true, was it?"

"In truth I had not expected the other lords to accept Theucinian's claim so quickly," he admitted. "I thought there'd be more resistance, but it seems I'm not the only one who disliked Markos's father." He paused. "We've sent a letter to the Margravina of Kynthessa. Perhaps she'll lend her support."

I'd had some small dealings with the Margravina, all of which suggested she would continue to play both ends against the middle. Kynthessa didn't want anything to do with a war in Akhaia. But I kept my doubts to myself.

"I still want to avoid bloodshed, Caro," Peregrine said. "But I'm afraid I can only promise to do my best."

I glanced up sharply. The mention of the word "blood" had jogged my memory, and I recalled there was something I'd been meaning to ask him. "Who is the Lady Dressed in Blood?"

Peregrine's fingers stilled mid-tap. "Where did you hear that name?"

Taking Kenté's cryptic letter from the desk, I read it to him. Peregrine had never met my cousin, but he knew she was training as a shadowman.

His face was thoughtful. "Everyone knows the Lady Dressed in Blood. That is, they know *of* her. She's the most famous courtesan in the city of Trikkaia—and skilled in the art of poison, or so the rumors go." He stared out the porthole. "She's whispered to be the longtime mistress of Konto Theucinian. A lady who dresses all in dark red velvet."

I snorted, causing him to raise his eyebrows at me.

"Sorry," I said. "It's just that it sounds like a whole lot of crock to me. A story meant to scare children."

"Ladies of the night." His lip twitched. "And murder. Clearly they're telling very different bedtime stories in the Kynthessan riverlands."

"I'm just saying if I was a murderer, a *real* murderer, I'd be stupid to go around dressing in red and calling myself the Lady Dressed in Blood, wouldn't I?"

"Fair enough."

"But you've met her?" I pressed him. When I was gone, someone would have to keep Markos safe. "You know what she looks like?"

Peregrine rubbed his beard. "Yes, I know Melaine Chrysanthe.

That's her real name. But Caro, I think it unlikely she'd leave the capital, and certainly not to come here. Her second husband was a man of Valonikos, a good friend of the Archon, and he disappeared under—well, suspicious circumstances. She would not be welcome in this city."

That was slightly reassuring. "Promise me you'll keep a watch out."

He patted my hand, sympathy in his eyes. "I will."

After he left, I took a pen and scribbled the name in the margin of my log. *Melaine Chrysanthe*. I had to write Kenté with that snippet of information at once.

I wondered how long it would take the letter to reach Trikkaia. My thoughts turned to the riverlands in autumn, buzzing with drowsy insects. I could almost smell the sweet marsh grass and crisp fallen leaves. The journey up the River Kars to Trikkaia would be nothing to a cutter like *Vix*, a matter of a week or so.

Maybe instead of a letter, I could go visit Kenté at the Academy myself. Surely seeing my cousin again would be a welcome distraction. I might even run into Pa. He and Fee often sailed the cargo route from Iantiporos to Trikkaia. I imagined spending the night on *Cormorant* in my old familiar bunk.

My smile faded. It wouldn't be the same. I belonged to the sea now. I could never go back to the river. Not truly.

❧

Antidoros Peregrine was not my last visitor that day.

The sun had already set, orange beams slanting in the porthole.

As I squinted through the glowing dust motes, I thought he was a dream at first. I stared at him, pen suspended and dripping ink in a puddle on the desk.

"Don't worry," Markos said. "I'm not here to renew yesterday's conversation." He took a deep breath. "I came because I need a fast cutter." Crossing the cabin, he handed me a leather tube. "Specifically, a courier."

The tube was stamped with a blob of red wax in the shape of a mountain lion. Peeking inside, I saw several sheets of rolled parchment. "What's this?"

"My answer to the Archon's letter, accepting his offer. Begging the honor of his daught—" His voice caught on the word. Clearing his throat, he continued. "His daughter Agnes's hand in marriage."

"Markos," I whispered. "I'm so sorry."

He held up a hand. "Don't be. Your pen is dripping, by the way," he said, looking down his nose at me. "Did you know?"

With dark hollows bruising his eyes and a crutch tucked under his arm, he looked older. Graver. His hair was combed and tied at the back of his neck, though locks still fell in artful waves around his face. He wore an elegant red coat and lace cravat, and his boots with the gold lion buttons were spotless. He looked every inch an Emparch.

But I knew Markos. The more correct and formal he acted, the more he was hurting on the inside. Stiff manners were his form of defense. I understood exactly what it meant that he'd gotten so dressed up to come see me.

Putting the pen back in the inkpot, I found my voice. "Why me?"

"You're the only one I trust."

"Really?" I whispered.

He deliberately removed his eyes from mine, studying the edge of my carpet. "Yes."

My fingers tightened around the leather tube. I held his offer of marriage to someone else in my hand. I wanted to scream.

But then I caught the flicker of his pupils. He was watching me surreptitiously out of the corner of his eye. He *wanted* me to react. I'd told him I didn't have any feelings for him, and he was calling my bluff.

"All right." I set the letter on the table and stood up. "I'll be your courier. I swore to sail for you, and that hasn't changed. I'll leave at once. Tomorrow, on the morning tide."

He raised his eyebrows. "Are you sure there's nothing else you'd like to say, Caro?"

"Nothing at all." I pretended I felt as airy as my voice sounded.

This must be what people meant when they talked about a broken heart. My chest physically *hurt*. I hadn't expected that. I'd thought it was a figure of speech, but this was real. My body felt like a raging knot of pain.

"How peculiar," Markos commented, "because I thought I saw your eyes gleaming. Which, you must admit, would be funny, considering our entire relationship was just you feeling *sorry* for me."

"My eyes are doing nothing of the sort," I snapped, and that made the tears dry up.

He cleared his throat. "Well, then." Primly, he extended a hand to me. "Good journey to you."

I moved to shake his hand at the same moment he tried to pull me into his arms. Or maybe we both reached for each other. We collided awkwardly, my face pressed into his jacket and our hands stuck between us. His crutch clattered to the floor.

Looking up to stammer an apology, I bumped my head on his chin. Emotion flooded through me. The skin of his neck was warm and he smelled like Markos and—

He kissed me, pushing his hands into my hair. Stinging sweetness and deep regret. Desperation. How could you get all that from one kiss?

"I don't want anyone but you." His voice broke, so he dropped it to a whisper. "One word from you, and I'll rip the letter up."

"I can't," I said against his lips. Now we were both crying. "It's the right thing to do. You know it is."

"Caroline." He rested his forehead on mine. "I hate this."

Hardly anyone called me by my full name. I closed my eyes, savoring the way his accent rolled the *r*. Strange to think that, once the two of us parted, no one would say my name like that anymore.

"Why do I miss you so much," he whispered, "when you're still right here?"

We stood, heads together, for a long time. I closed my eyes, trying to memorize him. His mannerisms, his smell, the way he rubbed that spot on his forehead when he was upset. All the little things that made him Markos.

I stashed them away in my heart. Then I stepped back, disentangling my hands from his neck.

Markos yanked his jacket straight, wiping his eyes on his sleeve. Gripping the chair back, he made a grab for his fallen crutch. He missed, nearly losing his balance, and swore.

I lunged forward. "Stop, I'll get it—"

"I have to do it myself." Setting his teeth, he slowly bent to retrieve the crutch from the floor. He tucked it under his arm, breathing heavily, and finger-combed his rumpled hair.

I brushed the damp spot my tears had left on his shoulder. "Gods damn it, I—I messed up your jacket." I scrubbed at it with my sleeve. "You shouldn't have come down here. The ladder—your leg—"

"Stop trying to take care of me," he said sharply.

"At least let me help you back up on deck."

"No. I'll get one of the men to help me again," he said, his dismissal cutting me. "I think you've done enough."

Readjusting the crutch, he limped across the cabin. When he got to the door, he paused. "Caro . . . Be watchful. There's a chance this marriage offer is a trap."

"If you think it's a trap, then maybe . . ." I didn't finish, because I already knew what he would say. Markos would do his duty to Akhaia regardless of the danger. It was who he was.

He shook his head. "No, you were right. This is a chance I can't pass up. Just . . . keep your eyes open in Eryth, all right?"

I could barely speak over the lump in my throat. "I promise."

For a long moment he stood with his hand on the doorknob.

I waited for him to say something more, until I realized he was waiting for *me* to say something. After a while, he sighed and went out.

ↄ♫

The next morning my eyes felt like they'd been rubbed raw with sand. It was past midnight before we'd finished securing the provisions for the journey to Eryth and loading them into *Vix*'s cargo hold. It had been difficult to get everything together at the last minute, and by the time I'd flopped into bed I was tired and cross.

It didn't matter. I hadn't slept anyway.

Pulling on a cable-knit sweater, I climbed to the deck. To the east the horizon was lit with the barest of glows. Seagulls wheeled and shouted in the purple sky. A sign from the sea god, perhaps? But even as I watched, none of them flew near me. All across the harbor, lanterns sparkled like stars atop the masts. My instincts told me we'd have a fair wind today. I almost smiled through my headache, remembering how I used to be jealous of Pa and Fee when the river god told them things like that.

Farther up the deck, someone stood talking to Nereus. I squinted into the shadows. The figure was too small to be a man.

"Daria?" I strode up the deck.

She turned to face me. "Go away. I didn't come to say goodbye to *you*. Just Nereus." She crossed her arms, hugging herself. A tear slipped down her cheek. "You hurt Markos."

I cleared my throat. "It's complicated."

"When he came back from visiting you last night, he was crying." She glared tiny daggers into me. "He never cries. *Never.*"

That wasn't true, but I knew she wouldn't listen to me. I hovered, feeling awkward, as she scrubbed her face with the hem of her dress.

I wondered if it wasn't for the best that Nereus was leaving with me. During our months in Valonikos, Daria had grown a bit strange. Her clothes were always grubby, her long hair perpetually escaping from its plaits. She wandered the city in a man's tricorn hat, collecting pocketfuls of strange and disgusting objects. Nereus wasn't exactly a suitable companion for a nine-year-old girl.

"Well, goodbye anyway," I said.

"I hate you. I hope your ship sinks," she hissed, backing away like an angry cat. "Markos *loves* you. Why can't you just—just love him back?"

I followed her. "Daria, you were raised in the Emparch's house." My voice came out thick. "You know Markos wouldn't have been allowed to marry whoever he liked. He's doing this for Akhaia."

"But—I thought things would be different here." She began to sob. "P-Peregrine says—he says—everything was supposed to be *different* in Valonikos." I touched her shoulder, but she jerked away. "I don't want to talk to you anymore."

She spun, black braids whirling behind her.

I called after her, "Markos is only doing this so someday you can go home!"

She turned on the gangplank, glaring at me. "I don't want to go back to Akhaia." Her red-rimmed eyes lifted to *Vix*'s rigging, where my crew was unfurling the sails. "First you hurt my brother and now you're taking my friend away from me. You're ruining my whole life."

I watched her stamp down the dock. Somewhere in the harbor a bell clanged out the changing of the tide. It was time to sail.

At the end of the dock, Daria stopped. With her woolen shawl pulled tight around her thin shoulders, she vibrated with anger.

Reaching up, she yanked off her pirate hat. "I don't want this anymore." She tossed it in the harbor, where it landed with a splash, spinning on the water.

And then we raised sail and left Valonikos.

CHAPTER
EIGHT

I stood at *Vix*'s rail, drenched from head to foot. My face and hair were grimy with salt. Every time the cutter climbed a new swell, the spray crashed over me. I supposed I was cold, but I barely noticed. My heart was numb, so the rest of me might as well be too.

Something slid between my fingers. I glanced down at Nereus's battered flask.

"Drink it, lovie." He leaned on the rail, jacket collar turned up against the spray. His hair was frosted with specks of water. "It don't heal the wound, but I reckon you could do with some warming up."

The rum felt like fire going down.

"No offense," I croaked, "but if you've come up here to give me some words of wisdom, I don't want them." I closed my eyes, feeling the cool salt mist on my face. "Sorry. I'm not mad at you."

"You ain't mad at the boy either. Reckon that makes it harder."

I took another pull off the flask, feeling a little warmer. He understood.

"When we make a promise to serve, sometimes that promise is hard to keep. Whether you serve a god or an Emparch." He nodded at me. "Or both."

I didn't want to talk about Markos, so I focused my thoughts on the voyage ahead. "Have you ever been to Eryth?"

Nereus studied the horizon. No land was visible. The province of Eryth was located north of Valonikos, on a fat finger of land jutting out into the sea. We would be ten days sailing northeast.

"Been to the Archon's castle once, in another time." I couldn't read his expression. "Another life."

Nereus had once been an Archon's son, before he pledged himself to the sea god's service in exchange for unnaturally long life. In fact, he was very distantly related to Markos. It wasn't surprising that he'd journeyed to Eryth as the young nobleman Nemros Andela.

I'd never been there myself. Growing up on *Cormorant*, I'd visited every port in the riverlands. But you couldn't travel to Eryth by river, and wherries don't do well in the open sea. For the first time in my life, I was sailing into unknown waters. It made me uneasy.

The voyage passed quickly. I spent most of my time learning more about my crew. By our third day at sea, I knew that Castor made the best coffee, Patroklos preferred to be called Pat, and Damian could carve intricate sculptures from whalebone.

"Sailed on the *Alyssum* and the *Fancy*," Damian said, a gold tooth flashing in his mouth. "Whalers, they be, plying their trade far north of these parts. But my family's mostly navy men, going back and back." His eyes met mine. "Andela men."

"Mine as well, miss," the sailor called Leon agreed. "It's why we signed on. Anything we can do to help the young lion."

Impulsively I reached out to grip their arms. "Thank you for your loyalty."

I hadn't known the men had joined my crew because they believed in Markos. The noble lords of Akhaia, I thought sourly, could take a lesson or two in loyalty from these sailors.

Late in the afternoon of our tenth day at sea, Pat waved from the bowsprit. "Land ho! Off the port bow!"

I squinted through the spyglass as the province of Eryth inched nearer. The outline of a city, the buildings topped with golden domes, sprawled behind a bustling port. There was something else on a cliff near the city, two pillar-like shapes I could not make out. I passed the glass to Nereus.

"Just as I expected," he said after a moment, lowering it. "Nothing's the same except the monument."

"Monument?" I took the glass back, finally identifying the oddly shaped pillars. They were legs, wearing sandals with straps. I supposed those feet had once been attached to a giant statue of a man, but the rest of him had toppled long ago. "What's it for?"

He shrugged. "Men build such things to assure they ain't

forgotten. And yet I suppose none now living remember the fellow's name. Perhaps he was an Emparch of old." He spat over the rail. "Fools."

"Was it a whole statue in your day?" I asked.

Nereus shook his head. "No. Reckon most of it crumbled to dust long before my time. Don't matter how rich you are, nor how great. Everyone turns to dust eventually. Everyone and everything."

"Except you." I immediately regretted my words.

His face was a mask of regret. "Ayah," he said softly. "Except me."

"Nereus . . ." I hated to bring it up, but I had been wondering for a long time. "Does everyone she chooses live forever? Or just you?"

The moment the question left my lips, I felt foolish. My explorer ancestor Jacari Bollard had been chosen by the sea god, and it was well known that he'd died at the age of eighty-five. But I knew almost nothing about the god or her magic. If I didn't ask, how would I get answers?

"Never make a wish unless you're certain you want it," Nereus said, shaking his head. "It might come true. And that's all I'll say about that."

The sun had already begun to set by the time we sailed into Eryth harbor. No sooner had we made *Vix*'s mooring warps fast to the dock than the harbor master strode up. He must have been watching our approach.

The harbor master had brown skin and tightly curled gray

hair. He gave a perfunctory bow. "I don't recognize your ship, but I see you fly the lion flag."

I exchanged glances with Nereus. "Um, we're a courier ship. I have an important letter for Lord Pherenekian. What's the docking fee?" I took my purse of silver talents out of my coat pocket. "I'd like to pay it and be on my way to his estate at once. The message can't wait."

The harbor master named his price, and I watched my coin disappear into his pouch. He inclined his head. "I shall summon you a carriage."

"I don't require one," I told him. "We've been many days at sea. I prefer to walk."

"Miss will forgive me for saying that the Archon's castle lies well out of town," the harbor master said, "an hour's journey by horse."

"Oh."

I supposed we had no choice, then. Tucking the leather tube with the letter into my belt, I followed him down the dock. As I climbed onto the seat of the hired carriage, I cast a longing look back at *Vix*.

Even though I'd changed into a smart skirt and jacket ensemble with slashed velvet sleeves, I felt ill equipped to speak to so powerful a man as an Archon. I shifted uncomfortably on the cushions. The carriage bumped and swayed through cobblestoned streets, which eventually subsided into dirt. The houses on either side grew less frequent as we left the city behind. Twitching aside the brocade curtains, I peered out the window.

All I saw was thick dark. Exhaling loudly, I slumped in the seat.

"Stop fidgeting." Nereus's head was tilted back on the cushions, his eyes closed.

I couldn't help it. Traveling by road had always felt unnatural to me. As a wherryman's daughter, it had been drilled into me that if you couldn't get somewhere by boat, it wasn't worth going. Being chosen by the sea god had done nothing to change my opinion.

But it was more than that. *Vix* called to me. I pictured her gently bobbing at anchor and tried to conjure up the smell of the familiar salt breeze. The strangeness of this land, with its eerie ruined statues and jutting hills, jangled in the back of my mind. The farther the carriage wheels rolled from the sea, the more apprehensive I felt.

At least I told myself that's what it was. I was trying not to think about the true nature of my errand. About Markos.

An hour later the carriage pulled into a circular driveway. A uniformed footman jumped to open the door, offering his arm to me. Cursing silently, I took it, because climbing down from a carriage is blasted difficult in skirts and petticoats. We were ushered straight into the dining room where, at the head of the table, a man in a gilt-trimmed waistcoat examined us from above a bushy mustache.

"The Andela courier, I presume," he said without getting up from the remains of his meal.

The butler whispered in my ear. "Lord Pherenekian, Archon of Eryth."

Putting one arm behind my back, I bowed. "My Lord. I have the honor of being Captain Caroline Oresteia."

The Archon paused, knife and fork in the air, peering at me like I was an exotic specimen of bug. Belatedly, I remembered I was wearing skirts. I should have curtsied instead of bowed. Cheeks warming, I thanked the gods Ma was not here to witness my gaffe.

"Ship thief." The Archon set down his cutlery, peering at me through his spectacles. "Rescuer of Emparchs. Read about you in the papers, though one never knows if you can trust the things you see in print. Is it true you have a connection to the Bollards?"

"My mother is a Bollard," I said.

"Jacari Bollard was a great man." He pushed his chair back from the table and stood. "Explorer. Visionary. Great man, great man. The rest of the Bollards, they're in trade, aren't they?"

"They are the foremost merchant house in Kynthessa."

"Lovely, lovely." Lord Pherenekian beckoned me forward. "I take it you've come with a message from the young Emparch?"

With a start, I remembered why I was here. Shaking the rolled parchment out of the tube, I passed it to him.

The Archon skimmed the letter. "So he's said yes." He gave me a faltering smile. "Of course, only a fool would turn such an offer down. I'd hoped the younger Andela was not a fool. No man likes the idea of his daughter marrying a fool. Oh, pardon me . . ." He cleared his throat. "I do tend to ramble on."

Markos had told me to keep my eyes open, but so far I hadn't seen anything to suggest this was a trap. The Archon was friendlier than I had expected. In spite of myself, I decided I liked him. His bumbling personality reminded me of one of my old Bollard uncles.

My gaze was drawn over his shoulder to an enormous oil painting of a lady perched stiffly on a garden chair. Standing beside her was a little black-haired girl with the porcelain complexion only the Akhaian nobility seemed to possess.

The Archon saw me looking. "My late wife." He nodded at the portrait. "And my daughter, Agnes. I've sent for her. She— she'll be down soon." He cocked his head at me. "Perhaps in the meantime you and your man would like to come out on the terrace for a glass of port. I often have a drink in the evening, while taking in the view. And of course, the fresh air is very good for the health."

Nereus spoke up. "We thank you, your lordship." His back was straight and his voice smooth. "A bit of libation is just what we need after our journey."

I blinked in surprise. Sometimes I forgot he hadn't always been a pirate and a scalawag.

The Archon led us onto a terrace full of potted plants and plump sofas. Against the wall, a selection of bottles stood on a side table. He signaled to a servant, who immediately jumped to take down three glasses and fill them with burgundy liquid.

It was after sundown, but I could make out the outline of rolling hills in the distance. Spread out on the Archon's land, between the castle and the hills, were the flickering orange pinpricks of what looked like campfires.

"What are all those lights?" I asked.

"Ah yes, the fires, the fires. I've called my underlords and the landowners sworn to me. As you can see, they're preparing to march." The Archon's throat bobbed as he swallowed. "I supported Antidoros Peregrine years ago—that is, until he grew too bold and got himself exiled. But I've been biding my time since then. I still believe in a democratic Akhaia, and it's led me . . ." He gripped the balcony railing. "Well, it's led me here."

I gazed out at the lights scattered on the hillside. I hadn't expected the Archon to have already amassed his army, or that they'd be camped right here in his garden. It seemed an impressive number of men, surely enough to put Konto Theucinian on guard. Relief trickled through me. I'd done the right thing, pressuring Markos into accepting the offer.

The Archon adjusted his glasses, meeting my eyes. "But I won't bore you with politics. Tell me, young lady, is it true that young Andela entered into a flirtation with you? Or was that just Fabius Balerophon writing nonsense to sell papers?"

My face felt like it was on fire. "I—I don't know why you—you'd ask—" I stammered, unsure where to look.

Pherenekian smiled. "So he did. It's obvious enough from your reaction. Nothing to be embarrassed about."

I disagreed.

"All that's in the past now," I said hastily, when I found my voice again. "If—if that's what you were worried about, I can assure you it's over."

"Oh no, I'm afraid you mistook me. You see, it is most

encouraging to me that he likes you. For my daughter Agnes is . . ." He faltered. "Well, she . . . She's not precisely conventional. Her mind is of a scientific bent. Agnes is actually quite a genius, you see. The trouble is, no one else ever does see it." His voice dropped low. "No one but me. Captain Oresteia, I love my daughter. You must understand that I would do anything for her."

I glanced at the terrace door. "Is she coming?" I asked, desperate to change the subject. I wasn't sure why he was explaining all this to me.

His shoulders twitched as he fussed with his shirt cuffs. "Perhaps not." He hastened to explain. "She's not very keen on the idea of an arranged marriage, you see. You're a young lady yourself. Surely you understand."

I did, although it seemed strange for the Archon to be so unconcerned with his daughter's absence. Sipping my port, I glanced sideways at Nereus. Why didn't he just send one of his servants to fetch her? My smuggler's instincts tingled, but I reminded myself I didn't know these people. Nor was I experienced in the ways of the great Akhaian houses.

The Archon downed his glass rather quickly, setting it on the table with a loud clunk. Picking up a bell from the sideboard, he rang it.

"And now," he announced, "the maid will show you to your room. You and your man shall have any refreshment you require. I'm sure your journey has been long and weary."

"My apologies, Lord Pherenekian," I said, putting on my best Bollard manners, "but I shall have to decline. I must get back to my ship."

"Oh no, I insist! Rooms have been prepared for you." He tugged at his collar, and I noticed he'd gone very red. I wondered how much he'd had to drink before we arrived. "What kind of host would I be, to send you away at this late hour?"

Belatedly, it occurred to me that the only way back to the city was in the hired carriage. Who knew if it was even still here? I hadn't asked the driver to wait.

The Archon continued. "In the morning I shall have my carriage convey you and Agnes to your ship."

"To—to my ship?" I spluttered. "Why?"

The Archon's brows drew together in puzzlement. "For her journey to Valonikos."

CHAPTER
NINE

I almost dropped my half-empty glass of port.

"Wait—you mean—*now*?" I stammered. "Tomorrow? There must be some mistake."

I'd told Markos I would be his courier, but that was all I had promised. The last thing I wanted was to be cooped up on a ship for ten days with his bride. And even worse, this meant the marriage was no longer a hazy future threat. It would be *soon*.

"What have you been sent for," the Archon asked, "if not to fetch my daughter to her husband?"

"I thought I was delivering a letter." Panic rocketed through me. This situation had careened alarmingly out of my control. I cast about for an excuse, any excuse. "My Lord, I'm not sure how familiar you are with ships, but *Vix* is a one-masted cutter. She's very small. Practically *tiny*," I stressed. "There isn't room for an entourage of passengers. There's only one cabin and it's not suitable—"

"Surely you've room enough for a single girl."

"But what about you?" I blurted, confused. "And all your servants?"

"Me? Go to Valonikos? Out of the question." He waved a hand at the campfires. "I have plans to make. An army to manage." His lips twisted into a self-deprecating smile. "*I* wouldn't know what to do at a wedding. If my wife were still alive, it would be a different story, but as it stands . . . No, no. My presence would be quite inappropriate."

I stared in disbelief. Everything he'd said had given me the impression that he cared deeply for Agnes, yet he wasn't planning to attend his own daughter's wedding? He meant to ship her off, alone, to marry a man he had never even met. A horrible thought struck me—had *Markos* known about this? Belatedly it occurred to me that I had never read the letter. What if this had been the plan all along? Surely Markos would have told me . . . wouldn't he?

"But, sir—" I protested helplessly.

The Archon clapped his hands. "Oh, look, here's the maid. She'll show you to your rooms."

He turned away, and I knew we were dismissed. We followed a uniformed maid down a long corridor. The ceilings were nearly twenty feet high, and the white plaster walls and marble floors spotless. I didn't dare touch anything, lest the maid glare at me for leaving a smudge.

I leaned closer to Nereus. "That was strange, wasn't it? Why wouldn't he come to the wedding?" The Archon's odd behavior had put me on edge. "Something's not right."

He shrugged. "Maybe. Could be this is a trap, though I can't see how."

"Me either," I said under my breath so the maid wouldn't hear.

"Then again, perhaps he just wants to make sure his army's prepared for battle. Seems like he trusts you to get his daughter to Valonikos safe and sound."

"Whyever would he? He just met me."

Lord Pherenekian hadn't seemed very warlike to me. He struck me as a man who puttered about his estate, trimming his prize rosebushes or reading classical poetry. But people had hidden depths, I supposed. I shook my head. Whatever was wrong, I could not puzzle it out.

The rooms the Archon had assigned me were the height of luxury, with silken drapes and a lush carpet my bare toes could sink into. Tossing my boots in the corner, I flopped in an armchair. Just as I was thinking a bath might be nice, and debating whether to pull the bell rope for the maid, a knock sounded at the door.

Grabbing my pistols from the table, I shook out my skirts to conceal my bare feet. I opened the door to discover a cringing servant girl. At the sight of my guns, she squeaked and jumped back.

"What do you want?" I demanded when she didn't say anything. "Oh . . . sorry," I said, following her gaze to the pistols. Sheepishly, I stowed them away.

"The—the lady summons you," she stammered. "The Lady Agnes, I mean. To her library. I'm to show you the way, miss. That is, Captain."

I followed her down a hallway decorated with oil portraits. The Archon's ancestors, lined up to stare down at me, an interloper with common roots. I ignored the disapproving prickle of their eyes. I was half Bollard after all and used to being glared at by centuries of history.

We reached the end of the hall, and the servant girl pushed open a narrow door. It was a spiral staircase, lit only by bare candles flickering in niches. Trailing my hand along the curved center wall for balance, I started up the steps. The brick walls were draped in spiderwebs. Blinking, I emerged through a round hole in the floor of a brightly lit room.

Her library, the servant had said, but it was much more than a library. The octagonal tower room was packed with shelves. Alchemical equipment stood on a table—an alembic and a crucible, plus other instruments I did not know the name for. One cabinet was stuffed with scrolls, each painstakingly labeled in a correct hand, and another with glass jars full of cloudy liquid. I didn't much want to know what was floating in them. The walls were hung with diagrams. I spotted a star chart and an anatomical drawing of a man, his insides splayed out. A tabby cat wove around the table legs.

Across the room a monstrous desk squatted under a stained glass window. Agnes Pherenekian sat behind it, pen poised over a notebook.

Her sleek hair was dressed in a jeweled net at the nape of her neck. She had a long elegant nose and a pointed chin, and her powdered skin was a light olive shade. Looking down, I noticed her thumb was stained with ink. She didn't say a word, yet coiled energy vibrated around her.

Thinking back to the portrait in the dining room, I tried to reconcile the two. Both Markos and Sophronia Hypatos had given me the impression that Agnes wasn't a great beauty. The girl in the painting was plain, with a long pale face overwhelmed by thick braids of black hair. Likely the painter had exaggerated the lightness of her skin as a stylistic choice. It wasn't one I approved of.

With a sinking feeling, I had to admit Markos might be pleasantly surprised by his new bride. She'd clearly grown out of her awkward phase.

"The Rose of the Coast." Agnes pointed at me with the pen. "That *is* who you are, correct?"

Candlelight flickered on her red lips. I squinted—that wasn't paint, was it? I chided myself for the thought. A girl could like both alchemical experiments and face paint.

A small chest of glass vials perched on the desk, and several of the books on the table were open. Sketches of butterflies, moths, and insects, labeled with the same tiny round script I'd seen on the scrolls, covered the pages. The notebook page she'd been looking at when I came in, however, was blank. I supposed I'd interrupted her work.

And it *was* work. What I saw here indicated much more than a hobby. Her scientific studies appeared to be extensive.

"Ayah, my lady." I folded my hands behind my back. "What is it you want?"

Her lips tugged to one side. "Do you know, no one ever asks me that question. What do I want?" She narrowed her eyes at me. "I didn't expect you to be Markos Andela's messenger. Funny— I'd heard you were lovers, and yet he sends you to go fetch his new wife. Frankly, I'm sure *I* would have too much pride to do it, were I in your position."

Her words were like a slap in the face. I forced myself not to take a step back.

"I heard your grand tour was not successful in securing you a husband," I replied, grinding my teeth. "I can see why."

Agnes relaxed back into her chair, spinning the pen between her fingers. My words didn't seem to bother her. "It's true, I am cursed with the unenviable trait of always speaking my mind. I can't help it."

It seemed to me, I thought bitterly, that she could help it if she wanted to. No one could have meticulously labeled those sketches and used these precision instruments without possessing a degree of control.

Agnes laughed suddenly. "Oh, look at your face. Peace, Captain Oresteia. I only wanted to see how you'd react." She threw down her pen. "Let's call it a scientific experiment."

If this was her idea of science, I wasn't altogether certain I liked it. My gaze drifted to a glass display case, where dead butterflies were pinned to the backboard and tagged with their scientific names. One was a particularly bright shade of lavender.

Agnes saw me looking. "That is the *Papillo pura*, more commonly known as the purple crown. Pretty, but unfortunately also quite deadly. Its wings produce a poison that stops the human heart within minutes."

I nodded at the vials on the desk. "What are those?" I asked politely.

"Oh, I mix all my own inks," she explained. "Over the years I have perfected my own personal formula, which I've found to be quite resistant to fading."

"Your sketches are very good." I pushed aside a stack of books, tugging out a diagram of a dragonfly. A pang of homesickness went through me. The dragonfly was well rendered, reminding me immediately of the riverlands.

"Please refrain from touching the volumes," she said sharply. "Some of them are hundreds of years old. I only handle them with gloves."

I dropped the sketch like a child caught with a stolen cookie. I understood her plain enough. She didn't want me getting my dirty sailor hands all over her things.

"My lady," I said, changing the subject. "Why am I here? To play games? Or so you can interrogate me about Markos?"

She gave me a conspiratorial smile. "That wasn't my intention. I just want to know what I'm getting into."

The tabby cat leaped onto the desk. Agnes held out one finger to it. The cat sniffed it and hissed. It scrabbled back, tail lashing from side to side. Then it jumped off the desk, nearly knocking over the candlestick, and disappeared under a bookcase.

Some folks thought cats were good luck on a boat. Myself, I had distinct memories of being bitten by an orange-striped Bollard tomcat when I was six. They were temperamental creatures, armed with tiny knives. This one did nothing to change my opinion. I resented that Agnes had snapped at me for touching her books, yet she allowed the cat free rein of the desk.

Choosing my words with caution, I said, "What's between me and Markos is in the past, but what I can tell you from my . . . association . . . with him is he's thoughtful. And unconventional. And honorable to a fault. You would be lucky to be married to him. I mean, you *will* be lucky."

"Have you any idea what subjects he has studied?"

I squirmed uncomfortably. It occurred to me that I should probably know the answer to her question. "Um, classics mostly, I think. He reads a lot of political treatises. And he's good at sword fighting."

A smile flitted around her mouth. "I see. Well, I appreciate your candor. This marriage is my father's idea, not mine. I'm doing this to please him." Agnes stood, shutting her chest of inks with a click. "I just wanted to get a better idea of the sort of man I will be dealing with. And you have relieved my mind greatly."

"That's . . . that's good," I managed.

Her gaze traveled around her library. "I shall be sorry to leave all this behind though. I suppose I'll have to start over again when I get to my new house."

In truth, I did not know what to make of Agnes. I'd insisted that Markos accept the marriage offer, but somehow it hadn't occurred to me to wonder if the match might be a success. *Would* Markos like this girl? She was both interesting and pretty. And, I suspected, smarter than me. A hot streak of jealousy flashed through me. I didn't like the idea at all.

"I wanted to meet you because I was hoping I might count you a friend," Agnes went on. "In Valonikos."

It would sting whenever I saw them together, every day of my life. I couldn't be her friend. I wasn't even sure I could be Markos's friend anymore. Perhaps someday when it didn't hurt so much to think of the part of us we'd lost.

But I couldn't say that to Agnes. It would be unspeakably rude. "I don't know, my lady," I mumbled. "I—I need to go get some sleep. And I'm sure you have things to pack. Our carriage leaves at dawn."

"Let's bid each other good night, then," she said. "I look forward to meeting your Emparch."

"He's not—" I began automatically, and then halted.

"*Your* Emparch?" She arched her finely drawn eyebrows. "No, I suppose he isn't. Not anymore. Good night, Captain Oresteia."

CHAPTER
TEN

The morning sun had not yet cracked the horizon, but the wharf was alive with sound and motion. Cooks haggled with provisioners at the market stalls, while sailors shook out the sails of their ships to make ready for departure. The harbor at morning tide is always the first part of a city to wake up.

Agnes sat very straight on the opposite seat of the carriage, her small chest of inks on her lap. I'd expected the Archon to come at least as far as the port, to see his daughter off, but Agnes had appeared at the bottom of the manor stairs alone. We'd exchanged few words during the bumpy carriage ride to the harbor.

The Archon's behavior was strange, but what did it *mean*? I felt uncomfortably like I'd missed something important. While Markos had been a fish out of water in the riverlands, I was a stranger to the world of Akhaian nobility. Had there been some kind of sign that this was a trap—one that Markos or Sophronia would have seen instantly? My instincts told me something was not right in Eryth, but I could not lay a finger on what it was.

Well, we couldn't call off the whole plan because of a funny feeling. I'd just have to keep an eye on Agnes.

The carriage lurched to a stop at the end of the dock. Peering past the curtains, I glimpsed *Vix* in her berth, mast standing tall. Nereus hopped out to unstrap Agnes's luggage from the top of the carriage.

Clutching her box tightly under her arm, Agnes stepped down. "You will please be careful with my books and instruments," she instructed Nereus in a lofty tone. Seeing me glance at the box, she explained, "I always carry my inks myself. They are precious to me."

Nereus lifted her lone trunk easily onto his shoulder and we boarded the ship.

Pointing the tiller, I guided *Vix* out of the harbor. We were running before a fair wind, with the topsail raised and two foresails billowing out on the bowsprit. As the day wore on, I couldn't shake the suspicion that something was following us, and I had a pretty good idea what it was. The sky was already darkening when the drakon finally showed itself.

With a splash, the creature's massive green head split the waves, rising until its unblinking eye was level with mine. Its mane looked like feathers, but I knew they were actually webbed spikes. Through the gap in its lips, I glimpsed teeth like swords. The smell of rotting seaweed wafted toward me.

At the tiller, Damian nearly jumped out of his shirt. All the men had been warned the drakon might appear, but I doubted they'd ever seen one before. Casting a sideways glance at the beast, Damian scrambled to the opposite end of the bench. Sailors were superstitious about looking a drakon in the eye.

The drakon shook its mane, sending salty droplets into my face. When it spoke, the voice that came out was *hers*.

"Oh, little river rat," she whispered. I thought I heard pity in her voice. "What are you doing?"

She didn't have to explain what she meant. Gripping the rail, I said, "I promised Markos I would sail for him."

"Cats, cats, cats," she said flippantly. "He's not for *you*. You were meant for much greater things."

She always said Markos smelled of cats. The sea god and the lion god, who was the patron of Akhaia, were rivals, time out of mind. The last time they'd faced each other, the sea god had won so resounding a victory that the lion god had retreated under his mountain for six hundred years. Or so she'd bragged to me.

"You don't even know what a little fool you are," she continued. "I could tell you your fate. What a mistake you're making."

I gritted my teeth. "If you're just going to keep insulting me, you needn't bother."

"I said I would make you a master of the sea. I gave you my best warrior." I knew she meant Nereus. "But you turn around and use my gifts to serve this lion boy." She stuck out her long forked tongue, which had barnacles growing on it. "I can't abide cats. You know what you have to do."

I licked my lips, finding they were suddenly dry. "Do I?"

"Laughter," the god said in a voice that sounded like a herd of dying animals. "You say you mean to leave him, and yet still you sail at his beck and call. First it was a letter. Now you're playing fetch for him, bringing him the girl who will replace you." Her voice dropped low. "I thought you had more pride."

The words hit me where it stung. I saw clearly the temptation she dangled before me—sailing off to adventures unknown, leaving Markos and Akhaia behind in my wake. The rebellious part of my soul howled, pulling at the ropes that tied me, like a ship tossing in a stormy harbor.

It wanted to smash ships. To be free.

"A promise is a promise," I insisted, emotions clashing uncomfortably inside me.

"Fortunate favorite." The drakon's voice wove around me like a silk ribbon. "You can go anywhere on the whole ocean. Do anything. And instead you allow love to make you a laughingstock and a fool."

"No," I whispered.

"I knew a girl like you once," she said. "She died without the smell of the sea in her nose or the taste of salt on her lips. They buried her in the dirt a thousand miles from her home." The words echoed sorrowfully on the wind. *Home-home-home* . . . "Is that what you want?"

I clenched my hands around the rail.

"Break your ties with that boy," she hissed. "I command it. Don't ever forget I found you in the mud of the riverlands. I lifted you up."

My lip twisted with resentment. It figured that was how she would put it. To her the river god was a lesser god, content to putter around on his slow inland waterways. His chosen were simple folk—wherrymen, smugglers, and fishermen. *My* folk.

The drakon hissed, "Remember, I keep what I take."

"You might've said, once or twice."

Her voice turned cold. "You are mine, Caroline Oresteia. Never forget that." *Vix* shuddered as the drakon's tail caressed the hull. "Make your choice tonight. I will return in the morning."

The drakon flipped over.

"Wait!" I called after it.

But the god didn't hear me, or she pretended not to. Twenty feet of tail swished above the foamy waves, then ten. The very tip disappeared with a *splish* and a swirl of bubbles. She was gone.

"I can't just leave him," I said aloud to the empty sea. "I promised—"

I stopped. What exactly had I promised? Once I delivered Markos's bride to Valonikos, what reason would I have to stay? We had no future together. We couldn't. Not when I was bound to the sea and he was bound to Akhaia. Not when he was marrying Agnes.

Remembering the sea god's city full of sunken things, I wondered if I was merely a trophy to her, like her bones and shipwrecks and broken ruins. What would she do to me if I refused her?

A female voice spoke behind me. "What was that bump? I thought I felt the ship lurch."

Agnes stood at the top of the ladder, tightening a silk shawl around her bony shoulders. A flimsy thing like that wasn't going to be enough for a sea journey. Her hair was twisted artfully into a loose knot, and face paint lined her eyes, which were not the blue of northern Akhaia but brown like my own.

I glanced back at the sea. The drakon had vanished, without even a circle of bubbles to show that it had ever been there.

"Ayah?" I hated to pretend Agnes was the crazy one, but I didn't want to explain the drakon. "Everything's shipshape up here. Likely just a big swell," I lied. "You get used to the motion after a while."

"I know," she said. "I've traveled by ship before. Only I could swear I felt . . ." She tilted her head. "Who were you talking to?"

"No one." Releasing the rail, I tried to shake off my uneasiness. It was cursed strange, going from arguing with a god to polite small talk. "Just making a list, my lady. Um, provisions and the like."

Agnes joined me by the rail. "I talk to myself sometimes too. I fear people think I'm odd."

I hastily changed the subject. "Do you have everything you need? In your cabin, I mean."

Which was actually my cabin, because it was the only private one on the cutter. I would be bunking in the hold with the crew for the return trip to Valonikos.

"I like it," she said. "There's even a desk. Though," she admitted, "every time I sit down to read, it makes my head buzz awfully."

"You want to watch out for that. The next thing you know, it's your breakfast coming up."

"That's what I was afraid of." She studied me, a knowing smile curving her mouth. "In the Museum of Art in Eryth, there's a sculpture of a drakon. It was done by Orsino the Great."

"Oh—is there?" I stammered. "How odd. I thought no one had ever seen a drakon."

I heard amusement in her voice. "I suspect that is because people are awful liars."

"If you mean me," I shot back, "you might as well say so." I leaned on the rail. In the dark, the water below had no color. It was just a swirling mass of motion. "In the riverlands, where I was born," I said slowly, "folk say it's bad luck, even dangerous, to speak of a god."

"Who said anything about gods? I thought we were talking of marine life." She tapped her notebook. "I should like to sketch a drakon. For scientific purposes."

I shifted uncomfortably. The drakon wasn't a god . . . not exactly. A close associate of the sea god, or a servant maybe. But I didn't know if I would blithely classify it as "marine life." It seemed too analytical a way to describe such a magical creature.

"Although," Agnes went on, "a drakon has no scientific classification, of course. The Royal Society of Natural History does not recognize them."

"Oh?" I seized on the new subject, happy to steer her away from the drakon. "Have you been there? To the Royal Society, I mean?"

"No." She stared into the moving waves. "Had I been born a boy, I daresay I'd be studying with them to become a member."

We spoke no more about drakons after that. Later that night,

Agnes shut herself in my cabin, while I dropped into a bunk. The hold was stuffy, and the curtain I'd strung across the bunk for privacy only made it worse. I lay in the dark, sweat beading on my skin, acutely aware that Markos's future wife was on the other side of the wall.

When I'd pushed Markos into accepting the marriage, it had seemed like the right thing to do. I'd told myself I was making a noble sacrifice. I was doing it so an entire country might be free. But only now, confronted with the reality of Agnes, a flesh-and-blood girl right here on my ship, was I beginning to understand the consequences of my choice.

Panic rippled through me. I would never kiss Markos again. We would never banter back and forth at the breakfast table. Hot tears seared the corners of my eyes. Oh gods, had I made the biggest mistake of my life?

The sea god had told me to choose by morning. If I agreed, not only would I never kiss Markos—I would never *see* him again. I squeezed my eyes shut. I wasn't ready for that. It was too soon.

I already gave Markos up, I thought angrily at her. *I gave him up when I told him to marry her. I don't know what else you want from me.*

But I did know. She wanted me to forsake my promise. To never return to Valonikos.

The god claimed Markos wasn't meant for me, but Nereus had warned me against trusting her. Three months ago I'd believed with every bone in my body that my fate was in the riverlands. I'd been wrong. Was this really fate . . . or the god attempting to manipulate me?

On the other hand, I could choose to throw myself whole-heartedly into my new life with the sea. I longed to feel like I knew my place in the world again. What if leaving Markos behind was the only way? Was it worth the price?

Shoving the blanket off, I tried to resettle myself. But every time I closed my eyes, I saw the drowned city of Amassia, with its toppled towers and seaweed streets.

I remembered only too well what the sea god had done when another girl spurned the ocean in favor of an Emparch.

CHAPTER
ELEVEN

When I woke for my watch, the sky was already ominously gray. The wherrymen say the god in the river speaks to us in the language of small things. The sea god was not as subtle. A strong wind whistled in the rigging and buffeted the canvas. Dark patches flattened the sea.

Squalls flew quick as a flash toward us. I glanced at the mainsail. The men had already taken two reefs, shortening the sail to lessen the burden of the wind.

Holding on to a rope for balance, Nereus made his way along the deck. The hood of his oilskin coat was pulled low against the blowing spray and spitting rain.

Raising his voice above the waves, he asked, "What did you do to make her this angry?"

Water trickled down my neck. "She told me I had to choose."

"Then you best make your choice quick," he shouted.

The sea god was flaunting her power. The crew scurried around the deck, shoulders hunched against the weather. No one smiled or made jokes. They were experienced sailors who'd seen plenty of rough storms, but their sober faces told me how precarious our situation was. Remembering Agnes, I felt a stab of guilt—she was probably throwing up her lunch in the cabin.

"A word from you can stop this, you know," the god hissed in my ear.

My shoulders jumped. I glanced wildly around, but this time I saw no drakon or seagull. She was speaking directly to me. The crew gave no indication that they'd heard her.

Panic rose inside me. I was no closer to a decision than I'd been last night. Thinking of the day I'd vowed to sail for Markos, my chest ached. We'd been standing on the Valonikos docks with hands clasped, the sun shining and the wind whipping our hair. I remembered his words, months ago on Nemertes Water. *We're stronger together than apart. Don't you think?*

Tears burned my eyes. Before we'd ever kissed, Markos was my friend. Our adventures together on *Cormorant* had made us a team, and he still needed me. I couldn't abandon him. Not even for the god.

"So you intend to defy me, then," she said, so softly her voice might have been the wind in the ropes.

"I never said that." Sweat dampened my neck.

"I see it in your mind."

I grasped frantically for the words I wanted. "Not defy, exactly. I need more time. And what about Agnes? Just let me go back to Valonikos first. Give me a chance to *explain*—"

The wind's howl picked up, causing the ropes to thrum. *Vix* heeled alarmingly as a gust slammed her. Mind racing, I glanced up at the taut canvas. We were carrying too much sail.

Another squall hit us. *Vix* tilted on her side, the starboard rail going underwater. My boots lost their grip and I fell, sliding down toward the churning sea. I didn't doubt for an instant that it was intentional. Nereus lunged across the deck to loosen the sail.

"Damn you!" I screamed, bracing my feet against the rail as the ocean dunked me to my waist. "Maybe Markos and I weren't supposed to be together! Maybe it was impossible from the beginning." My voice broke. "But at least it was *my* mistake. It's my life. You can't make my choices for me!"

The wind stopped, like a candle flame whisking out.

"Oh, can't I?" the sea god hissed, her voice like ice.

Suddenly I saw myself, a dark speck clinging to *Vix*'s rail. Then my vision pulled back and widened, and I saw that *Vix* herself was only a speck compared to the vastness of the ocean.

I was smaller than a minnow to the god of the sea. And I'd made a terrible mistake.

The cutter lurched, a shiver going through her from stern to bow. *Vix*'s hull seemed to groan, vibrating the deck under my feet.

"What was that?" I cried, but the wind snatched my words away.

A sharp crack rent the air. *Vix*'s topsail crashed to the deck, landing on Pat. The men's mouths moved as they stumbled toward him through the battering rain, but the storm was too loud for me to make out their words.

Grasping a rope end, I pulled with all my strength. My boots finally found purchase against the slanted deck. I waded toward the sail, fighting the sluicing water that tried to suck me back. Jerking a knife from my belt, I yelled, "Cut all this away!"

I squinted up, but the rain and sea obscured the top of the mast from sight. Had it been snapped? The deck was a mess of wood, rope, and sopping canvas. The spar was definitely down—I saw its broken outline under the pile of sail.

And below that, the outline of a body. Damian and Castor sliced away the heavy pile of canvas, revealing Pat lying crushed under the spar. I closed my eyes. He'd probably been killed instantly, hit on the head when the sail came down.

I didn't have time to think about him now. We could sail without the spar and even the top of the mast, if only everything else held together. A taunting voice whispered in the back of my mind. *Blood on your hands.*

"Water's coming in," Damian shouted.

"What do you mean?" I demanded. "From where?"

"From that hit. We're wedged on a shoal."

He was right. We'd stopped moving. I remembered that strange bump and shiver. If *Vix* was stuck on something, each wave that hammered us would only make it worse. That was why the topsail had snapped off—too much wind with nowhere to go.

Running to the rail, I saw nothing. We were only a few miles off the Akhaian coast and the land should have been visible, but the storm had turned everything to directionless gray. A wave rose up, knocking me to the deck. I coughed and spluttered, my nose and throat stinging from the salt. Under me *Vix* moaned again, her timbers shaking, as if she was in pain.

We were being helplessly battered. The sails, I realized. They were only pushing us onto the shoal.

"Cut all the canvas!" I screamed, struggling toward the foot of the mast. With slippery fingers I set my knife blade between my teeth and bit down hard. Grabbing a line, I hoisted myself up.

A hand on my waist hauled me back down.

"It's too dangerous to go aloft, girl!" Nereus shouted.

Something white went spinning away into the maelstrom. One of the foresails, transformed into a tangled, whipping bird. It flew up and up until it disappeared into another pelting wall of rain. *Vix* was being ripped apart by the storm.

No, not the storm. By *her*. She was dismantling my ship, like a bully tearing the wings off a butterfly.

Water swirled around my knees. From the slant of the deck, *Vix* must have struck the shoal on the starboard side. She was going down by the stern, her bow rising out of the water. How badly was she staved in? And how deep was the water here?

Horror nearly bowled me over. Agnes was still in the cabin. How could I have forgotten her? If the deck was swamped, surely the cabin was rapidly filling with water. Turning to the hatch cover, I realized it was half-underwater.

"Agnes!" I yelled.

Behind me, wood scraped on wood. The dinghy was kept on

crutches on the deck, where it could be raised and lowered if we needed to row ashore. The crew loosened the ropes and set it free, bobbing on the water. Something was wrong. I counted—Damian, Castor, and Nereus.

"Where's Leon?" I asked.

Nereus only shook his head. "Swept overboard. He's gone."

Reeling, I stumbled toward the hatch. Two men were dead because of me. Tears blended with the salt water on my cheeks. The hatch cover was completely submerged by the time I reached it. Plunging my hands underwater, I pulled the handle as hard as I could. The cover came away with a sucking sound, the sea pouring like a waterfall down the ladder.

Agnes stood at the bottom of the ladder, an ax clutched in her hand. Her waterlogged sleeves clung to her arms, and her wet hair was slicked back. The sea was nearly up to her chest.

"Don't you dare cut a hole in my ship!" I screamed.

Tossing away the ax, she glared up at me, eyes black with fury. "It's a bit late for that, isn't it?" She made a grab at the ladder rung, but the spilling water knocked her back. "The hatch was stuck."

"I'm throwing you a rope. Hold on!"

I cast around for a spare line. Finding one floating nearby, I seized it and tied a quick bowline knot around the nearest rail. I tossed the other end down the hatch.

And looked up into a nightmare.

Vix's entire stern end was underwater and the dinghy was—I turned left and right, frantically searching the waves—gone. The boom dragged in the water, the wet canvas pulling heavily on it. I had to get to that halyard and bring the sail down, and I had no time to wait for Agnes.

Struggling out of my wet coat, I dropped it in the water. My boots felt like lead weights on my feet. Kicking them off, I lunged into the sea and swam to the mast. Using my knife, I slashed the halyard. The sail came crashing down. *Vix* leveled, her starboard side bouncing up. My actions had dislodged the ship from the shoal, but she was still tipped toward the stern.

She's going down.

Arm wrapped around the mast, I shoved the thought away. *Vix* and I belonged together. The life in her called out to the life in me. She couldn't sink.

"Where's the lifeboat?" Agnes screamed at me across the tossing water.

I didn't know. But a streak of hope went through me as I suddenly remembered Docia Argyrus. Perhaps there was a chance *Vix* could be salvaged. As long as she wasn't smashed on the rocks.

Anchor. I had to drop the anchor. Hopefully it would be enough to keep *Vix* safe on the bottom of the sea until I could get back to her.

A wave crested, slapping me in the face. I let go of the mast and swam toward the bowsprit, which pointed out of the sea at a steep angle. Feeling underwater, I found the winch handle. It slipped from my fingers. The sea was pushing me back.

Gulping a deep breath of air, I went underwater. My hands located the catch that released the winch. I fumbled blindly for the anchor rope, and then snatched my hand back. The wheel was spinning so fast it had nearly taken my skin off.

Kicking away, I pulled for the surface. When my head broke through, I was alone. Splashing in a circle, I saw the dinghy bobbing upside down.

"No!" I screamed, inhaling water.

Someone grabbed my hand.

"Hold on to me." Tension tightened Nereus's face as he clung to a floating barrel. "You hear me, girlie? Don't let go. She won't be harming me. You're safe as long as we're together."

I held tight to him as the waves battered us. A big one splashed over the barrel, dunking me. In my spluttering confusion, I lost my grip on his hand.

When I resurfaced, Nereus was already several feet away. "Caro!" he yelled, the wind whipping his voice away.

I splashed toward him, but despite my efforts, the sea lengthened between us. Something slick and round bobbed in the water—a chunk of *Vix*'s broken spar.

Oh, *Vix*.

Salt burning my eyes and throat, I hung onto the spar with both arms. The waves drenched me again, and that's when I knew for sure.

She meant to drown me.

CHAPTER
TWELVE

The hot sun on my face woke me.

I rolled onto my stomach, gagging. My mouth was full of sand and my forearms were red as baked shellfish, the skin scraped raw. I burned everywhere. The beach spinning around me, I hauled myself upright.

I immediately regretted it, squeezing my eyes shut against a wave of nausea. My throat convulsed as something struggled to come up. Pressing my hands tight over my mouth, I swallowed hard.

To my left, birds squawked in the treetops. I heard the tuneless buzzing of insects and the whisper of leaves, but no human voices. I crawled up the beach, hoping to catch a glimpse of a dock, the roofs of a distant town—anything.

The leaning bones of what had once been a ship loomed up ahead, protruding from the beach.

Oh no. *No*.

Not *Vix*.

As I wobbled closer, knees digging in the sand, relief washed over me. This was a much older wreck, her black paint nearly worn away by the pounding surf. Farther up the beach a spar was half-buried in the sand, tattered canvas flapping in the wind. I didn't think I could stand seeing *Vix* that way, broken into jagged pieces.

Then I spotted the body in the sand. On its arm was a dark blot—a tattoo I recognized.

"Nereus!" I yelled, but it came out as a croak. "Nereus?"

Even at that distance I knew he was dead from the strange way he seemed to have shrunk. But when I got closer, I knew it from the smell. Judging by how burned my own skin was, he must have been lying a long time in the sun. His legs were tangled in a piece of shredded sail.

He *couldn't* be dead. It wasn't possible.

Fighting the heavy wet sand, I struggled to turn him over.

I shook him. "Nereus."

His eyes were open, rolled back in his head. They were already glazed over. I'd seen dead men before, but never like this, after being in the sun for hours or days. I forced myself to examine the gash on his forehead, yawning open like a swollen mouth. The blood had been washed away by the sea, but his skin was mottled like spoiled meat.

Numbly I stared at the bloated wreck that had been my friend. Nereus had lived for hundreds of years. I hadn't even thought he *could* be killed. Remembering his words as we clung together in the water, I squeezed my eyes shut. *She won't be harming me. You're safe as long as we're together.*

It didn't make sense. Why would the sea god let Nereus die and not me? Unless—a horrible thought trickled through me— maybe she'd killed him for trying to help me.

"Oh gods," I rasped, hastily turning him back over to avoid his staring eyes. The scent of death was thick in my nose. "It's all my fault."

This was the price for defying a god. The enormity of what I'd done hit me like a physical blow. Agnes and the crew were almost certainly dead. My selfishness had destroyed six lives. How could I ever face Markos again? I'd drowned his bride and ruined what might have been his only chance at getting his father's throne back. Dots swam in front of my eyes. My stomach spasmed, and the beach tilted, pitching me onto the sand.

I threw up.

Salt water streamed out of my mouth, searing my throat. My arms shook uncontrollably. Unable to prop myself up, I fell on my side. Sand rubbed the million cuts and scratches on my body. Moaning, I dug my fingers into the beach in an attempt to make the world stop spinning.

Nausea rolled over me again. I didn't have the energy to lift my body, so I turned my head and coughed. Water surged up, spewing from my mouth and nose.

Whimpering, I pressed my forehead to the hot sand. My nose was running, and horrid-tasting water dribbled from my mouth. Helpless tears leaked from my eyes. My body was expelling all the salt water inside it. I was dying.

The sea god had taken Nereus and *Vix*. She'd taken everything from me. I deserved to die.

A male voice spoke up. "Ayah, they do be stinking, don't they? Corpses."

My hand flew instinctively to my right side. The belt holster was empty. I fumbled for my left hip, relieved to discover I still had the other pistol. My fingers shook so hard I couldn't grip it.

I looked up, the world tilting alarmingly, and recognition flashed through me.

The last time I'd seen this man he was clean-shaven, with a dashing waistcoat and tricorn hat. Both of those items were gone now. Dark haired and deeply tanned, he lounged in the crook of a nearby tree, wearing tattered breeches and a vest of soiled linen that had once been a shirt. A scruffy beard straggled down from his chin. The curved scar under his eye was the same, but someone had given him a twin—redder and fresher—along his left cheekbone.

Tugging my gun out, I aimed it at his head.

"I wouldn't be firing that pistol if I was you, love," drawled Diric Melanos, former captain of the cutter *Victorianos*.

Disoriented by heat sickness, I hesitated. Lowering the flintlock, I checked the barrel. It was full of sand. Adrenaline belatedly washed through me, making sweat bead on my neck. If I'd pulled the trigger, the pistol would have backfired on me.

It would have killed me.

I wondered why he'd stopped me. Certainly no one in the world had greater reason to want me dead than the man whose ship I had stolen.

"Welcome to paradise." Nimble as a cat, Melanos dropped to the beach and ambled barefoot toward me. The hot sand didn't seem to hurt him like it hurt me. "That is, I reckon this island would be paradise if it weren't for all the bloody sand. And the crabs."

"What crabs?" I asked.

He laughed. "You'll see, come nightfall."

"What are you doing here?" I demanded.

"I were marooned on this island. By your Bollard bitch of a mother, if you must know."

Dropping the useless pistol, I jerked my dagger from my belt and assumed a fighting stance.

"Put the knife away, love." He snorted. "What are you going to do, puke on me?"

He crossed the beach, the end of his walking stick sinking into the sand. As he came closer, I realized it was a makeshift spear, a rusty blade strapped to the top of a wooden pole with bits of rotten rope. Using the blunt end, he poked Nereus's back.

My throat convulsed. "What are you doing?" I managed. "Stop it."

"Best bury this fellow," he said.

"No." I struggled to get my stomach under control. "Not bury," I whispered. "He belonged to—to *her.*"

"That way, was it?" Melanos turned to face the horizon, voice softening. "Best push him out to sea, then. Where she can take him."

He bent over the swollen body, dragging it down the beach. I watched the water lap at the corpse, feeling like I should do something. Say a blessing. Beg Nereus's forgiveness. But I only whispered, "Current carry you."

As the body bobbed on the waves, I had the chilling realization that the sea god could have taken Nereus to the deep anytime she wished. The only reason she'd let him wash up on the beach was so I could see him. So she could rub it in my face. The thought that hit me next was just as unsettling. The god had marooned me on an island with a man who wanted to kill me.

None of this was a coincidence. It was punishment.

After the body was gone, Melanos turned to me. "Now, what have you done to my ship?"

"*My* ship."

"Ayah, because you stole it, you villainous little wench."

"I had a letter of marque," I said. "I took a prize, as was my legal right."

"'I took a prize.'" He mimicked me. "Don't seem to me as it was much of a prize, seeing as you ain't in possession of it now. You weren't captain for very long, were you? Not cut out for it, I expect. No great surprise there."

My reply stuck in the back of my throat. What could I say? He was prodding all my insecurities like one might pick at a scab.

He's right, a bitter voice whispered in the back of my head. *You only had the ship for three months before you sank it. You failed. You killed six people.*

"What was it?" Melanos asked cheerfully. "Mutiny? Incompetence? Oh come, tell your old friend Diric. I could do with some amusement to brighten my day."

White spots broke out in front of my eyes. Hot. It was too hot. I swayed on my feet.

Melanos noticed. "If I ain't mistaken," he said, "you're going to feel pretty poorly for the next few days."

"And I suppose you're going to put a cool washcloth on my forehead and make me soup." My legs trembled. I suspected that bit of sarcasm had taken the last reserves of my energy.

He snorted. "No, but," he said, raising one finger, "I promise not to kill you while you're asleep."

"My mother marooned you here for good reason. You're nothing but a filthy pirate." The spots crowded in, blurring my vision. "Your word is worthless to me."

"Ayah, but it's all you've got."

Melanos said something else, but it sounded like he was calling down a long dark tunnel. The white spots exploded in a blinding flash. The world collapsed, and I felt my knees hit the sand.

Then everything faded to black.

❧

When I woke, night had fallen. I was drenched in sweat, my cheeks burning with fever. As my eyes adjusted, I saw tree branches weaving above me. Pinpricks of stars were visible through the gaps in the shelter roof, which seemed to be made from a torn sail.

Open on two sides, the shelter was built from tree branches and heaped-up brush. I lay on a sand-crusted blanket with badly frayed edges. In the dark I glimpsed the outlines of things piled along the walls. A rusty pot. Broken crockery. A whole crate of bottles.

My rescuer—or was he my captor?—sat cross-legged on the sand floor, moonlight glinting on his eyes as he stared out at the beach. From the rhythmic crash of the breakers, I knew we must not be far from the water. The wind rustled the trees. Underneath those familiar sounds, I heard a clicking, scuttling noise I could not identify.

I propped myself up on my elbows. "Did you *carry* me here?"

"You're welcome." Melanos leaned against the tent pole. "Just as much of a bitch as your mother." He tossed a dirty bottle my way. "Water," he grunted. "Drink it."

My eyes narrowed at the insult, but I was too thirsty to refuse the water. I seized the bottle, gulping greedily. It tasted stale and muddy, but I didn't care. Probably he'd been collecting rainwater in a barrel somewhere.

"Don't you dare say anything against Ma," I rasped, wiping my chin. "Where are my weapons?"

"I haven't stolen them, if that's what you think." He nodded across the shelter, where my belt and holsters lay in a pile beside his pieces of salvaged junk.

Eyeing him warily, I asked, "Why not?" He hated me after all, and that pistol was gold plated. "I would've."

"Because," he drawled, taking a pull off the bottle. The smell of whiskey wafted across the shelter. I wondered where he'd gotten that. "One knife and a busted pistol wouldn't help you, if I wanted to kill you."

Fingers flying to my throat, I was relieved to discover Kenté's strange talisman dangling from its chain. He hadn't taken it either. If Melanos had intended to harm me, he could easily have done so while I was unconscious. That didn't mean I trusted him.

I studied him in the dim light. It wasn't just his beard that was long. His hair hung shaggily around his shoulders. It had been over three months since he disappeared from the custody of the law. Had he been on this island the whole time?

"What happened?" I asked finally. A cool breeze whisked in from the beach, stirring my damp collar and hair. My face felt like it was on fire. "After Katabata Island? The official story is that you escaped from the brig."

"Smuggled out in the dark of night by Bollard men. They brought me to her." He touched the red scar on his cheek. "Held me down while she gave me this, with her own dagger."

I examined his face. My mother had done that. The Bollards had a reputation for being ruthless, especially when it came to protecting their own.

"Don't ask me why I haven't gutted you, girl." He spat in the sand. "Guess I'm fearful tired of talking to myself, that's all it is. You stole my ship. Ruined my life. Always remember this: I ain't your friend." He tilted the bottle to swallow the last of the whiskey. "I'm no one's friend."

I gathered up the boldness to accuse him out loud. "You murdered the Emparchess."

"Ayah," he said slowly. "I reckon I did. By Xanto's great hairy balls, am I going to get to drink in peace tonight or do you plan to catalog all my other crimes as well?" Chucking the empty bottle away, he staggered to his feet and lurched toward the beach. "I'm going to take a piss."

For a moment I was relieved to be alone. Then my thoughts crowded in, and with them black despair. I was never going to see Markos again. To make it sting worse, I'd *failed* him. His hopes for an army, his chance of regaining the throne, Antidoros Peregrine's plan for bringing democracy to Akhaia—all that had died along with Agnes.

Guilt washed over me. How selfish was I, to be thinking of Markos right now? He was alive. Agnes was dead, along with Nereus and my crew. A tear leaked from my eye to roll hotly down my cheek. Their deaths were my fault.

And *Vix*. Never again would I stand at her rail, feeling her plunge into the swells, or watch dolphins racing her bowsprit. I would never feel the sun-kissed warmth of her deck or admire the delicate grace of her sails. Despite my shuddering sobs, few tears came out. Perhaps the fever inside my body had burned them all up.

"Gods-blasted crabs!" Melanos burst back into the shelter. Seeing my face, he exhaled loudly. "Oh, what are you crying about?"

My voice trembled. "I'm not."

"Don't make me regret not killing you." He bumped into the crate, dropping unsteadily to the sand. "I tell you, the gods cursed me the day I was born. Girls," he muttered. "*Crying.*"

I bit my lip, struggling to control my heaving shoulders. "My—my ship."

He snorted. "*My* ship." Retrieving another bottle from his stash, he sniffed it. "Half seawater, I reckon, but it'll do." Several minutes went by. Then he asked, "What happened to her?"

I saw no harm in telling him, but I left out the part about my fight with the sea god. And Markos. The lump in my throat ached. I couldn't talk about Markos right now.

"Hang on. You was a day out of Eryth, running along the peninsula down to Valonikos? Sounds like Four Mile Rock." He grunted. "Many's the boat that's wrecked up there. But . . ."

Hearing the confusion in his voice, I asked, "What?"

"Well, Four Mile Rock is weeks north of here."

I half sat up. "*Weeks?* That's not possible."

If he was right, that meant I'd drifted for miles and been unconscious for days. I pressed my temples, combing through my brain for a memory—an image—anything. I couldn't have lost that much time.

Melanos squinted at me over the bottle. "Your dearest mother had me locked up belowdecks, but I know these seas well enough to know where I'm headed. We was on a beam reach for ten days, and then we rode a following sea south. This cursed bit of rock is somewhere out past Brizos, if I make my best guess."

I absorbed his words. This was the god's doing. *Vix* had been wrecked within sight of Akhaia, but she'd vindictively dragged me out to sea, depositing me on the same island as Diric Melanos. I supposed I had to count myself lucky. When Arisbe Andela had defied her, the god had sunk an entire country. I pictured the drakon grinning at me, her teeth like razors.

Laughter.

When Melanos spoke again, it was almost a whisper. "Pity about the ship. She were the fastest little cutter on the coast. Ah, but weren't those the days? Rum-running on the Neck. Narrow escapes from the Lion Fleet. Cannons blazing." He lifted the bottle. "To *Victorianos*."

A tear dribbled down my cheek. To *Vix*.

CHAPTER
THIRTEEN

It took me a week to recover from my near drowning.

In the shade of Diric Melanos's shelter, I dropped in and out of feverish sleep. Once I woke to see Nereus silhouetted in the doorway, moonlight illuminating his tattoo. The mermaids from the tattoo came to life, snaking across the sand to touch my throat with their cold dead fingers, and suddenly they weren't mermaids at all. They were my crew, the men I'd killed.

I tossed back and forth. "No—I'm sorry—"

Opening my eyes, I saw Agnes leaning over me. She offered me a vial of butterfly venom, holding it to my lips. Part of her jaw had been nibbled away by fish, exposing the white bone.

"Go away," I mumbled, thrashing my head on the blanket. "I don't want to drink your poison."

"Shut up, girl," Melanos said sharply, breaking through the haze of my fever dreams. He pulled the bottle back. "It's only water."

"I'm so sorry," I sobbed. But the apparition was gone.

∽

Finally, one day, I woke up and my head somehow felt clearer. The sun baked the roof and the trees rustled in the wind. I wrinkled my nose. Just my luck to be sharing the only shelter on the island with a filthy no-good pirate. This place smelled like sweat.

Then I realized the smell was me.

Blinking in the harsh daylight, I threw off the blanket and climbed slowly to my feet. My legs felt weak and wobbly. Ducking out of the shelter, I emerged on the beach. The tent was situated at the edge of a forest that appeared to take up the whole center of the island. Shading my eyes, I squinted down the sandy stretch. A strange silence lay over it.

Sunlight danced on the moving surface of the water. Tentatively I stepped closer, allowing the ocean to lap my bare feet. Nothing happened. I smiled sheepishly. What had I expected the sea god to do—bite my toe off?

All at once I knew why the beach had seemed so quiet. I couldn't feel the sea anymore. The cries of the gulls—the whisper of the waves—my weather awareness—they were all gone. I strained outward with my senses as hard as I could.

Nothing. The sea god truly had abandoned me. I was surprised by how deeply it stung.

Well, chosen or unchosen, I had to get clean. I splashed into the surf, plunging to my neck. My shirt floated up, swishing around my armpits. I'd lost my jacket and boots in the shipwreck. I didn't dare remove my remaining clothes to wash them, for fear Melanos might pop out of the bushes at any moment. Examining the dry ends of my curls, I pulled my lips to one side. My hair was a mess. I proceeded to clean myself as best I could without fresh water or soap.

Afterward I poked around the beach while the sun dried my clothes. If Melanos was right about our location, none of this wreckage could have come from *Vix*. I spied a shoal, far off the western end of the island. Likely that was where the ship I'd seen on the beach had run into trouble. And past the shoal—

I gasped. Another island.

The second island was bigger than ours, with a jutting rocky hill in the center. What if there were people living on it? A settlement or a navy fort or a rumrunner's hideout? For the first time I felt a spark of hope.

Studying the island, my mind ticked and whirred like a clock. If only I could figure out a way to get there.

The circular bay between the shoal and the beach was dotted with wrecks in varying states of dilapidation. One was so big I could walk inside the skeleton of its hull. Exploring it, I found nothing useful. The wreck had probably been picked over, either by Melanos or survivors of its former crew.

I had better luck on the beach, where the tide had pulled the flotsam up high, depositing it in a wobbly line. I found a steel sword, dull from being turned over and over by the waves. The marking on the handle indicated it had belonged to someone in the service of the Emparch, for it bore a crude version of the lion crest, just like my matching gold pistols.

A sharp pang went through my heart. I only had one pistol left now. The other was probably at the bottom of the sea. Markos had given them to me. How long would it be, I wondered, before word reached him about the shipwreck? And what about Pa? Ma and Kenté? Tears flooded my eyes, and I shoved the thought away. I couldn't bear to picture their reaction when they heard I was dead.

Poking around in the sand, I gathered a pile of interesting items. A bag of marbles, clotted with sand and seaweed, and the remains of a sewing kit. A chest of spices and teas, spoiled by the sea. A crate full of bottles, only half of which were broken. A scarf of water-stained red silk. Shaking the sand off, I stuffed that in my pocket. Hopefully once it was clean, I could use it for my hair.

"Doing a bit of salvaging?" Melanos leaned on his spear. Spotting the bottles, he grinned. "I knew I rescued you for a reason."

"You didn't rescue me."

He pointed the spear at me. "I decided not to gut you like a fish, didn't I? Same thing."

I disagreed.

Ignoring my sullen glare, he uncorked one of the bottles and examined the label, which was too sea-worn to read. He sniffed it. Tipping his head back, he took a long chug. "Aha! Whiskey!"

"Honestly, I don't understand how you've managed not to die

of some disease by now," I said. "Why didn't you tell me there was another island?"

He shrugged. "Didn't see as it mattered." Hefting the crate under his arm, he trudged back toward the camp.

I ran to catch up. "What do you mean, it doesn't matter?" I gestured at the wrecked ships. "With all this stuff lying around, we could make a raft. One with a sail, even. I'm sure we can stitch enough scraps of canvas together." I rummaged through the items in my pockets. "Look, I found a sewing kit. The needles are a bit rusty but—"

He grunted. "Waste of bloody time."

"Perhaps you're content to lie about on this island for the rest of your life, drinking watered-down whiskey," I snapped. "But I'm not. If we climb that mountain, we might be able to see something. Smoke. Settlements. Other islands! We could signal a ship."

Reaching the shelter, Melanos dropped the crate on the sand. A crab the size of my fist scuttled out from under a rock, sidestepping toward him.

"Be damned!" he roared, kicking sand at it.

"Fine. If you're not going to help me," I said, "I'll build a boat myself. It's not like I have anything better to do. You can stay here and rot."

"Maybe that's the way I want it," he shot back.

Diric Melanos might have been able to forget about that island, but I could not. I didn't mean to live out the rest of my days on this beach, never seeing my friends or family again. Not if I could help it. Each day I swam in the sea, gradually regaining my strength. A hike around our island confirmed that it was tiny. It only took three hours to circumnavigate the entire thing. As I walked, I felt the other island lurking over my shoulder.

Whispering to me.

❧

Inside the shelter, Melanos kept a stash pile of items he'd salvaged in his expeditions around the island. It was mostly liquor bottles, precious few of them containing anything worth drinking. As the days crawled by, I began to save up my own collection. A wooden door. Four barrels. A piece of torn sail. All the rope I could find that hadn't been frayed by age or the ocean.

In the evenings, while Melanos cussed and threw flaming sticks at the marauding crabs, I polished the needles from my sewing kit. I would need them to patch together enough canvas for a sail. I felt him watching me, but he said nothing.

The truth was, I didn't know what to make of him. He claimed he'd kept me alive so he wouldn't go crazy talking to himself, but he seemed disinterested in conversation. He stared moodily into the fire, sometimes going hours without speaking. Secretly I wondered if he hadn't already gone crazy.

What did I know about him, really? He'd accepted gold from Konto Theucinian to hunt down the members of the Akhaian royal family. To that end, he had taken the shadowman Cleandros on board his ship, but I had the distinct impression they had not gotten along. Antidoros Peregrine once told me that Melanos had been a privateer in the skirmishes of '88, the holder of a letter of marque from the Emparch. Somehow things had gone sideways and he'd disappeared, only to reemerge several years later as a pirate and cutthroat. He had amassed a small fleet of ships that sailed under the flag of the Black Dogs, so at least at some point I assumed he'd had some charisma. I snorted, remembering how my cousin Jacky had called him the handsomest outlaw on the high seas.

If only she could see him now.

I couldn't count on Melanos to help me get off this island. The only thing he was interested in doing was drinking himself to death.

Roping my salvaged door onto the barrels, I created a raft of sorts. Getting the mast to stand up was the tricky part. Nothing worked, until one day I happened upon a cache of rusted nails scattered inside a half-rotted hull. With driftwood and the sturdiest of my rope, I built a base for the mast. Now all that was left was the sail.

I'd found the remains of one on the beach, but it badly needed repair. Maybe Melanos had some cloth in his heap of junk. Returning to the camp, I spied him passed out in the shade, whiskey bottle stuck in the sand beside him.

"Hey!" I said loudly, but he didn't stir.

As I stooped to enter the shelter, my gaze came to rest on a captain's coat. Battered and worn, it lay crumpled in the corner beside Melanos's crate of half-empty bottles. That would do nicely.

Dragging it out, I raised my knife to cut out a patch.

Melanos burst through the door, snatching the tattered coat from my hands. "What do you think you're doing?"

"I was just—"

A muscle twitching in his neck, he clutched the coat to his chest. "This is mine."

"Well, I thought it was salvage!" I resisted the urge to take a step back. "I was going to cut it up for my sail."

"*Sail*?" he spat. Flipping the jacket inside out, he frantically felt the lining. He loomed over me, raising his fist. "Do you know what you could have done?"

I steeled myself. But he didn't hit me. Turning, he left the shelter without a word, the coat in his arms.

⁘

By the next week my raft was ready for its maiden voyage. In the end, I'd found another bit of canvas that wasn't too rotten and patched the hole in the sail. It still wasn't very sophisticated, so I had to wait impatiently for a day when the wind would be behind me. The raft wobbled as I climbed on. Adjusting the sail with my crude mainsheet, I stuck a busted oar into the water to use as a rudder. The wind caught the canvas, lifting it.

As the raft glided toward the shoal, I peered down into the shallow water. The dark hulks of sunken ships loomed threateningly. I only hoped my raft wouldn't run up on a wreck and get snagged.

The island inched closer until finally my makeshift boat hit the sand, jerking me forward. Jumping onto the beach, I hauled the raft up far enough so the tide wouldn't take it. My sword swung from its rope belt, banging awkwardly on my hip. I'd tried to sharpen it on a rock, but it was still dull from being tossed by the waves. I didn't know if it would be enough to cut through the vines and bushes.

Surveying the beach, I saw no sign of civilization. The island was a green mound of trees, with the mountain jutting up in the middle. Staring grimly up at the rock face, I gripped my sword.

The first hour of climbing was easy enough. Cutting a swath through the bushes, I hacked my way toward the side of the mountain that looked less steep. The scratches on my arms stung.

Something bright flapped, launching itself at my head. I shrieked, shielding my face with my arms. The trees squawked and chittered, and I realized they were full of pale green birds with yellow heads and evil beady eyes.

"Shoo!" I said, feinting toward them with my sword. They ignored me, screeching with laughter.

Sweat drenched my back by the time I scrambled over the edge of the last rock onto the bare mountaintop. The sea breeze buffeted my face, cooling my damp forehead. Suddenly my legs, screaming with exhaustion from the climb, felt lightened. With fresh energy, I bounded up to the highest point, spinning in a circle.

I saw—nothing.

Disappointment hit me in the stomach like a punch. There was nothing but ocean in all directions. No smoke. No islands besides the scrubby little one I'd just come from, nearly blocked from view by a lone wind-bent tree. No ships.

I'd climbed all the way up here for nothing.

My legs collapsed under me. Pulling out my water bottle, I gulped the warm liquid down. It tasted bitter. I'd been so certain I would find something.

Then I spotted it.

On a rounded ledge below the tree line was a pile of rocks. I squinted, excitement tickling my neck. That formation didn't look natural.

It was a cairn, or the remains of one. It must have crumbled some years ago, leaving nothing but a lopsided heap of stones, half-buried in the dirt. Sunlight glinted on something metal.

On hands and knees, I crawled closer. Digging with my fingers, I cleared the packed soil away. My heartbeat pounded in my ears. With trembling hands I tugged the dirt-caked object from its resting place. It was bronze, with ridges carved in it. A plaque?

Raising it to my lips, I blew hard across the surface. The ridges were letters.

J.B.
ASTARTA
1466

Stunned, I stared at the words. Every Bollard knew that ship, and most other folks too. The great explorer Jacari Bollard had sailed *Astarta* around the world, eventually discovering the Southwest Passage to Ndanna. This must have been one of the islands he'd mapped during his explorations.

Captain Bollard had been here. Right where I stood. As the fresh wind tousled my hair, I felt suddenly hopeful. It was as if my own ancestor was reaching out from two hundred and thirty years in the past to whisper in my ear.

In the old days Ndanna was a long journey by wagon from Kynthessa, through a perilous mountain pass. It took many months for goods to travel there overland and for the marvels of Ndanna—tea leaves and colorful silks and mechanical curiosities— to come back east. There'd always been rumors of a Southwest Passage, but that part of the sea was a treacherous maze of endless islands, littered with the bones of ships and men. After a while, most everyone gave up. There was no sea route to Ndanna. The only thing waiting there was death.

But what was inside Jacari Bollard was different from what lay inside other men. And, as family legend tells it, he knew one thing. He knew he could sail there.

I set the plaque back on the cairn. Captain Bollard had not given up, and neither would I.

Wedging the metal object into place with two rocks, I stood. The plaque was a part of my history, but it didn't belong to me. I swallowed, a swell of emotion in my throat. It belonged here. Maybe someday it would give someone else hope.

It was funny. I'd spent so much of my childhood trying to make sense of my two different families, worrying about where I fit. But Oresteia or Bollard, river or sea—none of that mattered anymore. Not here on this island.

I looked down at the freshly stirred dirt. Even if I never saw my family again, I could still be proud of where I came from. Reaching up, I wrapped my fingers around Kenté's talisman and squeezed it hard. I could still carry them with me.

Turning in one last circle, I gazed out at the unending blue of the ocean. The cool wind whispered on my skin. When I lowered my eyes, I spotted a dried-up creek bed in the woods, lined with rocks but otherwise clear of both vegetation and parrots. Feeling as if Captain Bollard had granted me a little bit of his luck, I grinned and headed toward it.

With barely a warning trickle of dirt, the ground fell out from under me. A rock hit my ankle, causing hot pain to burst through it like a shot. My leg buckled under me and I careened down the rocky incline, scrabbling to grab a root or a branch.

Anything to stop my uncontrolled slide.

A tree trunk slammed into my hip, halting my descent. I gasped in pain and frustration. The tree bark tore into my palms, but I held on. Around me the rocks continued to clatter down the hill. For several long moments all I could do was cling to the tree as stones battered me and dust rose up in a cloud.

Finally the rockslide ended, the last pebbles trickling away down the dirt path. Everything stung. My hands were scraped raw, blood smearing my skin. My left ankle throbbed. Green parrots screeched mockingly at me from the trees. I rose, forcing myself to ignore the twinges of pain all over my body. I was terrified to put my feet anywhere, for fear I'd bring the whole hill down on top of me.

I'd been so stupid to come alone. What if I'd broken my leg?

I doubted Diric Melanos would have shown up to rescue me. With a wave of horror I realized I might have died in that creek bed, my skeleton never to be found.

Somehow I made it back to my makeshift raft. With shaking hands, I raised the sail and let the wind slowly puff me back to the smaller island. Dark orange sunbeams slanted across the water by the time I limped into camp. Bruises mottled my legs and arms, and my left sleeve had been torn off. My hands were covered in thick red welts. I didn't bother to tie up the raft. It could float out to sea, for all I cared.

Melanos squatted barefoot by the fire, a bottle wedged in the sand.

He glanced up at me. "Found a whole lot of nothing, did you?"

I didn't answer.

"Ayah, and didn't I tell you it was a bloody waste of time?" He poked the coals with a stick. "There's nothing over there but a busted old cairn and a lot of bedamned parrots."

A cold ball of rage condensed in the center of my chest. I whirled on him, kicking sand in his general direction. "Liar! You've been there, haven't you?"

He leveled a finger at me. "When did I ever lie to you? I warned you, didn't I? Said not to bother."

"You deliberately didn't tell me the truth." I was drenched in sweat, covered in scratches and parrot shit. And I'd almost died in that rockslide. "You let me build that boat and climb all the way up that mountain because you thought it was funny."

He glanced at my disheveled clothes, lip curling in a smirk. "It's a little funny."

I leaped to my feet, drawing my sword.

He stood, towering over me. "Put that thing away. You don't even know how to use it. What kind of a fool do you think I am? Of course I climbed that mountain, girl. The third day after your cursed mother marooned me here. It only confirmed what I already knew." His spit sprayed my face. "There's *nothing here*. You won't escape this island. No one's going to rescue you. You're going to die just like me—alone and pathetic, with sand in the crack of your ass and the crabs eating your toes."

Dropping the sword, I stumbled back. I'd never seen him like this.

"You'll die a nobody. Alone." He turned his back, voice dropping to a whisper. "And no one will remember you. Or care."

I slumped to the sand. Staring hard into the fire, I willed my tears not to spill over. Mere hours ago I'd been naive enough to believe there was a way off this island. Finding Captain Bollard's cairn had felt like a sign. That there was something special inside me. That I was meant for a different fate.

But maybe Melanos was right. Maybe we were both going to die here. And no one would remember our names.

CHAPTER
FOURTEEN

The next morning I swiped a bottle from Melanos's stash. Flopping down on the beach, I made a hole in the sand and stuck the bottle in. At least the view was pretty. Removing the bloated cork, I took a long gulp.

And almost gagged to death. Whatever was in that bottle, it tasted horrible. If it was indeed brandy like the label claimed, exposure to sun and salt water had long since spoiled it. I sipped again, slower this time.

Melanos watched me for several minutes before he spoke. "Ain't you a bit young to be drinking before noon?"

"Why shouldn't I? You do it all the time." I squinted at him through the sun glare. "As it happens, I reckon you got the right idea. If we're going to die, I figure what's the harm in hastening it along?" I stretched out on the sand, rearranging my headscarf so it wouldn't leave a sun line on my forehead, and closed my eyes. "Now go away."

I felt the sand shift beside me. "Ah. There's the trick. I would, except . . . I feel like you've got all cynical on me. I ain't sure I like it."

"You were the one who made me cynical," I said sourly, opening one eye. "*You* told me we were going to die here. Make up your mind."

For a long moment he was silent. "I went through this too," he said gruffly. "When I were first marooned here. It passes."

Annoyed, I sat up. "Oh, does it now? Then why are you in such a black mood all the time?"

He looked uncomfortable. "Am I?"

"Hope is a bloody waste of time," I mimicked him. "I've done such horrible things. Gods damn it, girl! Let me drink myself to death in peace!"

"Xanto's great hairy balls, I hope that's not what I sound like." He kicked my leg. "Get up."

"What?"

He pulled out the sword he had slung through the rope belt at his waist. Assuming a fighting stance, he pointed it at me.

"Oh, I see." I sighed, my mind pleasantly hazy thanks to the brandy. "You've finally gone mad."

"Last night," he said, ignoring my comment, "when you pulled that blade on me, you looked terrible."

I lifted my bottle, toasting him. "Thank you."

Melanos disappeared, and for a moment I thought he'd finally left me alone. Then sand flew in my face. The dull blade I'd salvaged from the shipwreck lay on the beach by my feet.

"Pick that up, girl," he growled.

"No." I glared up at him. "I want to sit in the sun and drink brandy."

He swore. "Get up. If we're stuck here together, I might as well teach you something." His gaze settled on my bottle. "Unless you got something better to do."

Rolling my eyes, I took the hopelessly dull sword and attempted to copy the way I remembered Markos standing.

Melanos sighed. "I was right. You don't have any idea how to use that."

I lowered the sword. "I know how to throw a knife and shoot a pistol. That's always been enough."

"Ayah? What if someone comes at you with a blade?"

I shrugged. "I'd shoot him."

"What if you run out of shot?" He sighed again. "I suppose this is my punishment for a life of crime. Stuck on an island with a stupid girl who can't even fight." He swiped his sword at me. "Now try to block me."

Before I had a chance to move, he knocked me to the sand.

"Ow!" My fingers stung where he'd hit them with the flat of the sword.

Melanos laughed at me. "That was awful. Again."

Shoulders grumbling at the weight of the sword, I struggled to my feet. Once more he lunged and once more I attempted to block him. This time his arm tangled with mine, and he leaned against me hard, forcing my sword arm down. He was bigger and stronger. I lost my balance and fell.

He stood over me. "Again." I realized he'd barely broken a sweat.

I wiped my forehead. "I don't *want* to learn this."

Especially from someone I didn't trust. A chill crept down my neck. With no witnesses, he didn't even need to make it seem like an accident. I reminded myself that his sword was just as dull and water-damaged as my own.

When the noon sun was directly above us, Melanos finally relented and let me stop. "We'll go again tomorrow," he declared.

I wondered if he was doing this on purpose to torture me. The more he knocked me down, the more suspiciously cheerful he'd become.

Every part of my body aching, I sank to the sand. I hated to admit it, but in spite of the pain I felt better. The exercise had made me feel alive again.

That night, as the horizon faded from orange to pink to purple, I stretched my sore muscles next to the campfire. Leaning against a tree trunk, I watched the crabs scurry around on the beach. When it got dark, they came out by the hundreds.

One particularly daring crab approached Melanos's bare toes. Quick as a flash, he grabbed it around the middle, avoiding its waving pincers, and threw it in the fire.

"That's cruel!" I exclaimed.

"We eat them every day," he pointed out.

It was true. Besides a few scrubby fruit trees, our only source of food on the island was those crabs. But I usually made sure to kill them before roasting them. It seemed less mean.

"I been here longer than you, girl. Reckon they've built up a powerful craving for the taste of me. They'd like to roast our toes on their fire and have us for supper, make no mistake. Some young lady crab is likely out there right now with a recipe for Caro stew," he said. "Count on it."

I almost smiled. It was the first time he'd ever called me by my name, instead of "girl" or "love" or "wench."

Melanos ducked back into the shelter to get a drink. My gaze came to rest on his tattered coat, which he'd slung over a rock. I remembered how upset he'd been when I tried to cut a piece out of it. What was he hiding in there?

Sneaking a glance at the shelter, I edged toward the coat. I dragged it off the rock and into my lap, examining it. There was a hole in the lining. I stuck my fingers in, wiggling them around. It was a secret pocket. I drew out a leather envelope, wrapped in string.

Before I could unwind the string, a deadly voice spoke behind me. "Hand it over, girl. Or I gut you."

Melanos stood on the sand, firelight flickering on his sword.

"So this is your big secret?" I tossed him the leather packet. "What is this thing anyway?"

He caught it. "Just something I been saving for a rainy day." Returning the envelope seemed to have mollified him, because he put the sword down. "Your mother and her men turned my pockets inside out, but they never found this."

He undid the ties and drew a piece of paper from the protective leather. It was yellowed from age. There was writing on it, but I couldn't read it.

"Probably after showing you this, I'll have to kill you," he said casually. "But, seeing as we're going to die on this island anyway . . ."

"It looks like a bunch of scribbles," I said.

Melanos looked offended. "It's a treasure map."

"Oh." I sighed, thinking of Docia Argyrus and her dreams of gold and glory. "You mean a wild goose chase."

He ran careful fingers over the map. Leaning back against a tree trunk, he closed his eyes. I saw his lips curl into a smile. "The greatest wild goose chase in the world."

"What's it supposed to—" I looked over at him, only to discover he'd passed out with the scrap of ancient paper clutched to his chest. It rose and fell with his breath.

The next morning, the map had disappeared. Melanos lay snoring on his blanket in the shelter. I wondered exactly how drunk he'd been last night. Perhaps he didn't even remember showing it to me.

Hefting his rusty sword, I tossed it at him.

"Ow!" He covered his eyes, blocking out the beaming sunlight. "What's wrong with you, girl?"

I tilted my head innocently. "You said we'd practice again today."

"Too. Early."

I grinned. "This was your idea," I reminded him.

He surged to his feet. "Gods damn the young."

Grabbing up my sword, I ducked out of the shelter. The sun shone yellow above the line of breakers. It was still strange being so close to the water without feeling the sea god's presence, like looking at a painting of a beach instead of being there. The breeze stirred my curls, while gulls hunted for crabs in the sand, ignoring me. Inhaling the fresh air, I looked out to sea.

And froze.

Dropping the sword in the sand, I raced back to the shelter. "Sails!" I gasped. "On the horizon!"

Quick as a flash, Melanos followed me down to the beach. The ship was too far away to discern much, but it was big. Two or three masts and square white sails. As I watched breathlessly, it inched closer.

"Red flag with a yellow blob on it." Melanos spat in the sand. "Gods *damn* it."

Disappointment stabbed me. The three-masted naval frigate flew the Akhaian flag. Sunlight flashed on the round mouths of artillery on her deck—long nines, it looked like. At the peak of her main mast flapped a red pennant with a golden lion, as well as several smaller flags along the stays with military insignia I didn't recognize.

I kicked the sand. "Why couldn't it have been a merchanter? Or a whaling ship? Anyone else."

I wasn't keen on being stranded on this island for the rest of my life, but I also didn't want to be hanged for crimes against the Akhaian Empire.

I heard the god's mocking voice. *Laughter.*

As we watched from the cover of the trees, the frigate sailed into the bay and dropped anchor. Sailors no bigger than tiny dots scurried up the masts, loosening and then furling the sails. The ship launched a gig, which moved toward the beach like an insect with its many oars sticking out like legs.

"They're stopping here," I breathed. "Do you think they saw our smoke?"

"Not likely." Melanos nodded at the boat, which was loaded with barrels. "Just a water stop."

Well, they wouldn't have much luck. A leaf-coated track indicated where a stream had been, but it was dried up. We collected rainwater in a salvaged barrel. I counted the men in the boat. Could Melanos and I take all seven of them? I didn't think so, even with surprise on our side.

Unless . . .

I looked speculatively at him. I was a known associate of Markos Andela, the man they knew as the Pretender. But Melanos had committed far greater crimes against the Akhaian Empire. He'd stolen a ship and engaged in piracy. Surely he had a large bounty on his head. Could I barter his life for mine? Reveal who he was, in exchange for passage off this island?

Exhaling in frustration, I knew I could not. He was mostly horrible, but I couldn't betray him like that.

Melanos lunged out of the bushes. "Hey!"

Waving his arms like a windmill, he galloped down the beach. The gig had just touched sand, and the men's heads snapped up at his shout. Melanos began to speak, gesturing with his hands, but I couldn't hear what he said. Turning, he pointed at me.

"Xanto's balls!" I swore. Diric Melanos had betrayed me before I had a chance to betray him.

Surging to my feet, I turned to run deeper into the woods, but it was too late. The soldiers had spotted me. I didn't make it more than twenty feet. Something struck my foot from behind, and I tripped.

A soldier hit me in the face with the butt of his rifle. Stunned by the flash of pain, I dropped to my hands and knees. Blood dribbled out between my lips, dotting the sandy ground. Seizing my hair by the roots, the soldier pulled me up.

"The Rose of the Coast." He grinned. "You're worth a hundred talents."

"A hundred talents, is it?" Melanos drawled, watching the soldiers drag me across the beach. "The Emparch must want her pretty bad."

My chin shot up. "Markos is the true Emparch," I spat, tasting blood.

Two of the sailors exchanged uncomfortable glances. I remembered Damian's words back on *Vix*. *My family's mostly navy men. Andela men.* It didn't sit right with everyone in Akhaia, what Konto Theucinian had done to the royal family.

The officer rubbed his beard, a mercenary glint in his eye. Turning to Melanos, he asked, "What's your game? Aiming for a share of the reward?"

"Me? Oh no." Lifting his hands in surrender, he put on an easy grin. "Myself, I'd be grateful for a ride off this gods-bedamned island. That's all I want. Just put me ashore in Brizos."

At the officer's sharp glance, he added, "Or anywhere you like, of course."

They hauled me into the boat and shoved me down on a thwart, none too carefully. The soldiers roughly unbuckled my belt. I squeezed my fists, fingernails digging into my palms. Fighting would only make things worse. With my hands bound, I couldn't do anything to stop them anyway. As they stripped me of my weapons, I felt Kenté's talisman on its chain under my shirt, and prayed they wouldn't discover it.

Melanos sat across from me in the boat. He shifted his eyes away from mine, and for a moment I thought I saw regret flit across his face. Looking up at the smooth curved hull of the frigate as we bobbed under it, I read her name in ornate gilt paint: *Advantagia.*

On board the ship, they lugged me down a long cramped hall, past a row of open doors. Inside one room, a clerk in a blue robe bent over a writing desk. The soldiers stopped at the last door.

The officer prodded Melanos. "You first."

I'd never seen a captain's cabin so huge. The room was paneled in polished wood, with built-in cabinets stuffed with charts and books. Sunlight gleamed through a row of windows on the back wall, and a gold sextant and globe decorated the desk. I wrinkled my nose. A bit ostentatious for my taste.

"It's her, all right." The captain tossed a sheet of paper onto his desk. "The so-called Rose of the Coast."

Craning my neck, I saw the caricaturist had exaggerated my

features and given me a blank, sullen expression. I looked like a criminal. Under the picture on the bounty poster was a printed paragraph. *Conspiracy against the Emparch. Possession of stolen property belonging to the Lion Fleet of Akhaia.*

I stopped reading. Stolen property? What stolen property? Then I realized they meant *Vix*. Once again I glared at Diric Melanos. He'd absconded with the ship and gone rogue, and then I'd stolen it from him. How had I ever gotten into this mess? I was a wherryman's daughter. My life had been perfectly happy when Akhaia was just a big vague country to the north, with an Emparch whose name I didn't remember.

I lifted my head. "I demand my right to an advocate."

The captain bestowed an amused smile on me. "This isn't Kynthessa. You don't have the right to an advocate in Akhaian waters." Drawing out another rolled-up bounty, he set it on the desk beside mine and turned to Melanos. "While you seem to have been correct in your identification of Miss Oresteia, you failed to mention who you were," he said. "Or did you really think the beard would fool us?"

"Ah." Melanos winced. "In point of fact, I'd rather hoped the reports of my death would have caused you to throw that away long ago."

The captain unrolled the parchment. "Captain Diric Melanos," he read aloud, scorn twisting his voice. "Wanted for treason, piracy, illegal salvage, adultery—"

"Oh yes, I remember her," Melanos said under his breath.

"—Smuggling, bootlegging. Shall I go on?" He threw the

bounty down. "This list of crimes is as long as my arm. You escaped custody in Kynthessa, but I imagine you'll find that a little trickier here in Akhaia."

I smirked. At least I had the satisfaction of knowing Diric Melanos was going down with me.

The captain picked up my pistol, turning it over in his hands. "Bold," he remarked, "bearing the mark of the mountain lion." Only a member of the royal family or household ever wore that seal. The captain's voice dripped with disdain. "I don't believe you have the right to carry this."

They tossed us in adjoining cells in the frigate's brig.

Melanos leaned against the wall. "I admit that didn't go the way I hoped."

"Good." I examined the place where the bars were bolted to the floor. Both wood and iron seemed solid. Too solid.

Exhaling, I slumped to the floor. What use would an escape be anyway? From the motion of the ship I knew we'd lifted anchor and left the island. We were in the middle of the ocean, our destination unknown. And this time no one was coming to rescue me—not Markos or the Bollards or Pa—because no one knew I was here.

Melanos patted the side of his battered wool coat. "At least they didn't get my insurance policy."

Shooting him a dirty look, I ran my tongue over my busted lip. As if I cared about his stupid treasure, which was a fish story if I'd ever heard one.

"I should've expected this," I said.

He cocked his head at me questioningly.

"That you'd betray me," I spat at him. "You betrayed your own country. The only thing you care about is yourself."

Closing his eyes, he rested his head on the cell wall. "Stop acting like you know me, girl."

We ignored each other for the next several hours. Through my shirt I touched Kenté's talisman, fighting back tears. I refused to cry in front of that traitor. I was gratified to notice Melanos didn't look too well—he kept swallowing and rubbing his forehead, which looked damp. I suddenly realized the lack of drink must be making him sick.

After a long silence, he spoke. "When I turned rogue," he said quietly, "I lost everything."

Something in his voice made me take notice. In all our days on the island, he'd never opened up about his history. I held my breath, hating him yet hoping he would say more.

"Lost my letter of marque," he continued. "My commission. My family disowned me, and there was a bounty on my head if I ever returned."

"I feel *so* sorry for you."

Melanos stared blankly ahead. "I couldn't give it up, you see. After the treaty was signed, the skirmishes were over. But my heart still lusted for the chase. I found I couldn't live without it, is all." He spat on the floor of the brig. "Never give a ship to a twenty-four-year-old boy." Catching the look on my face, he gave me a rueful half smile. "You're thinking I should've said 'man.' No, I was a boy. I understood nothing of the world."

Why was he telling me this? As a warning? I was nothing like him.

He shrugged. "And, well, that's how it started. You know what a privateer without a letter of marque is."

A pirate. Holding my breath, I silently willed him to continue. I wanted to know. To understand.

"And then one night, that shadowman came. I walked into my cabin and there he was, cool as a cat, smoking a pipe. He offered me a deal. See, old Andela, he were the one who signed the bounty on my head. I knew he wouldn't forgive me my crimes. But Theucinian would, if only . . ." He sighed. "If only I did one last job."

"Wait, you wanted to go back to Akhaia? Then what was all that about the rush of the chase?"

"Give it ten years," he said. "You won't be asking that question then." Lines crinkling around his hollowed eyes, he looked at me. "I know who you are, Caroline Oresteia. You're me, before the world got turned upside down. When nothing mattered but the open sea. What I wouldn't give," he said softly, "to feel like that again."

"Like what?" I couldn't help asking.

His voice was hoarse. "Like the world was new."

This time it was my turn to be silent. His story had sparked the tiniest ember of pity in me, but I wondered if that wasn't exactly what he wanted. Was this all a game to him, luring me in with words he knew would stir my heart? He was a murderer, I reminded myself. He'd fired on Hespera's Watch, sinking eleven wherries and killing Captain Singer and his wife. They were fellow wherrymen and they'd been innocent.

The door creaked open. It was the same officer who'd commanded the sailors on the beach. He kicked Melanos through the bars. "Get up, you! You're wanted for questioning." He gestured to his men, and they dragged Melanos out of the brig, leaving me alone with my bleeding lip and tumultuous thoughts.

I almost didn't notice when the door opened a second time.

"Hello, Captain Oresteia."

My head snapped up, and I blinked. Agnes Pherenekian stood in the doorway.

CHAPTER
FIFTEEN

For one shocked moment I thought she was a ghost—or my guilt, taking human shape to haunt me. It wasn't possible. The dinghy had flipped over. My mind leaped to the clerk I'd glimpsed on the way to the captain's cabin, scratching away in a book. Not a blue robe, I realized. A blue *dress*.

"You drowned," was all I could manage, my surprise rendering me stupid.

Agnes stepped into the pool of lantern light. The dress was shabby and ill fitting. It was clearly something the crew of the *Advantagia*, unaccustomed to having a woman on board, had scrounged up from their stores.

"Very nearly," she said. "The sailors were quite shocked to discover me floating on a piece of wreckage, hundreds of miles from where your ship went down."

Scrambling to my feet, I rattled the bars with my fists. "Quick, unlock the door! You have to get me out of here!"

Agnes glanced over her shoulder. "Hush! They'll hear. I don't know where the keys are."

I dropped my voice to a whisper. "At least tell me what day it is."

"I keep a notation in my journal." She pulled a notebook from her pocket, the same one she'd carried back on *Vix*. Its pages were crinkled and swollen from water damage. She read me the date.

I did the math in my head. I'd lost more than two months. Word of *Vix*'s sinking had probably reached Valonikos weeks ago. Everyone I loved thought I was dead. Shaking off the strange feeling, I asked, "Do you know where this ship is bound?"

"Fort Reliance," Agnes said. "It's an island near the edge of Akhaian territory. When we arrive, they're putting me off this frigate and onto a royal courier ship."

I thought of Arisbe Andela, sent from Amassia to Akhaia to marry an Emparch. I'd always pitied her, cursed by the sea god for a marriage that had never been her idea in the first place. Was that how Agnes felt, ferried from place to place by men of power? Remembering the instruments, scientific sketches, and inks that had been so important to her, I shifted uncomfortably. Surely they were at the bottom of the ocean now.

"Where are they taking you?" I asked. "Back to Eryth?"

Her lips curved into a wicked smile. "To Valonikos." The shadows of the iron bars striped her face. "To meet my husband. Of course, they don't know that. I've made up a story about visiting my dear elderly aunt."

"I could tell the captain," I muttered. "If I'm stuck in here for conspiracy against the Emparch, then you should be too."

"True," she agreed. "Unfortunately for you, I have the name Pherenekian and you do not. Who do you think the captain will believe?"

My mouth dropped open. She was taunting me.

I gripped the bars. "You could use your name to get me out of here!"

She stepped up to the cell, studying me like a dead moth under glass. The linen dress had no trim or lace, but her posture somehow made it seem more elegant than a ball gown. She was taller than me by two inches, which I hadn't noticed before, because I'd been wearing boots then.

"But why would I do that?" she murmured, her breath whispering on my face. "It is not a requirement that my husband be in love with me, but I would prefer if he wasn't in love with someone else."

"That's—" I spluttered, cheeks going hot. "I never said—"

"When the ship went down and I was the only survivor," she said, "I thought fate had provided me with a rather convenient opportunity to get rid of you. Now that you've turned up like an unlucky cent piece, well . . ." Folding her hands behind her back, she paced the length of the brig. "Hanged for treason at Fort Reliance is just as good a solution."

"I th-thought—" I stammered in disbelief. "You said you wanted us to be friends."

"Oh, Caro," she said innocently, a dimple showing in her

cheek. "Can I call you Caro?" Without waiting for a reply, she went on. "How can we ever be friends? The shadow of this boy I've never even met stands between us. And always will."

Agnes turned to leave, skirt sweeping behind her. Setting a hand on the door, she hesitated.

"Markos Andela is my only hope of finally pleasing my father, Caro. You're just . . ." I tensed, expecting her to make a disparaging remark about my common ancestry. But when she spoke, she sounded almost regretful. "You're just the girl who's in my way."

⁓

Fort Reliance was located on a small island with a tiny bay curved like a half-moon. The stockade was fortified with long nines, and behind it the fort rose up on a hill, backgrounded by thick forest. At one end of the harbor was a shipyard with a covered warehouse, where several navy ships were being refitted. In the yard beside it, the bright new skeleton of a ship sat in crutches. I wondered if the Margravina's spies knew the Akhaian navy was building ships, right outside her borders.

As the soldiers shoved me down the gangplank, I counted three other vessels. A second frigate, the mirror image of *Advantagia*, lay in the harbor, along with a tiny cutter and a hulking beast of a ship whose decks were dotted with cannons.

"Man-of-war," Melanos said behind me. "I'd say about a hundred guns."

Impressive as the man-of-war looked, it was the cutter, with its single mast and long jutting bowsprit, that tugged at my heart. She looked just like *Vix*.

That was when I decided I wasn't going to die here. Somehow I'd figure out a way to escape Fort Reliance. I would get another ship, even if I had to steal one, and find my way back to Four Mile Rock. I didn't care how long it took or how much it cost. *Vix* and I belonged together.

The sea had taken everything from me. And I was going to get it back.

We were thrown into the lockup in the basement of the fort. There we waited, but I had no idea for what—a trial? A hanging? A ship to transport us to Trikkaia? The only part of the fort I ever glimpsed was the dim brackish-smelling corridor, and for much of the time my sole company was Diric Melanos, who sulked silently in his cell opposite mine. My attempts at conversation were met with irritable grunts. A rotating parade of naval officers in red coats brought food twice a day and escorted me to the privy next door, but they told me nothing.

By the second week, I'd identified the weakest link. The officer who brought supper during the night watch was my age, his red jacket hanging baggily from shoulders that hadn't yet filled out. I noticed the way he threw pining glances at me when he thought I wasn't looking. I suspected he was concocting elaborate fantasies in which he imagined us in a tragic romance—the noble soldier and the roguish pirate.

I made up my mind. That officer was my ticket out of here.

Unwinding the scarf that bound my hair, I pinched my cheeks

and lips to make them redder. Glancing down at my shirt, I undid the laces from the top hole. Satisfied, I turned to the door of the brig and squared my shoulders, awaiting my supper's arrival.

"No, no, *no*."

I whirled to see Melanos lounging on the floor of his cell, squinting up at me through one eye. "I don't recall asking for your opinion," I said.

"You are trying to entice a man, aren't you?" He opened the other eye. "In case it has escaped your notice, I'm a man."

After a long stubborn moment, I gave in. "All right, what am I doing wrong?"

"Sweetheart, no soldier of the Emparch's navy is going to unlock this cell over one paltry buttonhole." He gestured at the laces on my shirt. "And I hope you weren't planning to talk, because the way you talk is all wrong. Too mannish. And your *posture*. You look like you're going into battle."

My cheeks flamed. "Enough." He was lucky there were two sets of bars separating us, or I would've slapped him across the face. "If you're such an expert," I snapped, "why don't you flirt with him?"

He raised his hands in surrender. "I'm just saying, if our freedom depends on your seduction skills, well, then, I'd best start preparing for a short swing at the end of a long rope."

"What do you mean, *our* freedom?" I muttered, but I unlaced a second buttonhole and relaxed my stance.

Before he could reply, the door opened and the young officer entered, bearing two trays of unappetizing food. His face reddened when he saw me, the trays wobbling dangerously.

I held out my manacled wrists. "These are hurting me," I sniffled, turning them over to reveal raw red patches where the iron had scraped my skin. "I'd trade anything for ten minutes f-free of them."

He halted. It was the first time I'd ever said a word to him. Watching me uncertainly, he asked, "Anything?"

I pushed myself against the bars. "Anything," I breathed.

Glancing nervously over his shoulder, he took a set of keys from the hook on the wall. "You can't tell anyone about this, miss. I'll lose my commission if . . ."

Opening the cell door, he unlocked the manacles. I let them drop to the floor, caressing my scabbed wrists, which did hurt. But it wasn't enough. The guard stood, quite inconveniently, between me and my way out.

"Is—is that better?" he stammered.

"Oh yes." I took a brief moment to revel in my new freedom, feeling the cool air on my chafed skin. Then I continued softly, "I know I'm a wicked girl, but you've been so kind to me. How'm I supposed to give you your reward, sir?" I licked my lips. Noticing the way he looked at me, I did it again, but slower. "If you don't come inside?"

I tried not to cringe. Nothing about my voice sounded genuine or even particularly seductive. Across the lockup, Melanos lay on the floor of his cell, ankles crossed. I shot him a nasty look. He obviously had no confidence in me.

Checking behind him to make sure no one was coming, the officer squeezed himself through the door. Taking a quick inventory of his weapons, I tried to calculate my next move. I doubted his pistol was loaded, and going for the sword would take too long. Then I spotted the manacles and the length of chain on the floor.

I dropped to my knees.

The officer started to unbutton his trousers.

"You have *got* to be joking," I said aloud. Seizing the chain, I lunged to my feet and bludgeoned him in the head with it. He grunted and slid to the floor.

Quick as a minnow, I darted out and grabbed the keys.

In the other cell, Melanos sat up. "Use the manacles. Lock him up now, while he's still out."

"I'm not a complete idiot," I snapped. Glancing down at the unconscious officer, who had a nasty bump on his head, I winced. "Sorry."

"You're no actress," Melanos remarked. "It wouldn't have worked on anyone else but that young fool."

Rolling the officer over, I wrestled him out of his red jacket and locked the manacles around his wrists. I jammed his tricorn hat on my head and shrugged the coat on. It fell to my knees, even larger on me than it had been on him. The boots didn't fit either, but I wasn't about to escape this fort barefoot. Yanking his flint-lock pistol out of the holster, I checked the barrel. It wasn't loaded, and he didn't have a bag of shot on him. Pathetic. I eyed the sword dubiously, remembering too well how badly my lesson with Melanos had gone. But I strapped it on anyway. There was no way I'd pass for a naval officer, but at least the coat and hat might momentarily fool them in the dark.

Peeking down the corridor, I saw no red coats. But going that way, without knowing the layout of the fort or where the soldiers were positioned, was too risky. I shut the door of the brig, swinging down the bolt to barricade us in. Across from the cells was a desk, and above it a window.

Diric Melanos watched me. "Well?"

"Well, what?" I climbed onto the desk, coat trailing behind me. He struck the bars, causing them to rattle. "Open my cell!"

"Why," I asked flatly without turning, "would I do that?"

Outside the window, eight or nine feet of slimy wall dropped steeply down to the seaweed-draped rocks below. In the distance the harbor sprawled, dark except for the twinkling lights at the tops of the masts. At high tide the sea might have smashed me against the wall, but now the tide was out, revealing a stretch of wet sand that shone in the moonlight.

"I helped get you out!"

"Help?" My voice jumped up an octave. "All you did was sit around and insult me. Do you think I've forgotten how you turned me in?"

He flashed me a smile. "You're just jealous you didn't think of it first." Tugging the ancient map from inside his coat, he said, "Get me out of here, and I'll give you one third of my treasure."

"A third?" I laughed. "You must not be right in the head. You mean *half*."

His lips tightened. "This map is mine."

"Ayah? Well, I'm sure it'll be a great comfort to you when you're hanged." I swung the window open, inhaling the sea air that wafted in. Crickets chirped shrilly in the forest. I was almost free.

"All right, all right! Half of the treasure!"

"Half of nothing is still nothing," I retorted. I didn't believe there was any treasure.

"Wait." He scrambled up, seizing the bars. "What about that girl they picked up in the ocean—Adella? Aria? Whatever her name is. The one you said was marrying your Emparch."

"Agnes," I muttered. I'd told him how she had betrayed me. "What about her?"

"You're just going to let her steal him out from under you?"

I paused, hands on the windowsill.

"Even twenty bricks of gold bullion would be enough to hire an army." His words tumbled over one another, as if he knew he had only moments to convince me. "He wouldn't have to marry her. With that much gold, he can still return to Akhaia, but on his own terms. Isn't that what he wants? What *you* want?" He curled his hands around the bars. "Get me out of here. Put a pistol in my hand! I'll help you get your Emparch back."

I closed my eyes. How could I not be tempted? I reminded myself I couldn't trust him. He'd betrayed me once. He would do it again.

"Twenty bricks of gold," I repeated, still gripping the windowsill. "And you know where it is. This is a real treasure, not a fish story?"

"Ever so much more than twenty bricks," he said. "The greatest find in all the sea." He held out the map, voice dropping to a whisper. "The *Centurion* herself."

In spite of myself a thrill ran down my back. Suddenly I was back in the salvager's office, watching Docia Argyrus reverently run her fingers across the drawing of the ship.

"People have been looking for that ship for nearly two hundred years," I said. "They found a whole lot of nothing."

"Ayah, but none of them had what I have." Reaching into the secret pocket in his jacket, he drew out something small and flat. "Proof."

I stifled an exasperated sigh. I *knew* he was lying. And yet something made me climb down off the desk and clump across the brig in my stolen boots.

I examined the coin. "It looks like a talent, only it's—"

Gold.

The coin appeared handmade, with uneven edges. It wasn't entirely round, and there were markings stamped into it—if you squinted sideways, that blob might be the lion of Akhaia. In my head I heard Docia's voice. *They used to mint 'em from gold. Before they was changed to three parts silver, one part copper.* It definitely looked old, and it was the right color, but I had no idea if it was genuine.

Pocketing the coin, Melanos said, "This coin were passed down from my great-great-grandfather. He's the one who found the shipwreck and drew the map. He were running with an unsavory crew at the time, and he knew if he told them what he'd found, they'd cut his throat in his sleep. But he managed to pocket this and one piece of gold bullion. The balance of the plunder he hid in a cave, always meaning to go back for it one day." He shrugged. "Turns out the one gold brick set him up pretty good.

Bought himself a trawler, he did, and a fine house. He married and, life being what it was, he never returned to that island. And his sons, well, they weren't seafaring men, and neither were my pa and grandpa."

"This *is* a fish story. I knew it." Every sailor had a tale like that about some fabled treasure or another. They were all a load of nonsense.

"Maybe it is, maybe it ain't."

"If what you're telling me is real, why haven't you gone after this treasure before now?" I demanded.

He shrugged. "Saving it for a rainy day. 'Course it didn't help that my own crew was no more trustworthy than my great-great-grandpa's." He tucked the map and gold coin away, straightening his coat. "Even if you don't believe me about the treasure, you still need me. How do you plan to get off this island?"

"I hadn't gotten that far yet." Annoyance leaked into my voice. "Steal a ship, probably."

"Ayah? And where will you go?"

I crossed my arms. "Valonikos. Markos thinks I'm dead."

"Wrong answer. You're going to Brizos."

I gritted my teeth but asked, "Why?"

"With the Lion Fleet hot on your tail, a stolen ship is as good as a death mark. Ain't no law in Brizos. On the Pirate Isle, you can exchange the ship for something untraceable. Give them the slip."

"I don't know how to get to—" I stopped, suspecting I knew exactly what he was going to say.

"I can get you to Brizos."

"Of course you can," I muttered.

"And I haven't even mentioned the most important reason you're going to let me out of this cell." He raised his eyebrows. "Which is that there isn't a ship on this island that can be taken across the ocean single-handed."

I'd wasted enough time on talk. I had to make a choice—and fast. My mind raced. Diric Melanos's promises meant nothing to me. I knew he had no intention whatsoever of giving me half the treasure from the *Centurion*, if it even existed. But during our weeks on the island together, he'd had ample opportunity to kill me. And yet he had not. As long as we needed each other, I figured I was safe.

"The gods damn me for a fool if I'm wrong." I sighed. "This is the stupidest thing I've ever done."

I opened the cell.

CHAPTER SIXTEEN

The peaceful stillness of night lay over the Fort Reliance harbor. Red and green lanterns illuminated the masts of the docked ships while below, dim light spilled from the portholes, slanting across the water. Somewhere men's voices rose and fell, though I couldn't make out the words.

Hand resting on my sword hilt, I started to sneak down the dock toward the ships.

Melanos grabbed my arm. "Not that way. Those ships carry a crew of twenty men or more." He nodded toward the distant shipyard. "With any luck we'll find something in there that's not too banged-up."

My luck had been pretty much nonexistent lately, and I was certain it was the sea god's fault. But I released my grip on the sword and followed Melanos to the shipyard, skirting the bubbles of lantern light.

Ships lay scattered around the shipyard in various states of construction, only their ghostly bones visible in the night. The doors of the cavernous warehouse had been rolled open so a ship might be sailed inside. Keeping to the shadows, we slipped into the warehouse. I glimpsed the sketchy outline of masts and spars—a boat in the water, tied up for repair.

"Here she is." Melanos stopped in front of it. "Our ride to Brizos."

It was a two-masted schooner, her black paint nearly worn off. Green muck stained the planks above the waterline, like a circle around a bathtub. The sail sagged in a lumpy pile around the boom, as if no one had bothered to stow it. I noticed a burned patch, badly repaired with jagged stitches. The ropes drooped and a makeshift tarp covered what I suspected was a hole in the deck. The carved letters on her stern read *Trusted Steed*, though one of the *e*'s in *Steed* was missing.

The schooner looked like it had been in a battle and lost. Badly.

I snorted. "More like the *Busted Steed*." Gesturing toward the harbor outside, my gaze lingered lovingly on the cutter. "What about that one?"

"I think the Akhaian fleet would miss that one, don't you?" He glared at me. "Stop complaining. It's seaworthy." The *T* lost its grip on the hull and fell into the water with a splash. "More or less."

I eyed the ship, now advertising itself as the *Rusted Sted*. "We're going to die."

Melanos had moved on to a long wooden shed. Wiggling the knob, he tried the door. It fell open.

In the shadows, I could barely make out a table and benches. Cabinets lined the walls, stacked with dishes. This must be a dining hall for the men who worked at the shipyard.

Grabbing an empty burlap sack, Melanos shoved it into my hands. "Take that lantern," he ordered. "Find some food and anything in a bottle that looks drinkable. We'll need three days' provisions if we're to make it to Brizos. Then get aboard and get those sails hoisted."

"What will you be doing?"

His teeth glowed white in the dark. "Arranging for our escape."

A cursory inspection of the dining hall revealed bread, cheese, a large jar of olives, and several corked bottles of unknown origin. Sweeping them into the sack, I boarded the *Busted Steed*. Ten minutes later, Melanos hopped the rail and joined me on deck.

"What are you waiting for?" he demanded. "Why haven't you raised the sails?"

I stared up into the web of loose ropes. "I never committed an act of piracy before," I said, unwinding the halyards from the cleat.

"Ayah? So you think my cutter just up and walked out of Casteria harbor?"

I noticed he now had a flintlock pistol stuck sideways in the waistband of his trousers, as well as a sword identical to mine, and decided not to ask where he'd gotten them.

"That was legal." I watched him raise the other sail, which shivered in anticipation as the breeze caressed it. "I had a letter of marque. This is piracy."

Taking out my stolen sword, I held it over the ropes that tied the schooner to the dock. And hesitated. There would be no coming back from this. If I stole this ship, I'd be just as guilty as the Akhaian fleet already thought I was.

Before I could cut the rope, something flashed in the corner of my vision. Flames licked up the side of a barrel on the *Advantagia*'s deck. As I watched through the open warehouse doors, the tiny finger of fire leaped onto a rope, heading for the rolled-up sails. Farther down, a second flame flickered on the deck of the cutter.

I raised my eyebrows at Melanos. "Your escape plan?"

A bell pealed out. "Fire!" men shouted, their voices echoing across the water.

"I don't know why you didn't set fire to that man-of-war," I said. "Now they're going to be coming after us with all one hundred of those cannons."

"They're going to try," he corrected me. Taking out his own sword, he hacked through the mooring ropes. "That beast is heavy and slow. They won't catch us."

Slowly, creakingly, the *Busted Steed* drifted away from the dock. Spinning the wheel to port, I glanced overhead. Once we cleared the warehouse roof, the wind should catch the sails . . .

With the *Steed*'s bowsprit pointing ahead of us, we inched out of the shipyard. Feeling the familiar tug of the wind, I tightened my hands on the wheel. The boom rattled over—two booms, I corrected myself, unused to sailing a ship with more than one mast. The schooner began to heel, tilting slightly as she picked up speed. Without running lights, we were nearly invisible in the dark. With luck, the Akhaians might not realize the ship—and their prisoners—were missing until tomorrow morning.

Hearing a shout behind me, I looked over my shoulder. In the dark, the soldiers resembled scurrying red ants. Something flashed, followed by the crack of a musket.

Instinctively I ducked, shoulders tensing. "They're shooting at us!"

Melanos grinned. "They do that when you steal their ships, darling."

A bullet skipped across the deck, throwing up a shower of splinters. I yelped, clinging to the wheel. "You think this is *funny*? Do something!"

Reclining on the seat, he said, "It's all right. We'll be out of range in a moment."

Another bullet whistled past my ear and lodged in the mast.

"A few moments," Melanos amended. "Perhaps you best get down on your belly."

Flattening myself on the deck, I glared at him. This was ridiculous. My heartbeat throbbed in my ears, adrenaline streaking through my body. Behind us, Fort Reliance took an excruciatingly long time to dissolve into darkness. By the time it finally did, I was drenched in sweat.

We sailed around the curve of the island, the trees and rocks blocking us from view. Stretching my stiff muscles, I got to my feet. Overhead the *Steed*'s tattered sail flapped. I suspected the schooner was listing slightly to starboard and yet, as I gripped the wheel, I couldn't help grinning. Wind puffing through my hair, I inhaled the familiar smells of salt, seaweed, and wet rope.

This was where I belonged, at the helm of a ship, her bow dipping through the oncoming waves. The clouds shifted, and for one glorious moment the moon shone through, illuminating a dazzling path all the way to the horizon.

Then I remembered the sea had tried to drown me, and that killed the magical moment. Glancing at the peaceful waves lapping the hull, I didn't sense any malicious intent from the god—in fact, I couldn't sense anything at all.

Whether that was a good or bad sign, I did not know.

Melanos roped the wheel in place and together we descended belowdecks to explore. Jumping down from the ladder, I landed with a splash in stinking ankle-deep water. The tarp covering the hole in the deck fluttered above us.

"Ugh!" I glanced in annoyance at my stolen boots, now soaked. Raising the lantern, I said, "Looks like they didn't pump out the ship the last time it rained."

"Optimistic of you," he remarked, "thinking this is rainwater."

"You mean the ship is leaking?"

He only shrugged.

"Anything would've been a better ride to Brizos than this." With the point of my sword, I prodded a pile of moldy-looking rags in the corner, praying it wasn't a body the Akhaian navy had somehow overlooked.

"Will you stop complaining for one—" A piece of burned wood detached itself from the hole in the ceiling, falling with a splash into the murky water. Melanos sighed. "You know what? You're right. It's shit."

He looked at me, and I looked at him. A moment of sudden friendliness passed between us, and I began to laugh. Likely it was just my relief at having escaped death by hanging.

Holding my nose, I waded into the next room. The captain's cabin smelled like bilge water and mold. With a sigh, I abandoned any dreams I'd had of sleeping in a comfortable bed for the first time in months. Both captain's and crew's bunks had been stripped of mattresses, and anyway it stunk down here.

I opened a cabinet, which revealed itself to be empty. "I don't suppose they left anything useful in here. What do you think happened to her anyway?"

Melanos rummaged through a chest stenciled with the flag of Akhaia. "Cannonball through the deck, I expect. Likely they towed her to Fort Reliance to finish the refit." He let the chest bang shut. "Empty." Approaching a mechanism in the middle of the cabin, he experimentally spun the handle. "Seems like the pump's working though. We'll try that tomorrow. Maybe if we're lucky, we won't sink after all."

I eyed the waterlogged cabin. Maybe. We climbed the ladder to the deck, where the air was fresh. My head buzzed with exhaustion. I stifled a yawn, but Melanos heard me.

"I'll take the first watch," he said, settling himself by the wheel.

I curled up on the deck under my red officer's coat, staring up into the stars. They were brighter out here, untouched by the glow of the city. Eventually, lulled by the rocking of the *Steed*, I sank into sleep.

The morning dawned clear and bright. I woke with my arm thrown over my face, the sun beating down on me. Struggling out from under the coat, I blinked at the dazzling sea. Each wave was crested with sparkling light, making my eyes water.

Diric Melanos lay on the bench behind the wheel, boots propped on the railing.

"Didn't you sleep?" I asked.

"Been keeping six-hour watches my whole life," he said. "Reckon my body's too used to it to stop now. Didn't you keep a watch on your wherry?"

"Not really." I yawned. "We anchored at night." Shading my eyes to study the horizon, I saw nothing. "How far is it to Brizos?"

"Three days' sail from Fort Reliance." He pulled himself to a sitting position. "There are things you need to know about Brizos, girl. It's ruled by—"

I rolled my eyes. "By Akhaia. I know that."

He smirked. "If you'd ever been there, you'd know Akhaia holds that island in name only. It ain't called the Pirate Isle for nothing. No, the real power in Brizos is Dido Brilliante—Long Dido, that's what most folks call her. And she's . . . well."

"She's what?" I demanded.

"Different," he said cryptically. "Let's just say it's best we don't do anything to get on her bad side."

I'd heard stories of Dido Brilliante. Long Dido was only one of her names—some folks called her the Queen of Brizos, or the Pirate Queen. But I didn't know which parts of her legend were gossip and which were real. My mother's lip twisted scornfully whenever she mentioned her, so I understood they'd had more than one encounter in the past.

I wondered what Melanos wasn't telling me.

Later that morning, scrounging in the *Busted Steed*'s pathetic cabin, I found a few faded charts. Stashed away in a moldy cabinet, they looked like mice had gnawed them. Tucking the maps under my arm, I climbed the ladder into the sunlight.

I spread the charts flat on the deck, smoothing the creases. Locating the Akhaian Peninsula, I set a finger on Four Mile Rock and bent to examine the squiggly markings. At the wheel, Melanos watched me.

"If you're right," I said, "*Vix* is lying off the shoal here." I tapped the chart. "According to this map, that whole area has a depth of no more than twenty feet."

"So it says." There was doubt in his voice. "Shifting sands. Changing seas. You can't always rely on a chart."

"If we get the treasure—" I halted. Since when was I talking about the treasure as if it was real? I couldn't let my longing for

Vix muddle my head. "I could hire a salvage crew. Maybe Argyrus and Sons—"

"Ayah?" He grinned. "I thought the treasure was a fish story."

"Forget I mentioned it," I snapped. "I'll pay with my own coin, then."

He shook his head. "It's a fool's dream. She's rent in two by the shoals, most likely. She'd have to be patched and fitted with a new mast. New canvas."

I gritted my teeth. He'd been carrying that stupid fake map for years, and he thought *my* dream was silly? I gestured at the *Steed*'s patched hull, which smelled like fresh resin and tar. "If this one could be raised, why not *Vix*?"

"Because, sweetheart"—I'd never heard the term of endearment uttered quite so sarcastically—"you're not the Akhaian Lion Fleet. The expense would cripple you, and that's if she can be raised at all. And speaking of the Lion Fleet, how do you propose to sail into their waters with a bounty on your head?" He spat over the rail. "*Victorianos* is at the bottom of the ocean. Many ships go down on that shoal. Most of them stay there."

I stared at Four Mile Rock on the map, blinking hard. *Vix* had once belonged to him. I swallowed, resentment bubbling inside me. Didn't he even care?

"Oh well." I rolled up the charts, pretending his words hadn't hurt. "It was just an idea, was all. Pity the treasure isn't real. One brick of gold would be enough—"

Melanos scratched his head, shifting uncomfortably on the seat.

"What?" I demanded.

"Well, about that. There's a bit of a catch." He hesitated. "The thing about the treasure is . . ."

"It doesn't exist," I said. "I *knew* it."

"Oh, it exists, all right. It's just . . ." Carefully he pulled the treasure map from his coat, unfolding the waxed leather case like an envelope. "See for yourself."

I attempted to flatten the paper scrap on the deck.

His voice jumped in alarm. "Don't *touch* it, girl! That thing's over a hundred years old."

I rolled my eyes, but shifted my fingers to hold it by the edges. Studying the map up close for the first time, I saw an oblong island with a hill in the center. A winding line marked a river, squiggling down to meet the beach. On the southern end of the island, rocks—or other small islands—dotted the water. Among them was a curved mark with an X under it. I squinted at the letters. CAVE. In the top right corner of the map someone had scrawled a rudimentary compass rose.

I glanced up. "Where are the coordinates? I see the island. And the cave. But—" I scanned the paper again for anything I might have missed. "No reference points. Nothing to tell us where this island is." Strangely, I felt a pang of disappointment. I hadn't really believed in the *Centurion*'s treasure, of course, but the idea of it had tickled my sense of adventure. "This might be anywhere in the whole ocean."

"There's writing in the bottom left corner." Melanos pointed. "I reckon my great-great-granddad scribbled down latitude and longitude."

Only a faint brown smudge remained. "It's all worn off."

"And that's the catch. Always reckoned someday I'd go to the Royal Library and dig up everything they have on the *Centurion*. But . . ." He shrugged. "One thing led to another and I never got around to it. Nor could I, now that I got a price on my head if I ever return to Akhaia."

"Liar," I said. "You went back to Akhaia when you tried to kill Markos."

"Ayah, I did, and that job was cursed from start to finish," he said darkly, grabbing up his map and folding it into the protective wrapping. From his tone, I surmised the conversation was over.

It was almost a pity I didn't believe in the treasure. Docia Argyrus would've loved to get her hands on that map. Surely, with her knowledge of the *Centurion* and her collection of artifacts, she'd be able to tell me whether it was real or not. When we got back to Valonikos . . .

My heart fluttered. Markos was in Valonikos. I ached with my whole being to see him again. I pictured him standing on the beach, gazing out at the distant sea. Mourning me.

The more I reflected on my strange misgivings in Eryth, the more I was convinced the Archon could not be trusted. Whether Agnes was part of whatever was going on, I was less certain. She'd struck me as acting purely out of her own interest.

I shook off my concern for Markos. He was smart, I told myself sternly. If this was a trap, surely he or Antidoros Peregrine would be able to see through it. Before I could sail for Valonikos, we needed a better ship. Brizos had to come first.

The island appeared at sunset on the third day. At first it was a mere bump on the horizon, but as we sailed closer the blur distilled itself into individual buildings against a backdrop of thick tangled forest.

Brizos looked like . . . a wooden shack with another shack built on top of it. Then the townsfolk had constructed more shacks, tying them lopsidedly together with bits of old rope, and topped the whole thing off with another shack. Everything was made of unpainted weatherbeaten boards, and the balconies and walkways drooped alarmingly. The whole city seemed in danger of collapsing on itself at any moment.

I'd heard sailors in the riverlands say the Brizos harbor master was an infamous drunkard who got fat off bribes from smugglers and pirates, and my first sight of the docks did nothing to contradict that impression. There was nothing here of the rigid order of Siscema, or the easy flow of Valonikos. The port was chaos—ships packed into every available berth, barrels swaying atop high carts, and people cursing.

I glanced at Melanos. We should have been turning into the wind and slackening the sails to make our approach. "We're not going into the harbor?" I asked.

"In a stolen ship bearing the Akhaian lion crest?" He steered past the docks, aiming for the far side of the cove. "How do you plan on explaining that?"

"I thought you said Akhaia isn't really in control of Brizos."

"Doesn't mean they don't have men stationed here. Or that they're completely stupid."

We anchored across the cove, hidden by the trees, and lowered the dinghy to row ashore. I sat on the back thwart, staring morosely at the three inches of water swishing around my feet.

Of *course* there was a hole in the dinghy too.

Melanos hopped nimbly onto the dock. "Now, when we get in front of the Queen," he said, "you let me do the talking. And whatever you do, girl, don't mention anything about the *Centurion*."

He made a bowline knot, throwing the loop around a post. Glancing up, he swore.

I set my hand on my pistol. "What?"

Steel clattered behind me. I turned, stolen coat circling elegantly around my knees, to see five unsavory-looking men standing on the dock, weapons drawn.

The leader of the group stepped forward. "Diric Melanos, you old swindler. Didn't think you'd be bold enough to set foot in Brizos after the last time."

I shot Melanos a sour glance, yanking out my pistol. "Is there anyone you haven't betrayed?"

"Probably not," he said lightly. He spun so his back was to mine. A second group of men filed down the pier from the other side. We were trapped.

Markos and I had once fought the Black Dogs back-to-back like this. An ache rose in my chest, but I ignored it. This wasn't the time.

"I've orders to bring you downstairs," the leader said. "*Herself* wants to see you."

"Who?" I demanded, although I had a pretty good idea.

I lowered my pistol. There was no point when we were out-numbered ten to two.

The man grinned, revealing a sparkling ruby where his front tooth should have been. "Who else? Dido Brilliante, the Queen of Brizos."

CHAPTER
SEVENTEEN

The Queen's men led us to a rickety three-story building. Porches wrapped around it like lace trim on a lady's gown, with gaps where the railing was missing. It looked perhaps slightly less like a shack than the surrounding houses, but it was certainly no palace.

Once inside, I blinked as my eyes adjusted to the dark. The building seemed deserted, with a few guttering candle lanterns providing the only light. A strange wet smell hung over the place. Boot tracks led across the muddy floorboards to a door at the end of the hall. Past the door a wooden staircase disappeared into darkness.

One of the men prodded me in the back, and I stepped down. Counting the stairs, I tried to figure out how far we descended, but I lost track somewhere after the first hundred. Surely we must be far under the city of Brizos.

At long last, we emerged into a cavern. Dripping stalactites hung like black icicles from the ceiling and seawater dampened the rock floor. Blue glass lanterns dangled from ropes, casting an eerie underwater glow. A raised boardwalk, draped with lavish rugs of many colors, marked a dry path through the cavern, ending at an enormous enclosed platform. A circular bar stood in the middle, surrounded by stools and tables. Bottles with labels both familiar and exotic rose up on a high shelf crowned with a human skull and arm bones. On the far end of the tavern was what looked like a raised dais, and beyond that a house had been built right into the wall of the cave, its door outlined in heavy timbers.

As we entered the bar, a hundred smells assaulted my nose—pipe smoke, brackish water, spilled rum, mud, leather, and sweat. It was packed with people, the boisterous clamor of voices echoing off the walls and ceiling.

A brown-skinned bald man wearing a clockwork helmet watched us from a barstool. Golden gears clicked into place on his eyepatch, whirling in a circle. He gave me a slow nod as we passed. Hearing a *clip-clop*, I glanced to my left. The waiter who carried a tray of ales had the shaggy legs and black hooves of a goat. Two frogmen in straw hats squatted on stools, a dice game on the bar between them. The pale woman tending bar had blue swirling tattoos all over her face. No, I realized, catching a flash of color on her forearms as she flipped a mug and set it on the bar—all over *everywhere*.

"Will you please," Melanos said through his teeth, "stop gawking and look like you've been somewhere before."

I bit back a sarcastic reply. I'd sailed all over the riverlands on my father's wherry. But Dido Brilliante's crowd was . . . more colorful than even I was used to.

I saw instantly why they called her Long Dido. Over six feet tall, she lounged on her cushioned throne, with her impossibly long legs outstretched. Black leather boots went up over her knees, and she wore a boldly patterned silk waistcoat. I couldn't make up my mind about the shade of her skin—at first I was sure it was pale, but then she turned her head, revealing a light brown complexion. And then the light hit her differently and her face seemed—I squinted—almost gray and somehow not quite human.

I stared at her hair, which had all sorts of things twisted up in it—big painted seashells, a silver talent, and an ornament made of spongy coral. Jewels glittered in a row up and down her right ear-lobe, while in the other ear she wore a gold hoop with something white dangling from it. Was that—?

The Queen saw me looking. "You be staring at Ten Ton Johnny's finger, girlie?" She laughed. "Sad he were to part with it, make no mistake. But a deal's a deal." Shifting her gaze to my companion, she grinned. "Ain't that right, Diric, you old dog?"

"As it happens, I have a deal for you." He flashed a smile at her and I saw a brief glimpse of why he was rumored to be charming. "Got a ship I'm looking to trade. Bit run down, but good bones. A great bargain for a lucky someone."

"Did you think I wouldn't forget you're the biggest liar on the high seas?" She sat forward, propping her elbow on her knee.

"That ship is marked, isn't it? You been stealing from the Lion Fleet again?"

She turned her attention back to me, and a strange shivery feeling splashed over me.

"This one seems a bit young for you, Diric," she said. "What's your name, girl?"

"Caro Oresteia."

The slight narrowing of her eyes was the only sign that she'd recognized my name. "Well, that explains why you look familiar." She waved a hand full of jeweled rings and scarred knuckles. "I know your mother. Sure, and didn't she confiscate a crate of fine rugs from Ndanna from my men? A crate what should've come to me."

I held my tongue. Should have come to her, my ass. She meant they were stolen, most likely from Bollard Company. My mother's world was governed by rules and contracts. I saw at once why she would not be enamored with Dido Brilliante, who cared not a bit for such things.

"Why'd you bring her here, Diric? She'll only bring trouble down on us. Plenty of jumped-up traders make threats, but Tamaré Bollard has the muscle to back them up." She pushed a mug into my hands. "Have a rum punch, Bollard."

I was only half Bollard and I didn't want a rum punch, but I had the distinct impression that saying no wasn't an option. Accepting the drink, I took a tiny sip. I wanted to keep my wits sharp.

"As it happens," Melanos said, "the girl helped me out of a bit of trouble."

"What kind of trouble?"

"The Akhaian kind."

"I knew you were trying to pull the wool over my eyes," the Queen said sharply. "You *did* lift that ship from the Lion Fleet. Came here thinking I'd take your stolen goods off your hands, didn't you? Well, you may pretend to have a short memory, but I don't." Her voice suddenly reminded me of the sea god's, all shadowy cold depths. "I remember what happened the last time I helped you."

"I can explain that," he began, but the Queen of Brizos cut him off with a brisk nod.

Before I had time to react, four men grabbed Melanos and pushed him, struggling, up against the tavern wall. One moment they'd been in teasing conversation, and the next she was staring at him with deadly intent in her eyes. Which had darkened from gray to black. A foreboding chill whispered down my neck.

"Dido," Melanos gasped, "I was going to pay you back—"

She whipped a knife from her belt and hurled it at him. It landed in the wall, quivering. She'd pinned him by his shirt collar, narrowly missing his throat.

"That's enough from you for the present." Jumping to her feet, she projected her voice. "Let's have a game, shall we?" The bar fell silent. "Ten silver talents to anyone who can outline this man in ten knives without making him bleed!" She added, "Fifty if you can make him piss himself."

The crowd exploded in raucous laughter. I swore under my breath. Any number of them looked capable of winning the

Queen's wager, but . . . My gaze lingered on the bottles, glasses, and kegs scattered around the bar. Everyone here was drunk. Melanos would be lucky if he didn't end up with a knife in his heart.

I took a deep breath. "Let me try."

The Queen swiveled to face me, and again I was reminded of the sea god and her beady heron eyes. A long moment passed.

She bellowed with laughter. "I'm older than I look, girl, and there ain't much that entertains me anymore. But that . . ." She grinned. "That I was not expecting."

"You're right," I told her. "Tamaré Bollard is my mother. But my father is a smuggler and a gunrunner. I reckon he taught me how to throw a knife well enough. If I win, you buy the schooner off us." I desperately hoped she wasn't about to shoot me for my brash gamble. "If I lose, well, you still get your way, because Diric Melanos will be dead."

She threw back her head and laughed again. "All right, I'll take your wager, Caro Bollard."

"Oresteia," I corrected her.

She shrugged, as if it was all the same to her.

Pinned to the wall, Melanos raised one eyebrow, which I rather envied. I'd never been able to manage that trick. I did not, however, envy him for what was about to happen.

"I don't suppose it would matter," he said, "if I point out I never agreed to this."

Long Dido sat back down and threw a leg over the arm of her throne, crossing the other leg on top of it. Light glinted on the daggers strapped to her boots. "No."

Licking my lips, I turned to face Melanos. I was confident in my ability with a knife, but I'd never tried this with a real living person before. When I was little, Pa had taken me to a penny show in Siscema once. Among the tumblers and game booths and fried fish sellers, there had been a pretty lady in a white dress who'd stood handcuffed to a wheel while a tattooed man whipped knives at her. She hadn't flinched, not even when one landed too close and sliced off a lock of her hair. Later Pa had told me the man with the knives was her husband.

This was different. I didn't trust Melanos and he didn't trust me. Watching him glare murderously in my direction, it occurred to me it might be safer to kill him than nick him, or else he might kill *me*. My heart thumped so loudly I was certain the Queen and her court could hear.

I almost expected people to laugh at me behind their hands, but they didn't. They leaned forward excitedly. The frogmen had halted their dice game. Someone brought me a tray containing a pile of knives. I picked one off the top, flipping it over in my hand to test the weight.

Behind me, the crowd whispered wagers. "One talent against the girl. She looks a bit green, eh?"

"I'll take it. Sailors are a good hand with knife tricks."

"That slip of a thing? Doubtful."

I tried to shut out their voices. Taking a breath to calm my jangling nerves, I flung the first knife. *Whump*! It landed a foot away from Melanos's ear.

The Queen pretended to yawn. "They aren't all going to be that far out, are they? Make this more interesting."

I hadn't meant for that knife to land so far away, but now I had a better handle on the distance and the weight of the weapons. Hefting a second knife in my hand, I slowed my breathing and focused on Melanos. The noise of the crowd subsided.

With a thunk, the knife buried itself in the wall less than an inch from his shoulder.

"Gods damn it, girl!" Melanos glared at me.

The Queen clapped her hands. "What are you complaining about, Diric? She's doing a first-rate job. Now, only eight more."

The next knife went through Diric's sleeve and he winced, cursing. "I should've killed you on the gods-damned island."

To punish him for that remark, I aimed the next one between his thighs. It flipped end over end, sticking in the wall an inch below the crotch of his trousers. Sweat beaded on his brow.

"Hey!" a woman in the crowd yelled. "There be some of us girls in Brizos who would miss that!"

I threw the next five knives, the pile on the tray dwindling until there was only one left. The last knife clipped his shirt, right next to his hip. I held my breath, frantically hoping a blossom of red would not appear.

Someone slapped me on the back. "Well done!" Around me, people muttered and money changed hands. Sweat broke out on my neck, and my knees buckled with relief.

Melanos stepped out from between the knife hilts, ripping his shirt in the process. He didn't seem to care. Striding past me, he grabbed a jug off the nearest table.

"Where are you going?" I asked.

"To get very drunk," he growled. "And celebrate the fact that I still have my tackle, no thanks to you."

I would've said it was thanks to me that he *did* have his tackle, but I kept my mouth shut. Several women were eyeing him, and I suspected he could have his pick—if that was indeed the kind of celebration he meant.

Turning away, I saw Dido Brilliante watching me from her throne. She beckoned me closer. Reaching out with the point of her dagger, she drew the brass chain from under my shirt. My first instinct was to shiver at the touch of cold steel against my skin, but I sensed that would be a mistake.

"Interesting bit of pretty." She examined Kenté's talisman. "Felt it whispering, I did, when you walked in."

I wondered what she knew that I did not. I'd never noticed the talisman doing anything remotely like whispering. There was something about the Queen that I couldn't exactly name— something wild and strange.

In a flash of my mind's eye I saw a barnacled thing lumbering across the ocean floor. Heard the faint echo of something like whale song. Felt a sense of indescribable age. And one huge black knowing eye looked back at me.

We lived in a world of strange things, where a god's children might have knobby frog fingers or goat hooves. People usually shrugged and didn't think much of it. But what else was out there in the deep, in the primordial dark, lurking in the wet muck that the sunlight never touched? What kind of creature was Dido Brilliante?

Unsettled, I resisted the impulse to take a step back. Now I understood why Diric Melanos had only said enigmatically that she was different, and refused to explain further.

"I collect such things," she murmured, flipping the talisman over. "Did Diric tell you? Curious trinkets, rare books, automatons from Ndanna, and the like. Magical bits and bobs. You might call it a hobby of mine. I reckon some of the things in my treasure room are, oh, hundreds of years old." She winked. "Always keep the things I take, I do."

At those words, my head shot up.

She knew why instantly. "Oh yes, I know *her*," she said, so low only the two of us could hear. "You might say we're old acquaintances, time out of mind. She spoke to you, did she?" She sniffed deeply, as if inhaling a sea breeze. "Funny I didn't smell it right away. You're one of her chosen."

I swallowed. "I used to be."

"Hmm," was all she said. Releasing my necklace, she leaned back in her throne. "Come back tomorrow. We'll talk about your ship."

I tucked the talisman under my shirt, not knowing exactly what to make of her. A man approached the throne, jostling me with his shoulder. The Queen turned her attention to him, and I understood I was dismissed. Before I left, I seized two of the knives, still planted in the wall where I'd hurled them. Yanking them out, I stuck them into my belt.

Melanos sprawled in a chair, a woman in his lap and a bottle in his hand.

I stopped next to him. "Are you coming?"

"Sorry, what?" he said against the woman's lips, pretending he hadn't heard me. I knew perfectly well what this was—my punishment for flinging knives at him. That was what I got for throwing in my lot with pirates who were no better than they ought to be.

It looked like I was on my own. My calf muscles ached by the time I reached the top of Dido Brilliante's eight million stairs. Wiping sweat from my forehead, I pushed through the door of the abandoned building and into the streets of Brizos.

From the stories Pa had told me about the Pirate Isle, I knew it wasn't wise to take an evening pleasure stroll through Brizos without being heavily armed. But with the pistol and knives stuck diagonally through my belt, I didn't expect anyone to challenge me.

Hands in pockets, I ambled down the boardwalk. Lamplight and fiddle music spilled out from a tavern door. Hearing a trickling sound, I realized a man was pissing in the street and gave him a wide berth. A cat darted among the shadows, its paws silent on the planks.

Across the boardwalk I spotted a food cart, and my stomach growled in longing. I'd taken two strides toward the cart before I remembered I had no money. Feeling up and down my sides for any likely lumps, I rummaged through the pockets of my stolen coat. Finally I dug up a paltry handful of Akhaian coins. Not enough for a lamb sandwich, but I could buy roasted corn and a piece of sesame bread.

Something boomed, the sharp noise ricocheting off the walls of the shacks.

The building behind me exploded in splinters. I screamed,

dropping to my knees in the muddy street. The building collapsed, enveloping me in a cloud of dust. The man selling lamb sandwiches glanced back and forth between his cart and the harbor, and then took off running. His patrons also scattered.

Dazed, I touched the back of my neck. My fingers came away bloody. I must have been hit by a flying splinter.

A frigate lay in the harbor, ghostly white smoke drifting from her cannons. As people darted and shouted in the street, I knew tomorrow morning would be too late to get rid of that schooner.

The Lion Fleet was here.

The cannon boomed again, followed by a whistling sound. I covered my head, steeling myself for the impact. It hit somewhere to my right, the boardwalk trembling under my knees. Swallowing against the ringing in my ears, I wiped my face. For a moment I was so stunned, all I could do was stare down at my hands, which were streaked in sweat and dirt.

"Come on, we have to move."

Squinting into the smoky night, I saw a woman's hand extended down to me.

She smiled. "Always good to see a familiar face, Caro Oresteia."

CHAPTER
EIGHTEEN

"What are you talking about?" I asked, barely able to hear my own words. The cannonball had done something to my ears. "I've never seen you before in my life."

The woman was middle-aged, with an angular face and thin lips. She wore a gown of deep purple, trimmed in ribbon. As I watched, her face melted away to reveal a girl with an upturned pierced nose, deep brown skin, and amber eyes. Her dark hair was braided and twisted in an elaborate knot on top of her head. The earring that dangled from her left lobe was nearly three inches long, a column of jet beads with a shiny black crescent moon and star suspended at the end. A sprinkling of matching jet pins sparkled in her hair, reminding me of the night sky.

"Sorry," Kenté said. "I forgot about that."

I was so stunned to see my cousin that it took me a moment to realize what it meant. Somehow she'd known I was alive. And not only alive, but *here*, half an ocean away.

"How—when—what are you doing in Brizos?" I spluttered.

"Looking for you, of course. Everyone said you'd drowned." She grinned, which was not exactly the reaction to my tragic death I would've preferred. "It was in the papers, even in Trikkaia. But I knew it couldn't be true."

Taking her hand, I scrambled to my feet. "Explain."

"Well, if you'd really drowned, you would be at the bottom of the sea. Lying quite still as the fish nibbled on your corpse."

"This is not what I meant by explaining," I said, brushing dirt off my trousers.

"And yet every time I checked on you," she went on, "I was quite certain you were moving. Traveling southeast. Every night I'd close my eyes and find you."

I'd been so happy to see Kenté that I had forgotten her annoying tendency to talk in riddles. "Hold on—*how*?"

"My talisman," she said, as if I was the one being cryptic. "You obviously got it."

"Wait, you mean this?" I dug beneath my shirt. The chain was tangled in an awkward knot around the lumpy gold charm. I pulled the entire thing over my head.

Taking the talisman in her hand, Kenté kissed it. "Oh, hello, you."

Another sharp cannon blast echoed across the water. Seizing her arm, I dragged her briskly toward the harbor. "If you get killed by a cannonball, it won't matter if I'm already dead. The Bollards will murder me again. Let's *go*."

We both ducked as a cannonball hurtled over our heads, landing with the rattle of splintering wood.

Slinging the necklace back over my head, I asked, "So this thing has some kind of shadow magic in it? That's how you were able to find me?"

"Didn't I say so in my letter?" she said innocently as we hurried down the street.

"No." I glared at her. "You said it was supposed to protect me from enemy shadowmen. You purposely neglected to tell me you were using it to track my every movement. As you well know."

"It protects you a *little* bit."

I kept glaring.

"Nothing can really protect you from a shadowman." She wrinkled her nose. "Well, nothing I can do yet anyway. But by telling me where you are," she hedged, "in a very technical sense, the talisman could be interpreted as a *form* of protection . . ."

"So you're saying you lied to me."

"Really, Caro," she said, her face illuminated by a flash from the guns. "If I told you the truth, you might have stuck it in a drawer and not worn it. I don't know how you can possibly be upset about this. I'm here, aren't I? Everyone else in the whole world thinks you're dead, except me. I'm here to rescue you. You ought to be saying thank you."

"Did you come with the Bollards? Did you bring a ship?"

Kenté grimaced, but said nothing.

"Then how exactly are you rescuing me?" I demanded.

"Look, I knew you were somewhere east of Brizos." Keeping pace with me, she gestured at her chest. "*I* knew, when no one else did. I hired passage on board a ship as soon as I realized you were alive. I planned to search all the islands until I found you."

"Did you tell Ma and Pa I'm alive? Or Markos?"

Kenté shook her head. "I didn't want to get anyone's hopes up. I had to find you first."

We skidded around a corner, the harbor suddenly spread out before us. Shock immobilized me as I stared at the wreckage. The streets zigzagged down to the docks, lit by burning buildings. One merchant brig had a hole in the deck, black smoke pouring out. Another ship's mast was cracked, tilting dangerously. A warehouse had gone up in flames. The sailors on the frigate, squinting through the twilight, couldn't possibly know which ship was the *Busted Steed*. They were destroying the whole island on the small chance their cannonballs would hit us.

My fingernails dug into my palms, remembering another evening just like this one, when *Cormorant* had rounded the bend into the fiery ruins of Hespera's Watch and my whole life had been turned upside down.

Kenté halted in the street, causing me to nearly collide with her. "The guns. Why've they stopped?"

She was right. Crickets chirped in the trees, and somewhere a dog barked. The quiet was suddenly ominous. I craned my neck to get a glimpse of the frigate, but the smoke and the dark prevented me from seeing anything. A shiver of foreboding crawled down my back.

Jerking my stolen pistol out, I said, "It can't mean anything good."

A woman screamed. Soldiers were in the street, spreading upward from the docks with muskets in their hands. The sharp crack of gunfire sounded. One man yelled, "For the Queen!" and charged an officer with a sword. Several shots rang out and he fell in the street.

An officer barked out orders. "Find the fugitives."

On the balcony of a nearby building something sparked, followed by a puff of smoke and a boom. Men were firing down on the officers. At least some of the pirates weren't giving in without a fight.

A young soldier scurried up to his superior. "Sir," he said, "Brilliante's scalawags are fighting back."

"I don't care if you have to burn her place down," the captain yelled. "Find that traitor girl! The Emparch's been tolerant of this lawless place long enough."

I swore under my breath.

"Oh," said Kenté. "The fugitive is you." She sighed heavily. "Of course it is."

We pelted down an alley to the harbor, where we discovered we weren't the only ones keen to get away from Brizos. The docks were thick with people, shoving and jostling to get to their boats. One man carried a sack of coins slung over his shoulder, clinking as he ran. Soldiers swarmed over the docks like red ants, their coats bright splashes against the dark.

I gestured to Kenté. "The boat's over h—" I tumbled to a stop, staring at the blank space on the dock. The dinghy was gone. "Gods *damn* him."

Diric Melanos had made his escape from the Lion Fleet, leaving me to my fate.

The soldiers were getting closer. I turned to my cousin. "They have a bounty poster with my face on it! Quick, can you hide us in the shadows?"

Kenté balled her hand into a fist. Darkness leaped up, swallowing her legs. It traveled like tendrils of black fire up her body until only her torso was visible. I'd never seen her do anything like that before. "Of course," she said. "Get ready."

I eyed her disembodied head warily. "What does it feel like?"

"Like snakes crawling all over you," she replied with a smirk, before her head disappeared.

"Really?"

"No, *not* really." Her voice sounded testy. "Now, do you want me to save your life or not? Stand still."

Someone shouted my name.

The *Busted Steed*, only one sail flapping on the second mast, bucketed toward the dock with Diric Melanos at the wheel.

"Caro!" he yelled again, slackening the sail so the schooner slowed to a crawl. He sounded relieved, but surely I was imagining it. Grabbing a coil of rope, he tossed it over the side. It unraveled in the air, landing with a slap on the surface of the water. "Jump! I'll haul you on board."

"Is that Diric Melanos?" Kenté demanded.

"It's all right, I'll explain later." Peeling off my heavy red coat, I kicked it over the edge of the dock. It sank, twirling into darkness, to the bottom of the harbor. That coat wasn't going to bring me anything but trouble.

"What do you mean, it's all right?" she squeaked. "He tried to murder us!"

"Just trust me."

"But—"

A shot whizzed past me. We didn't have time for this. With a shove in the direction of my cousin's voice, I pushed her off the dock. She surfaced, spluttering and no longer invisible, and spat out seawater. Her skirts billowed around her head. Shooting me a dirty look, she stroked hand over hand toward the schooner.

A voice spoke behind me. "Sorry I couldn't help with the ship."

I whirled to see Dido Brilliante, hat pulled low to hide her face. She stood alone on the dock, hands in pockets. Half the Akhaian navy was combing the island for her, yet she looked for all the world as if she was out for a stroll.

"Looks like I've got to lie low for a while," she said. "But I'll be back. This is my island." She gave me a strange smile. "Always has been. If you ever return to Brizos, the password to my headquarters is 'Leviathan.' Tell them Dido Brilliante owes you ten talents."

With that, she strode past me. I wondered which ship was hers, but she didn't pause at any of them. She kept going until she reached the end of the dock and then—

She jumped, disappearing in a circle of bubbles. I waited for her to resurface, but she did not. Fifty feet out, a giant black tail flapped in the water, kicking up a mountain of spray. Then it slipped beneath the waves, leaving me alone and stupefied on the dock.

"Caro!" Kenté screamed, treading water. She seized the rope Melanos had thrown. "Let's go!"

I leaped into the sea. Cold hit me like a slap as the water closed over my head. My boots dragged me down like weights. I pulled with all my strength toward the surface and broke through, gasping. Sleeves clinging to my arms, I swam for the rope. My clothes ballooned around me in the water. I grabbed the rope and held on as Melanos hauled me up.

Safe on the *Steed*, I dumped water out of my boots and wrung out my shirt. A few feet away on the deck, Kenté ruefully eyed her drenched skirts. The harbor was in chaos, with ships tacking back and forth, narrowly missing one another in the dark. Two cutters had gotten their bowsprits tangled; their crews shouted and tugged at ropes. Everyone was in a hurry to get away from the Lion Fleet.

Untangling the halyards on the foremast, I suddenly regretted that we'd spent our time in Brizos trying to get rid of the *Busted Steed* instead of tidying up her mess. I hauled down on the rope and the sail rose jerkily to the top of the mast. In one swift motion, I tied the halyard off on the cleat and ran barefoot to tighten the staysail. With all her sails up, the schooner gained speed and heeled to starboard, water bubbling under her hull. I watched the smoking harbor fall away behind our stern.

The frigate remained at anchor, showing no signs of pursuit. A grin danced across my lips. The Akhaian attack had left the harbor in such frantic disarray that they hadn't been able to spot the one ship they were looking for.

"*Now* will you tell me why we aren't killing Diric Melanos?" Kenté demanded. "And why he isn't killing us?"

Briefly I told her the story of how I'd been shipwrecked and woken up on the island, gotten captured by the Lion Fleet, and escaped Fort Reliance on a stolen ship. When I got to the part about the treasure map, Kenté's eyes widened.

"Oooh," she breathed. "The wreck of the *Centurion*. What Bollard Company wouldn't give to get their hands on that map."

"Ayah? Well, don't get too excited," I said. "The *Centurion* is probably a wild goose chase." I nodded toward Melanos. "The point is we need each other. At least until I can get back to Valonikos."

That was another problem. How long a journey did we have ahead of us—a week or more? We had no food or water left. I swallowed down my frustration. We kept narrowly escaping one mess only to land right in the middle of another. I yearned for just one day to catch my breath.

Making my way back to the stern, I almost tripped on the pile of goods tossed haphazardly on the deck. A basket of fruit, several loaves of bread, a few blankets, and a collection of bottles lay beside a small strongbox, the kind a store might keep its profits in. The lock had been bashed apart.

Flipping open the lid, I saw coins gleaming in the moonlight. "Their town was being attacked, and you *looted* them?"

Melanos shrugged. "Doubt they'll be missing it."

I glanced at the stolen goods. He wasn't wrong. Still, it

rankled—the idea that he'd taken these things from folks whose homes and businesses were under siege.

"Though we won't have enough provisions to make it to Valonikos," he went on. "Not now that there's three of us." He and Kenté exchanged appraising looks. I could tell he remembered her. She and I had stolen *Vix* from him. "Reckon we'll have to make a stop in Iantiporos. It's the safest port. Even the Lion Fleet won't dare go against the Margravina, not with her own navy sitting in the harbor."

Seeing the disapproval on my face, he threw up his hands. "If you ain't happy with the way I do things, you take the wheel." Abruptly he let go, and I barely managed to catch the wheel before it spun the ship into an uncontrolled jibe. He swiped a bottle off the pile of stolen property. "What did I ever do to the gods," he growled, "to deserve being stuck on a sinking ship surrounded by girls? It's like—like being in a brothel," he said darkly. "Only not in a fun way."

He stomped belowdecks, the hatch slamming behind him.

Kenté watched him go. "Are you sure you trust him?"

"Not even a little." I settled my hands on the wheel. "I don't believe he intends to give me half of that treasure, if it really exists. He's going to betray me. I just don't plan on letting him."

"Good luck with that." Her expression softened. "In the papers," she said carefully, "they said Markos was engaged to marry the Archon of Eryth's daughter. What happened between the two of you?"

"I don't want to talk about it," I snapped, tightening my grip on the wheel. After a moment, I relented. "He wanted to turn down the marriage because of me. He was going to throw away his throne—his country—everything. You know how Markos is always so noble and stupid. He wasn't thinking straight. I decided to make the choice for him." My throat tightened. "So he wouldn't have to."

Kenté's face fell. "Oh, Caro. Are . . ." She hesitated. "Are you still in love with him?"

"When did everything get so complicated? Back on *Cormorant* with Pa, my life made sense. Now everything's a mess." My voice cracked. "How am I supposed to know if I'm in love with him, let alone the kind of love worth defying the gods for? When I don't even know who I am anymore."

She squeezed me in a warm hug, our damp clothes sticking together. All at once I felt sorry for yelling at her earlier. Having Kenté here was like getting a little piece of myself back.

She let me go and sat cross-legged on the bench, a ball of blue-tinted light appearing in her palm. Clearly she'd learned a pocketful of new tricks at the Academy.

"How are you doing that?" I asked. "Aren't you only able to manipulate the dark? And sleep," I added. "Night stuff."

"I'm not *making* the light," she said, nodding up at the moon. "I'm only pushing the darkness away from the light that's already there."

I didn't know enough about the nuances of shadow magic to understand the difference. "I never got a chance to answer your letter. How are things going at the Academy? Did you find out about the Lady Dressed in Blood?"

"I know a little more. For starters, her real name is Melaine Chrysanthe."

"I knew that," I said. "Antidoros Peregrine told me."

"She's the Emparch's—" Kenté shook her head. "Sorry. It's just out of habit—everyone in Trikkaia calls him that. She's Konto Theucinian's mistress. It's rumored they may even have children together. She's said to have had five husbands who all died early deaths." She waggled her eyebrows dramatically. "*Mysterious* deaths. And there are stories circulating in the capital that last month a prominent minister in Markos's father's cabinet, who refused to support Theucinian's claim to the throne, died the very day after a banquet at the palace. A banquet *she* attended."

"And Theucinian has sent her after Markos."

She spun her ball of light. "That's what the headmaster's visitor said, but . . . it doesn't fit, does it?"

"What do you mean?"

"She murders men by seducing them," Kenté reminded me. "But she's twenty years older than Markos. He's not likely to fall for that." She grabbed my sleeve. "This girl Agnes . . . you definitely saw her, right? Is it possible she's the Lady Dressed in Blood, in disguise?"

I shook my head. "She's not very nice . . . but she's our age."

I suspected Agnes had her own reasons for marrying Markos, ones that had nothing to do with the Akhaian succession. *Markos Andela is my only hope of finally pleasing my father.* I couldn't blame her for wanting that. I did, however, blame her for casually leaving me to my death.

"Well, then." Kenté released my arm. "Perhaps the Lady plans to infiltrate Lord Peregrine's household somehow. Sneak poison into their food."

Chewing my lip, I watched bubbles slip by on the surface of the sea, illuminated by my cousin's circle of light. Her words made me uneasy. There was no way of knowing what the Lady Dressed in Blood was plotting. Someone *had* tried to poison Markos. But the kitchen staff swore they'd seen a man . . . If only I was by Markos's side, where I could protect him.

Kenté and I chatted for several hours before agreeing to take shifts sailing the *Steed*. It was past midnight when I climbed belowdecks to catch a few hours' sleep. I was surprised to find Melanos still awake, slumped at the table. He stared moodily at the wall, spinning the whiskey bottle in a circle.

Gathering my courage, I faced him. "I want to ask you something."

He only grunted.

"Before, when you came back for me, I admit I couldn't believe it." I hesitated. "You sounded almost like you cared."

He waved a hand dismissively, but not before I caught a guilty glint in his eye. "Of course I care. I thought you might be dead."

Tonight I'd witnessed a woman transforming into a whale and a girl holding light where there should have been none, but this was even stranger. The Black Dogs had been disbanded and most of them arrested. I'd stolen this man's ship. Destroyed his life. What reason did Diric Melanos have to care if I was dead? Furthermore, why hadn't he put a bullet in me himself?

"What," I said slowly, "aren't you telling me?"

"Confound you, girl." His fingers twitched around the bottle. "Let me drink in peace."

"No." Seizing the whiskey, I pulled it away from him. "You're helping me for a reason. On the island you said it was because you were sick of talking to yourself. Fine. But you could have easily taken the ship and left me behind in Brizos. You didn't. I want to know why."

A long moment passed.

"The only reason that matters." His voice was so low I could barely hear him. "You're my only hope, Caro Oresteia."

My mouth went dry. "Of what?"

"Of getting it all back." He tipped the chair, resting his head against the wall. "It was no one's fault but my own. Knew what she was like, I did. Fickle. She likes her sparkly new baubles." He glanced at me, resentment in his eyes. "Her shiny treasures. She warned me not to lay a hand on you, but I was arrogant. You see, I was so close. So near to everything I wanted, I could almost taste it. All I needed to do was kill that boy and his sister."

You must be the wherry girl, he'd said when we first met in Casteria, *that I keep hearing so much about.* I had assumed he meant from folks in the riverlands. But he was talking about the god.

Diric Melanos had once been chosen by the sea god too. And been banished because of me.

The truth flooded in. Now I knew why he hadn't killed me on the island when he'd had the chance. This whole time Melanos had believed that by helping me, he could somehow redeem himself with the sea god. I almost snorted. Fat chance of that, when she hated me just as much as she hated—

Then I realized. *He didn't know.*

My pulse pounded in my ears. She who lies beneath had marooned me on that island to punish me for my defiance. But he didn't know that. And I couldn't let him find out. My palms grew clammy on the bottle.

"Captain Melanos—" I began, hoping he hadn't noticed my hesitation.

He rolled his eyes. "You might as well call me Diric, girl."

"Diric." The name felt strange on my lips. I slid the whiskey bottle across the table. "Thank you for the food. And the blankets. And—thanks for coming back for me."

His only reply was to rummage in his pocket. Tossing a bag of ammunition at me, he said gruffly, "For you, girl. *If* you can manage to overlook where it came from."

Likely he'd stolen it along with the provisions, but I took it without comment. I guessed this meant we were trusting each other now.

That night I dreamed I stood in the middle of a city street. A man strode ahead of me, hands in pockets. His long hair had been bleached by the sun, and seaweed clung to his jacket. His gait was that of a sailor accustomed to rolling with the sway of a deck. There was something familiar about him.

"Hey!" I shouted, ducking around a loaded wagon. "Wait!"

The man turned, and I caught a glimpse of a mermaid tattoo on his arm. My heart stopped.

It was Nereus. He opened his mouth to speak, but no words came out. Then his arms turned to bones and his face to a gaping skull. The word swirled around me like slimy seaweed.

Laughter.

CHAPTER
NINETEEN

I'd been to Iantiporos on hundreds of cargo runs with Pa and Fee, but this time was different.

Peering over the railing, nothing about the view seemed familiar. On *Cormorant*, we used to approach the city from the west by sailing across Nemertes Water, a brackish bay surrounded by flat wetlands. By contrast, the sea approach displayed majestic cliffs with white breakers crashing at their feet. I glimpsed high on a hill the imposing facade of the senate building, which folks called one of the wonders of the modern world.

On my signal, Kenté dropped the mainsail, while Diric steered the *Busted Steed* into an empty berth. "Make fast the mooring warps," he ordered.

I scrambled over the rail, rope in hand. Twisting it into a

bowline knot, I looped it around a post. For the first time it occurred to me that we'd never discussed who was captain of the *Steed*. I guess I'd stepped back into the first-mate position out of habit.

Turning toward the city, I inhaled deeply. The smells of salt, tar, bilge water, and wet rope were the same in every port. But this was Kynthessa, my country. A homesick pang hit me as I caught a whiff of muddy marsh grass. Across from the dock was a frogman tavern, the Sailor's Leap. I'd visited it more than once with Fee. As I watched, two frogmen pushed through the swinging door, chirping in their own language.

I craned my neck to look down the docks. Behind the big seagoing ships, a cluster of wherry masts poked up. Little blobs atop the masts indicated wooden windmills, but they were too far away for me to distinguish, nor could I read the painted names.

My heart swelled with longing. What if Pa and Fee were over there? Or Thisbe Brixton or Captain Krantor on *Jolly Girl*. The Oresteias had been sailing the riverlands for eight generations. The wherrymen were like a family to me.

Tears welled up in my eyes. *Home.*

Abruptly I turned away from the wherries. It was a foolish dream. The sea had disowned me, but I didn't belong to the river either. I didn't know where I belonged.

After the sails were properly lowered and stowed, Diric opened the chest of stolen coins. "We can't afford new canvas, nor have we the time. But we can at least replace some of these rotten ropes." Several coins disappeared into the pocket of his battered coat. "I'll see about arranging for provisions."

"I'll go buy the ropes," I offered.

He flipped me a silver talent. "While you're at it, get some clothes that fit." He gestured at my tattered shirt and stolen boots. "Girl clothes. And, I don't know, take a bath."

Looking him up and down, I grinned. "*You* take a bath."

"Bah," he muttered, waving a hand at me.

Kenté and I set off down the gangplank. As we passed each dock, I peered curiously down the rows at the ships. Square-rigged merchanters waited in their berths as cargo was rolled aboard. I couldn't imagine what it would be like to sail on an enormous ship like that, with three masts and a crew of forty. The pennants atop the masts were varied—I spotted the blue and green of Kynthessa, the Akhaian lion, and the yellow sun of Ndanna, among others. Farther out in the harbor, even more ships lay at anchor.

The afternoon sun beat down on the cobblestones as we turned into the crowded street. The city had the same architectural style as Valonikos, with whitewashed stucco buildings and tiled roofs. But the houses here were more spread out and the city was greener, with sculpted trees lining the streets. We took our time poking our noses into different shops. I purchased a new shirt and trousers, plus a fine wool dress and corset I daresay even my mother would've approved of. Eyeing the rows of shiny leather boots, I sighed, wishing I could afford them. The bundle of new rope I paid for with the last of my money, tossing a coin to the boy in the store, who would deliver it to the *Steed*.

Leaving the shops, Kenté and I wandered deeper into the city. Down the alleys, I caught tantalizing glimpses of ornate courtyards and gardens. Although it was a port city, there was something sedate and orderly about Iantiporos. Blue uniformed watchmen stood on the corners, muskets on their shoulders.

You never quite forgot this was the Margravina's city, because she didn't want you to forget.

On the next block we came upon a sprawling marble building, resplendent with columns. Matching classical statues of a woman under a fountain, water pooling around her bare feet, stood on either side of the door.

"Baths," I breathed.

One half of the public bathhouse was dedicated for women's use. An attendant clad in an old-fashioned toga stood beside a potted palm tree. Kenté put a coin in her basket, and she passed us scented towels.

As we pushed through the door into the baths, a wave of hot steam hit my face. The women lounging in the bathhouse in varying states of undress had skin ranging from deep brown to olive to north Akhaian pale. I would always love the riverlands, where I'd grown up, but I had to admit I enjoyed the more diverse population of the port cities. It was easier to be anonymous here, where no one looked askance at me, trying to puzzle out my parentage.

We walked barefoot across the slippery marble floor, between pools bordered with blue patterned tiles. Leafy potted plants surrounded the baths, and murmured conversation echoed off the low ceiling, along with the music of trickling fountains. There were people who found the steam of the public baths stifling and the incense sneeze inducing. To me, after weeks shipwrecked on that island and locked in the brig, this was paradise.

Shedding my ragged clothes, I sank into the bath. For a long time I floated in a blissful place between sleep and wakefulness, enjoying the feel of clean water caressing my skin.

Kenté set her chin on the edge of the pool, playing with the heap of necklaces and hairpins she'd removed from her person. One bracelet consisted entirely of brass buttons, and from another dangled a row of lockets in different geometric shapes.

"Do they all do something?" I asked.

"The lockets are just for storing shadow magic. But the others . . . well, I've been tinkering with illusions. Face changing, disguises, and the like. I've even succeeded in making an illusion of death." The chains jingled under her fingers. "Any of these three charms will give you lovely dreams." She gave me a knowing look. "I noticed you kept tossing around last night."

"I slept fine," I snapped. I was hesitant to talk about Nereus's appearance in my dream.

"Try one tonight and report back to me," she said, ignoring my testy remark. "I can always use ideas for improvement." She plucked a charm out of the stack with a lopsided smile. "Oh, but not this one though. That's about Julius—it's private."

I grinned, seizing on her embarrassment. "Who's Julius?"

"Someone who is none of your business, Caro." She sighed, sinking deeper into the water. "He has the most velvety brown eyes."

I leaned my head on the ledge. A swirling oily film lay over the water. It smelled of something decadent and floral—lilies, maybe. "Do you like the Academy?"

"I do, although I wish it wasn't in the Akhaian capital." She wrinkled her nose, the gold stud glinting in the candlelight. "I have *opinions* on the Theucinian Emparchy, and sometimes it's hard to bite my tongue when people talk about politics."

"You don't think you're in any danger, do you?" I lifted my head. "I mean, because you're related to me?"

"I'm not *that* related to you," she said, which was technically true. We were distant cousins.

"True, but everyone knows my mother is a Bollard," I pointed out.

"But they don't know I helped rescue Markos and Daria. Who would tell them? Most of the Black Dogs were hanged, Cleandros is dead, and Diric Melanos was presumed to be dead." She made a slow circle in the water with her fingertip, the ripples reflected in her eyes. "Still, I'm careful with my letters. I only send them with people I trust."

"Have your parents softened any?" I asked. "About the Academy?"

Kenté had once been terrified to tell her parents about her shadow magic, for fear of their disapproval. There were certain expectations for those of us born into the Bollard family, and unfortunately they centered around trade agreements, not enchanted hairpins.

She smiled. "Let's just say they've come to understand how a shadowman might prove useful to Bollard Company."

It made sense. The Bollards traded in information as well as wine, tea, and silks. A shadowman could become invisible or use an illusion to take on a different face. As a spy Kenté could be invaluable to the family.

"Is that all you want to do with your magic?" I winced at my choice of words. Unlike me, Kenté had grown up within the walls of Bollard House, and her loyalty to it was stronger than mine. "I didn't mean *all*," I said hastily. "I just meant—"

Briskly she shook her head. "I have my own ideas about how I plan to serve the god of the night. Plans which don't involve shipping contracts." She glanced guiltily around the bathhouse. "Ugh. I hope there aren't any other Bollards in here, I'll feel bad." She went on. "I'm willing to play along for the moment though. For one thing, now that my parents have given their approval, I've suddenly found myself in possession of a great deal of pocket money."

This talk of the Bollards reminded me that my parents still thought I was dead. "Bollard Company has an office here, don't we? Where is it?"

"Wharf Street," Kenté said right away. "By the harbor. On the other end, where the big ships and barges dock."

Captain Jacari Bollard's explorations had brought him great fame. Since his day, Bollard Company had only continued to grow until it was the largest trading company in Kynthessa, boasting hundreds of ships. The family had offices in nearly every port, although most of their business was conducted from the main branch in Siscema.

"We should go there straight away," I decided. "They can send a message to Ma, and while I'm there I can leave a letter for Pa. He stops here every couple of weeks. They'll know how to find him."

Kenté rose, dripping, from the bath. Wrapping herself in

towels, she sat cross-legged behind me on the floor and lifted a clump of my hair. Formerly a cloud of reddish-brown corkscrew curls, it hung in a tangle, the result of overexposure to sun and salt water. And also, I reflected, not being combed for weeks.

"We need to do something about this," she said. After helping me wash my hair, she expertly combed oils through my curls and began to braid them into a thick plait. "Your hair is too dry," she lectured me. "And full of knots."

"Deserted island," I reminded her.

I closed my eyes and leaned back, a smile curling across my face. I'd missed my cousin doing my hair. It was a pleasant, homey luxury I'd never expected to enjoy again. Kenté's fingers tugged a resistant chunk of hair into the braid, causing me to wince. Maybe I hadn't missed her *that* much.

As we left the bathhouse, I felt loose-limbed and relaxed. I was dressed in my new shirt and trousers, the rest of my purchases tucked under my arm. My old clothes I'd asked the bath attendant to throw out. Good riddance to them. I never wanted to see those rags again.

Descending the steps, we walked straight into a knot of people clustered on the sidewalk. The crowd buzzed with anticipation, standing on tiptoe to see over everyone else's shoulders.

Someone pointed at an elegant carriage. "That's him coming!"

"What's going on?" I asked a brown-skinned woman in a scholar's cap.

"They're saying it's the young Emparch in that carriage." She pointed up the street. "The Pretender, some call him now. Folk say he's here to beg the Margravina for help." Nodding at a nearby clock tower, she added, "Just in time too. The Margravina closes the castle gates at six."

My heart flipped over in my chest. I turned away, unable to stammer a reply. Waves of shock thumped through my body. Markos was *here*?

Behind us two girls giggled. "I heard she was lost at sea."

"That's not what really happened," the other one said. "*I* heard she drowned herself when she found out he'd sworn to marry another."

"*And* he fights to avenge his family." The first girl sighed. "It's all so romantic and tragic."

My face flushed hot. They were talking about me. I balled my hands into fists.

Kenté held on to my sleeve, restraining me from turning. "Don't," she whispered. "It's gossip, that's all. It isn't their fault."

The carriage rolled closer, the horses' hooves clopping sharply on the cobblestones. The seal of Kynthessa, a shield of green and blue divided by a winding river and crested by two crossed swords, was painted on the door. I held my breath as the carriage drew even with us. I could almost see inside . . .

It was him. I recognized the familiar outline of his profile as he sat stiffly on the seat.

"Markos!" I gasped.

I shoved desperately through the crowd, dodging elbows and curses. By the time I'd pushed my way to the front, the carriage had rolled on, changing the angle so the curtains obscured his face. But there was someone else on the opposite seat, facing backward. A girl, hands folded demurely in her lap.

Agnes.

I knew she'd spotted me from the way her eyes widened. She lifted her chin and smirked at me. The carriage rattled up the street toward the Margravina's castle, hiding them both behind the velvet curtains. I struggled to follow it, but the street was crowded and it was like swimming against the current. My heart tumbled into the bottom of my feet, all my hopes crashing down. After all this time, to be *so* close to him . . .

Kenté caught my sleeve. "Was that her? Was that Agnes?"

I could only nod. Helplessly I watched the roof of the carriage as it bobbed up the hill and out of sight.

"Well, that's a good thing, isn't it?" She raised her voice over the murmuring crowd. "It means he knows you're alive."

"No," I whispered. "I don't think he does."

The crowd had begun to disperse. Kenté set her hand on my shoulder. I knew she only meant to comfort me, but I shook her off. Pushing my bundle of clothing into her arms, I broke into a run. There was no hope of catching up with the carriage, not on foot, but I knew where they were headed.

The Margravina's castle was built into the side of the hill, the spire of the tallest tower barely visible above the roofs of the lower city. I pounded through the streets, dodging uneven cobbles and slow pedestrians. My boots were the wrong size and I wasn't accustomed to running. Wincing, I pressed my hand against the sharp stitch in my side. I only knew I had to get to Markos.

The castle was separated from the city by a roofed bridge, decorated with marble columns. Guards were stationed at the entrance to the bridge, standing like toy soldiers with swords resting on the shoulders of their uniform coats. The carriage must have already crossed, because it was nowhere to be seen.

Frantically I raced up to the nearest man. "Did a carriage come this way?" I gasped. My heartbeat raged hot in my ears. "Markos Andela's carriage? I *need* to see him. Right away."

Something cold touched my hand.

"Steady, sailor." The other guard tapped me gently with the flat of his sword. "You can't just come barging in here."

"You don't understand," I pleaded. "He knows me. But he thinks I'm dead. Can you at least give him a message for me? It's *important.*"

Pelting through the streets had completely undone the effects of my bath. Sweat dripped down my neck and a curl of hair had escaped my braid to bob in my eyes. In my trousers and hand-me-down boots, the guards probably thought I was a ship's girl or an apprentice, too young to be taken seriously.

"I'm Caro Oresteia," I tried again. "Please, tell him that name. He knows me. The Margravina knows me." Which was stretching the truth, to say the least, but I had to try. "She once gave me a letter of marque."

The guard's lip twitched as he tried not to laugh. He exchanged amused glances with his friend. "Very well," he said, extending his hand. "Give me this letter of marque."

"I—I don't have it anymore." I swallowed, humiliation

washing over me. Why had I ever thought this would work? Of course I couldn't just walk into the Margravina's palace. I was a nobody. If only Kenté was here—maybe then we could use shadow magic to sneak past the guards. But glancing over my shoulder, I realized she wasn't coming. I must have lost her in my hurry to chase the carriage.

Defeated, I turned and walked away. Behind me I heard the guards' snorts of laughter, and my cheeks grew even hotter.

I'd found Markos. But I had no way of getting to him.

The walk back took much longer, what with my too-large boots and aching muscles. *Wharf Street, where the big ships and barges dock.* That's where Kenté had said Bollard Company was located. As I limped in that direction, I only hoped she would have the good sense to also head there if we got separated.

This was the plan, I reminded myself as I trudged down the hill. This was what Markos was supposed to do. Marry Agnes. Get an army. Become Emparch. Nothing had changed.

Tears stung my eyes. Except *everything* had changed. I'd nearly drowned in a shipwreck, been tossed in a brig, and had cannonballs shot at me by the Lion Fleet. Life was precious. For so many weeks, I'd thought I would never see Markos again, and now that he was here—

"Caro!" Kenté gasped, jogging up to me in the street. Sheepishly I realized I'd abandoned her with all the packages from our earlier shopping. Hanging onto my shoulder, she tried to catch her breath. "You're—too gods-damned fast. You ran off and left me with all this stuff. Did—did you find him?"

I shook my head. "They wouldn't let me in." My eyes focused on her heap of necklaces. Shadow magic didn't work in the daytime, but that was what Kenté's lockets were for. They had shadows stored inside. "You've got to have something that can help us get into the castle."

A loud voice cursed at us, and we jumped onto the sidewalk just in time to avoid being hit by a wagon full of sacks. Somewhere a bell tolled, ringing out a somber rhythm.

"I do, but . . ."

"What?" I demanded.

"The bells," she said, nodding at the distant clock tower. I remembered what the scholar had told us about the castle gates being closed. The bell was tolling out the time. Six o'clock had just come and gone. Even a shadowman could not pass through a locked gate.

Somthing hit my chest with a *thunk*, causing me to stumble.

I whipped my head up.

A man stood at the entrance to a nearby alley, his face hidden by a black hood. Lowering a miniature crossbow, he turned and ran. His cloak fluttered behind him.

A tiny dart was lodged in the leather gun strap I wore across my chest. It hovered, feathers still quivering, just above my heart.

"What's this?" Kenté started to pull it out.

"Don't touch it!" I grabbed her hand. "It's probably poisoned."

With a muffled squeak, she dropped the dart to the cobblestones. "I should've realized that," she admitted, kicking it into the gutter with the toe of her shoe.

I took out my bag of shot and loaded my pistol.

"Caro!" Kenté seized my arm. "You can't go running around the streets of Iantiporos with a gun!"

"Xanto's balls," I swore, taking off down the alley. "I don't care. Someone just tried to murder me."

"Will you wait a second?" she panted. "You're going to get yourself killed. Or arrested." Removing one of her lockets, she threw it to the ground. It burst open on the cobblestones, and she immediately vanished.

I glanced down to see my ill-fitting boots disappear into the shadows. Strangely the magic didn't feel like anything. Somehow I'd expected it to be cold, like someone pouring a bucket of water over me. I swallowed, averting my eyes. It was disconcerting, having no body.

Splashing down the muddy alley, we emerged in a busy street. I scanned the crowd for that dark rippling cloak and spotted it a block away, fluttering around a corner.

"There!" I gasped.

We followed the would-be assassin to a row of connected buildings. One was a fancy hotel, judging from the rectangular placard and the uniformed doorman. The house next door was equally ornate, with white columns and scrollwork around the windows. Its grandeur was somewhat diminished by curling paint and an overgrown front garden. The first floor windows were boarded up, and a sign in front read, To Let.

The man in the cloak glanced over his shoulder to make sure the doorman was looking the other way, and then hopped the fence. He stalked across the garden and ducked between the boards, disappearing into the unoccupied house.

"Some kind of hideout," I guessed. We waited for several minutes, but he didn't reappear.

I couldn't see Kenté, but I felt her behind me. "Should we follow him?" she asked.

I tried to think. "No," I decided reluctantly. "We don't know who he is or if there are more of them. We could be walking into a trap."

The sound of a door closing made me look up. But it was only a woman in a red and gold brocade dress, a veil obscuring her hair and face, descending the stairs of the hotel next door. Stepping into the street, she raised a gloved hand to hail a carriage.

I turned back to the house, studying the barricaded windows. "Someone knows I'm not dead," I murmured.

Kenté's voice was sober in my ear. "Someone, I think, who very much wishes you'd stayed that way."

CHAPTER
TWENTY

After the mysterious attack, we recovered in a restaurant overlooking the harbor. Kenté ordered dinner and a bottle of wine, while I slumped in my chair, staring sullenly at the floor. I didn't care about eating. A shameful part of me wished we hadn't come here at all. I just wanted to hide in the *Steed*'s moldy cargo hold and succumb to tears.

Kenté set a reassuring hand on my arm. "Caro, it'll be all right."

I refused to be calmed down. "But he's going to *marry* her!"

She dipped a spoon in her shrimp stew. "Of course he is. Wasn't that the whole idea? Especially now that he thinks you drowned, why on earth wouldn't he marry her?"

Methodically I tore up my bread, wadding it into little balls and tossing them in a puddle of olive oil. "You're supposed to be on my side."

We sat at a table for two next to a row of potted cypress trees. To the left a cobbled alley led downhill, where the tiled roofs of Iantiporos were spread out like a lady's skirts. The garden of the restaurant was festooned with hanging lanterns, their patterned sides casting lacy shadows on the pavement. The food should have been a welcome piece of home—seafood stew, eels on toast, and fried fish with a seasoned dipping sauce.

It all tasted like ashes in my mouth.

Kenté swiped a discarded newspaper off a nearby table, flattening out the wrinkles. The ink was smudged by fingerprints and food stains.

"I can't believe I'm having hysterics," I said, "and you're sitting there reading the paper."

She skimmed the first page, and flipped to the next. "Caro, you've never had hysterics in your life."

I kicked the table leg. "I might start."

"No, you won't. Oh!" She jabbed her finger on an article near the bottom of the page. "Here's a bit about you . . . well, sort of." The type was so cramped I couldn't have read it even if it wasn't upside down. "It seems the Penniless Emparch has found love again," she read aloud, "after the intrepid girl privateer known as the Rose of the Coast drowned in a shipwreck, putting a tragic end to the star-crossed romance that has captivated readers since—"

"Gods damn it!" I exploded. "I *told* you. I told you she had no intention of telling him I'm not dead."

"It's possible," Kenté observed around a mouthful of food, "you might have some unresolved feelings."

"I wouldn't mind so much if he wasn't marrying *her*! It's just—she's—she's awful!" I spluttered. "She left me to be hanged!"

"No." My cousin pointed at me. "That's not what your feelings are about."

She was right.

I swallowed. "I messed up." My voice came out small and choked. Now that Markos was here, so infuriatingly close, I realized the enormity of what I'd done. "I really messed up. And it might be too late to fix it."

Kenté pushed her empty plate away. "So I guess we're doing this."

I looked up at her. "Doing what?"

She laid a finger next to her nose, her old sign for secrets and mischief, and grinned. "Breaking into the Margravina's castle."

I did not deserve my cousin. Who had sailed miles and miles across the sea to find me. Who cheerfully ignored all my sarcastic moods. And who would break into the most heavily guarded castle in the country just because she thought it would make me happy.

My voice wobbled. "Really?"

"Of course, really." Standing, Kenté tossed a pile of coins on the table. "We'll do it first thing tomorrow when the gates open. Come on, let's go."

The sun was setting behind the spires of the Margravina's castle, turning the sky golden, by the time we made it back to the *Busted Steed*.

"Where have you been all day?" Diric demanded. I started to

explain how we'd seen Markos, but he interrupted. "I don't care about your bedamned love life. I thought you was going to help me fix the rigging."

I glanced at the hammer and nails scattered around. Bright new planks covered the hole in the deck. I'd half expected him to be in a tavern somewhere, but Diric had already begun repairs on the *Steed*. Coils of stiff yellow rope were stacked on the deck. The boy from the shop must have delivered it.

"Well, I bought the rope anyway," I said with a guilty shrug.

"Ayah," Diric muttered. "At least you managed that, but it's almost dark. You was off fussing over your Emparch, and now it's too late to get any work done."

"I don't *care* about this stupid ship!" My frustration spilled over. "Not when Markos is here." My throat ached. "You wouldn't understand."

"I understand enough," he said. "I thought you was a captain and a buccaneer, but you're just a silly girl."

I opened my mouth to deny it, but a flicker of motion over Diric's shoulder halted me.

On the dock a sailor ambled between the ships, hands in pockets. A mermaid's tail curled around his arm.

Shock rippled through me. It was exactly like my dream, except this time I *knew* I was awake.

Nereus.

"Hey!" I yelled, racing to the rail. He didn't turn.

"Caro, what is it?" Kenté asked behind me, but I didn't have time to explain.

Vaulting over the rail, I took off down the dock. As I shoved through the sailors, I struggled to keep Nereus in my sight. First he went right, then left, dipping behind clumps of people and stacks of barrels. The faint smell of seaweed wafted over the crowd.

Blinking, I came to an abrupt stop.

Nereus had disappeared, but in his place a girl bustled down the dock, swearing as she kicked her skirts out of the way. She lugged a basket of sandwiches, and under her arm she carried a bundle of maps. As she turned, I got a good look at her face.

"Docia!" I shouted, breaking into a run. "Docia Argyrus!"

Her eyes widened. "Caro!" Her basket tumbled to the dock, and she encased me in a warm hug that smelled like salt and damp cotton. "We heard *Vix* went down with all hands off Four Mile Rock. Where have you *been*?"

I decided to leave out the part where I'd been captured by the Lion Fleet and committed an act of piracy. "I was lucky," I told her. "I got washed up on an island, and I've been working my way back ever since."

"Oh, Caro," she said. "I'm truly sorry. About *Vix*."

I hesitated. "I was thinking . . . perhaps she might be salvaged."

Doubt flickered across Docia's face. "It would be possible," she said cautiously. "Maybe. But . . . the expense . . . Well, a salvage job like that costs a lot." She didn't sound very hopeful.

"Whatever are you doing in Iantiporos?" I asked, shoving away images of *Vix*'s sails waving forlornly underwater while fish darted in and out of the wreck.

Blowing a hank of dark hair out of her eyes, she bent to gather

her basket. "I'm here on a job." She nodded down the dock. I recognized her family's salvage barge, the *Catfish*. Her two older brothers were laughing as they raised the sails. "We be heading up Nemertes Water to scout a wreck."

My gaze dropped to her basket. "Sandwiches?"

She pressed her lips in a line. "It's better than staying home in Valonikos." Looking past me, her expression changed. "That's Diric Melanos." Her lips flattened with disgust. "Recognize him from his poster. I thought he was supposed to be dead."

I glanced over my shoulder. Diric had followed me, with Kenté a few steps behind him. I realized I'd jumped overboard and taken off without a word of warning.

"It's all right," I told Docia. "He's with me."

"With *you*?" Her voice was incredulous. "Weren't he the one who tried to murder you?"

"It's a long story—" I began, but she cut me off.

"Have you forgotten the wherries he burned?" she demanded. "Because I haven't. I worked that job with my father. Some of those people lost everything." She shook her head, disappointment clouding her face. "How could you?"

"He helped me escape from—it's *really* a long story." I shifted uncomfortably, aware that it just sounded like an excuse. But the sight of Diric had reminded me about the map.

If it was real, surely Docia would know.

Excitement mounting, I turned to Diric. "This is Docia Argyrus," I explained. "She's a salvager and an expert on the *Centurion*. There's a good bet she knows something we don't. Show her the map."

I saw the distrust in his eyes. But he shrugged, pulling the map from inside his coat.

Docia cast a pitying look at me. "What's this about the *Centurion*? He's been telling you a pack of lies, Caro. I thought you was smarter than this."

Heart pounding, I passed the map to Docia. "Diric's great-great-grandfather claimed he found the wreck. This is a map to where he hid the treasure." I waited a beat while she examined the drawing. "Well, what do you think?"

She pursed her lips. "This is a fish story. No latitude or longitude." With an incredulous snort, she waved at the map. "No reference points of any kind. Nothing but a piece of trash." She focused her eyes on Diric. "Just like him."

I gestured to Diric. "Show her the coin!"

His expression was dubious, but he brought out the lumpy gold piece and flipped it to me.

I caught the coin, presenting it to Docia. "Well?"

She looked back at the *Catfish*. "Caro, I have to go."

"Will you just look at it?" I pressed the coin into her hand.

Sighing, she turned it over. "Can't be sure without my books." She stroked the gold piece, running her thumb over the bumpy decoration on its face. When she glanced up at me, her eyes were wide. "Hang on, this might be genuine. See the marking here, on the back." Her words came out faster and faster. "See, these antique gold talents was minted by hand. That's why the edges are so rough. It's the right era—look how the lion on the seal is different. As for the gold, you could get an alchemist to test it."

"Docia!" her brother hollered. "Hurry up! We can't sail without our dinner."

Her gaze lingering on the gold piece, she gave it back to me. "Coming!" she yelled.

"Just one more minute," I pleaded. "Did they ever find something—anything—from the *Centurion*? Some kind of clue to figure out where she went down?" I remembered that day in the office. "What about your map you were making? With the tides?"

She sighed. "Ain't I been trying to puzzle out that mystery for years. There's one thing though," she said. "They recovered the ship's log. What I wouldn't give to get my hands on that."

"How'd they find the log?" I asked. "Wouldn't it have gone down with the ship?"

Docia adjusted her basket of sandwiches. "When the frigate went down, they had time to launch the captain's gig. The bodies of the captain and the first mate were found, months later, drifting in the middle of the sea. They was only skeletons by then."

I made a face at the gruesome image. "What happened to the log?"

Docia shrugged. "Well, it were taken to the Royal Library in Trikkaia—"

Shaking her head, Kenté spoke up for the first time. "Which will be crawling with Theucinians."

"—Where it stayed for a hundred years," Docia continued. "Before it got sold to a private collector."

"Who?" Diric asked. "Where is it, girl?"

She shot him a nasty look. "Don't matter. You won't be able to get near it. It's said Dido Brilliante's headquarters is nearly impregnable. They call her the—"

"The Pirate Queen," Diric finished.

My neck tingled with excitement. The *Centurion*'s log was in Brizos. We'd been right there, and we hadn't even known.

Docia was still glaring at Diric. "What did he promise you, Caro? Half of the treasure?" She spat on the dock. "A likely story. He'll only put a bullet in your back."

"It's not like that," I protested. "You don't understand."

"I understand that those wherrymen he murdered were your friends," she said. "And you're betraying their memories for gold. For a wild goose chase."

Whirling, Docia turned her back on me. I watched her run to the *Catfish*, handing up the basket of sandwiches. Her harsh words had stunned me momentarily, but now guilt rushed in. She was right, wasn't she? Diric Melanos had killed those wherrymen. He'd killed Markos's *mother*. Why had I defended him?

What was I even doing here?

CHAPTER
TWENTY-ONE

That night, in the lamplit cabin of the *Busted Steed*, Diric was as animated as I'd ever seen him. Humming a bawdy tune, he unrolled a chart on the table. It depicted Brizos and the surrounding islands.

Looking around, I realized how busy he'd been today. On the way to Iantiporos, we'd pumped the cabin free of nasty-smelling water. Now that it had been aired out, it was much more pleasant. The bare wooden bunks were lined with the blankets Diric had stolen in Brizos. But while Kenté and I were gone, more amenities had appeared. Fresh food and dishes lined the shelves. I even caught a whiff of coffee. The water jar had been refilled with fresh water, and there was a small collection of medical supplies on the sideboard. The *Busted Steed* almost looked capable of tackling a sea voyage.

Diric uncorked a bottle of rum and sloshed it into a mug.

"A drink for me." His scarred face lighting up in a grin, he poured another mug. "And one for Miss Bollard." With a flourish, he poured a third. "And one for Caro—" He noticed I wasn't smiling. "What's wrong with you, girlie? Time for a toast—to gold and glory!"

"I'm not going back to Brizos."

Spluttering, he lowered the bottle. "What?"

"Markos is here," I said, steeling myself. "Telling him to marry Agnes was a mistake." My voice wobbled. "I was falling in love with him, and I threw it away."

Seeing him today had made everything magically become clear to me. I didn't even care if Markos and I were impossible anymore. I just wanted him back.

"Do I understand you rightly, then?" Diric took a gulp of rum, slamming his mug down. "You're forfeiting your half of the treasure. A chance at getting your ship back. All because of this *boy*."

Kenté watched me across the table. Light glinted on her nose ring, but she said nothing.

I lifted my chin. "Yes."

"But now you *know* the gold is real, gods damn it."

"I know." I swallowed. "And I won't blame you for going after it without me. The Queen's hideout is impregnable, ayah, but we both know she isn't there." For the first time since that night, I remembered Dido Brilliante had given me the password to her headquarters. I doubted Diric would need it. There was likely no one left to tell it to. "You do what you have to do. But me, I have to stay."

"Now see here." Diric's voice was unsteady, but I couldn't tell if it was rum or emotion. "We talked about this. You was going to get half the gold from the *Centurion* and use it to win your boy's throne back. Make things right between me and the gods."

"You murdered the Emparchess!" I jumped to my feet, shoving my chair back. "Even if you help Markos become Emparch, he'll never forgive you for that. *Never.* And nor will the gods. No amount of gold can ever make up for the horrible things you've done."

"You can't just walk away," he said roughly. "I *have* to help you."

For some gods-damned reason, he had fixed all his hopes on me. Well, I didn't want them. I didn't want any of this.

"I'm not your redemption, Diric Melanos," I spat. "Ayah, you can help me, all right. By sailing far, far away and never returning."

Turning my back on him, I climbed the ladder to the deck.

⁓

The next morning dawned overcast, with thick gray clouds threatening rain. Unfolding the paper package, I shook out the dress I'd purchased yesterday. Made of fine wool cloth, with a striped panel and ribboned half sleeves, it had a low-cut bodice trimmed in lace. It was exactly the kind of dress my mother always wanted me to wear.

"Ugh," I gasped, grabbing the bunk post and sucking in my

breath as Kenté laced my stays. She wasn't being very gentle about it. "I regret this already."

She yanked on the laces. "You're going to the Margravina's castle. You can't just wear trousers and boots."

I gritted my teeth. "We'll be invisible."

"Oh, fine," she said flippantly. "Markos hasn't seen you in months, but I'm sure you'll make quite an impression if you show up looking like a street rat."

Twisting over my shoulder, I made a face at her.

After I was laced into my dress, Kenté puttered around with the coffee pot. Then she spent five minutes rearranging the dishes on the counter. From the cabin table I watched her bite her lip.

"What?" I asked finally, setting down my cup.

"Are you sure you're doing the right thing? Forsaking the treasure, that is?"

I rolled my eyes. "Don't tell me Diric Melanos has charmed you with his lovely manners and handsome face."

"Hardly," she said. "I'm not Jacky." Our other cousin had been quite enamored with the stories of the dashing captain of the Black Dogs. "But Caro, he didn't kill Markos's mother. Cleandros did. You can lay many crimes at the feet of Diric Melanos, but not that one."

"Are you sure?"

"Cleandros bragged about it to me. I suppose you never heard him." She tilted her head, reflecting. "It was after he shot you. He said nothing had given him more satisfaction than lighting that crate on fire, except killing you."

"What a nice sentiment."

If Diric had not killed the Emparchess, why hadn't he denied it? Twice I'd accused him of the crime, but he had said nothing about any of this. It didn't make sense.

Stepping from the gangplank down to the dock, I glanced over my shoulder at the *Busted Steed*. I guessed this was good-bye. She looked pathetic, with her patched canvas and sagging ropes. Turning my back, I reminded myself sternly that I didn't like that sad old bucket of a ship. Diric Melanos was welcome to her.

Even if the treasure was real, so what? He was never going to let me have half. I hadn't believed him back at Fort Reliance, and I didn't believe him now. All this talk about making things right with the gods was nonsense. He was a pirate and a murderer.

I squared my chin. I knew I was making the right choice.

"Come on," I said to Kenté. "Let's go."

A gunshot cracked the air. I threw up an arm to protect my eyes as splinters exploded in my face. Someone shrieked.

"Caro!" Kenté pounded down the dock.

I realized she was the one who'd screamed. The lead bullet had lodged in the figurehead of the ship behind me. The wooden mermaid had a gaping hole where her right eye used to be. Belatedly a wave of fear bowled me over, weakening my knees.

I grabbed my cousin's arm for support. "I'm fine," I managed.

Out of the corner of my eye, I caught movement. A figure in a dark cloak cut through the crowd on the dock, knocking over a sailor with a crate of bottles. Two bottles slipped out and shattered, splashing ale everywhere. The cloaked man leaped from the dock into the street, moving diagonally.

"Our friend from yesterday?" Kenté gasped.

"That's it," I growled, lifting my dress to my knees. "I refuse to stand around and let him take potshots at me."

Kenté grimaced. "Caro, people are staring."

I straightened, clutching my flintlock pistol. "Let them stare." My side ached from bending over in stays, but I ignored the pain. I blew an errant curl out of my face. "I'm sure they've seen a girl's legs before. Come on."

Up the street the cloaked man slipped into the crowd. Splashing through the puddle of ale, I set off in the opposite direction. It began to sprinkle, fat raindrops speckling my bare forearms.

Kenté jogged beside me. "We're not going to follow him?"

I shook my head. "When people are shooting at me, I like to know why! He's headed *away* from his hideout," I explained, dodging through the drops. "I want to see what's in there. If we hurry, we can beat him back to it."

By the time we arrived at the unoccupied house, it was raining in earnest. The menacing sound of thunder rolled across the harbor. The hotel next door was crowded. Three carriages had pulled up outside, and the drivers stood chatting on the sidewalk, collars upturned against the weather.

I ducked into the alley. "Curse it, there's too many gods-damned people outside the hotel. We can't go in the front." I ran my hands over the boarded windows. "Someone will see. There's got to be another—" My fingers snagged on a rotten board.

Gripping the wood, I yanked as hard as I could. The board came away, causing me to stumble. Tossing it to the ground, I squinted through the hole. It was too dark inside to make anything out.

Kenté fingered her necklaces. "What if he doubles back here and catches us?" She clutched my arm. "Caro, what if it isn't even the same man? What if there's more than one person trying to kill us?"

There usually was, these days.

"Keep an eye out," I whispered. "And be ready to hide us."

Flintlock cocked and loaded, I squeezed through the opening. I blinked, my eyes adjusting to the dark. Ghostly sheets lay over the furniture, and dust had settled everywhere. On the nearest wall a lighter square indicated where a painting had once hung. It had either been removed by the former occupants or stolen by trespassers. Bits of ceiling plaster had crumbled and fallen, dotting the floor.

Gesturing silently with my pistol, I nodded toward the stairs, where footprints had disturbed the dust. Careful not to touch anything, we followed the trail up the winding staircase. Halting on the second floor, I glanced down the hallway. No footprints on this floor. My hand sweated on my pistol. We continued up the stairs to the fourth floor landing, which was scuffed with boot marks. The footprints led to a small wooden door. Darting forward, Kenté slowly turned the doorknob.

The attic, like the rest of the house, appeared to be deserted. The ceiling was low and slanted, and sheet-draped objects occupied the shadowy corners. On the far side of the room, under a shuttered circular window, sat a large rectangular table. Gun trembling before me, I crept across the creaky floorboards.

A small black chest lay unbuckled and open on the table. It had three levels, each stuffed with glass tubes and tiny bottles. Some had liquids in them, while others held dried herbs. The assassin had scrawled ingredients on the labels in a black, messy hand I couldn't decipher. I lifted the closest bottle from the chest, tilting it. Dark purple liquid slid up and down.

I dropped it back in its tray, remembering the dart from yesterday. Touching this stuff could be dangerous.

Light slanted between the shutters, spilling on the cover of a water-stained notebook. In a daze I ran my fingers over the items on the table. A lump of wax. A signet ring. A stub of a pencil. Picking up the ring, I turned it over in my hand. A mountain lion's tail curled in a circle around the seal. Its eyes were tiny rubies. I'd seen this crest many times before. It was on my pistols, the ones I'd lost.

"That's the seal of the Emparch," Kenté said, unnecessarily, behind me.

My heart pounded with dread. The notebook's spine was swollen, and the paper wrinkled. When I opened it, a familiar scent wafted out of it. The smell of the ocean.

With trembling fingers, I flipped the ruined pages. The notebook was full of dates and numbers, and hastily jotted lists of—I squinted at the messy handwriting—ingredients? Recipes? The dark scrawl was nearly illegible, and in places the pencil tip had torn the page.

"Purple crown," I read. "Nightshade. Hemlock. These are all—"

"Poisons," Kenté breathed excitedly. "The Lady Dressed in Blood. Do you think it's her?"

"How can it be?" I whispered. "When she doesn't know—"

I suddenly felt too sickened to finish. *That I'm alive.* Only one person knew that.

Agnes.

But it was a man who had shot at us—wasn't it? The truth trickled through me like icy water. One of Pa's first rules of smuggling was that people always see what they expect to see. Yesterday we'd watched a cloaked figure in a man's clothes enter this house, and several minutes later we'd seen a woman in a veil come out of the hotel. I was willing to bet that if we explored this attic, we'd find the two buildings were connected. The assassin had *seemed* to be a man, but we'd never gotten a look at his face.

"Oh gods," I whispered, my mind finally catching up to what my instincts already knew. "We have to find Markos. Now."

CHAPTER
TWENTY-TWO

My grandpa Oresteia once faced down a gang of river bandits with only a knife and a frying pan, but I daresay even he wasn't bold enough to break into the Margravina's castle.

My boots splashed through the puddles as we approached the bridge. "It's the same guard who stopped me yesterday," I whispered to Kenté, hands shaking with jittery nerves. "He's going to recognize me."

The two guards had retreated to a small sheltered area, protected from the rain. One crouched, warming his hands over a fire in a grate, while the other kept watch.

Kenté pulled a jet pin from her hair. "Well, he's not going to tell anyone." She threw the pin into the guard post.

Nothing happened.

"Um." I raised my eyebrows.

The guard by the fire nodded, pitching over on the floor. Then his companion slumped, helmet falling back until it clunked against the wall. They were both snoring.

Kenté jerked her head toward the bridge. "Come on. Hopefully no one will discover them for a while, thanks to the weather."

The rain picked up, pattering on the stones with an intensity that indicated this would not be a passing shower. Lightning flashed above us, followed by a rumbling thunder roll. The bad weather suited me just fine. Yesterday there'd been guards stationed beside every column on the bridge, but today they were huddled in the shelters at either end.

"You'd better hide us now," I whispered, pulling Kenté behind a column. "We still have to get past the other gatehouse."

Wreathed in shadows, we snuck past the remainder of the guards and into a courtyard. To our right horses stomped and snuffled in the Margravina's stables. Directly ahead of us a grand door was set in the stone wall. Eyeing it warily, I tugged my cousin's hand to steer her away from it. Best to avoid the main corridors.

My instincts turned out to be correct. An unadorned entrance on the far side of the yard led to the guard barracks. The rain had confined most of the Margravina's servants to their quarters. Several uniformed men crowded around a dice game, while others shined weapons or polished their armor. Boisterous voices rang off the walls. Carefully we picked our way across the crowded room, slipping through a door at the far end.

We'd made it into the castle.

The barracks were attached to a narrow servants' corridor that ran along the left side of the castle. Finding it empty, I exhaled. From here, I guessed we had to work our way toward the center. Water trickled down my forehead. Annoyed, I wiped it away. Nothing about my clothing was appropriate for this—I had no hat or jacket, and my weapons were stuffed awkwardly in the decorative sash of my dress. My bag of lead bullets was strapped to my thigh under heavily drenched skirts, more or less inaccessible, which meant I had only one shot.

Glancing at the floor, I grimaced. We were invisible, but the puddle of water we'd left on the doormat would be obvious to anyone who was looking. I took a step forward.

A shimmery wave shuddered and broke over me.

I halted. "What was that?"

Suddenly I realized Kenté was visible again. Looking down, I saw my own dress, soaked and dripping rainwater onto the tiled floor.

"Safeguard." Kenté examined the wall beside the door, running her fingers along the paneling. "Of course. It makes sense, doesn't it?"

The things that made sense to my cousin were usually incomprehensible to normal people.

"No. What do you mean?" I dragged her behind a cabinet full of dishes. Thank the gods the corridor had been empty when we'd reappeared.

"The Margravina has had this entrance enchanted, of course," she whispered. "To prevent her home from being infiltrated by shadowmen. That was a trap we just walked through. It stripped my illusion."

"So make us invisible again," I hissed.

She pursed her lips. "I doubt it'll be any use. Where there's one trap, there's probably more of them. We'll simply have to move fast, before we're seen."

I didn't like it, but I also didn't see that we had a choice. Markos was here somewhere—with a girl who had murderous intentions. We had to find him.

The Margravina's castle was a maze of sprawling columned rooms, hung with gauzy drapes and portraits that must have been fifteen feet high. Every few minutes a servant appeared at the end of the long hallway and we were forced to duck into an alcove or dive into an empty room. I began to despair of ever finding Markos. This place was huge.

Finally we heard voices coming from a doorway up ahead.

Pressing myself against the wall, I edged closer. It was a conservatory, full of carefully manicured trees and potted flowers. Bubbling water flowed prettily from a marble lady's outstretched hands. At the base of the fountain, marble fish leaped around her feet, while below in the murky water, real orange fish darted back and forth. Birds chirped in a golden cage nearby. The great rectangular window on the opposite wall might have dazzled the room with sunlight, if it hadn't been so stormy outside. Through the window I glimpsed a hedge maze and a sculpture garden, gloomy in the rain.

In the center of the room two chairs and a sofa had been set around a tea table. Agnes perched primly in a chair, dark hair twisted into a lovely half-up, half-down style.

Seated on the sofa, his face in profile, was Markos. He lifted a blue and white teacup. Remembering the poison, my heart leaped into my throat.

"Markos Andela!" I cried, throwing my knife. It went spinning across the room and hit the cup in his hands, which exploded into a million pieces. The knife clattered to the floor. "Don't you dare drink that!"

"Ow!" Markos shook out his hand, revealing a bloody gash on his palm. "Caro?" He gaped at me like he'd seen a ghost. "Why are you throwing knives at me?" He jumped up from the sofa, shards of porcelain falling from his lap. "*Why aren't you dead?*"

For one long moment all I could do was stare at him. His hair had grown out, and he wore it pulled back. It was the style of a common man, not an Emparch, but it looked good on him. *Everything* looked good on him. He wore a new jacket made of crisp brocade, gold leaves on burgundy, over a snowy white shirt that was open at the collar. One wavy piece of hair had escaped to hang in his face, and I longed to pick it up and tuck it back.

Something moved in my peripheral vision. With a terrifying lurch, everything came back to me.

"Stop her!" I yelled, but Agnes was already halfway out the garden door. A blustery gust of rain swept in. The maid in the corner only gawked.

I lifted my pistol, but Markos blocked me. "Put the gun down! What is *wrong* with you?"

"Gods damn you, Markos," I snapped, shoving him aside. It was too late. With a whisk of skirts, Agnes disappeared.

"On it," Kenté gasped, racing out the door. Through the rain-spattered window I watched them both dash into the maze. I picked up my skirts to chase after them—

Only to be brought up short by Markos's hand gripping my wrist.

"Let go." I struggled, but he was stronger than me. "You don't understand!" My voice broke. "She's trying to murder you. The tea—it's poison!"

An imperious voice spoke from the corner chair. "Explain. Yourself."

Markos released me immediately, backing away.

The voice belonged to an old woman wearing a lace cap. I hadn't noticed her because she was so tiny her head barely reached the top of the chair. From the door she was invisible, and up until now she'd been silent.

"Oh," I said. "Sorry, ma'am. I didn't see you."

Markos made a small choking noise. "Caro, you're speaking to the Margravina of Kynthessa."

I stared, my mind suddenly blank. Ridiculously, my only thought was that I'd broken her teacup. It was quite shattered in pieces on the floor.

So this was the Margravina. She was olive-skinned and white-haired, weighed down by the heavy jewels—a sapphire necklace and earrings, in a huge old-fashioned setting—draped on her person. Markos had once told me she looked like an old bat, but her dark eyes had snap and intelligence. Something about her features and the texture of her powdered hair made me study her more closely. Blinking, I realized she was of mixed heritage, like me. It made sense—royal people married other royal people. Somewhere in her lineage there was probably a lord of Ndanna or another southern country.

"Caroline Oresteia." The Margravina studied me through her lorgnette. "Oh yes, I know about *you*." Her voice was much bigger than her size. "I gave you a letter of marque. Stealing the Black Dogs' ship and making off with their plunder was not exactly what I had in mind."

I bobbed a curtsy, which was hopelessly awkward. Despite my mother's best efforts, I'd never gotten the hang of it.

"Stand up straight, girl. You look ridiculous." The Margravina waved her hand. "Now, why are you throwing knives at my tea set? It's three hundred years old, and the pattern is quite irreplaceable."

"Agnes Pherenekian is not who you think she is," I said in a rush. "She's an assassin, sent by Konto Theucinian." I whirled to face Markos. "I couldn't let you drink that tea. It might be poisoned."

"I've been traveling with her for days. If she was going to poison me," Markos said evenly, "why didn't she do it then?"

Doubt prickled me. "I—I don't know."

The Margravina rang a tiny silver bell. "If there's any truth buried in this fish story, we'll find it." A footman appeared in the doorway. "Get the guard captain," she barked. "Now." Gripping her gold-handled cane, she stood.

Markos bestowed a bow on her. "I apologize for Caroline's . . . well, for Caroline, in general. And the tea set. I'll handle this."

The Margravina snorted. "I doubt it." With that, she swept out of the room.

Markos watched her go. "Sorry," he said, turning to me. "She's . . ."

"Terrifying," I finished.

He didn't laugh. In the weeks since the shipwreck, I'd pictured our reunion a hundred times, but my imagination had never come up with anything like this. We stood four feet apart, eyeing each other warily.

Markos shook his head. "This—this is unbelievable." Blood flowed, forgotten, from the cut on his hand. "Are you telling me she's not Agnes? That girl isn't the girl you met in Eryth?"

"Ayah, she's Agnes all right," I said darkly. "But none of this has been what it seemed. I doubt her father ever meant to give you an army." Picking up a napkin off the table, I pressed it against his cut. "Markos, you're bleeding."

He yanked his hand back. "I know that."

Grabbing more napkins, he blotted the damp stains on his trousers. I winced. He was covered in tea and blood.

"Sorry," I said. "I got carried away."

"You *think*?" Bewildered, he stuck a hand in his hair. A pang went through my heart at the familiar gesture. "Caro, your ship sank nearly three months ago. When your body didn't wash up along with the others, I admit I held out a tiny bit of hope. But then Agnes—she said you went down with the ship. Where have you *been* all this time?" he asked hoarsely. "Why did you never even try to contact me?"

Somehow I knew this wasn't the right moment to tell him about Diric Melanos. "I promise I'll explain everything." I tucked my pistol in the belt of my sodden dress. "But first I have to find Kenté. And Agnes."

"I'm coming with you," he said, as I'd known he would.

"No. You're not safe out there." Reaching toward him, I touched his chest. It was warm, and I longed to bury my face in it. To tell him I'd been wrong to let him go. To tell him everything. "I'll be right back. Don't leave the Margravina's castle. And," I added, "whatever you do, for the love of the gods, *don't* marry Agnes."

His eyes darted away from mine. "Caro." I saw him swallow. "We're already married."

CHAPTER
TWENTY-THREE

I stalked through the maze, mud sucking at my boots. It was early afternoon, but the storm had darkened the sky. On either side of me, tall hedges shivered in the breeze. Rainwater was rapidly filling the shallow dimples in the path where the grass had been flattened by footprints.

I heard Markos's voice in my head, over and over. *We're already married. We're already married.* Viciously I kicked through a puddle. *Married.*

As I rounded a corner, lightning flashed on a ghostly figure in front of me. Panicking, I stifled a shriek. My heart hammered in my chest. It was only one of the Margravina's sculptures, a creepy marble rendering of an athlete whose arms had been lost to time.

Recovering, I continued deeper into the maze. "Kenté?" I called, hardly daring to raise my voice. The only answer was the wind stirring the hedges.

I twirled, fingers sweating on the pistol grip. Nothing was behind me.

Stupid. Both Agnes and my cousin were likely long gone. There was nothing in here but me and my fear. With a rueful shake of my head, I lowered the gun and forced myself to keep going.

When I emerged from the maze, a stiff wind buffeted me, whipping my skirts around. Shading my eyes from the pelting rain, I tried to get my bearings. The Margravina's gardens ended on top of a bluff overlooking the sea. The path curled around the cliffside, dotted here and there with marble benches. A giant bronze spyglass stood mounted on a post. On a clear day the view was probably spectacular.

My heel slipped in the mud and I lost my balance. Skidding down the path toward the cliff's edge, I slammed into a hard object. Thank the gods someone had thought to build a railing. Gripping it, I pulled myself up.

By the time I reached the city, my new dress clung to my body, drenched in mud. I smelled like wet wool and sweat. My mouth twisted in a grim smile. Lately all I did was ruin clothes.

Spots danced before my eyes. Pressing my hand against the stitch in my side, I wheezed a shallow breath. When I got back to the *Busted Steed*, I resolved to fling these stays overboard, where they could sink to the bottom of the harbor, for all I cared.

Then I remembered I'd told Diric Melanos to go to hell. The *Steed* would be on its way to Brizos by now, and him with it.

Kenté and I had never discussed where we would meet if we got separated. I gripped handfuls of sodden skirt in my fists, fighting off my increasing alarm. I'd been so preoccupied with Markos that I'd let her go after a murderer alone. Spinning in the empty street, I pressed my fingers to my temples. *Think.*

There was one place Agnes was certain to return—the attic. She'd left her notebook and poisons there. Remembering how she'd clutched her chest of "inks" to herself on the ride to the harbor in Eryth, I knew she wouldn't leave the tools of her trade behind. *Inks!* I thought to myself now. How naive I had been.

I reached the house, ducking through the hole in the boards. Water streamed from my skirts to turn to mud on the dusty floor. Ahead of me wet footprints led up the stairs. Pistol drawn, I edged through the attic door. There was no one here. The chest still sat on the table, but the notebook and the ring were gone. Several gaps marked where vials had been removed from the chest. The knot of dread in my stomach grew larger.

Back outside in the alley, I discovered the rain had finally let up some. I stood helplessly among the puddles. Where would my cousin go if she was in trouble? The Bollard offices? So many things had happened, we'd never made it there to send my letters.

"Wharf Street," I whispered, the sound of my own voice somehow steadying. "Right."

My only warning was the light shuffle of footsteps on the

cobblestones. I heard a shriek, quickly muffled. Something clattered to the street behind me.

I whirled to discover Agnes Pherenekian struggling in the arms of Diric Melanos, the muzzle of his pistol pressed into her neck.

He was the last person in the world I'd expected to see. "What are you doing here?"

"Was on my way back from the tavern when I spotted this one skulking around the ship." He saw Agnes eyeing the crossbow she'd dropped and kicked it out of her reach. "Knew she was up to no good, so I followed her."

He'd saved my life again.

"I mean, why are you still in Iantiporos?" I asked. "I thought you'd be long gone."

"Well . . ." He shrugged. "Reckon I'm an old fool. Figured you might change your mind."

I was gratified to see that Agnes looked somewhat disheveled. The kohl lining her eyes was smudged, giving her a hollow corpselike appearance. Mud coated the hem of her dress, and her hair had tumbled down. She squirmed in Diric's grip like an animal in a trap.

"The whole thing was a setup, wasn't it?" I said. "Your father was never going to give Markos an army."

Throat fluttering, she glanced at Diric's pistol. "Of course he wasn't," she spat, turning back to me. "I must say, you're terrible at staying dead. First I thought you drowned, and then I thought they were going to hang you at Fort Reliance, but now here you are mucking up my plans again." She smiled, displaying a row of perfect teeth. "Boys to marry, husbands to murder, you know."

"If you wanted me gone so badly," I asked, "why didn't you kill me back on *Vix*?"

"Who says I wasn't going to?" She ceased struggling and tilted her head, studying me. "It would've been a shame to kill you though. People like you only come around once in a lifetime. Consort to an Emparch. Favored of the gods." She saw the surprise on my face. "Oh yes, Markos told me all about that. Anyhow, I sensed you wanted to be something more than a mere Emparchess. So you see, we're alike, in a way."

I would rather have had something in common with a cockroach. "We're nothing alike. You're a traitor, Agnes Pherenekian."

"Ayah?" Diric laughed. "Is that who she said she was?" He tightened his grip on her. "Recognized you the moment I saw you. Quite the family resemblance."

My body turned cold. "What," I asked him slowly, "do you mean?"

Suddenly I remembered the portrait on the wall of the dining room in Eryth, of the little girl Agnes, who had been so plain. And how oddly the Archon had behaved during my time there, almost as if he'd been afraid. *I love my daughter. You must understand that I would do anything for her.* What if those campfires on the lawn hadn't belonged to his men at all? What if they were someone else's soldiers, sent to Eryth to make sure the Archon would cooperate?

The last piece of the puzzle dropped into place. The notebook. The scrolls and diagrams in Agnes's library had been labeled in a neat meticulous hand, but the writing I'd seen in the attic was a messy dark scrawl.

The Archon had been telling the truth when he said he would do anything to save his daughter. This just wasn't his daughter.

My voice came out hoarse. "Who is she?"

Diric dug the pistol into her neck. "Her real name is Araxis Chrysanthe. Her mother's a nasty piece of work. They call her the Lady Dressed in Blood."

I thought back to what Peregrine had told me. *Everyone knows the Lady Dressed in Blood . . . She's whispered to be the longtime mistress of Konto Theucinian.* My gaze flew to Araxis's finger, where she wore the lion signet Kenté and I had found in the attic. I realized what I should've known all along.

"Gods," I whispered. "You're Theucinian's daughter." Spinning to face Diric, I demanded, "You knew? Why didn't you say something back on the *Advantagia*?"

"Never saw her, did I?" He shrugged. "You told me about a girl named Agnes."

He was right. She'd been careful to save her visit to my cell for a moment when he wasn't there.

Diric set his finger on the trigger. "Best kill her. This one is nothing but trouble."

"Not yet," I said. Not when she might have answers. Studying her, I continued slowly, "So then you must be Markos's—"

"Cousin? Oh yes." She smirked. "I went to bed with him

anyway, if that's what you want to know. The Andelas and the Theucinians aren't *that* closely related."

I bit down hard on my lip. I should've let Diric pull the trigger.

"I'm still going to kill Markos," she taunted me. "Just like I killed your cousin."

Whipping her head back, she hit Diric in the face with a sharp crack. He doubled over, grunting in pain. Araxis swiped her foot in a circle so quickly I had no time to react. Diric toppled to the ground. She sprang away, not bothering to retrieve her crossbow. Footsteps splashing, she ran down the alley.

I raised my pistol and fired a shot. It glanced off the cobblestones with a shower of sparks. Araxis kept running.

"Kenté," I gasped, immediately abandoning the thought of chasing her. *I killed your cousin.*

Oh gods. I had to find Kenté.

Diric got to his feet, swearing. A red spot bloomed on his forehead, but he ignored it. "The *Steed*." He nodded toward the harbor. "Let's go."

As we hurried toward the *Busted Steed*, the docks seemed as if they'd gone into hibernation. Watchmen in high-necked sweaters shivered on deck under canvas awnings, and lamplight shone yellow from the portholes. The black water was pitted by raindrops. Alone among the ships, the *Steed* was dark.

I heard a snap, the smell of sulphur drifting toward me. Diric had lit an alchemical match. Its flame, unbothered by the rain, gave off a round circle of light. I strode up the gangplank, pistol at the ready.

"Kenté?" I called, danger senses jangling.

Diric set a hand on my shoulder. "Stay behind me," he rasped, pulling his gun. I'd never heard his voice so sober and deadly.

In the guttering match light I spotted a drop of blood on the deck, then another. Farther ahead there was a bigger puddle, strangely smeared, as if someone had slipped in it. Pistol shaking in my hand, I struggled to breathe.

Diric swore.

A figure lay crumpled on the deck. Kenté's wet purple dress clung to her still body. She was facedown, one hand outstretched. Her boots were twisted at an unnatural angle.

I wondered who was screaming so cursed loud and wished they would stop. Then I realized it was me.

Diric dropped to his knees. Stripping off his jacket, he wrapped Kenté in it to protect her from the pelting rain. "She's warm," he told me. "She's alive." He gathered her into his lap, slapping her face none too gently. Her eyelids fluttered.

"Kenté!" I shook her limp shoulder. "Wake up. Wake *up*."

She moaned. "I feel . . ." Beads of sweat glistened on her forehead. Her hand fell open and a dart tumbled to the deck, the metal tip bloody.

"Below," Diric ordered. "Get blankets and water."

I didn't stop to question him. My fingers numb on the ladder, I climbed down to the cabin. Lurching to the bunks, I gathered a pile of blankets. Then I tucked a jug of water under my arm and scrambled up on deck.

The puncture wound was on the back of Kenté's right shoulder.

It had stopped bleeding. The skin around it was puffy and slightly the wrong color. I stifled an angry sob. Araxis had shot my cousin from behind.

Diric picked up the dart, sniffing the end. "Don't smell like anything. But . . ." He shook his head. "No way to be sure with poison."

He covered Kenté with the blankets. "Try to get some water down her."

I tapped her face until her eyes opened. "How do you feel?" Holding the water jug to her lips, I watched her swallow.

"The shadows want me to dance," she murmured, eyes unfocused.

I squeezed her hand. She'd managed to take a little of the water, but I was terrified it wouldn't be enough.

"I pulled the dart out," she whispered. "Do you think I'm still going to die? What does it feel like?" Her face and neck looked swollen. "If I'm dying?"

I whispered, "I don't know."

Kenté's chest shuddered. "I don't want to die."

Diric pushed me gently but firmly aside and picked her up. "Bollard Company," he said grimly, tucking her over his shoulder. "What's the address?"

"It's on Wharf Street. You can't go to the Bollards." I scrambled to my feet. "They'll murder you."

"It's her or me." He carried Kenté down the gangplank and onto the dock. "She needs a physician. The best in this city. Your family will know what to do."

Kenté's head bobbed on his shoulder, liquid leaking out of the corner of her mouth. "No physician would dare turn us away!" I protested, jogging after him. "Not when she might be dying!"

His mouth flattened. "Neither of us look very reputable."

It was true. My skirt was splashed in mud to the waist, and he still wore his tattered and patched overcoat.

My gaze fixed on Kenté's hand, flopping limply. I whispered, "It was just one little dart."

Twice on the way to Bollard Company, Diric had to put Kenté down so she could throw up—if you could even call it that. Her throat convulsed. Horrifying green spittle flowed from her mouth, and her eyes floated back in her head.

"Oh gods," I choked. "Don't let her die."

Darkness pressed around us. I wasn't a shadowman, and I'd never spoken to the god of the night. But I closed my eyes and sent up a prayer now.

God of the shadows. Save her.

The Bollard Company headquarters was sandwiched between a millinery shop and the shipbuilders' guild. On a tasteful plaque next to the door was an embossed wine barrel, with three stars in an arc over it.

"Poison!" I gasped as I burst through the door. "We need a physician. *Now.*"

I stood dripping on the carpet of a wood-paneled lobby. At the desk, a woman leaned over an account book, scribbling with a pen. On the opposite wall, a portrait of my ancestor, the great explorer Jacari Bollard, resplendent in red cape and fine hat, judged everyone who walked through the door with his stern oil-painted gaze. A model ship sat in a glass-fronted cabinet beside a brass automaton made of tiny gears. In the hearth a fire crackled, lending the room a smokiness that complemented the scent of spiced tea.

My mother dropped her pen, knocking the inkpot to the floor unnoticed, and jumped to her feet. Her hands trembled as she stared at me. "Caro?"

CHAPTER
TWENTY-FOUR

I opened my mouth to speak, but a crowd of people flooded the room, pushing between us. A woman shrieked, tugging Kenté from Diric's arms. Clearly our relations in Iantiporos knew her well. They laid her on the sofa, and someone ordered a servant to go for the physician.

"Tamaré Bollard," Diric drawled behind me.

I tore my gaze away from my cousin's limp body. Diric stood with his hands in the air, encircled by my mother and two of her men. Three pistols were in his face.

Ma's hair was shorn close to her head, a row of gold hoops running up the outer edge of her ear. The dangling bottom earring was a gold disc engraved with a cask and three stars. She was taller than me and her complexion was darker, but her nose had the same curve and her chin the same shape as mine. The Bollard crest on her earring matched the one on her pistol, which was pointed at Diric.

"What have you done to her?" Ma's jaw was rigid. "By the gods, this time I'm *really* going to kill you."

The scar stood out, angry and red, on Diric's cheek. "Last I saw of you was the stern of your ship as you sailed away, leaving me to die. I ain't intending to let you finish the job tonight."

I stepped between them. "Ma, we don't have time for this! He didn't do it. He's not your enemy."

Ma's voice was as cool as ice. "Anyone who harms our family is our enemy." But she removed her finger from the trigger. "Caro, get out of the way." Her mouth twitched in annoyance. "You're standing right in my shot."

"Don't shoot. He saved my life." My heart hammered. "Let me *explain*."

"You do that," Diric said. "But you'll pardon me if I ain't planning to stick around." He looked at Kenté, and his voice softened. "I hope she makes it." Backing toward the door, he threw me a ragged salute. "I owe you one, Caro, so I'll wait twenty-four hours before I sail. If you change your mind, you know where to find me."

He dropped something on the floor. The room went black, as if someone had tossed a dark blanket over us. The fire whisked out. People shouted, footsteps scuffling on the floor, and the door hinges creaked.

Ma swore under her breath. "Get a gods-damned lamp," I heard her order.

A shaky flame sprang up, but it was too late. The door hung open, rain blowing in to pool on the floor. Diric Melanos was gone, just as I knew he would be. Bending, I picked a hairpin out of the crack in the floorboards. It was one of Kenté's. He must have grabbed it from her hair as he carried her. Did *all* her jewelry have shadow magic attached to it?

Ma shook her head. "That conniving son of a—"

She didn't finish, because just then the physician came bustling through the door, leather bag clutched in her hand. A harsh astringent smell followed her. At her direction, two of the Bollards carried Kenté upstairs.

As their footsteps subsided, Ma wrapped me in her arms. "We heard *Vix* was lost with all hands." She crushed the breath out of me. "I thought you were dead."

"*Vix* is gone." My voice broke. "She sank off Four Mile Rock." The whole story poured out. I finished by telling her about Araxis and her chest of poisons and darts.

"Oh, Caro." She wrapped my cold hand with her warm dry one.

I buried my face in her shoulder. Her perfume was sharp and woodsy, somehow more masculine than feminine. It smelled like cedar-paneled boardrooms, wine barrels, and money. I was certain my tears had ruined her silk shirt, but she said nothing.

"Come upstairs." She settled her arm around my shoulders. "You need to tell the physician what you just told me."

My voice wobbled. "She's going to die."

"Not if we can do anything about it," Ma snapped, as if it was entirely unfathomable that someone would have the audacity to die on her watch.

At the top of the stairs, a servant materialized with a pile of dry clothes. Grimacing, I realized I'd left a muddy trail on the stair runner. In the privacy of a spare room, I peeled the wet dress from my shoulders, stripping down to only my stays and underthings.

Unlike Bollard House, the family estate located upriver in Siscema, no one really lived here. The upstairs rooms above the offices were for agents of the family to use when they came to Iantiporos on business. In truth I hadn't expected to find my mother here— she must be in town to oversee a trade negotiation.

Ma cleared her throat, indicating the pile of clothes. "These are mine. I daresay you'll have to roll the trouser legs up, but . . ." She shrugged. "I thought you'd be more comfortable in them than a dress."

My mother and I had clashed more than once over my clothes. As chief negotiator for the most powerful trading company in the land, she rarely wore skirts herself. Tonight she was dressed in a gold-trimmed black waistcoat, a silk shirt and cravat, and trousers. In spite of that, she'd persisted in pushing ladylike things on me for years. I used to resent her for it, thinking she meant to imply that my life on the wherry with Pa wasn't good enough. But now I suspected she'd done it for a very different reason. Ma, who had never been particularly traditional, saw me as a second chance to experience the path she had not taken.

"Thanks." I shimmied into the trousers. Grabbing the short leather boots, I shoved my feet eagerly into them. My mother and

I wore the same size. It had been months since I'd had shoes that fit.

"How on earth did you come to be tangled up with that blackguard Melanos?" Ma asked. "By all the gods, I wish he'd stayed where I put him."

I raised my eyebrows. "On an island to die alone?"

She avoided my gaze. "No more than he deserved."

"As it turns out, I was shipwrecked on that very same island."

"Well, that was bloody poor luck," she said.

I didn't think it was luck at all. It was the sea god sticking her meddling hands into my business. But I wasn't in the mood to explain that right now.

"We were arrested for treason by the Lion Fleet," I told my mother, "and then we escaped and stole a—" I realized this was Ma I was talking to. "Well, never mind that part."

She snorted. "Just like your father. Always getting into scrapes." She watched me buckle my pistol to the belt, waiting a beat before saying, "I'm sorry you lost the cutter. But perhaps we can turn it into an advantage. We'll set you up on one of the larger brigs as apprentice to the captain. In a few years you'll make first officer," she said briskly. "And then we can talk about your own trading ship." She squeezed my shoulder. "It's going to be all right, Caro. We'll fix this."

Ma was an arranger. It was just how her mind ticked. I knew if I wasn't careful she'd have my entire life laid out for me by the time I finished getting dressed.

I shook my head. "I need to fix this on my own."

Unwilling to waste time unlacing my corset when Kenté might be dying, I tugged the linen shirt on over it. My lips pulled to one side in a half smile when I saw the cask and stars embroidered on the pocket.

Straightening my collar, Ma sighed. "You always act like I'm your enemy when I'm only trying to help." I sensed she wanted to say more, but she did not. Finally she reached for my hand. "Come on, let's see how Kenté is doing."

The next three hours passed in a blur. We watched helplessly while the physician forced Kenté to swallow milk and the contents of several medicine bottles. Squeezing poison and pus from the puncture wound, she applied a foul-smelling poultice. Someone slipped a cup of tea into my hands, and I sipped numbly, my face stiff from dried tears.

The physician finally stood, tucking her bag under her arm. "I've done all I can. Time will tell."

"That's *it*?" My voice cracked.

She regarded me coolly, and I remembered this wasn't personal for her. She saw death every day. "The fact that she's still alive is a good sign. I think it's quite likely she'll pull through. What she needs is rest, so her body can fight this." She glanced at my mother over my head. They went out together, the door closing behind them.

The room was finally quiet. Alone with my cousin, I took her hand.

"Caro," she croaked, struggling to lift her head.

I pressed her back on the bed. She felt so light. "You have to rest."

Kenté's lips moved, but at first nothing came out. "It's all so . . . fuzzy," she whispered. "Forgetting something important." Her eyes dipped shut. "Markos. That's it."

"What about him?" I asked.

"Something I wanted to tell you . . ." A long moment passed, during which I thought she was sleeping. Then she said, "The letter I sent you. That's it." Her eyelids fluttered open. "I'm falling asleep. It's . . . inconvenient. Sent a letter to Markos too. But I don't know . . . if he got it."

Tears welled up, burning my eyes. "Don't worry." I squeezed my cousin's hand. "I'm sure he got it. You need to rest."

"Hate this." Her lips barely moved. "That I'm missing . . . the adventure."

Ever since Kenté revealed her shadow magic to me, a part of me had assumed she was invincible. But nestled in the pile of blankets, she looked skinny and small. All at once I remembered she was only sixteen.

I rested my forehead on her arm, finding the skin hot and feverish. A sob bubbled up inside me, causing my shoulders to shake. She'd run away from the Academy and crossed an ocean to rescue me. Grabbing the talisman around my neck, I clung to it.

This was all backward. I should've been the one taking care of her.

Wiping my face on my sleeve, I remembered Markos was waiting for me at the Margravina's castle. I had to go. The bedroom had one dormer window. Unlatching the shutters, I swung them outward with a creak. Overlapping roof tiles sloped down, slippery in the rain. I threw my leg over the windowsill.

The storm had subsided, and the clouds drifted away from the moon. The wet roofs of Iantiporos were a shimmering playground at my feet. And beyond them lay the harbor, a sprawl of ships and masts and twinkling lanterns.

If you change your mind, you know where to find me.

Suddenly it seemed so simple. The treasure was the key to everything. All this time, Diric had been right. With those gold bricks, I could get Markos his throne *and* get *Vix* back. I didn't have to choose.

I was beginning to believe the sea god had marooned us together on that island for a reason. At first I'd assumed it was to punish me. After all, her gulls no longer perched on the railing, watching me with beady eyes. The sea didn't whisper to me anymore. Her drakon had abandoned me. And yet . . . Remembering my vision of Nereus, my blood turned chill in my veins. I'd followed him down the dock and he'd led me right to Docia. Right to the one person who had the answers we needed.

Diric Melanos and I were *meant* to find this treasure. Together. I was sure of it now.

"Going somewhere?"

Ma stood silhouetted in the door. I paused halfway out the window.

"Whatever you're up to," she said, "you should know that Diric Melanos can't be trusted." She crossed her arms. "He's a bloodthirsty pirate, Caro."

For some reason, I felt like being honest. I turned back to my mother. "He has a map to the *Centurion*'s lost treasure, Ma. And we're going to find it."

"The *Centurion*? That's a fool's errand," Ma said. "The ship is at the bottom of the ocean." Something like longing flashed across her face. "And the treasure is just a fish story."

"Maybe." I shrugged. "You want to come with us?"

Myself, I suspected Ma had a little bit of adventurer inside her. After all, she'd taken up with Pa, who was a smuggler and a rogue. I suspected it came from being descended in a direct line from Jacari Bollard.

But I already knew what her answer would be.

Ma schooled her expression back to cool neutrality, a skill she had honed in boardrooms and banks across Kynthessa. Slowly she shook her head. "You'll never make it. The whole Akhaian fleet is probably looking for you."

I saw *Vix* lying under the sea off Four Mile Rock. "This is something I have to do." I hopped from the window onto the roof. "Tell Pa I'm alive. Tell him I love him. And—" My throat suddenly felt thick.

Ma sighed. "I love you too, you incorrigible scalawag."

I threw her a grin, and dropped into the alley below. Shadows edged the street, deep enough to conceal an assassin. There were too many guards in the Margravina's city to openly carry a pistol, even at night, but I kept my hand on mine just in case. Araxis Chrysanthe could be anywhere.

I'd told Markos I would be right back, but that was hours ago. He was going to be furious with me.

Rounding the corner, I found myself at the harbor's edge. The ships at this dock were huge, their curved hulls looming in the dark far above my head. Nearby a fleet of long, flat barges creaked and bobbed at their moorings. The closest one was familiar, the printed letters across her stern reading *Catfish*. There was a light in the cabin window.

All at once I knew what I had to do.

I strode up the gangplank. Without knocking, I pushed through the door of the cabin. Equipment leaned against the walls and wet rope was strewn everywhere. The cabin smelled like mud and seaweed. Seated at a cluttered table was Docia Argyrus, working figures in the glow of a single lantern.

She dropped her pencil. "Caro!"

"Come with us," I blurted. "You're an expert on *Centurion* lore. You know salvaging and shipwrecks. Come to Brizos."

"I can't," she said in a small voice. "I got responsibilities. To my family. You're asking me to go tearing off on some outlandish quest, in the company of a murderer."

"Oh, really?" I asked. "Where's your family now? Where are your brothers?"

She lowered her gaze to the account book, and swallowed. "Down at the pub."

"While you sit here and do all the work?" I flicked a page of the book. "They're taking advantage of you, and you know it. Is this what you want—to do figures and make sandwiches for the rest of your life?" I didn't understand her hesitation. "You said it yourself—the *Centurion* is a find that could make a salvager's career."

Docia squeezed the pencil in her fist. "They're my *family*. I—I can't just up and leave. I thought you were my friend, Caro." Her voice came out choked. "A real friend would understand."

I'd offered her the chance of a lifetime—the chance to go after her dream—but now *I* was the one who wasn't a real friend? I wasn't angry. I was so disappointed it cut me like a knife.

"What was all that talk about leaving Argyrus and Sons," I demanded, "and setting up your own salvaging company?"

Her cheeks reddened. "Well, I meant someday. Not now. Not *tonight*."

"My pa always used to say the day your fate comes for you, you'll know," I told her quietly. "Well, I reckon this is it. And you're just going to sit there and let it pass you by."

"What would your pa say about Diric Melanos?" she fired back. "What would he say about you sailing off with the man who killed your friends?"

I opened my mouth to reply, and then closed it because there was nothing to say.

Docia tucked a strand of hair behind her ear. "I'm not going to Brizos on your wild goose chase." She shook her head. "Not with you and certainly not with the likes of Diric Melanos."

My nostrils flared. "Fine."

I went out, letting the door bang shut behind me. And I didn't look back.

CHAPTER
TWENTY-FIVE

By the time I reached the Margravina's castle, it was past midnight.

I found Markos pacing the bedroom of his suite. The remains of dinner lay half-eaten on a table nearby. Behind him an elaborate four-poster bed groaned with curtains and pillows. He'd discarded his jacket and loosened the top button of his shirt. Most of his hair had shaken free of its band to fall around his shoulders.

"Explain." His voice quivered, and I understood he was very angry.

"Markos—" I began, but he cut me off.

"You said, 'I'll be right back.'" His jaw twitched, that telltale line appearing between his eyes. "That was *twelve hours ago.*"

I was too tired for it, but apparently we were fighting.

"Well," I said, "that was before I found out you married your greatest enemy's bastard daughter, who is coincidentally your cousin, who poisoned *my* cousin, and who was going to poison you." I stopped to take a breath, clutching my side. "And who is a colossal bitch, as it turns out."

"Wait . . . *what?*"

My worry for Kenté was an ugly knot in my chest. I hoped she would be all right. But I forced myself to swallow my fear while I recounted everything that had happened since I'd last seen Markos. I purposely omitted Diric Melanos, since that would only make him more upset. I could explain him later.

"Also," I said, stifling a yawn, "I feel the need to mention that I did *all* of this in a corset."

I'd hoped that would make him laugh. Instead he dropped onto the end of the bed. "She's a Theucinian?" His shoulders slumped. "You're certain?"

"She admitted it," I said quietly. "In fact, she seemed proud of it." I shook my head. "I suppose her mother was the one who arranged for that empty house to stash her poisons in. Who knows, perhaps she even owns it. Where did you think Agnes—I mean Araxis—disappeared to yesterday, after you arrived at the castle?"

"I don't know!" He stuck his hand in his hair. "I didn't ask. She—she said she needed to freshen up."

"She was your wife," I muttered. "It seems like you should've known she had, I don't know, a murder lair."

"Caro, I barely knew her."

"Well, maybe you shouldn't have married her, then."

His head shot up. "I very clearly recall that it was you who told me to marry her in the first place," he reminded me. "And anyway, you were dead."

I remembered how Araxis had gloated about going to bed with him. The idea of Markos touching her made me sick. But they'd been married for days, if not weeks. I hesitated. "Markos, you didn't—"

"What?"

"Um . . ." My cheeks flamed. Suddenly I couldn't look him in the face. "Consummate the marriage?"

I heard the hurt in his voice. "How could you think I'd do that?"

"She lied to me," I breathed, relief flowing through me.

He bit his lip. "And you believed her?"

"Well, it's what you wanted, isn't it?" I folded my arms across my chest. "To marry her and get her father's support for your throne?"

His knuckles turned pale on the bedpost. "No." It was that cold stiff voice I hated. "But it was certainly what *you* wanted."

His words cut me. "That's not fair. The Archon's offer seemed like such a great opportunity. I didn't want your judgment clouded by—I mean, I reckoned if *I* was the one who broke things off, it would be easier for you to make the right decision." Seeing his face, I whispered, "Markos, don't look at me like that."

He twisted his hand in his hair, messing it up. "That day in

Valonikos, when I tried to tell you I loved you, you said you'd only been staying with me out of pity. You said it had been *fun*."

He'd never said the word "love" out loud to me before. Never. It felt exhilarating, but also bittersweet. It had not escaped my notice that he'd used the past tense.

"I didn't mean it." I reached for his arm.

"But you still said it," he countered, jerking it away. "You can't just—just come back from the dead and pretend like it never happened."

I held my breath. "How mad are you?"

"When I gave you my mother's bracelet, I was trying to tell you how I feel about you," he said hoarsely. "But you acted like you hated it. Then you said all those awful things, on purpose, to drive me away." He gestured between us. "Caro, this means something to me. *You* mean something."

"I lied." My voice cracked. "I never wanted us to split up. I only did it for you."

"But I never asked you to." He squeezed his hands into fists at his sides. "And now, months later, you come back from the dead and do the same thing all over again. Today you ran off without explaining and left me standing there alone—"

"For your protection!" I protested.

"I'm not made of eggshells!" he yelled, a muscle twitching near his jaw. "Just because I grew up in a palace, you think I'm a sheltered child. Is that it? You think I'm foolish and helpless?" He picked up the teapot from the table. "Well, I don't need you to make my decisions for me. I'm capable of protecting myself."

I eyed the teapot. "You're not seriously going to throw that at me, are you?"

"I don't know." He glared at me. "What do you think?"

I shrugged. "It might help."

He cast the teapot onto the floor, where it exploded into shards. Bits of porcelain clattered into the corners of the room. At the sound, a servant appeared in the doorway. He got one look at Markos's face and scuttled out of sight.

Myself, I suspected that the sooner Markos and I were gone from the Margravina's house, the better. I daresay we would not be invited back. We were hell on tea sets.

With a hollow laugh, Markos said, "It didn't make me feel any better."

My heart fell further. He hadn't laughed at any of my funny remarks. He was barely even looking at me.

"Maybe once I thought you were spoiled and naive," I began softly, only now realizing how deeply I'd ruined things between us. "But it's been a long time since I thought that."

"What about the bracelet?" he rasped. "You—you acted so strange when I gave it to you. It made me think you really meant it when you said you were only staying with me out of pity. I started to doubt everything."

"Markos, I'm always going to be a sea captain. No more, no less," I said, throat tightening. "Your mother was an Emparchess. I didn't feel like I was the right girl for that kind of gift. *That's* what I hated, not the bracelet."

"Oh." He fixed his gaze on the floor. "I wish you'd just told me."

Staring at the broken teapot, I swallowed hard. "Look, I made a mistake when I pushed you away. I reckoned if I made the choice for you, it would hurt you less. But I just wound up hurting you more. I'm sorry."

For a long moment he said nothing. Then the ghost of a smile touched his lips. "Are you trying to tell me you were being noble and stupid?"

"I don't know what came over me," I said. "That's usually your job."

Reaching across the gap between us, Markos took my hand.

A tiny thread of hope curled through me. "I just want us to be a team again." He drew a deep breath. "Like we used to be."

I wanted that too, more than anything.

"Are you sure Araxis hasn't poisoned you?" I trailed my fingers down his face. "You look pale."

He leaned in, pressing his cheek against my hand. "I always look pale." Then he smirked down at me from his impossibly tall height. "Do you know what Fabius Balerophon wrote in your obituary?"

"If I ever meet him," I said under my breath, "I'll write *his* obituary."

"He said we were one of the great modern love stories."

I snorted.

"It was very poetic. 'A great modern love story,'" Markos repeated with a flourish. "Oh, Caro." Lifting my hand, he kissed it. A ribbon of sensation rocketed from my head to my toes. "I don't have the right to kiss you. Not when I'm married to her."

"You just finished telling me we were a great modern love story." I twined my hands around the back of his neck. "You'd *better* be kissing me."

His lips crushed mine, firm and hot. Opening my mouth to him, I twisted his tousled curls through my fingers and tried to pull him closer. He set his hands on the small of my back, pressing me against his chest.

"Oh gods." I could hardly breathe. "Unlace me."

He grinned. "Are you flirting with me?"

"No, I most definitely am not." I turned, giving him access to the laces of my stays. "Take this thing off before I pass out."

I felt his fingers deftly pluck at the buttons of my shirt. It fell apart and then—finally—he undid the first set of crisscrossed laces. The stays loosened, and I gasped. Closing my eyes, I inhaled breath after breath of freedom.

His lips touched my bare shoulder.

Suddenly I remembered the *Centurion*. "How do you feel about long sea voyages?" I asked.

"What?" His lips stilled on my skin.

"I have a plan," I told him.

"So do I." I felt him laugh against my neck and suspected our plans weren't exactly along the same lines.

I rolled my eyes. "I was being serious."

He encircled my waist with his arms. Contentedly I leaned my head back until it fell against his chest, and closed my eyes. I'd missed his warm familiar smell.

"I'm coming with you." I felt his chest vibrate as he spoke. "Wherever you're going. But right now I don't care about Araxis

Chrysanthe. Or sea voyages. They'll just have to wait..." He kissed my neck. "... Till ..." He ran his hands up my legs. "... Tomorrow." We fell on the bed, and he rolled on top of me. "Say my name."

"Markos," I whispered.

"Louder than that."

We were right in the middle of the Margravina's guest wing. "People will hear."

"Ask me if I care," he growled. We kissed desperately, breathlessly. "I think," he said, the words tickling my ear, "you'd better say *all* my names and titles. And each time you get one wrong, you'll have to perform a forfeit."

I could never keep any of his titles straight. He knew that perfectly well.

"That's not a fair game," I objected as he kissed his way down my stomach. A thrill ran through my body. "All right, all right. Markos Andela. Emparch of Akhaia, Archon of—of—you're the Archon of something too, aren't you?"

"Three somethings, in fact."

"Oh damn." I lifted my hips to press myself closer to him. "I can't think when you're doing that."

"You'd better think harder." I felt his breath on my skin. "I promise you the next forfeit is going to be positively filthy. Protector of Trikkaia. You missed that one." Flipping onto his back, he pulled me on top. "Lion of the Ankares. There's another forfeit. Guess you'd better take some more clothes off."

"Now you're just making things up." I wriggled out of my trousers. "I don't believe that's a real title."

"Of course it's a real title. Honestly, Caro. You delivered that letter to the Archon. Didn't you read it?"

I made a face. "Your titles take up an entire paragraph."

He grinned. "How unfortunate for you. I guess we're going to be doing this a very long time, then."

⁓

Much later, we lay in bed talking.

"At least there's this." Markos played with my hair. "I don't think the marriage is legal. If one of the parties who enters into the contract has misrepresented who she is, that should nullify the agreement. And well, it helps that we never . . ."

I shuddered. "Don't finish that sentence."

"I'll visit a lawyer tomorrow. He can officially declare us . . . I don't know, unmarried."

"The sooner the better," I said.

Markos's certainty that the marriage was not legal did a great deal to undo the anxious knot in my chest. But there was still one in my stomach. I realized I'd barely eaten since breakfast. Sliding from bed, I padded across the room to the table.

"Even if I'm not married to her, this is still a disaster." Markos flopped back against the pillows. "Now I suppose I have to go back to Valonikos and tell Antidoros that the Archon of Eryth won't support my claim. To tell you the truth, I'm not even certain the Margravina does." He exhaled. "I suspect this entire affair has annoyed her."

I rummaged through the dishes, spotting grapes and cheese. Hands full of food, I looked up at him. "Sorry."

"It's not your fault." He smiled, while I admired his bare shoulders from across the room. "She was determined to remain neutral regardless of whether you broke her teacup. I suppose I can see why. Kynthessa's already had one war with Akhaia. They don't fancy another."

I returned to bed with my scavenged food, rolling onto my stomach and kicking my feet in the air. "Theucinian wouldn't attack Kynthessa, would he?" I popped a grape into my mouth. "You said he was an imperialist. You think he's longing for the glory days of the empire?"

"He may be, but he's not stupid," Markos said. "The Margravina is far too powerful. I do worry about Valonikos though. It's just a city-state, and being surrounded by Akhaia on three sides makes it . . ." His voice trailed off.

"What?" I asked.

"You're eating grapes naked in bed. I got distracted." He cleared his throat. "Anyway, I'm right back where I started. With none of the Akhaian lords willing to publicly support me."

"But you're not." I sat bolt upright in bed, realizing he didn't know about the treasure. His gaze drifted to my chest. "Markos, that's not very gentlemanly." I wrapped the sheet around myself. "Pay attention. I told you before, I have a plan about that. It involves," I began dramatically, "legends of lost shipwrecked treasure. What do you think of *that*?"

"I think it sounds like a lot of nonsense," he replied immediately. I suppose I should've expected as much.

I grinned. "This one's not." I told him about the map and the

Centurion. "I can't tell you where I got it, but I will say this. Docia Argyrus has seen a coin from the wreck, and she says it's genuine."

The moment her name crossed my lips, I remembered our harsh words on the barge. The friendship had been so new. I wondered if it would ever recover from this.

"How mysterious." Markos shot me a glance across the pile of grape stems. "What aren't you telling me? You're not married too, are you?"

"Ha-ha." I ran my bare toes up his leg. "Very funny."

I hated to lie to him. But I'd only just gotten back in his good graces. Things were still too shaky between us for me to bring Diric Melanos into the picture. Tomorrow. I would tell him tomorrow.

"All right, all right." He snaked an arm around me, pulling me close. "I trust you."

Just then the whole awful evening came back to me with a thud, causing my body to go rigid. How could I have forgotten Kenté? Reaching up, I squeezed the talisman. It wasn't right for me to feel so happy. Guilt settled in a sickening lump in my chest. Not when my cousin might still die.

Markos felt me tense up. "What's wrong?"

"I shouldn't stay here. I need to get back to Kenté," I whispered, burying my face in his shirt. My shoulders trembled. "Oh gods, what if she dies?"

He kissed the top of my head, stroking my hair. "Caro, you staying up all night isn't going to help her. The physician's done all she can. Get some rest, and we'll go see her first thing in the morning." He brushed a tear from my cheek with a gentle thumb. "All right?"

As I nestled my head on his chest, savoring the warmth of his body, my panic began to subside. I had missed him so much. Not the romantic things so much as the little things. His smell. The way his low voice rolled the *r* in my name. How fun it was to banter back and forth with him. In Valonikos, I'd felt awash with uncertainty, wondering how Markos fit into my life. But now I was so grateful to have him back, I didn't even care anymore.

I closed my eyes, letting out a contented breath. We could work that out later.

"Are we going to sleep?" His words vibrated under my ear.

"Shh."

As I drifted into the haze of almost sleep, my thoughts returned uneasily to Diric Melanos. I hoped Markos meant it when he said he trusted me.

Tomorrow we'd find out.

CHAPTER
TWENTY-SIX

Markos was the one who noticed our shadow first.

"There's someone following us." He squeezed my hand hard. "Don't turn around. I think it's Agnes—I mean, Araxis."

The first beams of sunrise slanted over the harbor, and a chill lay over Iantiporos. We were on our way to the Bollard Company headquarters to check on Kenté. I kept compulsively touching the talisman around my neck. Last night I'd been able to stop worrying about her, at least for a few hours. But this morning my concern for my cousin lay like a cloud over everything.

"Gods damn her." Sweat prickling the back of my neck, I glanced furtively out of the corner of my eye. I didn't see much, just the ripple of a black cloak disappearing behind a building.

A shot rang out. I caught a flash of red behind us.

Markos grabbed my arm, pulling me down the street. "Where's your ship?" At his belt he wore his two swords. With a whisper of steel, he took one out and said, "We have to leave Iantiporos. Now."

I struggled in his grip. "I can't just go without seeing Kenté!"

"Those are Akhaian soldiers." Markos steered me toward the docks. "Caro, we can't risk it!"

"But the city guard—" Another shot glanced off the wall of a nearby building.

How dare they fire on us in the Margravina's city? Glancing wildly around, I realized the city guard was nowhere in sight. It was dawn, and the streets were almost empty. Akhaia and Kynthessa were not at war, and the Lion Fleet came and went from this port as it pleased. I wasn't surprised that there were Akhaian soldiers in Iantiporos, but I was unsettled by the discovery that Araxis had this much influence over them. Enough to risk a diplomatic incident by shooting at us in the street.

With one last glance in the direction of Wharf Street, I reluctantly turned toward the harbor. I just had to hope Kenté was all right. Ma wouldn't let anything happen to her.

The docks swarmed with sailors. Mist hovered over the water, while men called to their crews high up in the rigging of the ships. At the far end of the dock, a wherry had already cast off, her black sail filling sluggishly as she turned toward Nemertes Water.

I stopped in front of the *Busted Steed*. "This is us. Markos, wait." I seized his sleeve before he could step on deck. "There's something I need to tell you."

But it was too late.

He looked up at the schooner, and stiffened. His breath caught, and I watched emotions crawl over his face. Shock. Loathing. Determination.

I turned, though I already knew what I would see. Diric Melanos stood on the deck.

Before I could stop him, Markos strode up the gangplank and punched him in the nose.

I scrambled after him. This morning was not going the way I'd hoped.

Markos slammed his fist into Diric's face a second time. "You killed my mother." A third time. "You tried to kill my sister." A fourth. "And you cut *my gods-damned ear off.*"

"Markos, stop!" I pleaded. "Let me explain."

Diric staggered back. His fingers hovered over the bridge of his nose, which was almost certainly broken. Straightening, he planted his feet on the deck. "Take as many shots as you like, boy. If it will help."

I swore. Calling Markos "boy" would only make him hit harder. "Don't!" I said sharply. "The soldiers, remember? We don't have time for this."

Markos's shoulders heaved. "I should cut your head off and throw it to the sharks." With a swish of steel, he drew his sword.

"By Arisbe's left tit," Diric cursed, wiping blood from his lip, "I said you could hit me. But if you cut me with that, I swear I'll end you."

Arisbe had been Markos's ancestor. Diric couldn't have

chosen a worse thing to say. Markos's nostrils flared, and tension trembled in the air. I held my breath, desperately hoping they weren't about to kill each other.

"Please, by all means, try," Markos sneered, looking down at Diric. "You're a traitor. And a murderer."

I stepped between them. "And we can't get to Brizos without him. Put the sword away *now*." I turned to Diric. "Any minute, Araxis is going to catch up to us. She's got soldiers combing the gods-damned streets. Help me get the sails up. We have to go."

Markos lowered his sword, slamming it into the sheath. Tentatively I touched his arm, but he refused to look at me. "Not now," he choked.

Turning his back, he walked away. A moment later the hatch cover banged shut.

Diric and I hurried to unlace the mainsail. I glared at him as we loosened the ropes. "And you! Isn't it enough that you're intent on drinking yourself to death? Stop wallowing in your own self-pity. I know you didn't kill the Emparchess," I said. "Why didn't you tell him?"

"Ayah, it's true I didn't light the fire." He hauled down on the halyard, avoiding my eyes. The sail climbed to the top of the mast. "But I did nothing to stop it. I might as well have killed her."

"How many times were you going to let him punch you?" I demanded.

Tying the rope off on the cleat, he laughed. "You think it hurt when he hit me? Nothing hurts anymore. I'm dead inside." He pinched his nose, which was dripping blood. "And I deserve to be hit."

The sail flapped like thunder above us. "That's between you and the gods," I said. "All I know is, if we're going to make it to Brizos, I need you." His hopelessness frightened me. "Don't do anything like that again."

The morning after bad weather, there's always a rush to leave port and get under way. We were forced to wait while several vessels floated away from the docks, blocking us in. Stifling a frustrated sigh, I watched a four-masted bark turn at a glacial pace, as if the helmsman hadn't a care in the world. There was no sign of Araxis on the docks, but I knew that wasn't going to last.

Spotting a gap, Diric deftly maneuvered the *Steed* into it. "Sorry about your Emparch," he said with a grimace. "Guess I ruined things a bit."

I swallowed. "I'll talk to him. It'll be fine." I wished I believed myself.

"You do that." Diric adjusted the wheel, the wind filling the *Steed*'s sails. "Meantime I'll be sleeping with my knife. Just in case."

"Markos is much too honorable to kill you in your sleep," I said.

"Ayah? And I'm much too cautious a fellow to take your word on that." He wagged a finger at me. "Don't think this means we're splitting the take three ways. Whatever he gets still comes out of your half. You decide how much. It ain't my concern."

I made a face at him. It figured he'd be worried about the gold.

The *Busted Steed* caught the wind up the channel, making for the northern end of Enantios Isle. Standing at the rail, I gazed into the moving gray water as it slipped by under our hull. Once we cleared the end of the isle, it would be nothing but open sea all the way to Brizos.

Relaxing a little, I let my thoughts turn for the first time to our destination. A chest full of gold bullion would be worth millions of talents. The bricks shone in my mind's eye, shiny and alluring. Snatches of images flashed through my head. Markos marching into Trikkaia at the head of an army of mercenary soldiers. *Vix* with a fresh coat of paint, the waves crashing on her bow.

We would be as fast as the wind. We could own the whole ocean.

Unless I was wrong about the sea god. Perhaps it wasn't our fate that we find this treasure. I cast a nervous glance at the rolling waves. Perhaps she was luring us to our doom.

I looked back over the stern. Several ships were in view, white sails shining in the sunrise. They spread out behind us, all bearing east on slightly different headings. I suspected one of them had Araxis Chrysanthe aboard.

How much, I wondered, had she overheard when she was skulking around our ship, disguised as a man? An awful thought struck me. Had she been there two nights ago when we sat in the cabin discussing the *Centurion*? What if she knew about the gold? And the ship's log?

If she did, then this wasn't just a treasure hunt anymore.

It was a race.

༄

Later that morning, I descended the ladder belowdecks. Bracing my hands on the walls for balance, I felt my way deeper into the schooner's cabin. I saw no sign of Markos in the dark bunks. Finally I reached the door to the captain's cabin, tucked into the curved bow of the ship.

Biting my lip, I knocked. "Markos?"

He didn't answer. I let myself in, slipping sideways through the door. The cabin was tiny, with a bunk on one side and a built-in desk and bookcase on the other. Cobwebs stretched across the empty shelves. Neither Diric nor I had bothered with this cabin, since it was so inconveniently far away from the ship's wheel. He'd been bunking in the main cabin, while Kenté and I—

A pang went through me. Kenté and I had been sleeping head to head in adjoining bunks, whispering late into the night through the cracks in the boards. Sleeping there without her wouldn't be the same.

Markos sat on the edge of the bunk, forehead in his hands.

I approached hesitantly. "Are you feeling sick?" We'd passed Enantios Isle, which meant we were on the open sea, where the motion of the ship was rougher.

He lifted his head to glare at me. "I don't get seasick."

I sat next to him on the mildewed mattress. "Look, I'm sorry I didn't tell you."

"This is not just a betrayal. It's . . ." He looked away. Blood oozed from a cut on his hand, and his knuckles were beginning to bruise.

"He didn't kill your mother," I said quietly. "Cleandros did. I know it probably doesn't matter to you—"

He snorted. "Well, you're right about that." He curled his hand into a fist. "It doesn't matter. All this time you've been sailing around with the man who watched my mother die. How *could* you?"

It was the same question Docia had asked me, and I still didn't have an answer. Diric Melanos had saved my life, and Kenté's. But it wasn't like weights balancing on a scale. People were not exchangeable like coins. Even if he saved a hundred lives, that didn't truly make up for the fact that he'd taken so many others. It was more complicated. If I closed my eyes, I could still see the smoldering wherries at Hespera's Watch and the Singers lying dead under ghostly white sheets. Strange now to think back on that day, when this had all begun.

I stared down at my hands, reflecting on the deaths I'd caused. Thanks to my headstrong ways, I'd killed my own crew. Perhaps I only wanted to believe Diric could be forgiven for the horrible things he'd done because it meant someday I could be forgiven too.

Swallowing down my uneasy thoughts, I turned to Markos. "He saved my life," I said. "And I saved his. What matters right now is finding the treasure. With that much gold, you won't need to marry. You can hire an army and take back the throne on your own terms. We're all in this together, whether you like it or not."

"I don't like it."

Markos's face was as still as stone. I yearned to touch him, to feel again the easy joking partnership between us. I hoped I hadn't destroyed that permanently this time.

Holding my breath, I set my hand on his arm. Briefly I recounted the full story of my shipwreck and escape from the island, leaving nothing out this time. I finished by explaining how Diric had wound up in league with the shadowman.

"He'd been banished from Akhaia as a traitor," I said. "The shadowman was going to offer him a pardon. He regretted the things he'd done—well, some of them anyway. He wanted to go home."

"Are you really making excuses for him?" Markos jerked his arm away. "He killed those wherrymen too. He burned your friends' boats and ruined their lives."

Once again I remembered the acrid smell of smoke over Hespera's Watch. "I haven't forgotten," I said, burying my hurt at the way he'd shaken me off. "It's not an excuse. It's an explanation. What would you give," I asked slowly, "to go home?"

Markos rested his head against the wall, closing his eyes, and did not answer. After several minutes of silence, I left.

❦

On the sixth day we sighted Brizos, a low bump on the horizon. I glanced astern to reassure myself that we were still alone. I'd identified two merchants, low with cargo, as being bound for Brizos, but we'd left them behind two days ago. The third ship had veered off yesterday, and we hadn't seen them since. If Araxis was indeed aboard, she was no longer following us. I wondered what she was up to.

Markos lowered the spyglass. "It's about time the Lion Fleet took Brizos in hand. It was a long time coming. The island is in Akhaian waters after all."

He passed the glass to me, and I passed it to Diric. Which pretty much summed up how the past five days had gone. The two of them refused to address each other directly, leaving me stuck in between.

"You weren't here," I told Markos, remembering the splintering crash of the cannonballs. "They fired on the city without a warning."

"Frigate in the harbor." Diric swept the glass across the crescent-shaped cove. "And—yes—a ten gun sloop. Lurking behind the frigate. Reckon that's the one we got to worry about." He looked up at the *Busted Steed*'s rigging. Despite our best efforts, it still looked slightly dilapidated. "She can outrun us if it comes to a chase."

We both glanced at the faded bolt holes on the deck where the *Steed*'s cannons had been removed for her refit. Without guns of our own, we'd have no way to fight back.

Diric spun the wheel. "Come about! Back out to sea."

"We're giving up?" I unwrapped the mainsheet from its cleat.

"I didn't say that."

The booms of the two sails creaked over, and wind filled the canvas with a familiar slap. We were sailing on the opposite tack, the sails swung out on the starboard side, pointing away from the island. To the sailor who was no doubt keeping watch on the anchored frigate, we looked as if we'd never planned to stop at Brizos.

Diric grinned at me. "You been forgetting how you was raised, girl. Ain't your pa a smuggler himself? You of all people ought to know—we always got our secrets."

CHAPTER
TWENTY-SEVEN

Diric's secret spot turned out to be an empty cove.

There was no beach, only the broken remains of what appeared to be a man-made canal, its crumbled walls angling steeply into the water. Seaweed and barnacles coated the ancient stones. We sailed between the walls, surrounded on both sides by flooded forest. The still water was clogged with green muck.

Through the trees I glimpsed a ruined structure that, from the looks of things, had long been abandoned. The trees had taken it back, their leafy green tops poking through holes in the roof. I flinched as the branches tugged the *Steed*'s rigging, hoping we wouldn't get stuck. Leaves scraped the sails, dropping to the deck.

Diric noticed me studying the fallen ruin. "Some lord or

another's keep," he grunted. "A hundred years ago, when Akhaia ruled this island, I reckon it were a grand estate. Before the Queen drove the lords out."

I supposed this had once been the lord's private docking place. The posts and cleats for tying up had long since rotted away. We set anchors fore and aft, and then lowered the *Steed*'s leaking dinghy and climbed in. A gap in the canal wall revealed a shallow green swamp. The tide had seeped in, swirling lazily around tree trunks marred with waterlines from years of flooding.

Diric rowed through the swamp until the dinghy's bow came to rest on solid ground. Keeping the sparkling sea on our left, we hiked through the forest. Through the trees I spotted the masts and banners of the Lion Fleet, a waving red threat. As we approached the city, my hands drifted to my weapons. I had no idea what we'd find there.

Brizos had been plastered over with a veneer of orderliness. Clusters of troops marched through the muddy streets in formation, muskets on their shoulders, while the original residents of the island scuttled by in the shadows, giving them a wide berth. I could almost smell the tension in the street. Akhaia had its boot on the neck of Brizos. No longer a city without law, it squirmed resentfully under the watchful eye of the garrison now occupying the waterfront.

A pang went through me. The last time I'd been here was with Kenté. I hated not knowing how she was doing.

"I don't like this," Diric said under his breath. "It ain't right. This is Dido's island."

Markos looked as if he wanted to argue the point, but I quelled him with a sharp glance. I was already edgy enough. The last thing I needed was the two of them fighting—and drawing attention to us.

The Queen's hideout loomed ahead. All its windows were busted out and a great hole yawned in the wall. One of the balconies had collapsed.

"And I don't like *this*," I whispered as we climbed through the window. The whole street seemed deserted. "Where are all the people?"

Shaking a match from his pocket, Diric lit the lantern. "Likely everyone with a ship is long gone. Don't blame 'em. I'd have cut out of here too." He nodded toward the stairs. "Who knows what we'll find down there?"

Dim light flickered on the ruined walls. I averted my eyes from a gruesome blotch that looked like a bloodstain. Dido Brilliante may have changed form and escaped under the waves, but it seemed not all her men had made it out. I swallowed. That blood, too, was on my hands. The Lion Fleet had attacked the city because of me.

As we descended the creaking stairs, Markos trailed his hand along the mossy wall. "How deep does this staircase go?"

"Underground," I told him. "Into the heart of the island."

The cavern had been ransacked. The bottles on the bar looked like they'd been smashed with the butt of a musket and emptied on the floor. Listening to the hollow echo of our footsteps, I remembered what a boisterous place this had been only two weeks ago. Now the stalactites reached toward us like ghostly black fingers. In the silence, water dripped. With only our one lantern, the cavern seemed huge. Anything might be lurking in the corners.

Shivering, I stepped closer to Markos. We edged around the upended tables and broken lanterns. The Queen's throne had been knocked on its side.

Diric raised the lantern, revealing unpainted timbers. "This is it."

The first time I was here, I'd thought this was a house built into the back of the cave. Studying it closer, I realized I'd been wrong. Rough logs the size of my body blocked out a rectangular doorway. The hole at the back of the tavern led to a tunnel. The planks and timbers had been placed here long ago to brace the door. It looked like an old mine—though I didn't know what metal they could possibly have been mining on an island in the middle of the ocean.

I went through the door first, cold seeping into the soles of my boots. The floor was rock. "Pass me the lantern."

Lifting it high, I turned in a slow circle. I stood in a small room, barely wider than the tunnel itself. To my left, empty bottles littered a table and a weapon rack lay on its side. Glass from a shattered lamp crunched under my feet. The tunnel gaped like a black mouth in the opposite wall.

I stepped through and looked up—

Right into the eye sockets of a grinning skull.

Stifling a yelp, I fumbled and nearly dropped the lantern. The skull was one of hundreds, mortared into the wall. From the grime coating the bones, I suspected they were very old. The tunnel was lined with shallow alcoves. Inside them I caught flashes of white, wrapped in rotten rags. Not a mine, then. A crypt.

"What're you looking at, girl?" Diric poked me in the back. "Keep moving."

"You know perfectly well what I'm looking at," I growled.

Sticking his hands in his pockets, he nimbly hopped around the bones on the floor, as if it was a sunny day and we were out for a walk in the country. "You ain't scared of a bunch of dead men, are you?"

I felt the whisper of Markos's breath on my neck. His warm hand encircled mine. I glanced up at him gratefully. Of course I wasn't scared of the bones. Not much anyway.

We continued down the tunnel. I stared resolutely at the floor, ignoring the silent eyes of the dead. My pulse thumped madly in my ears and sweat gathered on my neck. *Don't look, don't look.* I focused my gaze ahead.

I smelled the salt water before I saw it. Raising the lantern, I realized the tunnel had ended. Light played on the surface of a circular pool, around which rock ledges rose on all but one side. The far wall had a stone door cut in it, with strange lettering in an arc over the top. Squinting at the words, I couldn't make them out. Either the letters had been partially worn away or it was no language I knew.

Excitement tingled on my skin. "This *has* to be the Queen's secret stash."

Rounded stone steps curved around the pool, leading to the

door. I took them two at a time. Moisture pebbled the stone door in front of me. I gave it an experimental shove. Nothing happened.

Markos gestured down. "Look."

The stone floor was thick with muddy boot prints.

Diric bent to touch the marks. The dirt crumbled in his fingers. "Dried. These were made days ago. Likely the soldiers got this far, but they couldn't figure out how to get the door open."

I grinned. "Looks like our luck's finally changing."

"Or not." Markos raised his eyebrows. "Considering *we* don't know how to get it open either."

My smile faded. Turning back to the door, I ran my hands over the smooth damp stone. There had to be some kind of indent—a hidden button or a handle or—

Something splashed behind me. Whirling, I drew my flintlock.

"*Chee-chee-chee!*" A squeal echoed off the cave walls.

Two dolphins bobbed in the pool, bottlenoses pointed in the air. I exhaled in relief, lowering my gun. The dolphins swam in a circle, their slick gray skin gleaming in the light. I wondered how they'd gotten in here. Perhaps there was an underwater passage connecting this place to the sea. Dido would've known. If only she was here.

One of the dolphins swam to the edge of the pool. Tapping the rock with its flipper, it looked up at me with curious beady eyes.

Staring back at it, I had the strange feeling it wanted to tell me something. All at once I remembered the Queen's parting words.

If you ever return to Brizos, the password to my headquarters is "Leviathan." Tell them Dido Brilliante owes you ten talents.

The dolphin chittered, bumping my toe with its nose. Dido had never said exactly who she meant by "them." I'd assumed it was her men, but what if . . . ? My heart beat faster. Sailors always said dolphins were supposed to be intelligent creatures.

"Um," I said out loud, feeling extremely foolish. "I'm trying to get into Dido Brilliante's room. Where she keeps . . . well, the things she takes. Look, I don't want to steal any of her treasure." The dolphin tipped its head, fixing me with one black eye. "All right, I do," I admitted after a moment, "but just the one thing. I'm looking for a logbook. It's very important." Why was I bothering to explain myself to a fish? This was a stupid idea. "Uh . . . *Leviathan*?" I tried finally.

The dolphin looked pleased, or at least I thought it did. Its smile grew slightly wider.

Rusty gears rumbled and stone scraped on stone. The door ponderously creaked open. Squeeing, the dolphin flipped over with a splash.

"Well, that's something you don't see every day," Diric said dryly.

Markos stooped to peer into the dark swirling pool. "How did it do that?"

"Magic," I said immediately.

"Caro, dolphins cannot do magic. I'm sure there's a button or a lever under the water—"

I shook my head. Only Markos could see a dolphin open a door and then go on about how it wasn't magic.

The room beyond the door was immense, with a ceiling that rose up like a cathedral. It wasn't quite what I'd imagined. Instead of glittering chests of gold and gemstones, the space was packed with marble statuettes of gods in various poses, paintings, porcelain dishes in lovely patterns, a winged helmet, a ship's figurehead carved like a lady—and that was just what was visible in the circle of lantern light. Shelves lined the room, stuffed with dusty books. It seemed wealth didn't interest the Queen so much as antiquities.

"Xanto's balls," Diric murmured. "Never thought I'd lay eyes on Dido Brilliante's treasure room. Looks like a bunch of junk to me."

I studied the shelves. Grasping the spine of the nearest book, I pulled it toward me. Dozens of spiders scampered out from the hole where it had been. Making a face, I flicked away cobwebs and opened the book.

"*Being the First Treatise by Xenophon on Metaphysical Cosmology*," I read aloud. "Well, that's not it."

I replaced the book. No doubt Antidoros Peregrine, being a philosopher, would be interested. But I wasn't. As I turned back to the shelves, the enormity of our task suddenly set in. I sighed. There had to be hundreds of books here.

Nodding to Markos, I pulled another volume. "You start on that end of the shelf."

Together we worked through two shelves of books. Time inched slowly by as I pulled each book from the shelf, opened it to the first page, and then discarded it onto an increasingly haphazard pile. Diric hovered behind us with the lantern.

Markos flinched. "Some of these volumes are worth hundreds of talents, Caro."

Glancing at his stack, I realized it was much neater. "Well, I—"

He cut me off. "Did you hear that?"

I couldn't hear anything over the throb of my own pulse in my ears. Then a trickling sound echoed through the cavern—a pebble rolling across the stone floor.

Like someone had kicked it.

Diric lifted the lantern, scanning the shadows for any sign of movement. "Rats, most likely." But he set a hand on his gun.

Markos drew his swords, abandoning his shelf to guard my back. "The ones at this end are all too new." He nodded at a set of unlabeled red leather volumes. "Red is the color of Akhaia. Try those."

I yanked a book from the shelf, trying to ignore the prickles of panic on my neck.

Diric brushed something off the shoulder of his jacket. "Find the book and let's get out of here. This place is full of spiders."

"Don't tell me you're afraid of spiders," Markos scoffed.

"I ain't scared of them," Diric said, affronted. "I just don't put up with their shit." He whirled, whipping out his flintlock. "What was that?"

I didn't hear anything. "Probably the spiders, come to eat you," I said under my breath.

Markos set his jaw, staring into the dark. "Go faster, Caro."

I tried the next book. A water stain blossomed over the top right quarter of the moldering cover. I opened it, displaying a wrinkled handwritten page. The crest of the Akhaian Lion Fleet was stamped in the center of the page. *Please please please.* Under the crest the captain had written the name of the ship.

Centurion.

I blew dust off the crumbling cover. "This is it," I whispered. Holding my breath, I lifted the delicate book. I was scared it would fall to pieces in my hands. "The Year of Our Emparch 1505-06," I read, squinting at the page. The *Centurion*'s captain wrote in an old-fashioned spidery hand, the ink yellowed by water and age. "I need better light."

A bullet whizzed past my left ear, ricocheting off the lantern casing. Diric dropped the light. It hit the floor, with the tinkling of shattered glass, and went out.

Someone grabbed my wrist. I smelled Diric's stale musky scent close to my ear. "On the ground," he growled. "Now."

He tackled me to the floor, his weight knocking the breath out of me. The darkness pressed in close around us. For several excruciating heartbeats, nothing happened.

Then, "Ow!" Diric grunted. "Get off me, boy."

"Get off *her.*" I heard the distinct thump of an elbow meeting flesh.

Diric's weight shifted off me, and I sat up. "Will you two stop fighting?" I hissed. "People are trying to kill you. And one of them's about to be me."

"I am trying," Markos said stiffly, "to defend your honor, Caro."

"Ayah? I don't have any honor," I shot back. "So I'll ask you to please refrain from killing my captain."

"Who also doesn't have any honor," he muttered.

"Markos." I tucked the moldy log under my arm. "Shut up."

We had to find a way out of here. I wiggled forward, the coldness of the stone seeping through my trousers. As I hugged the log to my chest, I prayed the door had not been blocked by whoever was in here with us.

I had a pretty good idea who that was.

If the intruders were soldiers from the Lion Fleet, we would've heard the clinking of buckles and the heavy fall of boot steps. But our attacker was light-footed and silent. I was willing to bet Araxis Chrysanthe had caught up to us.

Getting to my feet, I felt my way around the corner of the long shelf. When I got to the end, I saw that the door to the treasure room was open a crack, illuminated by dancing light. Our pursuer had left a lantern behind in the room with the dolphins. In silence, we followed the cluttered shelves until we reached the stone door. I turned sideways to wedge myself through.

A dart struck the wall in front of me, its metal tip sparking. Behind us in the dark cavern, Araxis had seen our outlines silhouetted in the doorway.

"Run!" I gasped, clattering down the steps past the dolphin pool and racing into the tunnel of bones. Desperately I clasped the logbook. In the pitch dark, I rammed my elbow into the wall, raking it on rock or jagged bone. It stung, but I had to keep going.

Suddenly light sprang up behind me. I turned, fumbling for my pistol. It was only Markos, who'd grabbed the lantern Araxis had left by the dolphin pool. I glanced at my elbow, dripping blood from a long deep scrape. Why hadn't I thought of taking the lantern? Now she would have to feel her way out in the dark. It would definitely slow her down.

Markos set his hand on my waist to steady me, then spotted the blood. A line appeared between his eyes. "You're hurt?"

"It's just a scratch," I said. "She didn't hit me."

I felt his breath whisper on my hair, the barest hint of a kiss. His hand slid off me, and we continued to run until we burst, panting, into the room at the entrance to the tomb. It took me a few dazed moments to realize what was wrong.

Light. The room was full of light.

Three soldiers blocked the doorway. Seeing us, they drew their swords. It seemed Araxis had brought backup.

Swords, I thought with exasperation. Why did it have to be swords?

The closest soldier charged me.

"Caro!" Diric tossed me his blade.

I caught it, letting the book tumble to the floor. With an upward slash, I blocked the soldier's sword with my own. Markos spun across the room to engage the other two men, twin blades in his hands. I only hoped the *Centurion*'s log wasn't too badly damaged.

The soldier's eyes widened. Clearly he hadn't expected much of a fight from me. Raising his sword, he swept it toward my body. Again I met his swing, muscles trembling as I struggled to hold him back. I measured his size against my own, instantly judging that he had both reach and weight on me. With barely any practice with a sword, there was no way I could win this fight.

I'd have to cheat. I stomped hard on his foot. He stumbled, off balance, and I swept my leg around, taking out his ankles. I set my blade, quivering, at his throat.

Markos, having dropped the second soldier, was fighting with the third. Shoving with both swords, he forced him to stagger back. Before the soldier could gather himself to reengage, I whipped my knife from my belt and flung it at him. It landed with a gruesome thunk in his thigh, causing a fan of blood to spray Markos's jacket.

Grabbing his leg, the man toppled, screaming, to the floor.

Markos wiped blood from his face. "Was that necessary?" He stared at my blade. "And since when do you know how to use a sword? Although I admit that wasn't any style I'm familiar with. I'm not sure it's a style at all."

Behind me I heard a grunt and a gurgle, and knew it was Diric finishing off the man I hadn't killed. I wasn't inclined to look. Dropping my sword to the floor with a clatter, I brushed dirt off the *Centurion*'s log. Thank the gods, the binding was still intact.

"Let's go," I breathed. "Quick."

We sprinted up the stairs. By the time we reached the top, my lungs felt like they were about to explode. My scraped arm stung. I shifted the ship's log to the other side so it wouldn't get blood on it. On the landing I stumbled, nearly losing my footing. Markos caught me.

Shoving the book into his hands, I bent to brace my hands on my knees. Spots danced before my eyes. For several long moments, all I could do was draw heaving breaths. Straightening, I examined my injured arm.

"Gods damn it." The cut was nearly six inches long, the blood mingled with green slime and dirt.

Diric's grim voice made me look up. "We've got bigger problems."

In the dusky twilight, ships were moving in the harbor. As we watched from the doorway, the Lion Fleet weighed anchor and left the docks. Gliding slowly out to the edge of the bay, they took up position in an arc. Despair trickled through me. There were at least twenty ships. And they'd just set up a blockade around the port of Brizos.

We were trapped.

CHAPTER
TWENTY-EIGHT

Back on the *Busted Steed*, I set the battered book on the table. My hands shook as I brushed away cobwebs.

Opening the log, I flipped past page after page of tiny faded script, much of it mottled by water. "Here it is," I said to Markos and Diric. "The last entry."

It was perhaps two-thirds of the way through the book. The bottom half of the page was filled with writing, while a yellow water stain crawled across the top half. Heart pattering in anticipation, I read out loud:

"*For we knew what was on the horizon. Hurricane! . . . That deadliest of storms, which strikes a shiver into the hearts of seamen.*" Honestly, the *Centurion*'s captain had quite a flair for the dramatic. I resumed reading. "*The officers were divided on how to proceed.*

Balantes was insistent upon maintaining our course, a dangerous prospect but one which needs be considered as alas we find ourselves regrettably behind schedule. After great deliberation it was settled that we should come about and make with all haste to return to the nearest land, whereupon if the god finds it her pleasure to take the ship to the deep, at least the crew might escape with our lives. May that Great Lady Who Lies Beneath guide our wheel and shower her mercy upon we poor most wretched of souls."

"The coordinates." Diric gripped my shoulder. "Standard fleet procedure is to make a notation of latitude and longitude at the beginning of every entry."

I stared at the page in growing horror. The water stain blotted out the entire first half of the entry. The ink had been washed away. "No," I breathed, flattening the paper. "It's gone."

Frantically I turned the page, but of course there was nothing more. The whole crew had perished.

"Waste of my cursed time." Diric pushed the book off the table. It fell upside down on the floor, sprawled at an awkward angle.

I sprang up from the table. "Don't!"

"Get out of my face, girl," he snarled. "You're as worthless as the book."

"Don't you dare speak to her that way." Markos's voice was low and deadly. "This isn't her fault. You're the one with the useless map. Spinning stories of gold and glory, when all you are is a failure."

Diric stepped into his face. "A failure, am I? Is that right, boy?

I'll tell you what I failed to do. Failed to twist my dagger in your mother's heart."

Markos hissed sharply. The cabin hummed with tension.

Diric went on. "Failed to put a pistol to the little lady's head. Ayah, your sister. The shadowman wanted me to, but I guess I *failed* at that." His voice rose. "And if I were a halfway decent pirate, I would've taken your girl here into my bed, and then slit her throat."

"Stop it!" I cried. "Diric, stop!"

"Believe me, boy," he growled. "It's lucky you are that I'm such a gods-damned failure." Grabbing his patched jacket from the back of a chair, he shrugged it on.

"Where are you going?" I demanded.

"To find a tavern." He ripped something from inside his jacket. Crunching it in his hand, he tossed it to the floor. "And get a damn stiff drink."

After he'd climbed the ladder to the deck, I stooped to pick up the crumpled paper. I recognized the shape of the island, the river, and the X that represented the cave.

All at once I realized the truth about this map. It had been his childhood dream, handed down from his great-great-grandfather, perhaps what inspired him to go to sea in the first place. Through his years of privateering, blockade running, and exile, he'd held on to it. He scoffed at romance and laughed at sentimentality, yet he had never thrown the map away. It was the one thing that had kept him from breaking.

The map had meant everything to him. And he'd left it behind.

"Caro, what—" Markos began, but I was already halfway up the ladder. I spotted Diric pacing toward the stern of the ship, and ran to catch up.

He threw a leg over the *Steed*'s rail. "Curse it, girl, can't you let me go to hell in peace?"

"You can't go into Brizos," I protested. "They're looking for us."

"Bloody pathetic pirate I'd be if I couldn't get a damned drink without running afoul of the Lion Fleet." He climbed hand over hand down the rope ladder. "Stop trying to save me. You can't save a man the gods have cursed. Especially," he spat, "when you been cursed yourself."

"How long have you known?" I asked quietly.

He exhaled, shoulders falling. "I've always known."

Letting go of the rope, he dropped into the swampy water. Green muck swirled around him as he splashed toward the shore. I stared after him, bewildered. Why wasn't he taking the dinghy?

Then I knew. He was leaving it with us. He didn't intend to come back.

I called after him, "But you said—"

He stopped, waist deep in the water. "You wanted a reason why I wouldn't betray you, and I gave you a simple answer."

"I wanted the *truth*."

He didn't turn around. "The truth is a man wants to look in the glass and not hate himself, just once before he dies."

He pulled out his sword, moonlight flashing on steel, and

walked into the forest. I listened as he hacked and cursed his way through the underbrush. Then he was gone.

I gripped the rail of the *Busted Steed*. He wasn't wrong to hate himself. He'd murdered innocent people. He'd even tried to kill me, once or twice.

But if there was no redemption in this world for Diric Melanos, how could there be any for me? *You've never betrayed your country*, a voice in my head whispered. *You're not a murderer.* And yet . . . Not an hour ago I'd taken a life. When I'd quarreled with the sea god, I had sent my whole crew to their deaths at the bottom of the sea. Their faces flashed through my mind. Castor, Pat, Damian, and Leon.

Tears burned my eyes. And Nereus, who'd lived for hundreds of years before he met *me*. I was no less guilty than Diric Melanos.

"You're crying," Markos pointed out unnecessarily when I returned to the cabin.

Wiping my eyes furiously on my sleeve, I ignored him. The ancient log lay on the floor. I picked it up, straightening the bent pages. "It's nothing."

"Look, Caro." I felt Markos hesitate behind me. "If there's something between you and him—"

"*No.*" I took his hand, rubbing the callus on his thumb. "It's not that. I'm worried about him, is all."

I bit my lip. The map was the only thing that had given him hope. I was afraid of what he would do, now that it was gone.

Markos raised his eyebrows. "Worried. About Diric Melanos."

"I know this has been hard for you." I slid my arms around his waist, nestling my head under his chin. Sometimes it was nice that he was so much taller than me. Closing my eyes, I inhaled his familiar smell.

"It's just—I don't understand. Were you really so blinded by gold that you'd throw in your lot with him?" I felt his chest move as he sighed. "A traitor and a murderer?"

I kissed him softly on the lips. "Do you truly believe," I whispered, "we can't ever be forgiven for the things we've done?"

"Yes," Markos replied. I touched the spot under his ear with my lips. "No," he said after a minute. "I don't know. I can't think when you're doing that. Which I'm sure is your intention."

Stepping back, because this was too serious for kissing, I said, "Without him I might have died of fever on that island. I would've been captured by the Lion Fleet the first time we came to Brizos." I counted on my fingers. "And Araxis Chrysanthe would have cut my throat in the alley. That's three times he's saved my life."

He still looked troubled. "Saving your life doesn't make up for his other crimes."

I remembered Mrs. Singer knitting in her chair on the deck of the wherry *Jenny*, black hair flowing down her back. "No. But it matters." I swallowed. "It makes a difference, somehow."

He gently seized my wrist. "You're bleeding."

So eager had I been to finally read the *Centurion*'s log, I'd forgotten the scrape on my arm. The cave wall had raked the skin, leaving a crusty open wound. Dried blood caked my forearm, staining my sleeve. It hurt, now that I thought about it. I'd been too excited about the treasure to care—and afterward too gutted by disappointment.

Markos pushed me into a chair. He rummaged through the supplies on the sideboard, fetching a jar of salve. He filled a bowl of water and set it on the table.

"I'm fine," I protested. "Why are you fussing over me?"

"Because." He dabbed salve on the wound. "I want to take care of you." He must have felt me stiffen, because he tilted my chin up with his fingers. "I know you don't need me to. I know you can take care of yourself. But I want to."

As his careful fingers washed and dressed my cut, I realized this was what I'd feared the most. I'd been afraid if I allowed myself to be vulnerable with him, I'd lose a part of myself. But right now I didn't feel lost at all.

Markos wrapped a piece of fabric around the cut. As he tied it off, his fingers brushed the inside of my wrist. The touch was gentle, but it went through me like a shock. Our faces were so close together I could barely breathe. The whole journey to Brizos, we'd been sleeping in separate bunks. My body ached for his, but it was more than that. I missed *him*. My love for him was a dark reckless thing inside me—a thing I'd been too scared to give a name to.

I didn't want to be scared anymore.

Softly he ran his fingers over my curls. "I'm sorry I've been angry the last few days. I just . . . I don't want you to get hurt because you put your faith in someone who isn't worth it."

"*I'm* sorry," I said. "I should have realized forgiving him would be harder for you than it is for me. I was insensitive and I was wrong and—" I hesitated. The whole world seemed to hesitate. "And I love you."

I pressed my lips to his, expecting it to be the most romantic kiss of my life. But he didn't kiss me back. Instead I felt him grinning. "That's the first time you've said that."

"You're supposed to say it back," I whispered, our lips barely touching, "not sit there making me feel stupid."

"I love you, Caroline." He kissed me.

I closed my eyes against the delicious feel of him. Sensation rocketed through me like fire, lighting up all my nerve endings. Wrapping his arms around my waist, he lifted me from the chair. I slid my hands inside his coat, running them up and down his back. His muscles shifted under my fingers, and he pulled me closer. A throb went through my body so hard it made me catch my lip between my teeth.

We stood in the cabin kissing for what seemed like forever, until we stumbled to the bunk. As his weight pressed down on me, I sucked in a breath. Tangling my fingers in his hair, I kissed him hard. He tugged my shirt from my trousers, fingers hot against my stomach.

And finally, for the first time, nothing was separating us at all.

⁂

Markos slept, his arm heavy and warm over me. I kept my eyes closed and tried to let the rise and fall of his breath lull me.

It was no use. I couldn't sleep, not with the captain's log on the table, calling to me. Outside, the swamp water lapped at the

Busted Steed's hull. Easing out from under Markos's arm, I sat up. It was funny. For a moment, the whisper of the tide had almost reminded me of how the sea god used to call to me.

But that wasn't possible. She'd abandoned me.

Cool air caressed my bare skin as I slipped out of bed. Grabbing Markos's shirt from the floor, I padded barefoot into the cabin.

I flipped backward to the log entries leading up to the hurricane. There had to be something more here. I couldn't accept that we'd sailed all the way back to Brizos for nothing. Propping my elbows on the table, I stared at the book until the letters blurred. My head drooped in a nod.

I forced myself to focus. The page was dated a week before the final entry. Trailing my finger down the faded ink, I began to read.

Uninhabited and much forest'd the isle lay, tho surveyed it had been by Bollard's men, near forty years gone.

Bollard. I started awake, instincts tingling at the mention of my ancestor. It was, admittedly, not much help. Jacari Bollard had surveyed many islands.

We made anchor in the bay, the unnamed isle being long known along the trade routes as a source of fresh water. But verily we did come to regret mooring on that forsaken shore, for it came upon the men to undertake—

Hard as I squinted, I couldn't make out the next line. The ink had been washed away. What were the *Centurion*'s crew undertaking? I resumed reading.

—To take the air and admire the view from the heights. And alas, it was after the party had found Bollard's mark— Again there was

an infuriating water stain. *Hesperos we lost in a fall from the peak, may She Who Lies Beneath take his soul to the Deep.*

I sat up, senses buzzing. "The peak," I said out loud, my heart skittering in my chest. "Bollard's mark."

My neck tingled. What if this wasn't just another island Captain Bollard had surveyed? What if it was the *same island*?

Near our island there'd been a shoal littered with a hundred shipwrecks, some of them ancient. I checked the log again. It all fit perfectly. The view from the heights. Bollard's mark.

Slithering through the deep like a drakon, that's how your fate comes for you. This whole time I believed the god of the sea had unchosen me. I thought I'd been abandoned.

I was such a fool. None of this was a coincidence.

"Laughter," I whispered.

I reread the log, piecing it all together. The treasury ship had stopped at the island where Jacari Bollard had left his cairn so many years ago. They'd refilled their water, then raised the sails and gone on their way, bearing northwest toward the Akhaian peninsula. When the hurricane darkened the horizon, the captain made his choice to double back and take shelter on the last land they'd encountered. Only they never made it. Driven by the storm winds, the *Centurion* had probably wrecked on that shoal like all the others.

Markos spoke behind me. "Come to bed, Caro. That book is two hundred years old, and you're going to fall asleep and drool on it."

"I do not drool," I said, heart hammering. "And I think I've found it. The treasure."

He came to the table, the blanket trailing after him. Running my finger along the words, I read the passage out loud. Then I looked up at him expectantly.

Markos examined the crumpled map. "There's a mountain on here, and a river." He put a finger on it. "Was there a river on your Bollard island?"

I slumped back in the chair. "*Damn* it."

Why hadn't I thought of that? Markos was right. We'd been forced to collect rainwater in a broken barrel to drink. Neither of those islands had so much as a trickle of a creek.

Then I remembered. "There *was* a river, once." I grabbed his arm. "The rock slide—that's it! The river the captain wrote about must have—must have dried up over the centuries. Leaving just the rocky riverbed. I fell right down it."

A whole cave full of gold bricks. Hundreds of gold coins. And they would all be ours.

"We found it," I breathed. "We really found it. Every soldier in the world will fight for you now." Catching Markos's hand, I grinned up at him. "No lord will dare go against you."

I realized he wasn't smiling.

My heart froze in my chest. "Markos, what is it?"

For a long moment he didn't speak.

"The thing is . . ." He ducked his head. "I don't know how to say this. After all you've done for me."

"Markos." My blood was chilled. "What do you mean?"

Tugging his hand from mine, he examined the scabs on his knuckles. "When we first got to Valonikos, I was finally happy."

He took a ragged breath. "I was finally free. But then, Antidoros Peregrine—well, he had gotten the idea in his head that having me on the throne would be a better alternative than a revolution. I guess I never had the heart to . . ." He swallowed. "He looked at me and saw the future of Akhaia. *You* looked at me and saw an Emparch."

"That's because I believe in you," I said. "I'm right behind you. Whatever you need—" His face made me stop.

"I need you to listen," he said quietly. "Caro, when you look at the horizon, you see adventure. Opportunity. A whole world waiting to be explored." With a wistful look, he exhaled. "I just see . . . something that's not for me. A few days ago you asked me what I would give to go home. I didn't answer you." He paused for so long I thought he was finished. Then he said, "Because I don't want to go home. Not ever."

There was a knot in my stomach. "Markos . . . don't you *want* to become Emparch?"

"Gods, no." His smile was strangely giddy. "You know, that's the first time I've ever said it out loud. No, I do *not* want to be Emparch of Akhaia." Leaning against me, he began to laugh. "Not even a little."

How had I never realized how much this was crushing him? Shame washed over me. All this time I'd been telling myself I was doing this for him. When was the last time I'd asked Markos what *he* wanted?

"Well, that's a relief," I said with a grin. "Now we can keep all that gold bullion for ourselves."

"Caro, we're never going to get that treasure. The fleet is combing the island for us. We'll be lucky to escape with our lives."

I felt like remarking that it was the first time he and Diric Melanos agreed on something, but decided it was too soon.

"I'm not giving up." I curled my hand into a fist. "Not after everything we've been through."

Markos shook his head. "I just told you I don't want to be Emparch of Akhaia," he said, "and you're not even going to say anything?"

I took his hands in mine. "I once said you were the bravest man I know. You think this changes that? Do you really think I care about the name you were born with?" Impulsively I kissed him. "I care about the things you do. Who you choose to be."

"But I don't know—"

I shut him up with another kiss. "You'll figure it out."

I wondered how long he'd been keeping this from me. How could he believe this would change how I felt about him? Every ounce of blood in my veins wanted to shout for joy. I'd been convinced we were impossible, but now we weren't. Not even a little. How did he not know this was exactly what I'd always wanted? Just Markos.

No Emparchy. No throne. No war. Just him.

My lips stilled on his. "What if . . ."

I pulled back abruptly, the faintest glimmer of an idea hovering at the edges of my mind. But no—there was no way we could pull *that* off.

During the last few days I'd felt like a juggler, constantly struggling to keep everything up in the air. How to avoid the Lion Fleet. How to prevent Markos and Diric from murdering each other. How to beat Araxis at her own game. The pieces whirled around me, so close I could almost reach out and grasp them.

"Markos." My heart beat faster in spite of my doubts. "What if there was a way? To be free of Akhaia once and for all?"

He snorted. "As long as your plan doesn't involve trusting Diric Melanos."

I was silent.

Markos narrowed his eyes. "Caro?"

"Yes," I told him. "Yes, it does."

CHAPTER
TWENTY-NINE

It figured I'd find him in a place like this. The old men hunched over the tables looked as if they'd given up on life, and the moldy tomb-like smell permeating the tavern did nothing to dispel that impression.

"No use asking," Diric growled. "I ain't going to come back."

I took a deep breath.

"I know," I said. "You're going to betray me."

Outside the wind shifted, rain suddenly battering the window. The faded sign that read The Black Bittern creaked back and forth above the door. Through the wet glass I caught a glimpse of red jackets—a patrol of Akhaian officers, combing the Brizos streets for us. Hastily I turned back to the bar to hide my face.

Diric raised his eyebrows. "No, I ain't." He spat on the floor. "Though I'm sure that's what your boy Andela thinks."

"I know where the *Centurion* is," I said. Casting a glance at the bartender, I lowered my voice. "And we're going to get it—you and I."

In a whisper I told him what I'd found in the log. Taking the map from my pocket, I flattened it on the bar. It was creased with lines where he'd crumpled it.

Emotion flashed across Diric's face, quickly hidden. He smoothed the wrinkles in the map and tucked it back into his coat.

"You know what this means," he said hoarsely. The wind tossed rain at the tavern, causing the walls to creak. "If it really is the same island, then all this, right from the beginning, has been her doing."

"I always thought it was," I whispered. "Did you not? But I thought she meant to punish me, when she stranded me on that island with you. Now I'm not so sure." Something made me shiver, and it wasn't the cold. "She always said it came for you like the drakon, slithering in the deep. Your fate."

"I don't hear her anymore," he said in a low voice. I understood why. But surely if the god wanted to listen, whispering wouldn't stop her. "Haven't for months now. It's like having your gods-bedamned arm cut off."

I knew what he meant. "Me either."

He shook his head. "What if you're wrong? What if we're cursed, the both of us, and fixing to make off with an awful lot of her shiny things? She could be luring us to our deaths."

The sea god certainly did love shiny trophies. Like Dido Brilliante, she collected them. There was an entire drowned city under the ocean that she kept out of spite. But I couldn't shake the feeling that everything that had happened had led us to exactly this moment.

So many pieces of my plan could go wrong. Araxis might kill me. Markos might kill Diric. The sea god might send us all to the bottom of the ocean. I was flying by the seat of my trousers and I knew it.

In the back of my head, I heard Pa's voice. *You're an Oresteia. You're bold enough.*

A strange reckless courage flashed through me. I lifted my head. "You and me, we're the same," I said. "We're unchosen. Ayah, some may say we been cursed by she who lies beneath." I squeezed my fist around my glass. "But me, I say it's time we make our own fate. Did you ever stop to think maybe the sea god isn't trying to kill us at all? Maybe she's challenging us. Maybe we've got to *earn* this. What did she choose us for in the first place, if not to be warriors? I'm going after the treasure. Are you with me or what?"

His eyes twinkled. "Nice speech." Tilting his glass, he clinked it against mine. "What's the plan?"

I told him.

"No," Diric said as soon as I finished. "I won't let you give yourself up to her. I don't trust anyone with the name Chrysanthe."

"How else do you propose to get the blockade lifted?" I demanded. "Once Araxis and I are on our way, you and Markos set sail at once for the island. Get to that cave and remove as much of the treasure as you can." I grabbed his sleeve. "But you have to leave some. Enough so Araxis won't be suspicious."

He shook his head. "Can't abide the idea of letting her get her grubby hands on my gold, even if it's just a little bit."

"It's the most important part," I insisted. "The only way we all get out of this alive is to convince her she's won. Stash her portion of the gold somewhere on the island and lie in wait until we arrive. That's when you pull your pistol on me and we stage the fight. Say you'll trade her the gold in return for a royal pardon. And for the love of the gods, whatever you do, *don't* let Markos off the ship. I don't care if you have to tie him up. We can't trust her around him."

"It's not going to work. Don't forget, you and Araxis will likely be on one of the fastest ships in the fleet. Your boy and I . . . well, we'll be on board the *Busted Steed*." There was doubt in his voice. "And gold bullion is heavy. Reckon we'll need a sled or a lever or something." He rubbed his beard. "Removing the treasure will take too much time."

"I'll—I'll stall them somehow." I bit my lip. "Give them the wrong directions. Make them sail out of their way."

He grabbed my arm. "You're going to get yourself killed."

If we succeeded, we would never again have assassins firing shots at us or poisoning our food. We wouldn't have to watch our backs the rest of our gods-damned lives. Tears stung my eyes. And I would not be forced to watch Markos grow more and more hopeless every day, until finally he just faded away.

This was our chance to be free. We had to grab it.

I swallowed. "It's either me or Markos."

"Oh well." Diric lifted his glass. "To stupidity and love, I guess."

CHAPTER
THIRTY

I was alone when she found me.

With the clattering of gear, soldiers burst into the tavern. The booths were empty. Diric was long gone, leaving just the bartender and me.

Raising his hands, he backed up. "No muskets!"

The soldiers paid him no mind. I knew who they'd come for.

They dragged me off the stool, knocking my drink over. I didn't resist. Behind me, the toppled glass rolled in a circle, rum puddling on the bar. The men held both my arms, their rough fingers digging into my skin.

Araxis strode into the tavern, boot heels clicking on the floor. Behind her rain blustered in through the open door.

She wasn't wearing skirts anymore. Now that I knew she

wasn't the Archon of Eryth's daughter, she'd abandoned all pretense of being a lady. Her slim trousers were black, tucked into boots. I'd never seen anything like her jacket. It didn't look like a man's or a woman's but rather seemed to be custom made for her. It was short and black, with only one sleeve, leaving her right arm bare except for a leather cuff and several straps full of darts. Her crossbow hung from a hip belt.

I hated the entire look and coveted it at the same time.

Blowing a curl out of my eyes, I asked, "What happened to being dressed in blood?"

She pressed her lips into a red line. "That's my mother, not me." Surveying the empty tavern, she demanded, "Where are the others? Our informant said Melanos was with you."

"Your informant heard wrong," I said. "Diric Melanos and I have parted ways."

Her head swiveled back to me. "Where's Markos?"

"Not here," I answered unhelpfully.

She scanned the dark corners of the bar, as if at any moment Diric might burst out, guns blazing. "You really expect me to believe you're here alone?"

I imagined Markos's voice when someone annoyed him—regal and slightly bored. He ran cold, while I ran hot. Cold was what I needed right now.

"As it happens," I drawled, hoping she didn't notice the sweat on my forehead, "I'm here to make a deal."

Tapping her fingers on a chair, Araxis smirked. "I don't make deals."

"Maybe," I said, "you do when they involve a shipwreck full of gold bullion."

Her fingernails stilled in the air.

"I thought as much." My heart fluttered erratically. Somehow I had to make her go for it. Struggling in the soldiers' grip, I told her, "Like I said, I'm offering a deal. But I'll only speak with you alone."

She gave me a shrewd look, and then barked at the soldiers, "You're dismissed. Wait for me outside." She smiled. "But restrain her first." They cuffed my wrists with iron manacles and shoved me into a chair. When the door had banged shut behind them, Araxis turned to me. "Well?"

"You *were* listening that night in Iantiporos, weren't you?" Her lips twitched, but she said nothing. I assumed that was a yes, and went on. "So you know about the map. I'll give you the location of the *Centurion*'s gold. And you . . ." I took a deep breath. "You promise to leave Markos Andela alone. Return to Trikkaia and tell your father he's dead. Markos and I go free."

"You're lying. You and Melanos have some kind of plan."

I snorted. "He promised me half of the treasure. If you think he ever meant to keep his word, you're a fool." Watching her face for any signs of emotion, I continued. "But I am not a fool. I'm the daughter of a Bollard and a wherryman, and I reckon I know a good deal when I see one. You can have the treasure. All I want is Markos's life."

A flash of keen interest crossed her face, promptly banished. She shook her head. "I can't give you that. As much as I'd like a shipwreck full of gold bullion, my assignment has always been to kill the Pretender. You know that."

"What if I told you Markos doesn't want the throne of Akhaia? We'll sail away. Far away. You'll never see us again."

Araxis sighed. "He's still a threat to my father. As long as he's alive, the Theucinian line will never be secure on the throne. My father will hunt him to the four corners of the earth. He'll never stop hunting him."

"I'm not talking about your father," I said. "I'm talking about you."

She tilted her head but said nothing. I took it as a sign that she was listening.

"Fine, your father will hunt Markos till the end of his days." I licked my lips. "But *you* don't have to. This is enough gold for you to make your own fortune. You're a bastard." I hoped she wouldn't take it as an insult and do something unfortunate like slit my throat. Remembering what Daria had told me about Konto Theucinian's young son, I said, "No matter how well you serve your father, it'll be your little half brother who ends up on the throne, won't it? Not you."

"You think I haven't made my peace with that?" she snapped. "I've always accepted that I would live my life in Akhaia's shadow court, like my mother. She's royalty . . . in her own way."

But I thought I saw a flicker of something. Yearning. Jealousy. Suddenly my way forward lit up like a moon path across the sea. I knew what to say.

"Ayah, my mother is powerful too," I said. "When I was

younger I used to hate going to Bollard House. I felt like everyone there wanted me to be her."

"What do you know about my life?" she snapped. "I'm not stupid. I see what you're trying to do. Very clumsily, I might add. You're nothing like me."

I leaned back in the chair. "Probably not. *I* got a letter of marque and stole a cutter from the Black Dogs, which just so happened to be carrying a fortune in the cargo hold. I decided to make my own fate." I shrugged. "But I guess you don't wish to do the same. It's a gods-blasted shame Melanos will get all the treasure though." I winced. "Perhaps it wasn't such a good idea to steal *Vix* from him. Since he's just gone and stolen my schooner from me."

"Your schooner, which you stole from the Lion Fleet," she pointed out. "You're bluffing."

"Am I? You followed us to the Queen's lair. You were the one who shot at us, weren't you?" She didn't deny it, so I went on. "So you know I have the ship's log. Or I had it anyway." I made my hands into fists. "Melanos double-crossed me. He's taken it and the *Steed*. Markos and I barely escaped with our lives."

Araxis waved a hand dismissively. "The soldiers are searching the island for that stolen ship. They'll find it, and the *Centurion*'s log along with it. I need only wait."

"You think Diric Melanos is going to wait?" I wanted Araxis to understand that every moment we stayed here, we were wasting precious time. "He's been looking for that treasure his whole life. He might already be on his way."

"The blockade—"

"Please." I laughed. "I trust even you, sheltered in the shadow of the Emparch's court, are familiar with the reputation of the Black Dogs. Your little blockade means nothing to Melanos. He's been running blockades for eight years, and he's very good at it." Taking a deep breath, I launched into the conclusion of my pitch. "All I want is to be with Markos. I have the coordinates to the shipwreck. I'm a Bollard, the daughter of traders. So let's trade."

Sweat dampened my collar. I wasn't cut out for this. Just trying to keep all my lies straight was giving me a headache.

Araxis folded her arms, studying me. "All right," she said finally. "You lead me to the *Centurion* and Markos goes free." She held up a finger in warning. "But if Melanos gets the treasure first, the agreement is off."

"Deal." I stuck my manacled hands out, chains clinking. "First you have to tell them to lift the blockade on Brizos."

"That wasn't part of the terms."

"Of course it was," I said, like a professor explaining to a student who hadn't quite gotten the point. I wished Ma was here to see this moment. She would've been so proud. "You know Markos is somewhere on Brizos," I pointed out, "and you just agreed to let him go free. He can't leave unless you lift the blockade. I'm not giving you the coordinates until those ships are gone."

Araxis glanced out the window, where the soldiers' red coats were visible against the dark night. "I don't know if I can make that call."

"Oh?" I raised my eyebrows. "Sorry, I thought you commanded these men."

"They'll do what I ask." She fiddled with something on her finger—her lion signet. She stared intently at it, as if doing a complicated arithmetic sum in her head. "I just have to convince the captain."

I'd failed to consider that potential hole in my plan. The ring and her parentage seemed to give Araxis enough power to barter passage on a ship or commandeer soldiers as bodyguards. But what if it wasn't enough? What if the captain wouldn't listen to her?

"Oh, all right." Stepping forward, Araxis took my hand. I'd half expected it to be like shaking hands with a lizard, but hers was warm and a little sweaty. It struck me that maybe she'd been equally nervous. "I'll make it work somehow. Markos goes free and the blockade is lifted." She added, "But if the fleet finds Diric Melanos, they're free to execute him."

I shrugged one shoulder, secretly delighted with how well I was lying. "Please do."

"You're more conniving than I thought, Caroline Oresteia," she said. "I admit, it makes you rather more interesting to me."

She called the Akhaian soldiers back in. They jerked me out of the chair and marched me to the docks where, to my surprise, we boarded an armed sloop whose neat letters spelled out *Lightning*.

I turned to Araxis. "We're not going on that frigate?"

She leaned on the railing, watching the fleet glide away from its flanking position. Some ships returned to the Brizos docks, while others immediately raised sail and got under way, bound for parts unknown.

She shook her head. "The frigate is far too slow."

That threw a bit of a wrench in my plan. I'd simply have to talk my way around it.

Belowdecks, they tied me to a chair in the navigation room so I couldn't escape. I resisted the urge to point out that we were on the ocean—where would I go? From the motion and slant of the ship I knew we were riding a following sea, the wind behind us and slightly to starboard. We were probably past the Tea Isles by now.

Araxis entered the room, gesturing for an officer to unlock my manacles. I winced as he roughly obeyed. The bindings had rubbed the skin off my wrists, leaving raw red marks.

"Now you hold up your end of the bargain." She dumped a pile of charts on the table in front of me. "Where's this island?"

I requested a sextant, pencils, and paper. Then I made a big show of tracing lines across the maps, scribbling down numbers, and muttering to myself.

"We need to bear east-northeast," I announced finally, throwing down the pencil.

Araxis seized the paper, her forehead screwing up as she examined it. "You're certain?" I watched her sharply, hoping navigation wasn't one of the skills her assassin mother had taught her.

I hedged. "Well, I can't be completely sure."

"What did the log *say*?" She tossed the paper aside, impatience flitting across her face.

I leaned back in the chair. "That wasn't part of our agreement."

She signaled to the soldiers so fast that I didn't have time to duck. Sharp pain exploded across my face, radiating from my jaw.

Blood flowed out of my mouth. A wave of dizziness hit me, and I rocked forward to rest my forehead on the table. Drooling blood in a long line, I stared at my tooth, a tiny speck of white drowning in the red puddle on the floor. My lips were numb. I closed my eyes against the ringing pain.

"That's for insolence." Araxis's satisfied voice brought me back.

Wiping blood from my chin, I glared up at the officer who'd punched me. "Big man, aren't you?" I taunted him around my fat lip. "Hitting a girl tied to a chair."

He lifted his arm to backhand me again.

"No, don't." Araxis waved her hand. "I'm bored of this. And you got blood on my shoe."

Markos was missing part of his ear and now I'd lost one of my bottom teeth. I reflected that it was a good thing we'd never be Emparch and Emparchess. We certainly didn't look the part.

The door opened and the captain came in. I recognized him immediately as the captain of the *Advantagia,* the one who had laughed at me when I said I wanted an advocate. Strange that he was here, instead of on his own ship. And then I remembered Diric had set it on fire.

The captain stared in distaste at the blood on the floor. Nodding briskly at the officer, he ordered, "Get a mop and clean this mess up."

"But, sir," the man protested, "I ain't—I mean, I'm an officer. That isn't my job. Sir," he added, sensing the captain's imminent explosion.

That was another odd detail. Thinking back, I realized every one of the men I'd seen on this ship was wearing a ranking officer's coat. Surely that wasn't right. Where were the regular soldiers? And the sailors?

"Well, perhaps you might have thought about that before you caused the prisoner to bleed on my chart room floor." The captain pulled my scribbled notes across the desk, examining the numbers. Unlike Araxis, he saw at once what they meant. "These coordinates are in the middle of the ocean." Flexing his fingers, he flipped the paper aside. "Is this meant to be a joke?"

"No," I told him. My mouth throbbed. "Those are today's coordinates. Tomorrow I'll give you another set."

The captain glared, a muscle twitching in his neck. "You'll give the location of the island to me now."

"No," I said. "I'd prefer to stay alive until we reach the location, and you'll pardon me, sir, if I don't trust you." I took a guess. "A feeling which should be familiar to you, seeing as you neglected to bring the rest of the fleet with us."

The captain and Araxis exchanged glances, and I knew my suspicion had been correct. There were hundreds of sailors aboard those ships, men who'd taken a vow to serve their Emparch. Whether that vow extended to a shipwreck full of gold bullion . . . well, that was trickier. The *Advantagia*'s former captain had commandeered this sloop—a small, speedy vessel—and rearranged the crew to make sure it contained only his most loyal men. It explained why all the men aboard were officers.

"This deal wasn't my idea." The captain regarded me coldly. "But I admit to being intrigued by the prospect of recovering the greatest lost ship in Akhaian naval history. I'm willing to go along with your little game." He smiled. "But I trust you understand that further annoying me would not be in your best interest. Thanks to you, my ship is having to undergo extensive repairs. If this turns out to be a trick, I won't bother throwing you in a cell. You'll be hanged immediately."

The officers escorted me to a cabin, where they pushed me into a chair, binding my ankles to the chair legs. Then they left.

The cabin was simply adorned, with a built-in bed, chest of drawers, and a table with a round mirror on the wall above it. Araxis sat down, rummaging in a bag of little pots and tins. The ship dove across a swell. In the mirror I saw her purse her lips in annoyance, holding the lip paint well away from her face. She was having trouble drawing a straight line, what with the motion of the sea.

"So what happens now?" I ran my tongue over my busted lip. "You're just going to leave me tied to this chair for the whole voyage?"

"What's the point of talking?" She finished outlining her lips, stashing the paint pot in her bag. "I hate you. You hate me."

"I didn't always," I said.

Her eyes met mine in the mirror. "No, but you resented me for stealing your precious Markos." She sighed. "Oh, Caro. I truly wish we'd met under different circumstances. Both of us are girls caught in a struggle against fortune. Girls who latched onto a bigger destiny and pulled ourselves toward it with both hands." Her smile sliced like a knife. "Who couldn't be sunk, though gods and men and the ocean tried to defy us."

When I had spoken of our mothers and finding my own fate, it had clearly struck a nerve. Of course I'd been making it up as I went along, but Araxis seemed to have latched onto my words. She fancied us opposite sides of the same coin. I wouldn't say she liked me, but she was fascinated by me, as a bird might be fascinated by an interesting shiny object.

"That's very poetic," I growled. "But I haven't forgotten you tried to murder my cousin."

Her eyes shifted in the mirror. "I didn't succeed? Well, that's a pity."

"You must know that if you had, I would never have made this deal with you." My voice was cold. "And you'd be dead." If I found out Kenté wasn't all right, I swore I would travel to the far ends of the earth to find and kill Araxis.

Something flitted across her face that looked suspiciously like relief.

"Where is the real Agnes Pherenekian?" I asked. For a long time now I'd been wondering what had become of her.

"What does it matter?" Araxis shrugged. She fanned out her fingers, examining her nails. "She's a fat bluestocking nobody from the country. It was surprisingly simple, pretending to be her." Meeting my eyes in the mirror, she took a file out of her makeup bag. "You were easy to deceive. I rattled off some stuff about that butterfly—which I knew, thanks to my extensive study of poisons—and you were satisfied. Markos was a bit trickier. He asked me several very specific questions about the paper the real Agnes had published."

A wave of longing went through me at the mention of his name. It was just like Markos to do research about his future wife's interests.

"The cat knew." I remembered how it had hissed at her on Agnes's desk. "I should've listened to it."

"It didn't like me," she agreed. "Cats are notoriously finicky about strangers. *If* we ever find this treasure," she said, pointing at me with her nail file, "and *if* I don't kill Markos, you ought to tell him to be more careful in the future. He could take a lesson or two from that cat."

"But you both grew up in Trikkaia," I said. "You were cousins. I can't believe you never saw each other."

Her laugh came out as a bitter snort. "The daughter of a courtesan and the Emparch's son, at the same social gathering? It would have been inconceivable. A bastard child of the Akhaian nobility must remain out of sight. We lived in luxury, of course, in the fashionable part of the city. Lord Theucinian paid for absolutely everything. It was in that house that my mother trained me in her arts."

"Murder."

She shook her head. "Deportment. Etiquette. Languages." She tilted the nail file, lamplight glinting on the silver blade. "But later alchemy, chemistry, and poisons. Her *real* arts." She regarded me with curiosity. "I do wonder what you see in Markos. He's dreadfully dull and proper."

"You must have liked him a little," I said. "Or he'd be dead."

Araxis sniffed. "Not really. Why poison him when I could wait and murder him in the Margravina's own castle? Knowing *she* would be blamed for his death. Kill the Pretender and start a war with Kynthessa, all in one stroke. But then you showed up. Again."

My mouth hurt, and I didn't feel like talking anymore. "Terribly sorry."

She left me without another word, flouncing up from the chair and out the door. After a while, soldiers appeared to escort me to the head. They untied me from the chair, leaving my arms and ankles bound. Upon my return, I lay on a rough blanket on the hard floor, mouth throbbing with pain. Squeezing my eyes shut, I tried to sleep.

The next day when they dragged me into the navigation room, I made a big show out of consulting the charts and instruments.

"We've overshot it." I pushed the chair back with a scrape. "We need to come about and bear south." I handed Araxis a scrap of paper on which I'd scribbled a series of numbers. "On this heading."

She pursed her red lips, passing the paper to the captain. "I thought you said you knew where the island was."

I resisted the urge to say something sarcastic, preferring to keep the rest of my teeth.

"Look, I'm going off a bunch of scratchy notations in a moldering old book." I tried to look offended. "Which I only saw once before that dog Melanos stole it. Did you think this was going to be an exact science, like your precious chemistry?"

She lifted her hand to slap me, but the captain quelled her with a stern look.

"I'll not have any more hitting the prisoner," he reprimanded her. "I don't run that kind of ship." Just as I was wondering if perhaps he was on my side, he added, "If it turns out she's lying, she'll hang. But at least it will be a civilized death."

They returned me to the cabin.

That night, while Araxis was curled up asleep on the bed, I rocked back and forth in the sliver of moonlight that shone through the porthole. What if I'd made a mistake? Trusted the wrong people? I would end up dead, and Markos along with me.

There was nothing to do now but wait.

CHAPTER
THIRTY-ONE

Our fifth day at sea, we sighted the island off the *Lightning*'s port bow.

Above the trees rose the bald mountain peak, and to the left I recognized the smaller island where our camp had been. The shoal full of wrecked ships lay between.

The captain ordered a shore party of five men, plus myself and Araxis. On the way to the boat, I tripped three times over my ankle bindings, flinching as my bruised knees hit the deck. Araxis only smirked. The officers hauled me up by my armpits and shoved me onto a seat.

Six men was too many. My plan depended on getting Araxis alone. I bit my lip, nerves fluttering. I'd just have to worry about that later.

The captain didn't lift a finger while his crewmen manned the rudder and two sets of oars. His hat pointed like the bow of a ship toward land, the breeze ruffling the gray hair around his face. He looked like he was striking a pose, the pompous ass.

"You failed to mention this was the same island we found you on." The captain tapped his spyglass in his palm. "A striking coincidence, if I do say so myself."

"It's not the same island." I glared at him. "It's the island *next* to that island."

"Don't be pert with me, girl," the captain said. "The only reason you're coming along at all is because you've seen this supposed map. If your cave turns out to be a fish story, which I now very much suspect it is, you'll be swinging from the neck until dead," he said with relish. "I daresay that will shut you up."

Fidgeting on the seat, I fervently hoped the treasure wasn't a fish story. I had many plans for my future, and being hanged was not one of them.

I almost missed the cave the first time I looked. The entrance was only a triangular black hole in the rocky shoreline, possibly not even visible at high tide. The rocks around it were wet, clumped with seaweed and barnacles. Body tingling with excitement, I gripped the side of the boat.

The thrill of seeing the cave was short lived. The captain commanded two officers to hold lanterns aloft, and one by one they disappeared into the dark mouth.

Leaving me tied up alone on the beach.

With my bound hands I picked up a broken shell, hurling it

into the waves. It was cursed rotten luck. The first hour I sulked on the beach, manacles resting on my knees. When the second hour passed and still they didn't come out, my curiosity was aroused.

I saw no sign of Diric Melanos. If he was here on the island, he'd chosen to remain unseen. There were lots of places for a ship as small as the *Busted Steed* to lie low. I wondered exactly how long I was supposed to sit here and wait.

"Miss!" An officer picked his way over the slick rocks at the cave entrance. "You're to come inside at once!"

I scrambled up from the sand. "What's going on?"

Pulling a key from his belt, he opened the bindings. "*She* wants you." There was fear in his brown eyes. "It ain't right, what she's doing. It ain't right."

The rocks were slippery with seaweed. The officer steadied my elbow as we climbed toward the cave. When we reached the entrance, he took a handful of alchemical matches from his pocket.

"For you, miss." Dropping them in my hand, he backed away.

I looked up at the looming black crevice. "You're not coming in?"

"Ain't no amount of gold could make me go back in there, miss. I want to make captain someday." He shook his head. "Me, I don't plan on dying here."

What was going on in that gods-bedamned cave? Turning, I struck a match on the rock wall. It burst into a shower of alchemical sparks, quickly burning down to a steady flame. Holding up the match, I glanced around the cave. The floor was mostly rock, except where the tide had carried in sand and deposited it in wet ribbons. Seaweed and clams clung to the rocks.

I ventured in, ducking to keep from scraping my head on the ceiling. Wet sand sucked at my boots. The cave was barely three feet across. Luckily small spaces didn't bother me, having grown up on a wherry. Up ahead I heard voices.

The cave widened into a larger room, lit by a flickering lantern. I stepped into it, straightening, and saw at once why the officer hadn't wanted to come back. The room ended in a deep tidal pool, with a dark hole underwater about three feet down. The tide had covered the tunnel leading to the rest of the cave.

In the pool three bodies floated limply, facedown.

I dropped my match, softly snuffing it out with my boot. Dodging out of sight, I flattened myself against the wall. Araxis, the captain, and the last remaining officer stared into the pool. They hadn't noticed me yet.

"What are you waiting for?" Araxis demanded, advancing on the officer. She extended her hand. "This ring lets me speak with the voice of your Emparch. I'm *ordering* you to swim through that tunnel."

The man backed up, terrified.

Araxis raised her crossbow. "Gods-damned coward." A dart whizzed across the cave. The officer crumpled and fell, retching and clutching his throat. With a wave of nausea, I turned away, not wishing to see his final moments.

The captain straightened his jacket. "Clearly we were wrong to send common men. This is a test, you see." His lips curled in a smug smile. "Only those who are worthy shall be allowed to pass."

"You have the rank of captain." Araxis nodded to the medal on his coat. "And you've been decorated in war. Sir, surely if this is a test from the sea god herself, you'll pass it with ease."

I doubted she believed anything of the kind. She just didn't want to go through that tunnel herself.

The captain removed his boots, tucking his hat under his arm. He cut a grand figure, his red coat sparkling with buttons and medallions. "No one respects the sea more than I."

He waded into the pool until his chin touched the water, then gulped a deep breath and ducked under. For several long seconds only a rippling circle marked where he had been. Whispers danced on the cave walls, chilling and somehow inhuman. But the cave was empty except for Araxis and me.

With a bubbling splash, the captain's body burst from the water. It slowly turned over, revealing his mangled face. Something had bitten a chunk of flesh from his cheek, exposing white bone. Blood swirled in the water. The captain's eyes stared ahead, unseeing.

Araxis hissed, stumbling back. The whispers grew louder, bouncing off the cave walls, but she didn't react. My clammy hands shook. She couldn't hear them. Only I could. Suddenly I was certain this was the sea god's doing.

Remember, I keep the things I take.

These men had tried to take her treasure, and she'd judged them unworthy. I watched the tide swirl, minnows darting among the seaweed and floating bodies. This was her domain. What if I truly was unchosen? Then my fate would be no different from these men. If I tried to swim through that tunnel, she would drown me.

Water in my nose and mouth. Coughing, spluttering, clawing toward the surface. My lungs straining, bursting, the light fading—

I squeezed my eyes shut, stumbling on the rocks. That vision had come out of nowhere. Had *she* put it into my head? My pulse quickened with hope, and I strained outward with all my senses. *Wait. Come back.*

Nothing.

I shook my head to clear it. How pathetic was I? The god had sent me a vision of my own drowning—an obvious threat. But instead of being scared, I was grasping at the little scrap of her presence like a starving beggar.

Araxis's head snapped up. "Oh hello, Caro. Nice of you to join me." Raising her crossbow, she pointed it at my heart. "Your turn."

I watched the bodies bob, feeling sick to my stomach. "I can't."

"Who better to go through than you?" With her crossbow, Araxis gestured toward the water. "Fortunate favorite of the god."

"No, you don't understand." I shrank back against the cave wall. "I've been unchosen. If you send me in there . . ." I swallowed. "I'll end up just as dead as these men."

"I guess that's a chance we'll have to take." She nodded at the pool. "Unless you'd like to take a chance with my darts, but I assure you the poison is quite nasty."

Hesitantly I stepped in. Cool water swirled around my ankles. I closed my eyes, swaying at the gentle sensation. Once that feeling had meant something to me. I'd stepped into a pool like this and it had opened up a whole new world.

Not anymore.

I clenched my teeth and strode forward. Water rippled away from my legs to lap at the rocks. Around me the faces of the corpses were frozen in terror. What had they seen down there—under the water?

Araxis faked a yawn. "Let's not be all day about it."

Drawing a breath that I knew might be my last, I submerged myself in the water. Feeling my way along the rock, I propelled my body down until I came to the entrance of the tunnel. Growing up in the riverlands, I'd always been a strong swimmer. I knew I could hold my breath for a full minute. But I had no way of knowing how long the tunnel was, or if there was even air on the other side.

I opened my eyes and launched myself down the tunnel with a strong kick. The light from Araxis's lantern faded. Panic rose up inside me, but I had to conquer it. I had to survive. Stretching forward, I stroked hard with my arms.

My seeking hands met rock. A dead end.

No.

I screamed, but only a stream of bubbles came out.

Flailing, I spun in a circle. Above my head, my right hand hit rock. I grasped the corner of what felt like a ledge. Looking up, I thought I saw dim light. The way out was *above* me. I rocketed up, kicking like a frog. The confining rock fell away and I popped out into open water.

For a moment I was disoriented. I had no idea which way was up and which was down. My lungs screamed to breathe. I'd made it through the tunnel, but if there was no air in this part of the cave, I was done.

My hand burst through the surface, and then my head.

Chest heaving, I sucked frantic breaths into my burning lungs. I scrabbled with my feet and found the sandy bottom of the pool. I stood chest deep in the water.

In absolute blackness.

With shaking fingers I felt in my pocket for the rest of the matches. Arms extended in front of me, I sought blindly until my knuckles scraped a rock. It took me two tries to light the match.

I was in a pool inside a small cave. The water swirled around my waist, minnows flitting in the shallows. I looked up, and nearly dropped the match.

Sitting casually on a rock, his legs crossed, was Nereus.

He took a sip from his flask, looking for all the world like he was relaxing in *Vix*'s cabin with a game of cards and not lurking in a pitch-dark cave. The smell of rum wafted my direction.

"I saw your body." My mouth was dry. "We pushed it into the sea."

"Ah." He scratched the back of his neck. "About that . . . You remember when we met, I said I'd served her in a hundred lives."

"I admit," I said dryly, "I thought it was a figure of speech." I hesitated. "Nereus, I—I don't understand. Why am I here? I disobeyed her. I thought I was unchosen. But now . . . I don't know what to think."

"Unchosen?" Nereus winked. "I have a secret for you, Caroline Oresteia." His sparkling eyes met mine over the flask. "There ain't no such thing." He raised his voice, and the tone changed. "Ain't that right? I know you're there. Stop lurking in the corner like a cat."

For a moment I wondered who he was talking to. The match light danced on the water, playing on the cave walls. There was no one else here but him.

Then the sea god hissed, "You know I loathe cats."

Nereus threw a grin at me. He'd chosen the exact words he knew would rile her up.

I turned in a slow circle. "You tried to drown me."

"Did I?" Her voice echoed off the cavern walls. For once she wasn't a drakon or a heron or a gull. She was everywhere.

"You took my ship," I accused her. "And Nereus. You banished me to an island in the middle of nowhere and put hundreds of miles between me and Markos. You took everything that ever meant anything to me. And then you *disappeared*."

"I sent you to that island," she whispered, "to save someone I thought was lost to me."

I stifled a laugh. "I'm pretty sure if you ask him, he'll say it was the other way around." Remembering who waited for me outside in the cave, I said, "While you were *so* busy arranging my whole life, I wish you'd managed to drown Araxis. Who, you might have noticed, has been an enormous bother to me."

"The lion girl is annoyingly resourceful," the god said crossly. "Where you are concerned, however, everything has proceeded according to my plans. You wanted to sail the world, but you never even left Valonikos. You wanted that lion boy, but you were willing to stand back and let him marry another. You didn't know who you were." The water around my knees rippled, sending a shiver down my back. She whispered, "Laughter. You know now."

Hot anger coursed through me. "If I didn't know who I was, it's no one's fault but yours! Ever since you chose me, my whole life has been so mixed-up." My fists dripped water. "You abandoned me." I thought of Diric, alone for months on that island. "You abandoned us both."

"Laughter. *You* were moping about that boy. *He* was drowning in guilt and whiskey." She swirled the pool in satisfaction. "Look at the both of you now. My warriors."

I realized what her words meant. Inspecting the cave again, I saw footsteps in the sand, along with deep grooves. Something had been dragged across the cave. Something heavy. "He was here too, then?" I asked. "Diric Melanos?"

"Oh yessssss." Her words slithered around me like the drakon.

I turned to the water-filled tunnel. "But how did he get the treasure out?"

She said nothing.

And then I knew. Closing my eyes, I stretched out with my senses. I felt the rhythm of the sea, the pull of the breakers crashing and receding on the beach. Thousands of invisible creatures floated in the water, their presence like tiny pricks of light all around me. In the sky the gulls reeled and cried. In the depths a drakon roared.

In Valonikos I'd tried to move the sea and failed. This time was different.

Spreading my fingers, I lowered them into the water. The pool whirled around me, sending up a splash. It receded first to my knees and then to my ankles. The sand was dotted with bits of broken shells. Where there once was only water, a dripping rock tunnel led to the cave entrance. The footsteps and drag marks had been washed away.

Araxis splashed through the tunnel. "Who are you talking to?" A water droplet fell in her eye. She brushed it away, smudging her makeup. "Who's there?"

She didn't even glance in Nereus's direction. Turning, I discovered he was gone. Cursed annoying, the gods.

"Where's the gold?" she demanded.

"I—I don't know," I stammered. "Melanos said his ancestor hid the gold in this cave. Perhaps someone else found it and looted it long ago."

She drew her crossbow. "How unfortunate for you."

On the way out, I was silent. My role in the plan was to bring Araxis to the cave and get her alone—which had, admittedly, worked out more gruesomely than I had planned, thanks to the sea god's interference.

Now it was Diric's turn. Gods damn him, where was he? My body hummed with anxiety. If he didn't show, I was about to be very, very dead.

We burst out of the cave, squinting in the sudden light.

"That's far enough."

Diric Melanos stood on the beach, leaning against a wooden

chest. Through the broken lid shone the sparkle of gold. His tattered coat hung to his knees, and he held two flintlock pistols. The barrel of one gun was aimed at us, and the other . . .

I halted. "Markos."

Blue eyes flashing, he looked at me hungrily. My heart fluttered at the sight of him standing in the sand in his shirtsleeves, hair loose around his face. He was tall and handsome and—

He wasn't supposed to be here.

"Caro." His voice caressed my name, as if no one else was on the beach with us.

My danger sense tingled. This wasn't part of the plan. I reached for my pistol at my waist, and then remembered it wasn't there.

Diric poked his gun into Markos's back. "Shut up."

My pulse skittered a mile a minute, but I couldn't let Araxis know. Everything else had come together perfectly. Diric was waiting with the treasure. Araxis was alone. Everything was right, except . . . why had he brought Markos?

Markos grimaced. Not only was his jacket gone, but both his swords were missing. "Sorry, Caro. He caught me by surprise."

"It's not your fault." I swallowed down my fear. *Stick to the plan.* "What are you doing, Diric?"

He nodded at the Akhaian ship anchored in the cove, only its sails visible above the rocks. "You betrayed me—made a deal with the lions behind my back. I admit, I didn't think you had it in you."

"I betrayed *you*?" Struggling to control the tremor in my voice, I eased into my role. This was exactly what he was supposed to say. I just didn't understand why Markos was here. "You took the log and the map. You ran off with my ship."

"Sorry, love, but this treasure is mine." He shoved Markos hard, causing him to stumble to his knees in the sand. "I like you, girl. That part weren't a lie. But your precious Emparch makes you sentimental. Makes you weak. That's what you did, isn't it? Traded my family's treasure to save *him*." Settling his pistol at the base of Markos's neck, he turned to Araxis. "As you can see, Caroline ain't in possession of the treasure, so your deal with her is off. I'm here to make my own deal."

I could barely breathe with that pistol touching Markos's skin. "You bastard," I choked.

Araxis's eyelids flickered, and I realized it was a poor choice of words. But she chose not to comment. Instead she folded her arms. "Name your terms, Captain."

"Eight years I've spent in exile." Diric's voice was ragged. "I want to go home. To Akhaia. That's all I've ever wanted. So those are my terms—an official pardon from your father. And my freedom."

Crossing the beach, Araxis flipped open the lid of the chest. Rows and rows of gold bricks packed the left side. In a compartment on the right, a spill of gold coins lay tangled with what looked like tiny rusted buckles—the remains, I guessed, of leather purses that had rotted away long ago. Gold light bathing her face, she drew her fingers over the bricks.

"There's only one chest here." She looked up at Diric. "Where's the rest of it?"

"Reckon this was all my great-great-granddad ever found," he drawled casually, keeping his pistol on Markos.

"That ship was a galleon," Araxis sneered, "of the Royal Akhaian Treasury. There should be boxes and boxes of bullion. Heaps of gold coins." She kicked the chest, causing two coins to fall with a clink to the sand. "This is *nothing*."

Just the gold bricks in that chest would be worth millions of talents today. Perhaps it was nothing to her. To me it was a fortune the likes of which I'd never seen in my life.

Araxis raised her crossbow. Sunlight sparkled on the dart's metal tip. "My men will search this island. If you've hidden it somewhere, I'll find it."

"Then you best search the bottom of the sea." Diric shrugged. "It ain't here." His voice changed. "And I ain't stupid, girl. I seen my bounty poster. That chest alone is worth a hundred times the price on my head. And don't you be forgetting it belongs to my family, so you might say it's got sentimental value besides. I be willing to give you *half*, in exchange for my pardon."

Markos spat in the sand. "You're just a filthy mercenary. Caro *trusted* you."

"Had enough of you, I have." Diric cuffed him across the face.

"Don't!" I cried.

Markos's hand flew up to touch the smoldering red mark on his cheek. His nostrils flared, but he was quiet.

The sight of him getting hit seemed to cheer Araxis up. Smirking, she turned back to Diric. "Half the chest isn't enough. Caro was going to give me all of it." She drummed her fingernails on the crossbow. "Ugh, I wish I'd just killed the lot of you. All this haggling is tiresome."

Diric had one pistol on Markos's neck and the second pointed at Araxis, whose crossbow was trained on him. I had no weapons at all. It was a stalemate. I couldn't take Diric out, not when he had two guns. If I went for Araxis . . .

What *would* Diric do? He'd veered so far away from the plan, I didn't know what was going on anymore. A chilling thought slithered through my mind. Perhaps he did mean to kill us all and take the treasure for himself. We wouldn't be the first people he'd murdered.

Oh gods. I could hardly breathe. I'd trusted him. *What had I done?*

"Ah." There was a steely glint in Diric's eye. "Figured you might say something like that." He nudged Markos with his boot. "That's why I brought the boy. Sweeten the deal. Half the gold goes to me, and you get your *dearest husband* back."

"Done," she said right away, lowering the crossbow.

My voice broke. "*What?*"

Before I could move, Markos kicked his leg out. Diric grunted, stumbling in the sand. Desperately Markos scrambled backward toward me.

Snarling, Diric climbed to his feet.

"Don't do anything stupid," I gasped.

He laughed. "Oh, I ain't. This is the smartest thing I've done in a long time. I'm finishing my job." He raised his pistol. "I'm getting my gold." He set his finger on the trigger. "I'm going home."

Then he shot Markos in the heart.

CHAPTER
THIRTY-TWO

I used to spend sleepless nights dreading this moment.

Blood oozing through Markos's shirt to pool on the muddy ground. His chest shuddering under my hands. The unsteadiness of his breathing, the seconds growing longer and longer between each gasp.

Until . . . nothing.

"Markos," I gasped, bending my face to his. Hoping desperately to feel his breath on my cheek.

His head flopped to one side, blue eyes fixed on something in the distance. His hand, which he'd clasped to his chest when the gun went off, went limp and slid away. Dark blood flowed sluggishly between my fingers as I pressed down on the bullet wound, trying to push the life back into him.

It didn't work.

I remembered nothing of the trip back to the *Lightning*. The whole time I clung to Markos's body, my senses numb. I couldn't let him go. I'd trusted the wrong man and paid the most devastating price.

Later an officer told me Diric Melanos took his royal pardon and ran. The last they saw of the *Busted Steed* was her billowing sails headed south. At Araxis's command, the men searched the island for hidden treasure, but found nothing.

The crew wrapped Markos's body in a length of sheet and carried it down to the underbelly of the sloop. The hold was stacked to the ceiling with wooden crates, and barrels lined the walls. They laid him on the floor, stiff and still, in a gap between the boxes.

I'd never thought much about death before. I was not prepared for the coldness. The emptiness. Alone in the hold I tugged back the sheet, revealing his familiar face and tousled hair. His skin was waxy. Everything that had been *Markos* was—not here.

Not anymore.

It seemed as unfathomable as the ocean.

I smelled her presence in the cargo hold before I saw her. A whisper of perfume. The powdery scent of lip paint. Seizing the sheet, I rushed to cover Markos's face before she could see it. That didn't belong to *her*.

Araxis sat cross-legged on the floor. "I'm glad I didn't have to kill him. I know you won't believe me." She shot me a sideways look. "But I'm glad. He was . . . nice to me. A bit naive, but nice."

If she said another word, I would scream. "Stop. Talking."

We both stared at the sheet-draped body, illuminated by a candle. My eyes felt full of sand from crying. The timbers above us groaned and, far above, the rigging thrummed in the wind. The *Lightning* was bound for Akhaia.

Araxis rested her clasped hands on her knees. "I wish I hadn't poisoned your cousin."

"Why," I asked quietly, "would I believe you?"

A long moment passed. "I watched the two of you in Iantiporos," she said finally. "You and her. Listened to you talking. I might even have wished . . . Well, never mind. My mother says friends are only enemies who haven't turned on you yet."

"No offense," I croaked, "but your mother is a murderer."

She shrugged. "Why on earth would I be offended by that?"

I refused to look at her. "If you're asking for my forgiveness, I won't give it. You nearly killed Kenté. You *did* kill Markos." I sensed her mouth opening, and snapped, "I know you didn't pull the trigger, but all this happened because of you."

I squeezed my eyes shut. Easier to lash out at her than admit the truth—I'd been fool enough to believe Diric Melanos had actually changed. I'd *wanted* to believe it. And he'd used it against me. Markos was dead because of my stupidity. I had killed him, not Araxis.

Araxis tilted her head like a bird, uncomprehending and inhuman. "Forgiveness." She turned the word over in her mouth. "No, I don't need that."

We sat in silence, while she watched me as if I was some kind of curious specimen, and I wished she would go away.

"I think you know none of this is going to make your horrible father love you," I said.

I wanted to drive a stake into her heart, the same way she'd driven one into mine. But I didn't know if it was even possible.

Araxis's face was like a porcelain mask. She'd exchanged her peculiar black jacket and trousers for a plain gray shift. Her hair flowed over her shoulders like spilled ink.

"Is that what you think I need?" She stared ahead into the flickering candle. "Your pity?"

I said nothing, until finally she left me.

In the dark of the hold, timbers creaked and swayed around me. The stillness of Markos's body terrified me. And yet the thought of leaving him here—alone—frightened me more. The night seeped into me, taking hold in my bones. I refused to move, not even to get a blanket. Instead I held his cold hand until a thread of light beamed through the porthole.

My eyes focused on something white on the floor. Reaching out, I plucked it from the crack between the planks. It was just a button, probably dislodged from Markos's shirt. I let it fall to the floor.

My bones ached with stiffness. A headache throbbed in the center of my forehead. The candle had long since burned down and sputtered out. I blinked my gritty eyes. It was morning.

And still Markos lay motionless and cold. My adventures had begun with two bodies under a sheet, back in Hespera's Watch, and now they were ending with one.

The rest of the journey passed in a blur, until one day I heard the sailors shout and felt the canvas slacken. Seagulls cawed outside the porthole. Somewhere a bell was ringing. Peering at the red roofs of the distant city, I recognized it as Valonikos. It made sense, I supposed. This was a naval vessel, and it belonged at sea. Likely Araxis would disembark here and book passage on another ship, bound up the River Kars for Trikkaia.

Araxis descended the steps. She'd changed into the clothes of a lady, a red silk dress with gathered sleeves. Her hair was coiled in a golden net at the back of her head.

She sniffed the air. "The corpse isn't stinking yet. Lucky for you, else the air would be so thick you wouldn't be able to stand it down here." Her red lips twisted. "Oh. That wasn't very sensitive, was it?"

"If you're determined to be a bitch, then why don't you just kill me?" I asked without inflection. The world was flat and gray, and I didn't care anymore.

"Because, Caro," she said reasonably, as if we were discussing our dinner plans and not standing over Markos's dead body, "our deal was Markos's life for the treasure. As it turns out, I ended up with both. Winning puts me in quite a good mood, I find. So as soon as we dock in Valonikos, you're free to go."

My fingernails bit into my palms. "What about Markos?" I growled.

Araxis nudged his sheet-covered leg with her boot, as dispassionate as if she was poking a dead butterfly. "I'm taking the body to Trikkaia, of course. To present to my father."

It seemed ridiculous that I had any tears left, but they seared my eyes anyway. "What's he going to do to him?"

She hesitated. "Cut him into quarters, probably. Put his head on a stake. Display him on the walls of the palace so everyone will know what happens when you cross the Theucinian family."

"I'll die," I said flatly, "before I let that happen."

Araxis shrugged. "That's your choice, isn't it?"

"Isn't it enough that he's dead?" My voice broke. "You have to desecrate his body too? Let me take him," I pleaded. "Just let me bury—"

"I'm going to the harbor master to arrange for passage up the river. Say your farewell," she said coldly, "and get out of here before I return. Or I may change my mind and decide to bring my father your head as well. Remember, it's only because of my mercy that you're alive." At the top of the steps she paused. "Goodbye, Caro Oresteia."

With a whisper of silk, she was gone. Light footsteps treaded the creaky deck above me. Through the porthole I watched the back of her dress as she slipped down the plank and melted into the bustle of the Valonikos docks.

Tears filling my eyes, I fell to my knees beside Markos. How could I leave him? I couldn't bear to think of his body being torn apart and laughed at by people who hated him. And I wasn't ready to say goodbye. Twisting my hands in the sheet, I rested my head on his chest. I would never be ready.

The sheet moved.

I ignored it. I'd barely slept for days. I was imagining things. Markos's chest shuddered.

I tore off the sheet, my hands flying to touch him everywhere. His forehead didn't feel so cold, but surely that was wishful thinking. I'd heard sometimes bodies moved after they were dead. That's all it was.

Something fluttered under my fingers. Was that—a pulse under his sticky skin? "Markos?" I gasped, gently slapping his cheek.

He opened his eyes.

I sat down hard. "You were dead," was all I could manage.

Tentatively he flexed his arms. "Ugh, my mouth tastes horrible." He moved his jaw. Satisfied that everything was working properly, he grinned at me. "I admit, it's different being on this end for once. You're usually the one who's dead."

My heart was racing so fast I thought it might explode. "This isn't funny."

Struggling to a sitting position, he touched my cheek. "Caro, you look—" He stopped.

"Awful," I grumbled. "You can say it. I've been crying for days. Over *you*."

"I was going to say beautiful," he said. "I was trying to be polite."

"Stop complimenting me at once and tell me how you're alive," I rasped. "He shot you. I saw it."

"You *heard* it," he corrected me. "Melanos rigged the pistol. The whole thing was his idea. The closer we got to the island, the more edgy he became. Finally he asked me if I really thought the Theucinians would stop chasing me, even for gold. I was forced to admit the same worry had been plaguing my own mind. And so the two of us came up with this plan. Not," he added, "that your plan wasn't good. This one just, um, enhanced it. Closed up the final hole."

"But you punched him in the face." I couldn't understand why Diric cared whether or not the Theucinians pursued Markos. "He hates you."

He gave me a lopsided smile. "I suspect he did it for you."

"And you—you were willing to let him aim a pistol at you? You don't trust Diric."

"No." He caught my hands in his, which still felt like blocks of ice. "But I trust *you*."

"But you were bleeding everywhere. And you—well, you—" My throat closed, and I was unable to tell him how broken I'd felt when I saw his eyes staring with the emptiness of death.

"The blood was fake. Well, I daresay it was blood from something. Melanos disappeared into the woods and returned with it, and I wasn't particularly inclined to ask what he'd killed." Markos folded his shirt back, showing me an object awkwardly sewn inside. "I emptied out one of the medicine vials we had in the supplies, and he put the blood inside. When I heard the shot go off, I clutched my chest, smashed the vial, and well . . ." He indicated his blood-encrusted shirt. Kicking the sheet off, he got to his feet. "Ow." He grimaced. "My legs are asleep."

"Markos, you were dead." I refused to believe his story. "I sat with your body for days. You weren't there. I *know* it. All this about fake gunshots and fake blood—that doesn't explain—"

"As for that . . ." He glanced around the floor. "I don't know where it's gone. I suppose I dropped it."

"Dropped *what*?"

"The button."

My head snapped up. I'd found a button on the floor of the hold. Studying his stained shirt, I realized all the buttons were firmly in place. All at once I remembered Kenté's collection of pins and trinkets. The night she was poisoned, she'd tried to tell me something that had to do with Markos. Something about a letter.

I ground my teeth. "I'm going to murder my cousin."

"She sent me a letter explaining how it works," Markos said. "She bound an illusion of death into a button with a piece of string twisted through it. Pulling out the string sets off the illusion. Quite clever, really. She said I would fall into a deep sleep, appearing dead to anyone around me."

"And you didn't feel the need to share this with me?"

"Well . . ." He winced. "In truth I'd forgotten all about it. Her letter arrived right after I received word that *Vix* was lost. I wasn't thinking about anything except you. I stashed the button in my shaving kit for safekeeping, and then Agnes showed up and everything just sort of took off . . ." Tentatively he tried to set weight on his foot. "I've been awake for several minutes now. The sheet was tickling me awfully. But I knew I couldn't move until she was gone."

Something thumped on the deck above us. I glanced at the stairs. "We need to go, before she gets back. Can you walk?"

He leaned on the wall. "Just give me another moment. I feel stiff as a corpse."

"Not funny." I bit my lip, thinking hard. "I don't know how we're going to get you off the ship without them seeing you."

Markos stuck a hand in his pocket and pulled out something slender and shiny. "I don't suppose this will help?" He held one of Kenté's hairpins. "She sent me one of these too."

Grabbing it, I kissed it. All right, so I wasn't going to murder my cousin after all. Eyeing the vial inside Markos's shirt, I asked, "I don't suppose there's any blood left in there?"

"No." He gaped at me. "*Why?*"

"Because," I said, "you're dead. So it needs to look like I dragged your corpse out of here. Or else when Araxis comes back, she'll wonder."

He wrinkled his nose. "Disgusting, but practical."

"That's me." I grinned. "Do you have a blade on you?" He rummaged in his pocket, offering me a pocketknife. Before he could stop me, I slashed my own arm. Dripping blood on the floor, I smeared it with the sole of my shoe, making a wobbly line toward the steps.

"Caro! You should've let me do that."

"Don't be stupid. You've been dead." I tossed the hairpin to the floor. "Come on, let's get out of here."

Invisible, we tiptoed up the stairs and snuck down the gangplank. Once we reached the busy dock, I was finally able to breathe. Men shoved past us, rolling a giant barrel of ale. A small boy waved a newspaper over his head. The dock inspector shouted orders at someone while, in the distance, equipment clanged and hammers banged. In the familiar chaos of the harbor we could slip away unnoticed, a pair of silent shadows.

By the time the illusion wore off, we'd managed to put half a mile between us and the docks. We walked down a shabby street where the buildings leaned close and the doorways didn't have nice flowerpots. Myself, I wasn't sure Markos knew where he was going. This didn't look like a part of the city he had much experience with.

I glanced over at Markos. "Aren't we going to Peregrine's?"

He stopped walking. "No." His face was hard. "Not yet. Araxis may come looking for you, and I don't want to lead her to Daria. We'll find a hotel and disappear for a few days. Until we're certain she's gone." He nodded up the street. "The Majestic is somewhere this way. At least, I think it is."

Sometimes he really could be ridiculous. "We just finished faking your death. We're not *going to the Majestic*. It's the most famous hotel in Valonikos."

I led him to a small cheap tavern that rented rooms for fifty cents a night. The roof was missing half its tiles and someone had vomited on the doorstep.

Markos's lip twisted. "I understand your reasoning," he said with a sigh, "but I refuse to bathe here."

I didn't have the heart to tell him a place like this probably didn't have baths anyway. The room was tiny, with a narrow bed and one scratchy blanket. Despite being reunited after a harrowing separation, both of us were too tired to do anything more than fall into the bed and sleep.

Two days later a report of Markos's death appeared in the newspaper. Further down, it mentioned that triumphant envoys had departed for Trikkaia this morning to inform the Emparch that the Pretender was dead.

At sunset we borrowed a skiff and rowed down Valonikos

beach to a deserted spot, past the fishermen and bathers. Bare toes digging into the sand, I watched the sun set over the red-roofed city. Its twinkling orange glow lit up the waves. I raised the spyglass to my eye, sweeping it across the horizon. This was the agreed-upon time and place. All we had to do now was wait.

Markos glanced pityingly at me. "Caro, he's not coming." He lifted a hand to run it through his hair, and then stopped with a bemused expression.

Yesterday I'd gone to the market and purchased scissors, with the result that he now had short spiky hair—admittedly, not very evenly cut. He looked remarkably handsome, but not at all like himself. It seemed neither of us were used to it yet.

"The two of you were plotting behind my back, and your plan went off without a hitch. Not to mention that you let him shoot you, on purpose," I pointed out. "And you still don't trust him?"

"Not," he said, "when it comes to gold." He stepped up behind me, wrapping his arms around my waist, and kissed my neck. "Even if he doesn't show up, it will have been worth it. I'm free, Caro. Really and truly free, for the first time in my life. We don't need the gold. We have our whole lives ahead of us."

I restrained myself from rolling my eyes. Practicality had never been Markos's strong point. He could stand there and make romantic proclamations all he wanted. Myself, I preferred the money.

"He'll come." I looked back at the horizon. "I know he will."

And then I saw white sails.

With a laugh, I ran barefoot down the beach. Shading my

eyes, I squinted at the ship. Two masts, with two sails standing tall, and yet something was different.

It was the old *Busted Steed* all right, but she gleamed. Fresh paint shone on the curve of her hull. The canvas and ropes were stiff with newness. Her list to starboard was gone, and she crested the waves with a confident power I'd never seen before.

With a rueful smile, Markos shook his head. "I don't believe it."

Diric Melanos rowed ashore, accompanied by two crewmen. He nodded at the sailors, who lifted three chests from the bottom of the boat. They dragged them across the sand and, from the way they sank deep, I knew they were very heavy. The sailors loaded the chests into our skiff.

I took off running toward the boat.

Diric grinned. "Caro!" He was wearing a new jacket. I crashed into him and he lifted me, spinning me in a circle.

"The *Steed*!" I exclaimed when he set me down. "She's— fixed!" I couldn't stop staring at her. It was hard to believe it was the same ship. "She's lovely."

As I gazed at the *Busted Steed*, bobbing at anchor outside the line of breakers, I realized I owed her my life several times over. She was a good, faithful schooner.

But not, I suspected, meant for me.

"Oh, that old thing." Diric shrugged. His gaze lingered lovingly on the schooner. I knew he was proud of her, although he would never say so out loud. "Turns out a shipyard can get an awful lot of work done in a week's time, if you throw enough gold at them."

Diric turned to Markos. "I see you recovered from your death just fine, Andela." He clasped Markos on the shoulder. "Good show. You was a better liar than I expected."

"All I really had to do was stand there and let you hit me in the face," Markos said sourly. "And then shoot me." But he reached out to shake Diric's hand. "I admit I didn't think you were coming."

I glanced at Markos, then back at Diric. "For what it's worth, *I* thought you would show up."

"Ayah, well, I just got on her good side again, didn't I?" He kicked affectionately at the lapping foam around his feet. "Wouldn't want to ruin it."

My throat tightened. "That's not why you came."

"Now don't you go painting me as something I'm not." He wagged a finger at me. "I ain't a man of honor. Reckon I'll go on rum-running and smuggling."

"Smuggling is a time-honored tradition!" I said defensively when Markos rolled his eyes. "You're free to return to Akhaia now. Will you?"

The wind ruffled Diric's hair. "No, I feel like going south for a while. Sailing wherever *she* takes me. Been a long time since I smuggled some choice goods to the Clockwork City. Perhaps that's where I'll go."

His shoulders seemed lighter somehow, and his manner more free. I wanted to think he'd finally found his absolution for the horrible things he'd done, but likely it was just the gold.

Diric nodded to our skiff. "Well, there's your prize, Caro." He brushed sand from his hands. "Reckon I know what you're going to do with it. You promised you would, and I laughed at you. I ain't laughing now." Leaning close, he said, "Take care of her for me."

Throwing a lazy salute to Markos, he jumped in the dinghy.

After they rowed away, Markos turned to me. "Take care of who?"

The wind caught the *Busted Steed*'s sails, and emotion swelled in my throat. I couldn't answer.

Dropping to my knees in the wet gritty sand, I flipped up the buckles securing the nearest of the three chests. The lid creaked open, revealing row upon row of gold bricks. Nestled together they almost glowed, the orange sunlight setting them aflame.

"Xanto's balls," was all I could manage. "We're rich."

CHAPTER
THIRTY-THREE

I looked up at the glowing windows of Antidoros Peregrine's house. Glancing at Markos, I asked, "Are you sure about this?"

He took a deep breath. "As sure as I'll ever be."

The gold had proved too heavy for the two of us, so we'd had to hire a cart and pay three dockworkers to help unload the chests from the skiff and lug them up here. They pocketed their coin and ambled off, leaving us alone in Peregrine's courtyard.

I knocked on the door.

Peregrine's servant nearly fainted when he recognized Markos. "You—you're supposed to be dead," he stammered. "My lord has been locked in the library all evening, trying to decide how to tell the little lady."

Something clattered down the stairs and flung itself at Markos.

"Markos!" Daria shrieked, burying her face in his shirt. "I had a dream about you. At least, I think I did. I dreamed of a big talking cat." She beamed up at him. "And now you're here, so I was right. The lion must have been you."

He laughed. "Hush, little badger." Dropping to his knees, he squeezed her. "I'm back."

"You look so different." She plucked at his hair. "It's so *short*." Noticing me over his shoulder, she gave a dramatic sigh. "Oh, Caro. You're not very good at staying dead, are you?"

I shot a look at Markos. "Neither of us are these days."

Daria's hair was in two neat plaits, secured together with a ribbon bow, and instead of a motley assortment of junk she carried a book under her arm. I craned my neck to read the title. *The Modern Senate: A Primer.* Peregrine certainly seemed to have been a steadying influence on her.

"What happened to Agnes?" she asked me. "Did you shoot her?"

"Daria, that's not very nice," Markos chided her.

"I wish I had," I muttered. He elbowed me. "Ow! I mean, it turned out she was a traitor. She was working for the Theucinians the whole time."

"I didn't like her anyway," Daria said. "She called me 'pet.' "

"I call you badger," Markos pointed out.

She screwed up her face. "It is *not* the same thing."

Peregrine descended the stairs, rather less dignified than usual. After he and Markos clasped hands, he said, "I admit I hoped the announcement of your death was Theucinian propaganda. The last I heard you'd arrived safely at the Margravina's castle."

I interrupted. "Aren't you surprised *I'm* not dead?"

Peregrine smiled. "Well, Caroline, these things do seem to happen around you, don't they?" Rummaging in his pocket, he handed me a letter. "Here, this arrived the other day from Iantiporos."

Recognizing the sloppy handwriting on the envelope, I ripped it apart.

Cousin Dearest,

I hope this letter finds you safe and well, far from the clutches of the Vile Agnes. I've entrusted it to the keeping of Antidoros Peregrine, since it occurs to me that, whether you find the shipwrecked treasure or not, you and Markos will eventually return to his house to reunite with Daria. (Tell her I say hello.)

The physicians say I'm very lucky. The poison never took hold in my veins. When I woke up the next day, I felt much better, almost like a haze had been lifted. But to my horror I realized I'd forgotten to tell you about another little experiment of mine.

You know I've been experimenting with putting shadow magic into all my buttons and pins and things. Well, I made a button that gives the appearance of death. I had the idea that, as a last resort, we might use it to somehow fake Markos's death. Then perhaps the Theucinians will leave him alone. Before I set sail for Brizos to find you, I sealed one up in a letter and sent it to him. But then everything happened in such a rush in Iantiporos, I never found out if he got it.

Oh well. If the time arises when such measures become necessary, I'm sure you're clever enough to come up with a plan on your own.

Or are you?

Offended, I lowered the letter. "What does she mean, or are you?"

You have always been more about kicking over tables and throwing knives, while I have always been the one with an inclination toward Secret Plots. Ah well, I shall be rejoining you soon.

Until then, may the shadows hide you,

K.B.

Later, relaxed around the crackling fire in the library, we told Peregrine and Daria the whole story, starting with the shipwreck and ending with how we'd snuck from the *Lightning*'s cargo hold using Kenté's hairpin. Daria lay across Markos's lap, giggling as he tickled her.

"Believe it or not, I understand how you feel." Peregrine spun the stem of his wineglass. "You're young. Having the fate of a whole country on your shoulders is a great burden. But I would still hate for you to throw it all away."

Markos played with his sister's hair. "I'm not any good at

speeches. I'm not a revolutionary. Or a leader. You've thrown your support behind me, Antidoros, and I'm so grateful for that." Watching him from an armchair on the other side of the fireplace, I had never felt so proud of him.

Peregrine acknowledged him with a wry smile. "But?"

"But how would Akhaia be any different under my rule?" Markos asked. "I'd still be just another Emparch. I'm not even certain I'd be a very good one."

"You're nothing like your cousin."

"I know." Markos took a deep breath. "He wants to be Emparch, so much that he was willing to kill for it." Sensing his turmoil, Daria twisted her neck to glance at him in concern. "I don't. I'm so sorry." His voice cracked. "But I can't be who you want me to be."

"Yes, you can." Peregrine leaned forward, gripping his arm. "You're the future of Akhaia."

"No, I'm not." Markos's voice was certain. "You are." He shook his head. "I don't know why it took me so long to see. I understand what you were trying to accomplish, putting me on the throne as an intermediary step to democracy. But what our country really needs is someone who speaks for the people—someone they already trust." He turned to face Peregrine. "Even if it takes years. Even if it takes a revolution."

Daria sat up straight. "Markos," she said, "does this mean we're not going back to Akhaia?"

"I don't think so, badger. Not for a long time." The firelight flickered on his smile. "Konto Theucinian believes me to be dead. Which means, for the first time in my life, I'm free."

"What will you do?" Peregrine asked.

"Perhaps I'll go to the university in Iantiporos and read for a degree." He shrugged. "Perhaps I'll learn a trade."

I snorted at that.

He glanced at me. "You know, Caro, I am good at *some* things." Nodding at the chests on the floor, he told Peregrine, "Open them."

Peregrine unbuckled the nearest chest and lifted the lid. His face lit up with a golden glow. Giving Markos a piercing look, he said, "I can't take this."

"It's not for you. It's for Akhaia." Markos met his eyes, a sober expression on his face. "For the revolution."

"This—this is too much." Peregrine lifted a gold brick, turning it over in the firelight. "Each of these pieces of bullion is worth a small fortune. You must know that." He scratched the brick with a fingernail. "At least I assume it's solid gold all the way through . . ."

Peregrine was an intellectual, and his curiosity had been roused. No doubt he'd be poking that brick with a file and dropping it into an alchemical solution the moment we left.

"When my father banished you from Akhaia, he stole your fortune," Markos said. "I'm only making things right."

"I can emphatically assure you I didn't have this much gold."

"Well, you have it now." Markos grinned lightly, as if the weight of that gold had been lifted from his back. "I trust you'll use it wisely. And if you do march on Akhaia someday, I'll be right by your side. Just . . . not as Emparch."

He squeezed his sister's shoulders, and she rested her head on his chest with a contented smile. As he stretched out his legs, light glinted on the gold lion buttons on his boots.

All at once Daria's words from earlier tonight rushed back. *I dreamed of a big talking cat.* The mountain lion was the symbol of Akhaia, so she had assumed her dream was about Markos. But the sea god claimed the lion god had been asleep under his mountain for six hundred years, and he chose no warriors.

I looked at Daria, bouncing on the sofa, black braids falling over her shoulders.

And wondered.

✧

Purple dusk had settled over the city by the time I was able to steal away from Antidoros Peregrine's house. I'd left Markos there with his sister. They needed the time together and anyway . . .

This was something I had to do for myself.

As I strode through the streets of Valonikos, people scuttled out of my way. Likely it was the intense look in my eyes. I didn't care. The sack in my hand clung to the outline of the rectangular object inside. Glaring at the pickpockets in the shadows, I dared them to just try and touch it.

No one was going to take my ship away from me. Not this time. Not ever again.

I kept walking until at last I came to a door in the market district with a red sign and gold lettering. It was the door I'd been looking for.

A lamp burned in the office, casting a pool of light on a girl bent over an account book. She rubbed her neck, scratching something out with a pen. Her lips moved as she worked through the figures.

I walked in, dropping the sack on the desk with a clunk. "I have a salvage job for you."

Docia Argyrus knew what I'd come for.

Rising from the desk, she replaced her pen in its pot. She pulled the burlap sack aside to reveal a brick of gleaming solid gold.

"I see you found your prize," she said softly, tucking back a shank of hair that had worked itself loose from her bun. "And I missed the adventure. I'm so sorry, Caro. The next morning I woke up and realized I'd made a mistake. But by the time I got to the harbor—" She sighed. "They told me you'd already sailed."

I'd been so angry with her in Iantiporos. But what was she guilty of—trying to be loyal to her family? A vision of Ma standing in the upstairs window of the Bollard offices flashed before my eyes. There was nothing wrong with that. I couldn't blame Docia for the choice she'd made. But I could make things right.

"Wait here," she said in a resigned voice. "I'll get my father."

"Not Finian," I said. "You."

"You've no idea how much I wanted to come with you." Docia's voice was thick. Reverently she touched the gold. "You were right about my family. They never mean to let me be one of them. I suppose I shall sit in this office until I die and—" She broke off, staring. "Wait, *what* did you say?"

"Could you raise a ship from off Four Mile Rock?" I asked. "On the Akhaian peninsula?"

Sometimes when your fate comes for you, you just aren't looking. But you always get a second chance.

Docia lifted her head, eyes widening. "Of course I can." Her nostrils flared. "I can do anything my pa can do. But . . . you know I've never headed up a job on my own before."

I met her eyes. "Want to?"

"Caro, it will cost you." Docia shook her head. "Better to collect the insurance. Buy another."

"She wasn't given to me," I said quietly, "for that." I gestured at the sack. "You didn't see what else I brought you."

"Caro, this one brick of gold is worth a fortune. Far too much for one salvage job."

"Not the brick," I said. "Under it."

Reaching into the sack, she pulled out a piece of paper. On it I'd scribbled a series of numbers. "Coordinates. To . . ." She studied the notation. "I don't know, really. This looks like the middle of the ocean."

"If you sail to that spot, you'll find two islands. Between them there's a shoal. I reckon there must be hundreds of ships lying under the water off those rocks. One of them's the *Centurion*. I bet there's still plenty of gold down there too." I watched her face light up as she realized what she was holding.

"You go get your shipwreck, Docia." I grinned at her. "But first, I need you to find mine."

⁊

Two weeks later, we were at sea.

The *Catfish* bucketed slowly northeast along the Akhaian

Peninsula. The barge wasn't exactly the fleetest vessel, but that was fine. I was counting on her for strength, not speed. Peering over the rail, I almost expected to see the swishing tail of the drakon.

But the sea god remained ominously silent. I had not heard a word from her since that day in the cave. The gulls were back, however. They alighted on the cabin roof, tilting their heads to stare at me with beady eyes, so I knew she was watching me.

I clutched the rail. Waves splashed white on Four Mile Rock, the black tip poking out from the churning sea. I'd never actually seen it the night of the shipwreck. Staring into the murky green depths, I wondered how many other ships had gone to their fate here.

Markos came up behind me, setting his hands on my shoulders. "Is this where it happened?"

"Mmm." I didn't want to talk about that night. Instead I leaned into his warm chest. He smelled like wet wool and coffee.

Docia appeared on deck, wearing a funny-looking woolen suit that covered her from wrists to ankles. A coil of rope was slung over her shoulder. I'd never seen her in diving gear before.

"Well, this is it." She set a pair of goggles on her head. "Reckon it's time to see what's what."

Her brother Torin leaned on a winch. "There's an awful lot of wreckage down there. The rope might get snagged, and then you'd be trapped. Might be a tricky dive." He drummed his fingers on the machinery, and I realized he was bored. "I could go down first if you want."

"This is my job." Docia turned to him and grinned. "*You* stand here and hold the rope."

"I'm just saying it might be dangerous."

She waggled her eyebrows. "How exciting."

Docia was underwater for what seemed like forever. As the seconds wore slowly on, I fidgeted at the rail. Surely she would run out of air. The salvage crew, however, seemed to think nothing of it. All of them were capable of holding their breath for several minutes at a time.

Docia's head popped above the surface. "Ayah," she gasped after she caught her breath. Her hair was slicked back by the water. "She be down there all right. Mostly in one piece too."

"Depth?" her brother called down.

"Depth is good. I make it thirty feet. Check the rope."

The next morning the work began in earnest. Docia, wearing loose trousers and an oilskin coat, stalked the deck and hollered out orders. Four divers went down, tools strapped to their backs, inside a strange bell-shaped chamber. There wasn't much Markos or I could do to help, since I knew very little of salvage operations and he knew even less. He found the process interesting, however, and hovered around the deck pelting Docia's brother with questions.

I gazed at the lapping gray waves, squeezing the rail. I couldn't see *Vix*, but I knew she was down there. *I'm here*, I thought. *I'm coming for you.*

By the end of the week, they had patched the hole in her side. The divers cut away the tangled sails and lines, fixing ropes to her fore and aft. On the final day, the sea was black and the sky a flat gray. Cold wind blustered in from the north, crusting my hair with salt. It would soon be winter.

Waves lashed the *Catfish*. The sea wasn't going to give up *Vix* without a fuss.

The sea god trickled into my mind, like water pooling on sand. Above me seagulls circled, their cries clawing at my ears. Gripping the rail, I reeled. My heart raced like I'd been running. After weeks of silence, the god's sudden presence was overwhelming.

"What are you doing?" Her whisper sounded almost unsure, but that must certainly be a trick of my hearing.

"What do you think? I'm raising my ship."

"I sent her to the bottom." Now she sounded amused. Like the sea itself, she flipped capriciously between moods. I could never quite keep up. "You know I can snap the ropes and send her back without a touch."

"Ayah, I know." I raised my chin into the blowing spray. "So do it. But I'll be back tomorrow. And the next day. And the next day."

"Laughter. Then I will sink her again," the god's voice rumbled. Farther up the deck, Markos was deep in conversation with Docia's brother. They leaned over the rail, pointing at various ropes. No one could hear the sea god but me. "And again," she hissed. "And again."

"Like I said." I took a ragged breath, my gaze coming to rest on Markos. "Go ahead. Do it. But before you do, know this: I keep the things I love."

She knew I didn't just mean the ship. The wind gusted, and her voice was as icy as the spray. *"And I keep the things I take.* I gave you all that gold, a fortune beyond your wildest imagination, and still you defy me. Have you forgotten so soon?" A wave slammed into the hull, splashing up at me. "Your fate is to serve me, Caroline Oresteia."

"And why?" Defiantly, I faced the sea. "Because you chose me. You could have chosen any girl to be yours. But you wanted me." The waves churned below. "Well, it's time you understood that this is me. This is what you've got."

"Fool," she snapped. The smell of brine and seaweed curled around me, filling my nose with its damp stink. "You must know I can drown you in an instant."

"If you wanted to drown me," I pointed out, "I'd be at the bottom of the sea."

The sea surged ominously, the white foam swirling in a pattern I could almost understand. "Perhaps I didn't do a good-enough job the first time."

"No," I said. "That's not it. You told me yourself—you wanted to teach me a lesson. But you didn't want to kill me."

There was a long silence. "I did not foresee that you would be this much trouble. I practically gave you that ship," she said sullenly.

"That's not how I recall it."

The god was quiet again. Even the gulls ceased their squawking. The silence was so ominous, I noticed one of the *Catfish*'s crew glancing uneasily at the sea. Squeezing the rail, I stared out at the gray water. Somewhere under there was *Vix*. The ship of my heart. The first time I had faced down the sea god, I hadn't been able to find the right words. I hoped I could find them now.

"Back in the cave," I began slowly, "you told me I didn't know who I was. But I do know." I took a deep breath. "I belong right here, on the ocean. I belong on *Vix*. I'm going to fix her up with new sails and new rigging and new paint. And then we're going to sail the world together, me and Markos. And if you try to stop me, I'll fight you with everything I have." My throat swelled with emotion. "So now it's time for you to choose. What do *you* want—a servant or a warrior?"

Gulls circled and dove in the overcast sky, while the salt wind tore at the barge's sails.

"Laughter," the god said finally. "I like you this way, Caroline Oresteia."

Then she was gone.

Docia called to her men to get ready. The ropes the salvagers had attached to *Vix* tautened, thrumming with tension. Wood groaned and the winches creaked. The barge lurched under the sudden strain. I leaned over the rail.

"That's it!" someone yelled. "She's moving!"

Markos slipped his hand into mine, squeezing it reassuringly. But I couldn't tear my eyes from the water. I couldn't speak.

This was what I hadn't understood before. You had to know what you wanted—but knowing wasn't enough. You had to be willing to *fight* for it. To be so strong even the sea could not defy you. That is how strong we must be, to keep the things we love.

Something shifted in the depths, rippling and dark. A shape I could almost see.

"Haul away, boys!" Docia yelled.

My breath caught in my throat. My heart sang.

And then her bow broke the surface.

ACKNOWLEDGMENTS

They say the second book is the hardest, but what they don't tell you is that writing a sequel is kind of like writing fanfiction of your own characters. Which is to say, I had so much fun reuniting with Caro and friends for one more adventure.

Thank you to my husband for putting up with me on the nights when I was writing so much, my brain broke. On one occasion, I ran into the room, pointing at the floor by the wall and spluttering, "That! That thing! What's that thing?" He stared at me like I was nuts, then said, "The baseboard?" I shrieked and ran away. I also forgot all the members of the Wu-Tang Clan, and he didn't divorce me for it, so I will thank him for that too.

Thank you to my family, Twitter friends, real-life friends, and the 2017 debut group for all of your support. Nothing was as amazing as seeing friends from twenty-plus years of my life posting selfies in bookstores with *Song of the Current*.

Thank you to my agent, Susan Hawk, and the folks at both the Bent Agency and Upstart Crow Literary. You're the best!

Thank you to Cat Onder and Sarah Shumway, my two fantastic editors on this series. And thank you to all the awesome people at Bloomsbury who worked on this book in some capacity, including Diane Aronson, Erica Barmash, Anna Bernard, Bethany Buck, Liz Byer, John Candell, Alexis Castellanos, Phoebe Dyer, Beth Eller, Alona Fryman, Emily Gerbner, Cristina Gilbert, Courtney Griffin, Melissa Kavonic, Cindy Loh, Donna Mark, Elizabeth Mason, Pat McHugh, Linda Minton, Brittany Mitchell, Emily Ritter, and Claire Stetzer. Thank you to littlemissgang for the jacket design and Virginia Allyn for the maps, which are a dream come true.

Thanks to all the readers and bloggers who read and loved *Song of the Current*! Special thank-you to Uppercase Box, Book Loot, YA Chronicles, Turista Literário, and all the other book boxes that chose my book.

Thank you to Stan Rogers, for "The Mary Ellen Carter." The plot of this book is a shameless homage to the song, which has always been one of my anthems, reminding me to keep going.

And finally, a warning to future writers out there: never ever ever attempt to write a heist.